Critical acclaim for Joseph Finder

'Joseph Finder's visions of corporate America make riveting reading . . . Finder is in good form in this tense page-turner' *Sunday Telegraph*

'A thriller like this rides on its characters, and Finder creates full-blooded ones here . . . the novel's pacing is strong, with steady suspense . . . there are few thriller fans who won't stay up to finish this assured tale'
Publishers Weekly

'Non-stop action, brilliant twists and a 446-page guarantee you won't sleep until it's finished'
Daily Record

'Finder melds brilliantly orchestrated suspense with characterisation that has the richness of the best literary fiction' *Good Book Guide*

'Young Finder knocked out a masterpiece with his last book, *Paranoia* . . . Now he's presented us with *No Hiding Place* and proved that his debut was no flash in the pan . . . A book you need' *Ladsmag*

'The corporate thriller of the year . . . compulsive reading and the end is stunning and absolutely unguessable' Susanna Yager, *Sunday Telegraph*

'Combines a fresh voice, terrific characters, and high-octane suspense. Joseph Finder catapults himself into the front ranks of contemporary writers'
Harlan Coben

In addition to fiction, Joseph Finder continues to write extensively on espionage and international relations for the *New York Times*, the *Washington Post* and the *New Republic*. He lives in Boston with his wife and daughter. Visit his website at www.josephfinder.com.

By Joseph Finder

FICTION

The Moscow Club

Extraordinary Powers

The Zero Hour

High Crimes

Paranoia

Company Man
(*published in paperback as* No Hiding Place)

Killer Instinct

NON-FICTION

Red Carpet: The Connection Between
the Kremlin and America's Most Powerful
Businessmen

KILLER INSTINCT

Joseph Finder

An Orion paperback

First published in Great Britain in 2006
by Orion
This paperback edition published in 2007
by Orion Books Ltd,
Orion House, 5 Upper St Martin's Lane,
London WC2H 9EA
An Hachette Livre UK Company

A CIP catalogue record for this book
is available from the British Library.

Printed and bound in Great Britain by
Clays Ltd, St Ives plc

The Orion Publishing Group's policy is to use papers
that are natural, renewable and recyclable products and
made from wood grown in sustainable forests. The logging
and manufacturing processes are expected to conform to
the environmental regulations of the country of origin.

www.orionbooks.co.uk

For Emma, my baseball fanatic

When the student is ready, the Master appears.

— Buddhist proverb

Prologue

I'd never fired a gun before.

In fact, before this evening, I'd never even held one.

It was a Colt .45 semiautomatic pistol, and it felt heavy and awkward in my hand. Its grip was rough. I couldn't steady the weapon. Still, I was close enough to him now to put a bullet in the center of his chest. If I didn't – if I didn't kill him now – there was no question he'd kill me. I was no match for him, and we both knew it.

It was the middle of the night, and we were the only ones on the twentieth floor, probably in the entire building. Outside my office the maze of cubicles was dark. All those people who worked with me and for me, I'd probably never see again.

My hand was trembling, but I squeezed the trigger.

Just a few days ago, if you looked at me you'd see a successful corporate executive. A guy with a high-powered job married to a beautiful woman. A man for whom everything seemed to be going perfectly.

My idea of danger had been going to bed without brushing my teeth.

Now I didn't think I was going to live to see the morning.

So where did I go wrong? How far back did it go? First grade, when I hit that kid Sean Herlihy with a snowball? Fourth grade, when I was picked third to last for the kickball team?

No, I can tell you exactly when it began.

It was ten months ago.

PART ONE

PART ONE

1

Okay, so I'm an idiot.

The Acura went into a ditch because I was trying to do too many things at once. Radiohead's 'The Bends' was playing, loud, while I was driving home, too fast, since I was late as usual. Left hand on the wheel, while with my right hand I was thumbing my BlackBerry for e-mails, hoping I'd finally nailed a deal with a huge new customer. Most of the e-mails were blowback from the departure of our divisional vice president, Crawford, who'd just jumped ship to Sony. Then my cell phone rang. I dropped the BlackBerry on the car seat and grabbed the cell.

I knew from the ring that it was my wife, Kate, so I didn't bother to turn down the music – I figured she was just calling to find out when I'd be home from work so she could get dinner ready. She'd been on a tofu kick the last few months – tofu and brown rice and kale, stuff like that. It had to be really good for you, since it tasted so bad. But I'd never tell her so.

That wasn't why she was calling, though. I could tell right away from Kate's voice that she'd been cry-ing, and even before she said anything I knew why.

'DiMarco called,' she said. DiMarco was our doctor

at Boston IVF who'd been trying to get Kate pregnant for the last two years or so. I didn't have high hopes, plus I didn't personally know anyone who'd ever made a baby in a test tube, so I was dubious about the whole process. I figured high tech should be for flat-screen plasma monitors, not making babies. Even so, it felt like I'd been punched in the stomach.

But the worst thing was what it would do to Kate. She was crazy enough these days from the hormone injections. This would send her over the edge.

'I'm really sorry,' I said.

'They're not going to let us keep trying forever, you know,' she said. 'All they care about is their numbers, and we're bringing them down.'

'Katie, it's only our third try with the IVF stuff. It's like a ten percent chance or something per cycle anyway, right? We'll keep at it, babe. That's all.'

'The point is, what are we going to do if this doesn't work?' Kate's voice got all high and choked, made my heart squeeze. 'Go to California, do the donor egg thing? I can't go through that. Adopt? Jason, I can barely hear you.'

Adoption was fine with me. Or not. But I'm not totally clueless, so instead I focused on turning down the music. There's some little button on the steering wheel that I've never figured out how to use, so with the thumb of my driving hand I started pushing buttons, but instead the volume increased until Radiohead was blaring.

'Kate,' I said, but just then I realized that the car had veered onto the shoulder and then off the road. I dropped the phone, grabbed the wheel with both hands, cut it hard, but too late.

There was a loud ka-chunk. I spun the steering wheel, slammed on the brakes.

A sickening metallic crunch. I was jolted forward, thrown against the wheel, then backwards. Suddenly the car was canting all the way down to one side. The engine was racing, the wheels spinning in midair.

I knew right away I wasn't hurt seriously, but I might have bruised a couple of ribs slightly. It's funny: I immediately started thinking of those old black-and-white driver-ed shock movies they used to show in the fifties and sixties with lurid titles like *The Last Prom* and *Mechanized Death*, from the days when all cops had crew cuts and wore huge-brimmed Canadian Mountie hats. A guy in my college frat had a videotape of these educational snuff flicks. Watching them could scare the bejeezus out of you. I couldn't believe anyone learning to drive back then could see *The Last Prom* and still be willing to get behind the wheel.

I turned the key, shut off the music, and sat there for a couple of seconds in silence before I picked the cell phone off the floor of the car to call Triple A.

But the line was still open, and I could hear Kate screaming.

'Hey,' I said.

'Jason, are you all right?' She was freaking out. 'What *happened*?'

'I'm fine, babe.'

'Jason, my God, did you get in an *accident*?'

'Don't worry about it, sweetheart. I'm totally – I'm fine. Everything's cool. Don't worry about it.'

Forty-five minutes later a tow truck pulled up, a bright red truck, M.E. WALSH TOW painted on the side panel. The driver walked over to me, holding a metal clipboard. He was a tall, broad-shouldered guy with a scruffy goatee, wearing a bandana on his head knotted at the back and long gray-flecked brown hair in a kind of mullet. He was wearing a black leather Harley-Davidson jacket.

'Well, that sucks,' the dude said.

'Thanks for coming,' I said.

'No worries,' Harley said. 'Let me guess. You were talking on your cell phone.'

I blinked, hesitated for a microsecond before I said sheepishly, 'Yeah.'

'Damn things are a menace.'

'Yeah, totally,' I said. Like I could survive without my cell phone. But he didn't exactly seem to be a cell phone kind of guy. He drove a tow truck and a motorcycle. Probably had a CB radio in there along with his Red Man chewing tobacco and Allman Brothers CDs. And a roll of toilet paper in the glove compartment. Kind of guy who mows his lawn and finds a car. Who thinks the last four words of the national anthem are 'Gentlemen, start your engines.'

'You okay?' he said.

'Yeah, I'm good.'

He backed the truck around to my car, lowered the bed, hooked the winch up to the Acura. He switched on the electric pulley thing and started hauling my car out of the ditch. Fortunately, we were on a fairly deserted stretch of road – I always take this shortcut from the office in Framingham to the Mass Pike – so there weren't too many cars whizzing by. I noticed the truck had a yellow 'Support Our Troops' ribbon sticker on one side and one of those black-and-white POW/MIA

8

stickers on the windshield. I made a mental note to myself not to criticize the war in Iraq unless I wanted to get my larynx crushed by the guy's bare hands.

'Climb in,' he said.

The cab of the truck smelled like stale cigar smoke and gasoline. A Special Forces decal on the dashboard. I was starting to get real warm and fuzzy feelings about the war.

'You got a body shop you like?' he said. I could barely hear him over the hydraulic whine of the truck bed mechanism.

I had a serious gearhead friend who'd know, but I couldn't tell a carburetor from a caribou. 'I don't get into accidents too often,' I said.

'Well, you don't look like the kinda guy gets under the hood and changes the oil himself,' Harley said. 'There's a body shop I know,' he said. 'Not too far from here. We're good to go.'

We mostly sat there in silence while he drove. I made a couple of attempts to get a conversation started with Harley, but it was like striking a wet match.

Normally I could talk to anyone about anything – you name it, sports, kids, dogs, TV shows, whatever. I was a sales manager for one of the biggest electronics companies in the world, up there with Sony and Panasonic. The division I work for makes those big beautiful flat-panel LCD and plasma TVs and monitors that so many people lust after. Very cool products. And I've found that the really good sales reps, the ones who have the juice, can start a conversation with anybody. That's me.

But this guy didn't want to talk, and after a while I

gave up. I was kind of uncomfortable sitting there in the front seat of a tow truck being chauffeured around by a Hells Angel, me in my expensive charcoal suit, trying to avoid the chewing gum, or tar, or whatever the hell it was stuck on the vinyl upholstery. I felt my rib cage, satisfied myself that nothing had broken. Not even all that painful, actually.

I found myself staring at the collection of stickers on the dashboard – the Special Forces decal, a 'These Colors Don't Run' flag decal, another one that said 'Special Forces – I'm the Man Your Mother Warned You About.' After a while, I said, 'This your truck?'

'Nah, my buddy owns the towing company and I help out sometimes.'

Guy was getting chatty. I said, 'He Special Forces?'

A long silence. I didn't know, were you not supposed to ask somebody if they were in the Special Forces or something? Like, he could tell me, but then he'd have to kill me?

I was about to repeat the question when he said, 'We both were.'

'Huh,' I said, and we both went quiet again. He switched on the ball game. The Red Sox were playing the Seattle Mariners at Fenway Park, and it was a tight, hard-fought, low-scoring game, pretty exciting. I love listening to baseball on the radio. I have a huge flat-panel TV at home, which I got on the friends-and-family discount at work, and baseball in high-definition is awesome. But there's nothing like a ball game on the radio – the crack of the bat, the rustling crowd, even the stupid ads for auto glass. It's classic. The announcers sound exactly the way they did when I was a kid, and probably sound the same as

10

when my late father was a kid. Their flat, nasal voices are like an old pair of sneakers, comfortable and familiar and broken-in. They use all the well-worn phrases like '*high – fly – ball!*' and 'runners at the corners' and 'swing and a miss.' I like the way they suddenly get loud and frenzied, shouting things like, 'Way back! *Way back!*'

One of the announcers was commenting about the Sox pitcher, saying, '. . . but even at the top of his game, he's never going to come close to the fastest recorded pitch speed of one hundred point nine miles an hour, thrown by . . . ? Jerry, you must know that one.'

And the other guy said, 'Nolan Ryan.'

'Nolan Ryan,' the first guy said, 'very good. Clocked at Anaheim Stadium, August the twentieth, nineteen-seventy-four.' Probably reading off the prompter, some research fed him by a producer.

I said, 'Wrong.'

The driver turned to me. 'Huh?'

I said, 'These guys don't know what they're talking about. The fastest recorded pitch was Mark Wohlers.'

'Very good,' Harley said, nodding. 'Mark Wohlers. Hundred and three.'

'Right,' I said, surprised. 'Hundred and three miles per hour, in nineteen-ninety-five.'

'Atlanta Braves spring training.' Then he smiled, an easy grin, his teeth even and white. 'Didn't think anyone else knew that,' he said.

'Of course, the fastest pitcher ever, not in the major leagues –'

'Steve Dalkowski,' said Harley. 'Hundred and ten miles an hour.'

11

'Shattered an umpire's mask,' I said, nodding. 'So were you a baseball geek when you were a kid, too? Collection of thousands of baseball cards?'

He smiled again. 'You got it. Those Topps gum packs with that crappy stale bubble gum inside.'

'That always stained one of the cards in the pack, right?'

He chuckled.

'Your dad take you to Fenway a lot?' I said.

'I didn't grow up around here,' he said. 'Michigan. And my dad wasn't around. Plus we couldn't afford to go to games.'

'We couldn't either,' I said. 'So I listened to games on the radio a lot.'

'Same here.'

'Played baseball in the backyard?' I said. 'Break a lot of windows?'

'We didn't have a backyard.'

'Me neither. My friends and I played in a park down the street.'

He nodded, smiled.

I felt like I knew the guy. We came from the same background, probably – no money, no backyard, the whole deal. Only I went to college and was sitting here in a suit, and he'd gone into the army like a lot of my high school buddies did.

We listened to the game for a bit. Seattle's designated hitter was up. He swung at the first pitch. You could hear the crack of the bat. 'And there's a *high* fly ball hit *deep* to left field!' one of the announcers crowed. It was headed right for the glove of a great Red Sox slugger, who also happened to be a famously clumsy outfielder. And a space cadet who did things like

12

disappear from left field, right in the middle of a game, to take a leak. When he wasn't bobbling the ball.

'He's got it,' said the announcer. 'It's headed right for his glove.'

'He's going to drop it,' I said.

Harley laughed. 'You said it.'

'Here it comes,' I said.

Harley laughed even louder. 'This is painful,' he said.

A roar of disappointment in the ballpark. 'The ball hit the *back* of the glove,' said the announcer, 'as he tried to slide to make the play. This is a *major*-league error right here.'

We groaned simultaneously.

Harley switched it off. 'I can't take it anymore,' he said.

'Thank you,' I said, as we pulled into the auto body shop parking lot.

It was a kind of scuzzy place that looked like a converted gas station. WILLKIE AUTO BODY, the sign said. The manager on duty was named Abdul and probably wouldn't have an easy time getting through airport security these days. I thought Harley would start off-loading the carcass of my poor Acura, but instead he came into the waiting room and watched Abdul take down my insurance information. I noticed another 'Support Our Troops' sticker on the wall in here, too, and a Special Forces decal.

Harley said, 'Jeremiah at home?'

'Oh, yeah,' said Abdul. 'Sure. Home with the kids.'

'This is a friend of mine,' he said. 'Make sure you guys take care of him.'

I looked around and realized the tow truck driver

was talking about me.

'Of course, Kurt,' Abdul said.

'Tell Jerry I was here,' Harley said.

I read an old copy of *Maxim* while the tow truck driver and Abdul walked back to the shop. They returned a couple of minutes later.

'Abdul's going to put his best master tech on your car,' Harley said. 'They do good work here. Computerized paint-mixing system. Nice clean shop. Why don't you guys finish up the paperwork, and I'll get the car in the service bay.'

'Thanks, man,' I said.

'Okay, Kurt, see you,' said Abdul.

I came out a few minutes later and saw Harley sitting in his tow truck, engine idling, listening to the game.

'Hey,' he said, 'where do you live? I'll drop you off.'

'It's pretty far. Belmont.'

'Grab your stuff out of the car and jump in.'

'You don't mind?'

'I get paid by the hour, buddy. Not by the job.'

I got my CDs off the floor of the car and my briefcase and baseball glove off the backseat.

'You used to work in a body shop?' I said when I'd gotten back into the truck.

The walkie-talkie started blaring, and he switched it off. 'I've done everything.'

'How do you like towing?'

He turned and gave me an *Are you out of your mind?* look. 'I take whatever work I can get.'

'People don't like to hire soldiers anymore?'

'People love to hire soldiers,' he said. 'Just not ones with DDs.'

'What's a DD?'

14

'Dishonorable discharge. You gotta put it down on the application, and as soon as they see that, you're out the door.'

'Oh,' I said. 'Sorry I asked. None of my business.'

'No big deal. It just pisses me off. You get a DD, you don't get any VA benefits or pension. Sucks big-time.'

'How'd it happen?' I said. 'If you don't mind my asking.'

Another long silence. He hit the turn signal, changed lanes. 'Nah, I don't mind.' He paused again, and I wasn't sure he was going to answer. Then he said: 'The CO of my Special Forces A-team ordered half of us to go on this suicide mission, this broke-dick reconnaissance mission in Tikrit. I told the CO there was a ninety-nine percent chance they'd get ambushed, and guess what? The guys got ambushed. Attacked with rocket-propelled grenades. And my buddy Jimmy Donadio was killed.'

He fell silent. Stared straight ahead at the road as he drove. Then: 'A good kid, just about finished with his tour, had a baby he'd never even seen. I loved that guy. So I just lost it. Went after the CO – head-butted the bastard. Broke his nose.'

'Wow,' I said. 'Jesus. I can't blame you. So you got court-martialed or something?'

He shrugged. 'I'm lucky they didn't send me to Leavenworth. But nobody in the command wanted to draw any attention to what went down that night, and they sure as hell didn't want CID looking into it. Bad for army morale. More important, bad PR. So the deal was, dishonorable discharge, no time.'

'Wow,' I said again. I wasn't sure what CID was,

but I wasn't going to ask.

'So are you, like, a lawyer or something?'

'Salesman.'

'Where?'

'Entronics. In Framingham.'

'Cool. Can you get me a deal on a plasma TV?'

I hesitated. 'I don't sell the consumer line, but I might be able to do something.'

He smiled. 'I'm kidding. I couldn't afford one of those anyway, even wholesale. So, I noticed the glove you got back there. Sweet. Rawlings Gold Glove, Heart of the Hide. Same as the pros use. Looks brand-new. Right out of the box. Just get it?'

'Um, about two years,' I said. 'Gift from my wife.'

'Oh. You play?'

'Not much. Mostly on my company's team. Softball, not baseball, but my wife didn't know the difference.' Our team sucked. We were on a losing streak that resembled the Baltimore Orioles' historically pathetic 1988 season. 'You play?'

He shrugged. 'Used to.'

A long beat of silence.

'In school or something?' I said.

'Got drafted by the Detroit Tigers, but never signed.'

'Seriously?'

'My pitch speed was clocked at ninety-four, ninety-five miles an hour.'

'No way. Jesus!' I turned to look at him.

'But that wasn't where my head was, at that point. Enlisted instead. I'm Kurt, by the way.' He took his right hand off the wheel and gave me a firm handshake. 'Kurt Semko.'

'Jason Steadman.'

There was another long silence, and then I had an idea.

'We could use a pitcher,' I said.

'Who?'

'My company's team. We've got a game tomorrow night, and we sure could use a decent pitcher. How would you like to play on our team tomorrow?'

Another long pause. Then: 'Don't you have to work for the company?'

'Guys we play have no idea who works for us and who doesn't.'

Kurt went quiet again.

After a minute, I said, 'So what do you think?'

He shrugged. 'I don't know.' He was staring at the road, a half smile on his face.

At the time it seemed like a fun idea.

2

I love my wife.

Sometimes I can't believe that a woman as intelligent and sophisticated and, oh yeah, unbelievably beautiful, settled for a guy like me. She likes to joke that our courtship was the greatest job of salesmanship I ever pulled off. I don't disagree. I did close the deal, after all.

When I walked in, Kate was sitting on the couch watching TV. There was a bowl of popcorn in her lap and a glass of white wine on the coffee table in front of her. She was wearing faded old gym shorts from her prep school, which nicely set off her long, toned legs. As soon as she saw me come in, she got up from the couch, ran over to hug me. I winced, but she didn't notice. 'Oh, my God,' she said. 'I've been so worried.'

'I'm fine, I told you. The only thing that got hurt was my pride. Though the tow truck driver thought I was an idiot.'

'You're totally okay, Jase? Were you wearing a seat belt and everything?' She pulled back to look at me. Her eyes were a great shade of hazel green, and her hair was full and black, and she had a sharp jawline and high cheekbones. She reminded me of a young, dark haired Katharine Hepburn. Endearingly enough, she considered herself plain, her features too sharp and exaggerated. Tonight, though, her eyes were bloodshot and puffy. She'd obviously been crying a lot.

'The car just went off the side of the road,' I said. 'I'm fine, but the car got messed up.'

'The car,' she said with an airy wave, as if my Acura TL were a wad of toilet paper. I assume she inherited these aristocratic gestures from her parents. You see, Kate comes from money, sort of. That is, her family was once very rich, but the money never made it to her generation. The Spencer fortune took a big hit in 1929, when her great-grandfather made some really dumb investment decisions around the time of the Crash, and finally got finished off by her father, who was an alcoholic and only knew how to spend money, not manage it.

All Kate got was part of an expensive education, a cultivated voice, a lot of rich family friends who now felt sorry for her, and a houseful of antiques. Many of which she'd jammed into our three-bedroom colonial house on a quarter acre in Belmont.

'How'd you get back?' she said.

'Tow truck driver. Interesting guy – ex-Special Forces.'

'Hmm,' she said, that not-interested-but-trying-to-fake-it noise I knew so well.

'Is that dinner?' I said, pointing to the bowl of popcorn on the coffee table.

'Sweetie, I'm sorry. I just didn't feel like cooking tonight. You want me to make you something?'

I could visualize the brick of tofu lurking in the refrigerator, and I almost shuddered. 'Don't worry about it. I'll just grab something. Come here.' I hugged

19

her again. Braved the pain without wincing this time. 'Forget about the car. I'm worried about you.'

All of a sudden she started crying as I held her. She kind of crumpled. I felt her chest heave and her hot tears dampen my shirt. I squeezed her tight. 'It's just that I really thought . . . this one was going to work,' she said.

'Next time, maybe. We just have to be patient, huh?'

'Do you not worry about *anything*?'

'Just stuff I can do something about,' I said.

After a while, we sat down together on the couch, which was an uncomfortable but no doubt really valuable English antique as hard as a church pew, and watched some documentary on the Discovery channel about bonobos, which are apparently a species of monkey smarter and more highly evolved than us. Seems the bonobos are a female-dominated society. They showed footage of the female bonobo trying to seduce a male, spreading her legs and putting her butt up to the male's face. The announcer called that 'presenting.' I suppressed a remark about our own conjugal relations, which had become just about nonexistent. I don't know if it was the fertility treatments or what, but our sex life lately had turned into a kind of bed death. I couldn't remember the last time Kate had 'presented.'

I took a handful of popcorn. It was air-popped and lightly spritzed with I Can't Believe It's Not Butter. It tasted like Styrofoam peanuts. I couldn't politely spit it out, so I finished chewing and swallowed it.

The female bonobo didn't seem to be scoring, but she kept at it. She stretched out an arm and beckoned at the male with upstretched fingers like a silent film star playing a harlot. But the guy was a dud. So she went up to him and grabbed his balls, hard.

'Ouch,' I said. 'I don't think she's read *He's Just Not That Into You.*'

Kate shook her head and tried not to smile.

I got up and went to the bathroom and swallowed a couple of Advil. Then I went to the kitchen and served myself a big bowl of ice cream, Brigham's Oreo. I didn't bother to ask Kate if she wanted any, because she never ate ice cream. She never ate anything remotely fattening.

I sat back down and dug into the ice cream while the narrator said, 'The females kiss and hug and rub their genitals together with their special friends.'

'So where are the male bonobos, anyway?' I said. 'Sitting on the couch with the remote control?'

She watched me tuck into the ice cream. 'What's that, babe?'

'This?' I said. 'Fat-free tofu ice-milk substitute.'

'Sweetheart, you know, you might want to lay off the ice cream at night.'

'I never feel like it at breakfast.'

'You know what I'm saying,' she said, and touched her perfectly flat belly. I, on the other hand, was already developing a potbelly at thirty. Kate could eat anything she wanted and not gain weight. She just had this incredible metabolism. Women hated her for that. I found it a little annoying myself. If I had her metabolism, I wouldn't be eating bulgur and tempeh.

'Can we watch something else?' I said. 'This is getting me too horny.'

'Jason, that's disgusting.' She grabbed the remote and began flipping through the hundreds of channels until

21

she stopped at a show that looked familiar. I recognized the actors who played the beautiful high-school-age brother and sister and their divorced father, himself a divorce lawyer. This was that Fox show *S.B.*, about beautiful rich high-school kids and their broken families in Santa Barbara – proms, car crashes, divorce cases, drugs, cheating moms. It had become the hottest TV show of the season.

And it was created by my brother-in-law, Craig Glazer, the hotshot TV producer who was married to Kate's older sister, Susie. Craig and I pretended to get along.

'How can you watch that crap?' I said, grabbing the remote and switching the channel to some old *National Geographic*-style show about a primitive Amazonian tribe called the Yanomamo.

'You'd better deal with that hostility before Craig and Susie come next week.'

'Without my hostility, what's left? Anyway, they have no idea how I feel about him.'

'Oh, Susie knows.'

'She probably feels the same way about him.'

Kate cocked a brow provocatively but said nothing.

We watched some more of the nature show, sort of listlessly. The narrator said in a plummy British accent that the Yanomami were the most violent, aggressive society in the world. They were known as the Fierce People. They were always breaking out into wars, usually over women, who were scarce.

'I'll bet you like that, huh?' I said. 'Fighting over women?'

She shook her head. 'I studied the Fierce People in one of my feminism classes. The men beat their wives too. The women think the more machete scars they have, the more their husbands must love them.' There was always some book about feminism on Kate's bedside table. The latest was called something like *This Sex Which Is Not One*. I didn't get the title, but luckily there wasn't going to be a quiz.

Kate had gotten interested in obscure African and South American cultures in the last few years because of her job, I think. She worked for the Meyer Foundation for Folk and Outsider Art in Boston. They gave money to poor and homeless people who made paintings and sculptures that looked like they could have been done by my eight-year-old nephew. But they didn't give much money to their employees. The foundation paid Kate eight thousand dollars a year and apparently believed she should be paying them for the privilege of working there. I think she spent more in gas and parking than she earned.

We watched the show some more. Kate ate popcorn and I ate Oreo ice cream. The narrator said that Yanomami boys proved their manhood by 'blooding their spear,' or killing someone. They used axes and spears and bows and arrows. And blowguns carved from bamboo that shot poison darts.

'Cool,' I said.

The Yanomamo tribe cremated their dead and mixed the ashes into plantain soup and then drank it.

Maybe not so cool.

When the show was over I gave her the latest news about how the divisional vice president, Crawford, had just left the company for Sony and took six of his top guys with him. Which left a huge, gaping hole in my department. 'It sucks,' I said. 'Huge mess.'

'What are you talking about?' Kate said, suddenly interested. 'It's terrific.'

'You don't get it. Entronics just announced they're acquiring the U.S. business of this Dutch company called Meister.'

'I've *heard* of Meister,' she said, sounding a little annoyed. 'So?'

Royal Meister Electronics N.V. is an immense electronics conglomerate, one of our biggest competitors. They had a unit based in Dallas that sold the same things we did – the LCDs and the plasma screens and the projectors and all that.

'So Crawford's getting the hell out of Dodge. He must know something.'

Kate sat up, drew her knees to her chest. 'Listen, Jase, don't you realize what this means? This is your *chance*.'

'My chance?'

'You've been stuck at the level of district sales manager for *years*. It's like you're frozen in amber.'

I wondered whether she was dealing with the bad pregnancy news by throwing herself into my career. 'Nothing's opened up.'

'Come *on*, Jase, think about it. If Crawford's gone, along with six of his top guys, the sales division has no choice but to backfill some of those slots from inside, right? This is your chance to get into management. To really start climbing the ladder.'

'Greasy pole, more like it. Katie, I like my job. I don't want to be a VP.'

'But your salary's basically capped out right now, right? You're never going to make much more than you do now.'

24

'What do you mean? I'm doing pretty good. Remember how much I made three years ago?'

She nodded, her eyes fixed on mine, like she was weighing whether to say more. Then she said, 'Honey, three years ago was a freak. Plasma screens were just coming out, and Entronics owned the market, right? That's never going to happen again.'

'See, Kate, here's the thing. There's this corporate egg-sorting machine for guys around my age, okay? It starts dropping the eggs into the Large and Extra Large and Jumbo cartons, right?'

'So what are you?'

'I'm not going into Jumbo. I'm just a sales guy. I am what I am.'

'But if you get into management, baby, that's when you start making the real money.'

A couple of years ago, Kate used to talk to me about how I should focus on climbing the corporate ladder, but I thought she'd given that up. 'Those guys in upper management never leave the office,' I said. 'They have to put a LoJack on their ankles. They turn fishbelly white from being in meetings all the time. Too much sucking up, too much politics. It's not for me. Why are we talking about this?'

'Look. You become the area manager and then a DVP and then a VP and general manager and pretty soon you could be *running* a company. In a couple of years, you could be making a *fortune*.'

I took a deep breath, wanting to argue with her, but there was no point. When she got like this, she was like a terrier that wouldn't let go of its Nylabone.

The fact was, Kate and I had very different ideas of what a 'fortune' was. My dad was a sheet-metal worker at a plant in Worcester that made ducts and pipes for air-conditioning and ventilation systems. He rose as high as shop foreman, and he was pretty active in the Sheet Metal Workers Local 63. He wasn't a very ambitious guy – I think he took the first job that came along, got good at it, stuck with it. But he worked really hard, did overtime and extra shifts whenever possible, and he arrived home at the end of the day wiped out, unable to do anything more than sit in front of the TV like a zombie and drink Budweiser. Dad was missing the tips of two of the fingers on his right hand, which was always a silent reminder to me of how nasty his job was. When he told me he wanted me to go to college so I didn't have to do what he did, he really meant it.

We lived on one floor of a three-decker on Providence Street in Worcester that had asbestos siding and a chain-link fence around the concrete backyard. To go from that to owning my own colonial house in Belmont – well, that was pretty damned good, I thought.

Whereas the house Kate had grown up in, in Wellesley, was bigger than her entire Harvard dorm building. We'd once driven by the house. It was an immense stone mansion with a high wrought-iron fence and endless land. Even after her boozer father had finally killed off what remained of the family fortune with some lame-brained investment, and they'd had to sell their summer house in Osterville, on Cape Cod, and then their house in Wellesley, the place they moved to was about twice as big as the house she and I lived in now.

She paused, then pouted. 'Jason, you don't want to end up like Cal Taylor, do you?'

26

'That's a low blow.' Cal Taylor was around sixty and had been a salesman with Entronics forever, since the days when they sold transistor radios and second-rate color TV sets and tried to compete with Emerson and Kenwood. He was a human cautionary tale. The sight of him creeped me out, because he represented everything I secretly knew I was in danger of becoming. With his white hair and his nicotine-yellowed mustache, his Jack Daniel's breath and his smoker's hack and his never-ending stock of stale jokes, he was my own personal nightmare. He was a dead-ender, a timeserver who somehow managed to hang on because of a few tenuous relationships he'd built over the years, those he hadn't neglected anyway. He was divorced, lived alone on TV dinners, and spent almost every night at a neighborhood bar.

Then her face softened and she tipped her head. 'Honey,' she said softly, almost wheedling, 'look at this house.'

'What about it?'

'We don't want to bring up kids in a place like this,' she said. There was a catch in her breath. She suddenly looked sad. 'There's no room to play. There's barely a yard.'

'I hate mowing the lawn. Anyway, I didn't have a yard growing up.'

She paused, looked away. I wondered what she was thinking. If she was expecting a return to Manderley, she sure married the wrong guy.

'Come on, Jason, what happened to your ambition? When I met you, you were this totally fired-up, sky's-the-limit kind of guy. Remember?'

'That was just to get you to marry me.'

27

'I know you're kidding. You've got the drive, you *know* you do. You've just gotten' – she was about to say 'fat and happy,' I'll bet, but instead she said, 'too comfortable. This is it. This is the time to go for it.'

I kept thinking about that documentary about the Fierce People. When Kate married me, she must have thought I was some Yanomami warrior she could groom into a chieftain.

But I said, 'I'll talk to Gordy.' Kent Gordon was the senior VP who ran the entire sales division.

'Good,' she said. 'Tell him you demand to be interviewed for a promotion.'

'"Demand" isn't exactly my style.'

'Well, surprise him. Show him some aggression. He'll love it. It's kill or be killed. You've got to show him you're a killer.'

'Yeah, right,' I said. 'You think I can get one of those Yanomami blowguns on eBay?'

3

'We're screwed, man,' said Ricky Festino. 'We are so screwed.'

Ricky Festino was a member of what we called the Band of Brothers, a fellow salesman for Entronics USA's Visual Systems unit. Salesmen are supposed to all be outgoing and affable, backslappers, hail-fellows-well-met, but not Festino. He was an outlier. He was dour, cynical, bitingly sarcastic. The only thing he seemed to get into was contracts – he'd dropped out of Boston College Law School after a year, and contracts was the one course he liked there. That should tell you something about him.

As far as I could tell, he hated his job and didn't much like his wife and two little kids either. He chauffeured his younger boy to some private school every morning and coached his older boy's Little League team, which would theoretically make him a good dad, except for the fact that he was always complaining about it. I was never sure what motivated him except fear and bile, but hey, whatever works.

I couldn't figure out why he liked me so much either. To Ricky Festino, I must have seemed cloyingly optimistic. I should have made him seethe with contempt.

Instead, he seemed to regard me like the family pet, the only one who really understood him, a happy-go-lucky golden retriever he could bitch to while he took me out for a walk. Sometimes he called me 'Tigger,' referring to Winnie-the-Pooh's bouncy, irrepressible, and basically retarded friend. If I was Tigger, he was Eeyore.

'Why's that?' I asked.

'The acquisition, what do you think? Crap,' he muttered as he squeezed out a glistening dollop of anti-bacterial hand cleaner from a tiny bottle he carried with him everywhere. He rubbed his hands together violently, and I could smell the alcohol. Festino was an out-of-control germophobe. 'I just shook hands with that guy from CompuMax, and he kept sneezing on me.'

CompuMax was a 'system-builder,' a company that assembled and sold low-end no-name computers for corporations. They were a lousy client, mostly because they didn't spend money on name-brand components, and Entronics was too name-brand for them. Festino was trying to sell them a bunch of LCD monitors that Entronics didn't even make, that we got from some second-rate Korean firm and just put our logo on. He was trying to convince them that having the Entronics name on at least one of their components would make their systems seem classier and thus more desirable. A good idea, but CompuMax wasn't buying. My guess was that Festino didn't know how to pitch it, but I couldn't get too involved – it was his deal.

'I'm starting to get why the Japs think we Westerners are so unclean,' Festino went on. 'He was, like, sneezing into his hands over and over, then he wanted to shake. What was I going to do, refuse to shake his filthy hand? Guy was a human petri dish. Want some?' He offered me the tiny plastic bottle.

'No, thanks, I'm good.'

'Is it my imagination, or is your office a lot smaller than mine?'

'It's the décor,' I said. 'Same size.' Actually, my office was starting to look smaller all the time. The Entronics USA Visual Systems sales division took up the top floor of the Entronics building in Framingham, about twenty miles west of Boston. It's by far the tallest structure in town, surrounded by low-rise office parks, and the locals fought it bitterly before it went up ten years ago or so. It's a handsome building, but everyone in Framingham considers it an affront. Some wit had dubbed it the Framingham Phallus. Others called it the Entronics Erection.

He sank back in the visitor chair. 'Let me tell you something about this Royal Meister deal. The Japanese always have a master plan. They never tell you what it is, but there's always this long-range master plan. We're just those little round game pieces – what's that strategy game the Japanese play?'

'Go?'

'"Go," right. "Go." Go take a leap. Go screw yourself.' I could see dark sweat stains under the arms of Ricky's blue button-down shirt. The Entronics offices were kept at a steady sixty-eight degrees, summer or winter, and if anything they were too cold, but Ricky sweated a lot. He was a couple of years older than me and was going to seed. He was paunchy, a potbelly more advanced than mine hanging over his belt, a roll of neck fat spilling over the collar of his too-tight shirt. He'd started coloring his hair a couple of years ago, and the Just For Men shade he used was too black.

I sneaked a glance at the time on my computer screen. I'd told the guy at Lockwood Hotel and Resorts that I'd call him before noon, and it was 12:05. 'Hey, uh, Rick . . .'

'See, you don't get it. You're too *nice*.' He said it with a nasty curl to his lips. 'Entronics acquires Royal Meister's U.S. operations, right? But why? You think their plasma screens are better than ours?'

'Nope,' I said, trying not to encourage him.

I'd tell the guy at Lockwood that I was closing a huge deal, that's why I couldn't call him earlier. I didn't want to lie to the guy, but I'd hint around about a rival five-star luxury hotel chain I couldn't name that was also putting plasma-screen TVs in all their guest rooms. If I hinted right, maybe I could make him think it was the Four Seasons or something. Maybe that would light a fire under him. Then again, maybe not.

'Exactly,' Ricky said. 'It's their *sales force*. They kick our ass. The boys in Tokyo are sitting on their tatami mats in the MegaTower rubbing their hands at the prospect of buying a sales force that's more high-test than we are. So what does that mean? It means they get rid of all but the top ten percent, maybe, and move them to Dallas. Consolidate. Real estate in Dallas is a lot cheaper than Boston. They sell this building and throw the rest of us under a bus. It's so totally obvious, Jason. Why do you think Crawford went to Sony, man?'

Festino was so proud of his Machiavellian genius that I didn't want to let him know I'd already come up with the same theory. So I nodded and looked intrigued.

I noticed a slender Japanese man passing by my office, and I gave a casual wave. 'Hey, Yoshi,' I said. Yoshi Tanaka, a personality-free guy with thick aviator-frame glasses, was a *funin-sha,* an expatriate Japanese, transferred to the U.S. to learn the ropes. But he was more than that. Officially, his title was Manager for Business Planning, but everyone knew he was actually an informer for the Entronics management in Tokyo who stayed at his office late into the night and reported back by phone and e-mail. He was Tokyo's eyes and ears here. He spoke just about no English, though, which couldn't have been good for his spying.

He scared the shit out of everyone, but I didn't mind him. I felt bad for him. Being posted in a country where you didn't speak the language, without family – at least, I assumed he had family back in Tokyo – couldn't be easy. I couldn't imagine working in Japan and not speaking Japanese. Always being a beat behind. Never getting it. He was isolated, ostracized by his colleagues, all of whom distrusted him. Not an easy gig. A hardship posting, in fact. I never joined the others in Yoshi-bashing.

Ricky turned, gave Yoshi a smile and a wave, and as soon as Yoshi was out of range, muttered, 'God-damned spy.'

'You think he heard you?' I said.

'Nah. Even if he did, he wouldn't understand.'

'Listen, Rick, I'm late calling Lockwood.'

'The fun never stops. They still dicking you around?'

I nodded ruefully.

'It's over, man. Forget it. Stop pursuing them.'

33

'A forty-million-dollar deal, and you're telling me to forget it?'

'The guy just wants Super Bowl tickets. Any deal that takes this long is dead in the water.'

I sighed. Festino was an expert on deals that were dead in the water. 'I gotta call him.'

'You're like a hamster on a wheel, man. We're all hamsters. Any second now the guy in the white lab coat's gonna come and euthanize us, and you're still running around the wheel. Forget it, man.'

I stood up to encourage him to do the same. 'You playing tonight?'

He got up. 'Yeah, sure. Carol's already pissed at me for going out with clients last night. What's one more night in the doghouse? Who're we playing tonight, Charles River?'

I nodded.

'Gonna be another ignominious defeat for the Band of Brothers. We got no pitching. Trevor sucks.'

I smiled, remembering the tow truck driver from last night. 'I got a pitcher.'

'You? You can't pitch for shit either.'

'Not me. A guy who almost went pro.'

'What are you talking about?'

I filled him in quickly.

Rick's eyes narrowed, and for the first time this morning, he smiled. 'We tell the Charles River boys he's the new stockboy or whatever?'

I nodded.

'A ringer,' Rick said.

'Exactly.'

He hesitated. 'Pitching softball's different from baseball.'

'Guy's obviously an incredible athlete, Rick. I'm sure he can do fastpitch softball.'

He cocked his head to one side, gave me an appraising look. 'You know, Tigger, under that simpleton façade, you've got hidden reserves of craftiness. Never would have expected it. I'm impressed.'

4

The Lockwood Hotel and Resort Group was one of the largest chains of luxury hotels in the world. Their properties were a little mildewed, though, and in need of an overhaul. Part of management's plan to compete with the Four Seasons and the Ritz-Carlton was to put Bose Wave Radios and forty-two-inch flat-panel plasma TVs in every room. I knew they were talking to NEC and Toshiba too.

I'd been the one who'd pushed for a bake-off, and I arranged to send one of our screens to Lockwood's White Plains, New York, headquarters, for a head-to-head comparison with NEC and Toshiba. I knew our product performed at least as well as the other guys', because we were still in the running. But the Vice Presi-dent for Property Management at Lockwood, Brian Borque, couldn't seem to make a decision.

I wondered whether Ricky Festino was right, that Borque was stringing me along just for the Super Bowl and World Series tickets and the dinners at Alain Ducasse in New York. I half wished he'd just put me out of my misery already.

'Hey, Brian,' I said into the headset.

'There he is,' Brian Borque said. He always sounded happy to hear from me.

'I should have called you earlier. My bad.' I almost gave him the lie about the other hotel chain, but I didn't have the heart to go through with it. 'Meeting ran long.'

'No worries, man. Hey, I read something about you guys in the *Journal* this morning. You getting acquired by Meister?'

'Other way around. Entronics is acquiring Meister U.S.'

'Interesting. We've been talking to them too, you know.'

I hadn't known. Great, another player in this endless negotiation. It reminded me of this old movie I once saw in college called *They Shoot Horses, Don't They?*, about marathon dancers who dance until they drop.

'Well, that'll mean one less competitor, I guess,' I said, keeping the tone light. 'How was Martha's birthday? You take her to Vienna, like she wanted?'

'Vienna, Virginia, more like. Hey, I've got to be in Boston next week – you feel like catching a Sox game?'

'Sure.'

'You guys still get those amazing seats?'

'I'll do what I can.' I hesitated. 'So, listen, Bri.'

He heard the change in my tone and cut me off. 'I wish I had an answer for you, buddy, but I don't. Believe me, *I* want to do the deal with you guys.'

'Thing is, Brian, I'm getting a lot of pressure from senior management on this thing. The deal's been on the forecast –'

'Come on, man, I never said you could forecast the deal.'

'I know, I know. It's Gordy. He's really been pressuring me. He wants me to set up a meeting with your CEO.'

'Gordy,' Brian said in disgust. Kent Gordon was the Senior Vice President and General Manager of Sales for Entronics USA, a Six Sigma black belt, the most aggressive guy I'd ever met. He was ruthless and conniving and relentless – not that there's anything wrong with that – and my entire career lay in his hands. Gordy was in fact leaning on me hard to do this deal, since he leaned on everybody hard to do every deal, and it was entirely plausible that he'd want me to set up a meeting between him and the CEO of Lockwood Hotels. But it wasn't true. Gordy hadn't asked for that. Maybe it was only a matter of time before he did, but he hadn't yet. It was a bluff.

'I know,' I said, 'but, you know, I can't control what he does.'

'I don't recommend you do that.'

'My bosses really want to do this deal, and it doesn't seem to be going anywhere, and . . .'

'Jason, when I was on your side of the desk I tried that old trick plenty of times,' Brian said, not unkindly.

'Huh?' I said, but I didn't have the heart to carry the bluff all the way through. I touched my bruised rib cage. It was hardly painful anymore.

'Look, I wish I could tell you what's going on with this deal, but I'm out of the loop. The bake-off went great, your price points are fine. I mean, I probably shouldn't say it, but your price points are *more* than fine. Obviously there's stuff going on upstairs that I'm not privy to.'

'Someone up there's got a favorite or something?'

'Something like that, yeah. Jason, if I knew the whole story, I'd tell you. You're a great guy, and I know you've worked your ass off on this deal, and if the product didn't measure up, I'd be straight with you. Or if the numbers didn't work. But it's not that. I don't know what it is.'

A beat of silence. 'I appreciate your honesty, Brian,' I said. I found myself thinking about the egg-sorting machine again and wondering how they worked, exactly. 'What day next week you coming up?'

My immediate boss was a woman, which, in this business, is unusual. Her name was Joan Tureck, and she was an area manager in charge of all of New England. I didn't know much about her personal life. I'd heard she was gay and lived with a woman in Cambridge, but she never talked about her partner or brought her to company events. She was a little dull, but we liked each other, and she'd always supported me, in her low-key way.

She was on the phone when I came by. She was always on the phone. She wore a headset and was smiling. All the Entronics offices have narrow windows on either side of the doors so everyone can always see inside. There's really no privacy.

Joan finally noticed me standing outside her office, and she held up a finger. I waited outside until she beckoned me in with a flick of her left hand.

'You talked to Lockwood Hotels this morning?' Joan said. She had short, curly, mouse brown hair with wisps of gray near the temple. She never wore any makeup.

I nodded as I sat.

39

'Nothing yet?'

'Nothing.'

'You think maybe it's time to call in some reinforcements?'

'Maybe. I can't seem to get to score with them.' I immediately regretted the sexual metaphor until I remembered that it was actually a sports term.

'We need that deal. If there's anything I can do.' I noticed she looked unusually weary, almost beaten down. She had reddish brown circles under her eyes. She took a long sip of coffee from a cat mug. 'Is that what you wanted to talk about?'

'No, something else,' I said. 'You have a couple of minutes now?'

She glanced at her tiny wristwatch. 'I've got a lunch any minute, but we could talk until my lunch date shows up.'

'Thanks. So, Crawford's out of here,' I said.

She blinked, not helping me at all.

'And his whole posse,' I went on. 'You're probably moving up to the DVP job, right?'

She blinked, hesitated. 'Bear in mind that, with the Meister acquisition, we're going to be cutting back. Anyone who isn't a top performer.'

As I thought, I bit my lower lip. 'Should I start packing up my desk?'

'You don't have to worry, Jason. You've made club four years in a row.' 'Club,' or Club 101, was made up of those reps who'd outperformed, made 101 percent of their revenue numbers. 'You've even been salesman of the year.'

'Not last year,' I pointed out. Last year the oily Trevor Allard got it and won a trip to Italy. He took his wife and then proceeded to cheat on her with some Italian chick he met at Harry's Bar in Venice.

'You had a bad fourth quarter. Everyone misses a quarter now and then. Bottom line is, people buy from people they like, and everyone likes you. But that's not what you came in to talk about.'

'Joan, do I have a chance at the area manager slot?'

She looked at me with surprise. 'Really?'

'Yeah, really.'

'Trevor's already put in for that, you know. And he's lobbying pretty hard.'

Some of the guys called him Teflon Trevor, because he always got away with everything. He kind of reminded me of the unctuous Eddie Haskell in the old *Leave It to Beaver* TV show. I guess you can tell I waste a lot of time watching old reruns on TV Land.

'Trevor would be good. But so would I. Do I have your support?'

'I – I don't take sides, Jason,' she said unhappily. 'If you want me to put in a word for you with Gordy, I'm happy to do so; but I don't know how much he listens to my recommendations.'

'That's all I ask. Just put in a word for me. Tell him I want to be interviewed.'

'I will. But Trevor is – maybe more Gordy's type.'

'More aggressive?'

'I guess he's what Gordy calls a meat-eater.'

Some people called him other things that weren't so nice. 'I eat steak.'

'I'll put in a word for you. But I'm not going to take sides. I'm staying completely neutral on this.'

There was a knock at her door. She made her little beckoning sign with her fingers.

The door opened, and a tall, handsome guy with tousled brown hair and sleepy brown eyes stood there and flashed her a perfect grin. Trevor Allard was long and lean and muscled and arrogant, and he still looked like the crew jock at St. Lawrence he'd been not too long ago. 'Ready for lunch, Joan?' he said. 'Oh, hey, Jason. I didn't see you.'

5

Kate was already home from work when I got in. She was lying on Grammy Spencer's rock-hard couch reading a collection of Alice Adams stories. She was reading it for her book group, nine women she'd gone to school and college with who got together once a month to discuss 'literary' novels written by female authors only.

'I've got a game tonight,' I told her after we'd kissed.

'Oh, right. It's Tuesday. I was going to try this tofu recipe from the *Moosewood Cookbook*, but I guess you don't have time, right?'

'I'll just grab something on the way to the field,' I said quickly.

'How about a Boca Burger?'

'No, I'm fine. Really. Don't bother.'

Kate wasn't a great cook, and this new tofu kick was really bad news, but I admired her for cooking at all. Her late mother didn't even know how. They'd had a full-time cook on staff until the money disappeared. My mom would come home from a long day working as a clerk-receptionist at a doctor's office and make a big meal for Dad and me – usually 'American chop suey,' which was macaroni and hamburger meat and tomato sauce. I'd never even

43

heard of anyone who had a cook, outside of the movies.

'So I told Joan that I want to be interviewed for the job,' I said.

'Oh, honey, that's terrific. When's the interview?'

'Well, I don't even know if Gordy will interview me for it. I'm sure he wants to give it to Trevor.'

'He has to at least *interview* you, doesn't he?'

'Gordy doesn't have to do anything.'

'He'll interview you,' she said firmly. 'And then you'll let him know how much you want the job and how good you'll be at it.'

'Actually,' I said, 'I *am* starting to want it. If for no other reason than to keep Trevor from becoming my boss.'

'I'm not sure that's the best reason, sweetie. Can I show you something?'

'Sure.' I knew what it was. It had to be some painting she'd discovered at work done by some impoverished 'outsider' artist in some totally primitive style. This happened at least once a month. She would rave about it, and I wouldn't get it.

She went to the entrance hall and came back with a big cardboard package out of which she pulled a square of cloth. She held it up, beaming, her eyes wide. 'Isn't it amazing?'

It seemed to be a painting of a huge black tenement building with tiny people being crushed beneath it. One of the tiny people was turning into a ball of blue flame. Another one had a bubble coming out of his mouth that said, 'I am oppressed by the debt of the capitalist society.' There were oversized hundred-dollar bills with wings floating against a baby blue sky and on top of everything the words, 'God Bless America.'

44

'Do you see how brilliant this is? That ironic 'God Bless America'? That phallic building representing debt, crushing all the little people?'

'That looks like a phallus to you?'

'Come on, Jase. That massive physical presence, the engineering prowess.'

'Okay, I see that,' I said, trying to sound like I meant it.

'This is a painted story quilt by a Haitian artist named Marie Bastien. She was a really big deal in Haiti, and she's just moved to Dorchester with her five kids. She's a single mom. I think she could be the next Faith Ringgold.'

'That right?' I said. I had no idea who she was talking about.

'The luminosity of her colors reminds me of Bonnard. But with the raw, simple Modernism of a Jacob Lawrence.'

'Hmm,' I said, glancing at my watch. I picked up the American Express bill from the coffee table and opened it. 'Very nice,' I said. I looked at the bill, and my eyes widened. 'Jesus.'

'It's bad, isn't it?' she said.

'I am oppressed by the debt of the capitalist society,' I said.

'How bad?' Kate said.

'Bad,' I said. 'But you don't see me turning into a ball of blue flame.'

6

You could hardly collect a more competitive bunch of guys than the sales team of Entronics USA. We were all recruited for our competitiveness, the way certain species of pit bulls are bred to be vicious. The company didn't care if its sales reps were particularly smart – there sure weren't any Phi Beta Kappas among us. They liked to hire athletes, figuring that jocks were persistent and thrived on competition. Maybe used to punishment and abuse too. Those of us who weren't jocks were the outgoing, naturally affable types, the social chairman in college, frat guys. That was me. Guilty on all counts. I was on the Happy Hour Committee at U. Mass, which we called Zoo-Mass.

So you'd think that, for all the jocks on the sales force, our softball team would be formidable.

Actually, we sucked.

Most of us were in lousy shape. We took clients out to lunch or dinner all the time, ate well, drank a lot of beer, and didn't have time to exercise. The only guys who'd stayed in shape were Trevor Allard, our pitcher, and Brett Gleason, our shortstop, who was your classic big dumb jock. Allard and Gleason were good buddies who hung out together a lot, played basketball together every Thursday night.

It was considered uncool to be too serious about our softball games. We had no uniforms, unless you count the ENTRONICS – BAND OF BROTHERS T-shirts that someone had made and that hardly anyone ever remembered to wear. We all chipped in to pay an umpire fifty bucks, whenever he was available. There'd be occasional arguments over whether someone was safe, or whether a ball was foul, but the disputes ended pretty quickly, and we got on with playing.

Still, no one likes to lose, especially dog-eat-dog types like us.

Tonight's game was against the reigning champions of our corporate league, Charles River Financial, the behemoth mutual fund company. Their team was almost all traders, right out of college, and they were all twenty-two years old and over six feet tall, and most of them had played on the baseball team at some Ivy League college. Charles River hired them young, chewed them up and spit them out, and by the time they hit thirty they were gone. But in the meantime, they fielded one hell of a softball team.

The question wasn't whether we'd lose. It was how badly they'd mop up the floor with us.

We played every Tuesday evening at the Stonington College field, which was carefully maintained, far better than we needed or deserved. It looked like Fenway. The outfield grass was turquoise and lush, perfectly mowed; the red infield dirt, some kind of clay and sand mix, was well raked; the foul lines were crisp and white.

The young studs from Charles River arrived all at the same time, driving their Porsches and BMWs and Mercedes convertibles. They wore real uniforms, white jerseys with pinstripes like the New York Yankees, with CHARLES RIVER FINANCIAL stitched across the front in looping script, and they each had numbers on their backs. They had matching Vexxum-3 Long Barrel aluminum-and-composite bats, Wilson gloves, even matching DeMarini gear bags. They looked like pros. We hated them the way a Sox fan hates the Yankees, deeply and irrevocably and irrationally.

By the time the game got under way, I'd forgotten all about the tow truck driver. Apparently he'd forgotten too.

It got ugly fast. Allard allowed seven runs – four of them a grand slam by Charles River's team captain, a bond trader named Mike Welch who was a Derek Jeter look-alike. Our guys were visibly uptight, trying too hard, so instead of aiming for base hits they kept swinging for home runs and inevitably got pop-ups instead. Plus there was the usual parade of errors – Festino collided with a fielder, which was an out, and a couple of Allard's pitches were ruled illegal because he didn't have his foot on the rubber.

According to our rules, if a team is ten runs ahead after four complete innings, they win. At the end of the third inning, the Charles River studs were ahead, 10–0. We were discouraged and pissed off.

Our manager, Cal Taylor, sat there drinking from a small flask of Jack Daniel's poorly concealed in a well-used paper bag and smoking Marlboros and shaking his head. I think he served as manager only to have company while he drank. There was the roar of a motorcycle nearby, coming closer, but I didn't pay much attention to it.

Then I noticed, in the waning light, a tall guy in a

leather jacket with a mullet walk onto the field. It took me a few seconds to recognize the tow truck driver from last night. He stood there for a few minutes, watching us lose, and then during the break I went up to him.

'Hey, Kurt,' I said.

'Hey.'

'You here to play?'

'Looks like you guys could use another player.'

Everyone was cool with it except, of course, Trevor Allard. We called a time-out, and we all huddled around Cal Taylor while Kurt hung back a respectful distance.

'He's not an Entronics employee,' Trevor said. 'You can't play if you don't have a valid employee number. That's the rules.'

I wasn't sure whether Trevor was just being his usual priggish self, or he'd heard that I'd put in for the promotion that he probably figured had his name on it.

Festino, who enjoyed twitting Trevor, said, 'So? If they challenge him, he just says he's a contract employee and didn't know he wasn't eligible.' He took advantage of the break to furtively slip the little bottle of Purell out of his pocket and clean his hands.

'A contract employee?' Trevor said with disgust. '*Him?*' As if a bum had just wandered onto the field from the street, reeking of cheap booze and six months of body odor. Trevor wore long cargo shorts and a faded Red Sox cap, the kind that comes prefaded, which he wore backwards, of course. He had a pukka shell necklace and a Rolex, the same kind of

Rolex as Gordy had, and a T-shirt that said LIFE IS GOOD.

'You ever ask the Charles River guys for their photo IDs?' said Festino. 'How do we know they don't have their own ringers, from the Yankees farm team?'

'Or some guy named Vinny from the mailroom,' said Taminek, a tall, scrawny guy who did inside sales. 'Anyway, Hewlett-Packard uses ringers all the time.'

'Yo, Trevor, you're not objecting because this guy's a pitcher, are you, dude?' Gleason razzed his buddy. He was an overdeveloped lunk with Dumbo ears, a lantern jaw, a blond crew cut, and bright white choppers that were way too big for his mouth. He'd recently grown a bristly goatee that looked like pubic hair.

Trevor scowled and shook his head, but before he could say anything further, Cal Taylor said, 'Put him in. Trevor, you go to second.' And he took a swig from his paper bag.

All anyone had to say was 'new hire,' and there were no questions asked. Kurt didn't look like a member of the Band of Brothers, but he could have been a software engineer or something, as far as the Charles River team knew. Or a mailroom guy.

Kurt was assigned to bat third in the lineup – not fourth, like in a real baseball team, but third, because even in his Jack Daniel's stupor, Cal Taylor understood that three batters would probably mean three outs, and we wanted to give the new guy a chance to show his stuff. And maybe save our asses.

Taminek was on first, and there was one out, when it was Kurt's turn at bat. I noticed he hadn't been warming up but had instead been standing there quietly, watching the Charles River pitcher and captain, Mike Welch, pitch. As if he were watching tapes in the clubhouse.

He stepped up to the plate, took a few practice swings with his battered old aluminum bat, and hammered a shot to left-center. The ball sailed over the back fence. As Taminek, and then Kurt, ran home, the guys cheered.

Kurt's homer was like an electric shock from those ER paddles. All of a sudden we started scoring runs. By the top of the fourth, we had five runs. Then Kurt took the mound to pitch to a big, beefy Charles River guy named Jarvis who was one of their sluggers. Kurt let loose with a wicked, blistering fastball, and Jarvis swung and missed, his eyes wide. You'd never think a softball could travel so fast.

Kurt threw an amazing rise ball, then a change up, and Jarvis had struck out.

Festino caught my eye. He was grinning.

Kurt proceeded to strike out two more guys with a bewildering and unhittable assortment of drop curves and rise balls.

In the fifth inning, we managed to load the bases, and then it was Kurt's turn at bat. He swung lefty this time, and once again drove the ball somewhere into the next town, trimming the Charles River lead to one.

Kurt struck them out, one two three, in the sixth, and then it was our turn at bat. I noticed that Trevor Allard was no longer complaining about our ringer. He hit a double, Festino singled, and by the time I struck out, we were up by two. Finally, in the bottom of the seventh, Kurt had struck out their first batter and allowed two hits – only because of our lousy fielding – when their guy Welch hit a slow grounder. Kurt scooped it up, fired to second, where Allard caught it, stepped, and threw to first. Taminek caught it and held it high for the third out. A double play, and we'd actually won our first game since prehistoric times.

All the guys thronged around Kurt, who shrugged modestly and gave his easy smile and didn't say too much. Everyone was talking and laughing loudly, exuberantly, narrating instant replays, reliving the double play that ended the game.

The inviolable tradition after each game was for our opponents to join us for food and beer and tequila shots at a nearby bar or restaurant. But we noticed that the young studs from Charles River were heading sullenly for their German cars. I called out to them, but Welch, without turning around, said, 'We're going to pass.'

'I think they're bummed out,' said Taminek.

'I think they're in a state of shock,' said Festino.

'Shock and awe,' said Cal Taylor. 'Where's our MVP?'

I looked around and saw Kurt slipping out to the parking lot. I chased up to him and invited him to join us.

'Nah, you guys probably want to hang by yourselves,' he said. I could see Trevor, standing at his silver Porsche, talking to Gleason, who was sitting in his Jeep Wrangler Sahara, top down.

'It's not like that,' I said. 'It's totally loose. Believe me, the guys would love to have a drink with you.'

'I don't drink anymore, man. Sorry.'

'Well, whatever. Diet Coke. Come on.'

He shrugged again. 'Sure you guys aren't going to mind?'

7

I felt like I'd brought Julia Roberts to audition for the high-school play. All of a sudden I was Mister Popular, basking in the reflected glory. We all gathered around a long table at the Outback Steakhouse, a five-minute drive away, everyone jazzed from our comeback-from-oblivion victory. Some ordered beers, and Trevor asked for a single-malt Scotch called Talisker, but the waitress didn't know what he was talking about, so he settled for a Dewar's. Kurt gave me a look that seemed to communicate secret amusement at what a dick Trevor was. Or maybe I was imagining it. Kurt didn't know that Gordy drank single-malts too, that Trevor was just sucking up to the boss even though the boss wasn't there.

Kurt ordered ice water. I hesitated, then did the same. Someone ordered a couple Bloomin' Onions and some Kookaburra Wings. Festino went to the john and came back wiping his hands on his shirt. 'God, I hate those scary cloth roller towels,' he said with a shudder. 'That endless, germ-infested loop of fecal bacteria. Like we're supposed to believe the towel only goes around once.'

Brett Gleason hoisted his mug of Foster's and proposed a toast to 'the MVP,' saying, 'You don't have to buy another drink in this town again.'

Taminek said, 'Where'd you come from?'

'Michigan,' Kurt said, with a sly grin.

'I mean, like – you play in college or something?'

'Never went to college,' Kurt said. 'Joined the army instead, and they don't play much softball. Not in Iraq, anyway.'

'You were in Iraq?' said one of our top dogs, Doug Forsythe, a tall, slender guy with a thatch of brown hair and a cowlick.

'Yeah,' Kurt said, nodding. 'And Afghanistan. All the hot tourist spots. In Special Forces.'

'Like, killing people?' asked Gleason.

'Only bad guys,' Kurt said.

'You ever kill anyone?' asked Forsythe.

'Just a couple of guys who asked too many questions,' said Kurt. Everyone laughed but Forsythe, and then he joined in, too.

'Cool,' said Festino, yanking at the tendrils of a fried onion and dipping the straws into the peppery pink sauce before gobbling them down.

'Not exactly,' said Kurt. He looked down at his glass of water and fell silent.

Trevor had his BlackBerry out and was thumbing the wheel, checking for messages as he sipped his Dewar's. Then he looked up and said, 'So how do you guys know each other?'

I flinched. The cell phone, the Acura wiping out in a ditch – the true story could inflict lasting damage to my reputation.

Kurt said, 'Mutual interest in cars.'

I liked this guy more and more.

'Cars?' said Trevor, but then Cal Taylor looked up from his Jack Daniel's – a freshly poured tumbler from the bar – and said, 'In 'Nam, we called you guys Snake Eaters.'

'The closest you got to 'Nam was Fort Dix, New Jersey,' said Gleason.

'Screw you,' growled Taylor, finishing off his Jack Daniel's. 'I developed boils.'

'Is that the same as Navy SEALs?' asked Forsythe. He was greeted by a chorus of derision, and Cal Taylor began singing, in a slurred and warbling tenor, the 'Ballad of the Green Beret.' He stood up, held out his glass of J.D., and sang, 'One hundred men we'll test today . . . But only one wins the Green Beret.'

'"Only three,"' corrected Gleason.

'Sit down, Cal,' said Trevor. 'I think it's time to go home.'

'I haven't finished my supper,' Cal growled.

'Come on, old man,' Forsythe said, and he and the rest of the guys trundled Cal out to the parking lot, Cal squawking in protest the whole time. They called him a cab and promised that someone would get his car back to his house in Winchester.

Kurt turned to me while they were gone, and said, 'Why are you guys the Band of Brothers? Some of you guys vets?'

'Vets?' I said. 'Us? Are you kidding? No, it's just a nickname. Not a very imaginative one, either. I don't even remember who thought of it.'

'All you guys in sales?'

'Yep.'

'You good?'

'Who, me?'

56

'You.'

'I'm okay,' I said.

'I think you're probably better than okay,' Kurt said.

I shrugged modestly, the way he seemed to shrug without saying anything. I do tend to unconsciously imitate whoever I'm around.

Then I heard Trevor say, 'Steadman's fine. He's just not much of a closer anymore.' He sat back down at the table. 'Right, Steadman? How's that Lockwood deal going? Are we in the third year yet? This may be the longest negotiation since the Paris Peace Talks.'

'It's looking good,' I lied. 'How's it going with the Pavilion Group?'

The Pavilion Group owned a chain of movie theaters that wanted to put LCDs in their lobbies to run trailers and ads for concessions.

Trevor smiled with satisfaction. 'Textbook,' he said. 'I did an ROI test for them that showed a seventeen percent increase in sales of Lemon Slushies.'

I nodded and tried not to roll my eyes. Lemon Slushies.

'Tomorrow I've got a meeting with the CEO, but it's just a meet-and-greet formality. He wants to shake my hand before he inks the deal. But it's in the bag.'

'Nice,' I said.

Trevor turned to Kurt. 'So, Kurt, you guys skydive and all that?'

'Skydive?' Kurt repeated with what sounded like a little twist of sarcasm. 'I guess you could call it that. We did jumps, sure.'

'How awesome is that?' said Trevor. 'I've gone sky-diving a bunch of times. Me and some guys from my frat did a skydiving trip to Brittany the summer after we graduated, and it was such a rush.'

'A rush.' Kurt said the word like it tasted bad.

'Nothing like it, huh?' said Trevor. 'What a kick.'

Kurt leaned back in his chair, turned to face Trevor. 'When you're dropped off from a C-141 Starlifter at thirty-five thousand feet to do a jump deep inside enemy territory, doing a clandestine entry seventy-five kilometers east-northeast of Mosul, it's not exactly a *rush*. You're carrying a hundred seventy-five pounds of commo gear and weapons and ammo, and you've got an oxygen mask blinding you and your stomach's in your throat and you're falling a hundred fifty miles an hour.' He took a sip of water. 'It's so cold at that altitude your goggles can freeze and shatter. Your eyeballs can freeze shut. You can get hypoxia and lose consciousness in a few seconds. Sudden deceleration trauma. Death on impact. If you don't hold your arms and legs just right when you're free-falling, you might go into a tumble or a spin, and go splat. Maybe your chute malfunctions. Even really experienced soldiers break their necks and die. And that's if you don't find yourself under attack from SAMs and antiaircraft artillery. You're scared shitless, and anyone who says they're not is lying.'

Trevor blushed, looked as if he'd just been slapped. Festino gave me a sidelong look of immense pleasure.

'Anyway,' Kurt said, draining his water, 'I'm sure Brittany was loads of fun.'

Kurt was a huge hit.

Forsythe said, 'Hey, can you come back next week?'

'I don't know,' Kurt said.

'We too Little League for you, that it?' said Taminek.

'Nah, not at all,' Kurt said. 'It's just that I work nights a lot.'

'Doing what?' Forsythe asked.

I braced myself – the tow truck, the Acura in the ditch . . . But he said, 'I drive for a buddy of mine who owns an auto body shop.'

'We got to get this guy a job at Entronics,' Taminek said.

Kurt chuckled, and said, 'Yeah, right.'

The rest of the guys eventually went home, leaving just me and Kurt.

'So,' he said. 'Band of Brothers.'

I nodded.

'Good buddies?'

I shrugged. 'Some of them.'

'Pretty competitive bunch, looks like.'

I couldn't tell if he was kidding. 'Can be,' I said. 'At work, anyway.'

'That pretty-boy who sat across from me – what's his name, Trevor? – seems like a real dickhead.'

'I guess.'

'Saw him driving over here in his Porsche. So, was your boss here tonight too?'

'No. Most of the guys here tonight are just individual contributors.'

'Individual contributors?'

'Sales reps. I'm a DM, a district sales manager, and so is Trevor, only we have different territories.'

'But he's competing against you.'

'Yeah, well, it's complicated. We're both up for the same promotion.' I explained to him about the recent turmoil at Entronics and the AM job that had just opened up and the trouble I was having with the Lockwood Hotels deal. He listened without saying anything.

When I was done, he said, 'Not easy to have unit cohesion when you're all battling each other.'

'Unit cohesion?'

'See, in Special Forces, we'd work in twelve-man teams. Operational detachments, they call 'em. A-Teams. Everyone's got his job – mine was eighteen charlie, engineer sergeant. The demolitions expert. And we all had to work together, respect each other, or we'd never be battle-ready.'

'Battle-ready, huh?' I smiled, thinking of the corporation as a battlefield.

'You know the real reason soldiers are willing to die in war? You think it's about patriotism? Family? Country? No way, bro. It's all about your team. No one wants to be the first to run. So we all stand together.'

'I guess we're more like scorpions in a bottle.'

He nodded. 'Look. So we were on this armed reconnaissance mission outside Musa Qalay, in Afghanistan, right? Going after one of the anticoalition militias. A split team, so I was in charge. We had a couple of GMVs. Nontactical vehicles, I'm talking.'

'GMV?' Military guys speak a foreign language. You need a simultaneous translator to talk to them sometimes.

'Modified Humvee. Ground Mobility Vehicle.'

'Okay.'

'Suddenly my GMV's struck head-on by machine gun fire and RPGs.' He made a slight grimace. 'Rocket-propelled grenades, okay? Shoulder-launched anti-tank weapon. It was an ambush. My vehicle was hit.

We were trapped in a kill box. So I ordered the driver – my good buddy, Jimmy Donadio – to floor it. Not away from the ambush, but right *toward* the machine-gun emplacement. Told the guy on top to start firing off the .50 cal, just unload it on them. You could see the bad guys slumped over the machine gun. Then my GMV got hit with another RPG. Disabled it. The vehicle was in flames, okay? We were screwed. So I jumped out with my M16 and just started firing away at them until I was out of ammo. Killed them all. Must have been six of them.'

I just stared at Kurt, rapt. The scariest thing I ever faced in my line of work was a performance review.

'So let me ask you something,' Kurt said. 'Would you do that for Trevor?'

'Fire at him with a machine gun?' I said. 'I fantasize about that sometimes.'

'You get my point, though?'

I wasn't sure I did. I poked at the Bloomin' Onion but didn't eat any. I already felt queasy from all the grease.

He looked like he was getting ready to leave. 'Mind if I ask *you* something?'

'Go for it.'

'So when we were in country, our most important weapon by far was always our intel. The intelligence we had on the enemy, right? Strength of their units, location of their encampments, all that. So what kind of intel do you guys collect on your potential customers?'

This guy was smart. Really smart. 'They're not the enemy,' I said, amused.

'Okay.' A bashful smile. 'But you know what I mean.'

'I guess. We gather the basic stuff . . .' I paused for a few seconds. 'To be honest, not much. We sort of fly by the seat of the pants, I sometimes think.'

He nodded. 'Wouldn't it help if you drilled down? Like the way you're getting dicked around by Lockwood Hotels – like, what's really going on there?'

'Would it help? Sure. But we don't have any way of knowing. That's the thing. It's not pretty, but that's how it is.'

Kurt kept nodding, staring straight ahead. 'I know a guy used to work in security for the Lockwood chain. He might still be there.'

'A security guard?'

Kurt smiled. 'Pretty high up in corporate security, at their headquarters – New York or New Jersey, whatever.'

'White Plains, New York.'

'Lot of Special Forces guys go into corporate security. So why don't you give me some names, some background. Tell me who you're working with. I'll see if I can find anything out for you. A little intel, right?'

Kurt Semko had already surprised me a couple of times, so maybe it wasn't so far-fetched, I figured, that this tow truck driver who'd been kicked out of the Special Forces might be able to get the lowdown on Brian Borque, the Vice President for Property Management at Lockwood Hotels. It made sense that there'd be a network of ex-Special Forces officers who now worked in the private sector. Why the hell not? I gave him a bit of background and scribbled Brian Borque's name on a napkin. Kurt had an e-mail address, too – I guess everyone does these days – and I wrote it down.

'All right, man,' Kurt said, getting up and putting a

big hand on my shoulder. 'No worries. I'll give you a call if I find anything out.'

It was pretty late by the time I got home, driving the Geo Metro that Enterprise Rent-A-Car had brought over that morning. Kate was asleep.

I sat down at the computer in the little home office we shared to check my office e-mail, as I always did before I went to bed. Internet Explorer was open, which meant that Kate had been using the computer, and out of pointless curiosity I clicked on 'Go' to see where she'd been browsing. I wondered whether Kate ever looked at porn, though that seemed awfully unlikely.

No. The last place she'd been was a website called Realtor.com, where she'd been looking at houses in Cambridge. Not cheap ones, either. Million-dollar, two-million-dollar houses in the Brattle Street area.

Real estate porn.

She was looking at houses we could never afford, not on my income. I felt bad, for her and for me.

When I signed on to my office e-mail, I found the workup I'd done on Lockwood, and forwarded it to Kurt. Then I scrolled quickly through the junk – health-plan notices, job listings, endless personnel notices – and found an e-mail from Gordy that he'd sent after hours.

He wanted me to 'drop by' his office at 8:00 tomorrow morning.

8

The alarm went off at 5:00 A.M., two hours earlier than usual. Kate groaned and rolled over, put a pillow over her head. I got up as quietly as I could, went downstairs, and made the coffee, and while it was brewing I took a quick shower. I wanted to get into the office a good hour before my interview with Gordy so I could go over my accounts and get all the numbers in order.

When I got out of the shower, I saw the light in the bedroom was on. Kate was downstairs at the kitchen table in her pink bathrobe, drinking coffee.

'You're up early,' she said.

I gave her a kiss. 'You too. Sorry if I woke you.'

'You were out late.'

'The softball game, remember?'

'You went out for drinks afterward?'

'Yeah.'

'Drown your sorrows?'

'We won, believe it or not.'

'Hey, that's a first.'

'Yeah, well, that guy Kurt played for us. He blew everyone away.'

'Kurt?'

'The tow truck driver.'

64

'Huh?'

'Remember, I told you about this guy who gave me a ride home after the Acura wiped out?' It wiped out by itself. I had nothing to do with it, see.

'Navy SEALs.'

'Special Forces, but yeah. That guy. He's, like, the real thing. He's everything Gordy and all these other phony tough guys *pretend* to be. Sitting in their Aeron chairs and talking about "dog eat dog" and "killing the competition." Only he's for real. He's actually killed people.'

I realized I was telling her everything except the one thing I was most anxious about: my interview with Gordy in a couple of hours. I wasn't sure I wanted to tell her. She'd probably just make me more nervous.

'Don't forget, Craig and Susie are going to be here in time for supper tonight.'

'It's tonight?'

'I've only told you a thousand times.'

I let out a half groan, half sigh. 'How long are they staying?'

'Just two nights.'

'Why?'

'Why what? Why just two nights?'

'Why are they coming to Boston? I thought L.A. was God's country. That's what Craig's always saying.'

'He was just elected to the Harvard Board of Overseers, and his first meeting is tomorrow.'

'How could he be on the Harvard Board of Overseers? He's a Hollywood guy now. He probably doesn't even own a tie anymore.'

'He's not only a prominent alum but also a major contributor. People care about things like that.'

When Susie met Craig, he was just a poor starving writer. He'd had a couple of stories published in magazines with names like *TriQuarterly* and *Ploughshares*, and he taught expository writing at Harvard. He was kind of snooty, and Susie probably liked that, but she sure as hell wasn't going to live in genteel poverty, and I think he figured out pretty quickly that he was never going to make it in the literature business. So they moved out to L.A., where Craig's Harvard roommate introduced him around, and he started writing sitcoms. Eventually he got a gig writing for *Everybody Loves Raymond* and began making serious money. Then, somehow, he created this hit show and overnight became unbelievably rich.

Now he and Susie vacationed on St. Barths with Brad and Angelina, and Susie regularly fed Katie gossip about which movie stars were secretly gay and which ones were in rehab. They had a big house in Holmby Hills and were always out to dinner with all the celebrities. And he never let me forget it.

She got up and poured herself another cup of coffee. 'Susie's going to take Ethan around Boston – the Freedom Trail, all that.'

'She doesn't get it, does she? Ethan's not into Paul Revere. Maybe the Salem Witch Museum, but I don't think they show the real sicko stuff there that he's into.'

'All I ask is for you to be nice to them. You and Ethan have some sort of great chemistry, which I don't quite understand. But I appreciate it.'

'How come they're staying here anyway?' I said.

'Because she's my sister.'

'You know they're just going to complain the whole

time about the bathroom and the shower curtain and how the water from the shower spills out on the floor, and how we have the wrong coffeemaker and how come we don't have any Peet's Sumatra coffee beans –'

'You can't hold it against them, Jason. They're just accustomed to a higher standard of living.'

'Then maybe they should stay at the Four Seasons.'

'They want to stay with us,' she said firmly.

'I guess Craig needs to stay in touch with the little people every once in a while.'

'Very funny.'

I went to the cereal cabinet and surveyed its depressing, low-cal, high-fiber contents. Fiber One and Kashi Go Lean and several other grim-looking boxes of twigs and burlap strips. 'Hey, honey?' I said, my back turned. 'You've been looking at real estate?'

'What are you talking about?'

'On the computer. I noticed you were looking at some real estate website.'

No answer. I selected the least-disgusting-looking box, a tough choice, and reluctantly brought it to the table. In the refrigerator all we had now was skim milk. Not even one percent. I hate skim milk. Milk shouldn't be blue. I brought the carton to the table, too.

Kate was examining her coffee cup, stirring the coffee with a spoon, though she hadn't added anything to it. 'A girl can dream, can't she?' she finally said in her sultry Veronica Lake voice.

I felt bad for her, but I didn't pursue the subject. I mean, what's to say? She must have expected more from me when she married me.

We met at a mutual friend's wedding when both of

us were pretty drunk. A guy I knew from DKE, my college frat, was marrying a girl who went to Exeter with Kate. Kate had been forced to leave Exeter in her junior year when her family went broke. She went to Harvard, but on financial aid. Her family tried to keep everything a secret, as WASPs do, but everyone figured out the truth eventually. There are buildings in Boston with her family name on them, and she had to suffer the humiliation of going to public school in Wellesley her last two years. (Whereas I, a boy from Worcester who was the first in his family to go to college, whose dad was a sheet-metal worker, had no idea what a private school even was until college.)

At the wedding, we were seated next to each other, and I immediately glommed on to this hot babe. She seemed a little pretentious: a comp lit major at Harvard, read all the French feminists – in French, of course. She also definitely seemed out of my league. Maybe if we hadn't both been drunk she wouldn't have paid me any attention, though later she told me she thought I was the best-looking guy there, and funny, and charming, too. And who could blame her? She seemed amused by all my stories about my job – I'd just started as a sales rep at Entronics, and I wasn't yet burned-out. She liked the fact that I was so into my work. She said that I was such a breath of fresh air, that it really set me apart from all her clove-cigarette-smoking, cynical male friends. I probably went on too much about my master plan, how much money I'd be pulling down in five years, in ten years. But she was taken by it. She said she found me more 'real' than the guys she normally hung with.

She didn't seem to mind my dorky mistakes, the

way I mistakenly drank from her water glass. She explained to me the dry-to-wet rule of table setting, with the water and wine to the right of your plate and the bread and dry things to the left. Neither did she mind that I was a lousy dancer – she found it cute, she said. On our third date, when I invited her over to my apartment, I put on Ravel's 'Bolero,' and she laughed, thought I was being ironic. What did I know? I thought 'Bolero' was classic make-out music, along with Barry White.

So I was born with a plastic spoon in my mouth. Obviously Kate didn't marry me for my money – she knew plenty of rich guys in her social circles – but I think she expected me to take care of her. She was on the rebound from an affair she'd had with one of her college professors right after she graduated, a pompous but handsome and distinguished scholar of French literature at Harvard, whom she discovered was simultaneously sleeping with two other women. She told me later that she considered me 'down-to-earth' and unpretentious, the polar opposite of her three-timing, beret-wearing, silver-haired father-figure French professor. I was a charismatic business guy who was crazy about her and would make her feel safe, at least, give her the financial security she wanted. She could raise a family and do something vaguely artistic like landscape gardening or teaching literature at Emerson College. That was the deal. We'd have three kids and a big house in Newton or Brookline or Cambridge.

The plan wasn't for her to live in a fifteen-hundred-square-foot Colonial in the low-income part of Belmont.

'Listen, Kate,' I finally said after a moment of silence. 'I've got an interview with Gordy this morning.'

Her face lit up. I hadn't seen her smile like that in weeks. 'Already? Oh, Jason. This is so great.'

'I think Trevor has it sewed up, though.'

'Jason, that's just negative thinking.'

'Realistic thinking. Trevor's been campaigning for it. He's been having his direct reports call Gordy and tell him how much they want Trevor to get the job.'

'But Gordy must see through all that.'

'Maybe. But he loves being sucked up to. Can't get enough of it.'

'So why don't you do the same thing?'

'I hate that. It's cheesy. It's also devious.'

She nodded. 'You don't need to do that. Just show him how much you want the job. Want an omelet?'

'An omelet?' Was there such thing as a tofu omelet? Probably. Tofu and scrambled eggs too, I bet. This could be nasty.

'Yep. You need your protein. I'll put some Canadian bacon in it. Gordy likes his guys to be meat-eaters, right?'

9

On the way into work I popped a CD into the dashboard slot of the rented Geo Metro. It was one of my vast collection of tapes and CDs of motivational talks by the god worshipped by all salesmen, the great motivational speaker and training guru Mark Simkins.

I'd probably listened to this CD, *Be a Winner*, five hundred times. I could recite long stretches of it word for word, mimicking Mark Simkins's emphatic, sing-song voice, his nasal Midwestern accent, his bizarre, halting phraseology. He taught me never ever to use the word 'cost' or 'price' with a customer. It was 'total investment.' Also, 'contract' was a scary word; you should say 'paperwork' or 'agreement.' And never ask a prospect to 'sign' an agreement – you 'endorsed' the copies or 'okayed' the agreement. But most of all he taught that you had to believe in yourself.

Sometimes I listened to the discs just to get myself fired up, to stiffen my spine, give myself a tequila shot of confidence. It was as if Mark Simkins were my personal coach, cheering me on in the privacy of my car, and I needed all the confidence I could get for my interview with Gordy.

By the time I got to Framingham, I was swimming in

caffeine – I'd brought the extra-large travel Thermos – and totally pumped. I walked from the parking lot reciting like a mantra a couple of my favorite Mark Simkins lines: 'Believe in yourself one hundred per-cent, and everyone else will have no choice but to follow you.'

And: '*Expect* good things to happen.'

And: 'The only thing that counts is how many times you succeed. For the more times you fail and keep try-ing, the more times you succeed.' That one was like a Zen koan to me. I used to repeat it over and over try-ing to crack its wisdom. I still wasn't totally sure what it meant, but I repeated it to myself every time I got dinged on a sales call, and it made me feel better.

Hey, whatever it takes.

Gordy kept me waiting outside his office for a good twenty, twenty-five minutes. He always kept people waiting. It was a power thing, and you just got used to it. I could see him through the window, pacing back and forth with his headset on, gesticulating wildly. I sat there at an empty cubicle next to his secretary, Melanie, who's a sweet, pretty woman, very tall, with long brown hair, a couple of years older than me. She apologized repeatedly – that seemed to be her main job description, apologizing to everyone he kept waiting – and offered to get me coffee. I said no. Any more caffeine and I'd go into orbit.

Melanie asked me how the game went last night, and I told her how we'd won, without getting into detail about our ringer. She asked me how Kate was, and I asked her about her husband, Bob, and their three cute little kids. We made small talk for a couple of minutes until her phone started ringing.

At close to eight-thirty, Gordy's door opened and he came barreling through. Both of his stubby arms were extended in welcome, as if he wanted to give me a bear hug. Gordy, who looks sort of like a bear cub, only not cute, is a very huggy person. If he's not hugging, he's got an arm on your shoulder.

'Steadman,' he said. 'How're you doing there, buddy?'

'Hey, Gordy,' I said.

'Melanie, get my buddy Steadman here some coffee, could you?'

'Already offered, Kent,' said Melanie, turning around from her cubicle. She was the only one in the office who called him by his first name. The rest of us had largely forgotten he had a first name.

'Water?' he said. 'Coke? Scotch?' He threw his head back and brayed, a sort of open-mouth cackle.

'Scotch on the rocks sounds good to me,' I said. 'Breakfast of champions.'

He brayed again, put his arm around my shoulder, and pulled me into the vast expanse of his office. In his floor-to-ceiling windows you could see turquoise ocean and palm trees, the waves crashing against the perfect white sand. Really a magnificent view, enough to make you forget you were in Framingham.

Gordy sank into his ergonomic desk chair and leaned back, and I sat in the chair across from him. His desk was a ridiculously large oblong of black marble, which he kept fanatically neat. The only thing on it was a giant, thirty-inch Entronics flat-panel LCD monitor and a blue folder, which I assumed was my personnel file.

73

'So, man,' he said with a long, contented sigh, 'you want a promotion.'

'I do,' I said, 'and I think I'd kick ass.'

Believe in yourself one hundred percent, and everyone else will have no choice but to follow you, I chanted silently.

'I'll bet you would,' he said, and there was no irony in his voice. He seemed to mean it, and that surprised me. He fixed me with his small brown eyes. Some of us in the Band of Brothers – not Trevor or Gleason, who were famous suck-ups – referred to Gordy's eyes as 'beady' or 'ferretlike,' but right now they seemed warm and moist and sincere. His eyes were set deeply beneath a low, Cro-Magnon brow. He had a large head, a double chin, a ruddy face that reminded me of a glazed ham, with deep acne pits on his cheeks. His dark brown hair – another Just For Men victim, I assumed – was cut in a layered pompadour. There were times when I could imagine him as the tubby little kid in school he must have been.

Now he hunched forward and studied my file. His lips moved a tiny bit as he read. As he flipped the pages with a stubby paw, you could see a flash of monogrammed cuff link. Everything he wore was monogrammed with a big script KG.

There was no reason for him to be reading my file right in front of me except to rattle me. I knew that. So I repeated to myself, silently: '*Expect* good things to happen.'

I looked around the office. In one corner of his office he had a golf putter in a mahogany stand next to an artificial-turf putting mat. On a shelf in his credenza was a bottle of Talisker eighteen-year-old

74

single-malt Scotch, which he liked to brag was the only Scotch he drank. If so, he must have made a real dent in the world supply of it because he drank a lot.

'Your annual reviews aren't bad at all,' he said.

From Gordy, this was a rave. 'Thanks,' I said. I watched the surf crashing against the dazzling white sand, the palm trees swaying in the gentle breeze, the seagulls circling and diving into the azure water. Gordy'd had the latest Entronics QD-OLED proto-type PictureScreen installed in his windows, and the resolution and colors were perfect. You could change the high-definition video loop to one of a dozen scenes, any of which was better than the view over-looking the parking lot. Gordy liked the ocean – he owned a forty-four-foot Slipstream catamaran, which he kept in the Quincy marina – so his background films were always the Atlantic or the Pacific or the Caribbean. The PictureScreen was a real breakthrough in display technology, and we owned it. It could be manufactured in any size, and the screen was flexible, could be rolled up like a poster, and there wasn't a better, crisper picture available anywhere. Customers and potential customers who visited Gordy in his office always gasped, and not just at what a pompous jerk he was. It was strange, though, when you walked into Gordy's office at seven or eight in the morning and saw midday Caribbean sunlight.

'You were Salesman of the Year three years ago, Steadman,' he said. 'Club four years running.' He gave a low whistle. 'You like Grand Cayman?'

The Cayman Islands was one of the trips the com-pany sent the Salesman of the Year on. 'Great diving,' I said.

'Diving for dollars.' He tipped his head back, opened his mouth, did a silent bray.

'I'm impressed you were able to sell UPS those self-keystoning projectors. They wanted compression technology, and we don't do compression technology.'

'I sold them on future compatibility.'

'Booya,' he said, nodding.

That was Gordy's way of congratulating people. He was being too nice, which made me nervous. I was expecting his usual frontal assault.

'Morgan Stanley?' he said.

'They've got an RFP on the street, but they won't talk to me. Got to be an inside job. I'm just column fodder.'

'Sounds right,' he said. 'They're just specking the competition. Send 'em back their lousy RFP.'

'I'm not going to make it easy for them,' I said.

His smile twisted up at one end, making him look appropriately Mephistophelian.

'And it looks like FedEx hasn't delivered yet, huh?'

'FedEx wants a bunch of LCD projectors for their logistics center, to display the weather and all that, twenty-four/seven. I demo'd it for them in Memphis.'

'And?'

'They're jerking me around. They're looking at Sony and Fujitsu and NEC and us. Doing a side-by-side shoot-out.'

'Deciding on price point, no doubt.'

'I'm trying to sell them on quality and reliability. Better investment in the long run, all that. I'd say we've got a thirty percent chance of winning it.' That was a complete hallucination.

'That high, huh?'

'That's my take. I wouldn't forecast it, though.'

'Albertson's fell through,' he said, with a sad shake of the head. Albertson's is the second-largest supermarket chain in the country. They own thousands of supermarkets, drugstores, and gas stations, and they wanted to put in digital signage in a bunch of their stores. That would have meant fifteen-inch flat-panel LCD screens at every checkout lane – I guess so you wouldn't have to read the *National Enquirer* and then put it back in the rack – and forty-two-inch plasmas throughout the store. They were calling it a storewide 'network' that would 'provide our customers with relevant information and solutions during their visits to the stores.' Translation: ads. Brilliant idea – they wouldn't even have to pay for the equipment. It was going to be installed by this middleman, a company called SignNetwork that bought and installed all this stuff in stores. The screens would run ads for Walt Disney videos and Kodak and Huggies diapers. I'd been dealing with both Albertson's and SignNetwork, trying to sell them on the advantages of paying a bit more for quality and all that. No dice.

'They went with NEC,' I said.

'Why?'

'You want to know the truth? Jim Letasky. He's NEC's top sales guy, and he basically owns the SignNetwork account. They don't want to deal with any other company. They love the guy.'

'I know Letasky.'

'Nice guy,' I said. Unfortunately. I wished I could hate the guy, since he was stealing so much of our business, but I'd met him at the Consumer Electronics show a couple of years back, and he was great. They say people buy from people they like; after we had a drink, *I* was almost ready to buy a bunch of NEC plasmas from Jim Letasky.

He fell silent again. 'And Lockwood drags on like a case of the clap. You column fodder there too?'

'I don't know.'

'You're not giving up on this one, though, right?'

'Give up? Me?'

He smiled. 'That's not you, is it?'

'Nope.'

'Let me ask you something, Steadman. Hope you don't mind if I get too personal. You got problems in your marriage?'

'Me?' I shook my head, flushing despite my best efforts. 'We're great.'

'Your wife sick or something?'

'She's fine.' Like: What the hell?

'You have cancer, maybe?'

I half smiled, said quietly, 'I'm in good health, Gordy, but thanks for asking.'

'Then what the hell's your problem?'

I was silent while I pondered the best way to answer that wouldn't get me fired.

'Four years in a row you're Club 101. Then you're what? You're Festino.'

'What do you mean?'

'Can't close.'

'That's not the case, Gordy. I was Salesman of the Year.'

'In a great market for plasma and LCDs. Rising tide floats all boats.'

'My boat floated higher.'

'Your boat still seaworthy? That's the question. Look

78

at the last year. See, I'm starting to wonder whether you're hitting the wall. Happens, sometimes, to sales guys at this point in their careers. Lose that spark. You still have the fire in the belly?'

It's called acid reflux, and I was feeling it right now.

'It's still there,' I said. 'You know, like they say, the only thing that counts is how many times you succeed. The more times you fail and keep trying, the more times you succeed.'

'I don't want to hear any of that Mark Simkins candy-ass crapola here,' he said. Busted. 'He's full of it. The more times you fail, the more accounts you lose.'

'I don't think that's what he means, Gordy,' I began.

'"*Expect* good things to happen,"' he said, doing an unexpectedly good imitation of Mark Simkins, half-way between Mister Rogers and the Reverend Billy Graham, if you can imagine that. 'Well, in the real world that we're living in here, I expect a shitstorm every day, and I come prepared with my rubber poncho and *galoshes,* you get me? That's how it works in the real world, not in Candy-Ass Land. Now, you and Trevor Allard and Brett Gleason want to do a side-by-side? See who drives a bigger piece of the number? See who's up-and-coming and who's history?'

History. 'Trevor got lucky last year. Hyatt started buying big.'

'Steadman, listen to me, and listen good: You make your own luck.'

'Gordy,' I said, 'you assigned him the better accounts this past year, okay? You gave Trevor all the good chocolates, and you gave me all the ones with the pink coconut centers.'

He looked up at me abruptly, those ferret eyes glittering. 'And there's a hole in the ozone layer, and you were switched at birth, and you got any *other* excuses while you're at it?' His voice got steadily louder until he was shouting. 'Let me tell you something. There is shit about to rain down on us from Tokyo, and we don't even know what kind of shit it is! And if I promote the wrong guy here, it's *my* ass on the line!'

I wanted to say, Hey, I don't want this stupid promotion anyway. I just want to go home and have a steak and make love to my wife. But I'd suddenly realized that, damn it, I wanted the job. Maybe I didn't want the job so much as I wanted to *get* it. I said, 'You won't be making a mistake.'

He smiled again, and I was really starting to despise his evil little smiles. 'It's survival of the fittest around here, you know that.'

'Hell, yeah.'

'But sometimes evolution needs a little help. That's my job. I promote the fittest. Kill off the weak. And if you get this job, you've got to be able to fire people. Lop off the deadwood. Throw the deadweight overboard before it sinks us. Could you fire Festino?'

'I'd put him on a plan first.' A performance plan was the way the company told you to shape up or beat it. It was usually a fancy way to create a paper trail to fire you, but sometimes you could turn things around.

'He's on a plan already, Steadman. He's deadwood, and you know it. If you get the job, could you fire his ass?'

'If I had to,' I said.

'Any member of your team doesn't perform, *you* don't hit your numbers. One weak link, we all suffer.

Including me. Remember: There's no "I" in "team."'

I thought: *Yeah, well, there's an 'I' in 'idiot.' And a 'U' in 'stupid.'*

But I just nodded thoughtfully.

'See, Steadman, you can't be sentimental. You've got to be willing to push your grandmother under a bus to make your nums. Allard would. Allard's got that. So does Gleason. How about you?'

Sure, I'd push Allard's grandmother under a bus. I'd push Allard under a bus. Gleason too.

I said, 'My grandmother's dead.'

'You know what I'm saying. Motivating people to climb the hill for you isn't the same as carrying a bag.' *Carrying a bag* – that was insider-speak for selling.

'I know.'

'Do you? You got the fire in the belly? The killer instinct? Can you level-set? Can you incent your team?'

'I know how to do what it takes,' I said.

'Let me ask you a question: What kind of car did you drive to work today, Steadman?'

'Well, it's a rented –'

'Just answer the question. What kind of car?'

'A Geo Metro, but that's because –'

'A Geo Metro,' he said. 'A Geo. Metro.'

'Gordy –'

'I want you to say that aloud, Steadman. Say, "I drove a Geo Metro to work today."'

'Right.'

'Say it, Steadman.'

I exhaled noisily. 'I drove a Geo Metro to work today because –'

'Good. Now say, "And Gordy drove a Hummer." Got it?'

'Gordy –'

'Say it, Steadman.'

'Gordy drove a Hummer.'

'Correct. Is anything sinking in? Show me your watch, Steadman.'

I glanced down at it involuntarily. It was a decent-looking Fossil, about a hundred bucks at the kiosk in the Prudential Mall. I held out my left hand reluctantly.

'Take a look at mine, Steadman.' He flicked his left wrist, shot his cuff, revealed a huge, gaudy Rolex, gold and diamond-encrusted with three subdials on its face. Tacky-looking, I thought.

'Nice watch,' I said.

'Now look at my shoes, Steadman.'

'I think I get your point, Gordy.'

I noticed he was looking up at his door. He flashed a thumbs-up at whoever was outside. I turned around to see Trevor walking by. Trevor gave me a smile, and I smiled right back.

'I'm not sure you do get my point,' he said. 'The top sixty percent of the sales force hit their OTEs.' OTE was on-target earnings. 'Then there's the over-achievers, okay? The Club. And *then* there's the high-octane, the best-in-breed. The meat-eaters. Like Trevor Allard. Like Brett Gleason. Are you a meat-eater, Steadman?'

'Medium rare,' I said.

'Do you have the killer instinct?'

'You have to ask?'

He stared at me. 'Show me,' he said. 'Next time I see you, I want to hear about how you closed one of your big accounts.'

I nodded.

His voice got quiet, confiding. 'See, I'm all about BHAGs, Steadman.' He pronounced it bee-hags. It stood for 'big hairy audacious goals.' He'd read an article somewhere that quoted from some book. 'You have the ability to come up with a BHAG?'

'Very big and very hairy,' I said, just to let him know I knew what it meant. 'Absolutely.'

'You playing to play, or playing to win?'

'To win.'

'What's our company motto, Steadman?'

'"Invent the Future."' Who the hell knew what that meant? Like we sales reps were supposed to invent the future? They invented stuff in Tokyo, under the cone of silence, and shipped it over to us to sell.

He stood up to signal that our little meeting was over, and I stood up too, and he came around the desk and put his arm around my shoulder. 'You're a good guy, Jason. A really good guy.'

'Thank you.'

'But are you good enough to be on the G Team?'

It took me a few seconds to realize that G stood for Gordy. 'You know I am,' I said.

'Show me that killer instinct,' he said. 'Kill, baby, kill.'

Melanie gave me a sympathetic smile as I stumbled out of Gordy's office into the natural sunshine. Well, actually, it was gray and cloudy and starting to rain outside. Much nicer in the Caribbean, but I liked the real world.

I switched my cell phone back on as I walked back to my office. My cell started making that fast, urgent-sounding alarm sound that indicated I had a message.

I checked the calls received and didn't recognize the number. I called voice mail and heard a message from someone whose voice I didn't at first recognize. 'Yo, Jason,' a gravelly voice said. 'I got some information for you on that guy at Lockwood Hotels.'

Kurt Semko.

When I got to my office, I called him back.

10

'Guy's name is Brian Borque, right?' Kurt said.

'Yeah?' I was still feeling kind of numb from being beaten about the head and neck with Gordy's psychic rubber truncheon.

'My buddy's still in corporate security at Lockwood, and he did some poking around for me,' Kurt said. 'So dig this: Your man Brian Borque and his fiancée just came back from Aruba, right?'

'Yeah?' I vaguely remembered him saying he'd be out of the office for a week or ten days. 'He said he took his wife to Vienna, Virginia, I remember.'

'First-class tickets there and back, five-star hotel, all expenses paid, and by guess who?'

'Who?'

'Hitachi.'

I was silent for a few seconds as it dawned on me. 'Shit,' I said.

Kurt's reply was a slow, husky chuckle. 'Maybe that explains the runaround you've been getting.'

'I'll say. And he's been jerking me around for a year on this contract. Boy, that pisses me off.'

'Greedhead, huh?'

'I should have known. He was stringing me along

for Super Bowl tickets and everything else he could get out of me, and all the while I'm just his chick on the side, because he's in bed with Hitachi. He was never going to buy from us anyway. All right. Thanks, man. At least now I know.'

'No worries. So . . . what are you going to do about it?'

'Close it or kill it, that's the rule around here. I kill it and move on.'

'I don't think so. I don't see why you have to kill it and just walk away. See, there's something else you may not know.'

'Like what?'

'Seems Lockwood Hotels has a policy on not accepting gifts greater than a hundred bucks from a customer or vendor.'

'They have a policy like that?'

'That's why my buddy in corporate security knows about it.'

'Borque's in trouble, that what you mean?'

'Not yet. A file's been opened. That little trip to Aruba was worth a good five or six thousand bucks. I'd say that's a violation of company policy, wouldn't you?'

'What am I supposed to do with that? Blackmail the guy?'

'Naw, man. You help him out of his ethical dilemma. Lead him away from temptation. You . . . torque Borque.' He chuckled again. 'Then you're good to go.'

'How?' I said.

I called Brian Borque but got his voice mail and asked him to call me back as soon as he could.

In the meantime I checked my e-mail and plowed

through the usual meaningless company crap, but one subject header caught my eye. I normally ignore all the job listings – after all, I already have a job, and anything in my department I hear about long before they post it. But this one was a notice for a Corporate Security officer that had just been posted today.

I skimmed it quickly. 'Perform various duties such as ensuring the physical security of the facility as well as acting as first response to all emergencies including security, medical, bomb, and fire,' it said. 'Qualified candidates must have: High School Diploma or GED, good communication skills, and physical security background.' It went on to say, Prefer: Recent Military experience such as Military Police . . . Demonstrated leadership and experience with handguns a plus.'

I remembered what Taminek said at the Outback: 'We got to get this guy a job at Entronics.'

Interesting idea.

I saved the job listing as new in my e-mail in-box.

I was getting a little nervous waiting for Brian Borque to call me back, so I got up to stretch my legs. I took a quick walk down the hall to see the Technical Marketing Engineer, Phil Rifkin, to arrange for a demo I had to do in a couple of days.

Phil Rifkin was your quintessential audiovisual nerd, the Alpha Geek in our division. He was an engineer by training, was deeply familiar with all Entronics LCD projectors and LCD screens and plasma displays. He supported the sales force, answered stupid questions, taught us about the latest products, and arranged for the demos to go out of our repair facility. Sometimes he accompanied a sales rep on a demo if the rep was unsure how to operate one of our products or the customer was really high-profile. He was also our in-house technical guru when customers had questions we couldn't answer.

Rifkin worked in what we called the Plasma Lab, even though it wasn't just for plasmas. It was a long, narrow, windowless room. Its walls were covered with plasma and LCD screens. Its floor was a tangle of power cords and cables and huge spools, which everyone was always tripping over. I knocked on the lab door, and he opened it quickly as if he'd been waiting for me.

'Oh – hello, Jason.'

'Hi, Phil. I'm demo'ing the 42MP5 on Friday morning in Revere,' I said.

'So?' He blinked owlishly.

Rifkin was a small, thin guy with a huge mop of frizzy brown hair like a Chia pet. He wore horn-rimmed glasses and was partial to white short-sleeve dress shirts with two pockets and big collars. He kept strange hours, tended to work through the night, lived out of the vending machines.

Phil lacked all social skills. Fortunately he didn't need them in his job. In his own little world he was vastly powerful, a veritable Czar of all the Plasmas. If he didn't like you, there might not be a plasma display available to demo for your new customer. Or he might not have it prepped in time. You had to be nice to this guy, and I always was. I'm not an idiot.

'Can you make sure all the cables make it too?'

'Component cable or RGB or both?'

'Just component.'

'Make sure you warm the unit up for a couple of minutes first.'

'Of course. Do you think you could preadjust it? To full Rifkin standards?'

He shrugged, privately pleased but trying not to let on. He turned and I followed him in. He stood before a forty-two-inch mounted on the wall. 'I don't know what the big deal is,' he said. 'Leave the sharpness at 50%. I like to jack up the reds and blues and tone down the greens. Contrast at 80%. Brightness at 25%. Tint at 35%.'

'Got it.'

'Make sure to show off the zoom feature – the scaling's far superior to any other plasma out there. Much sharper. What's this for, anyway?'

'The dog track in Revere. Wonderland.'

'Why are you wasting my time on this?'

'I leave nothing to chance.'

'But a dog track, Jason? Greyhounds chasing a mechanical bunny rabbit?'

'Even animal-rights abusers like good monitors, I guess. Thanks. Can you have this prepped and on the truck by eight Friday morning?'

'Jason, is it true that we're all gonna have to pack up and move to the City of Hate?'

'Huh?'

'Dallas. Isn't that what's really going on with the Royal Meister acquisition?'

I shook my head. 'No one's told me that.'

'They wouldn't, would they? No one ever tells people on our level anything. We always find out when it's too late.'

Back in my office, my phone was ringing. Lockwood Hotels came up on the caller ID.

'Hey, Brian,' I said.

'There he is,' Brian said, sounding typically buoyant. 'You got the Sox tickets, right?'

'That's not why I called,' I said. 'I wanted to circle back to you on the proposal.'

'You know I'm doing what I can,' he said, his voice suddenly flat and clipped. 'There's all kinds of factors in play here that are beyond my control.'

'I totally understand,' I said. My heart started beating fast. 'I know you're doing everything you can to work the system for me.'

'You know it,' Brian said.

'And you know Entronics will price-compete on any reasonable proposal.'

'No doubt.'

My heart was thudding loud and my mouth was dry. I grabbed a mostly empty Poland Spring water bottle and drained it. The water was warm. 'Of course, some things we can't match and won't try,' I went on. 'Like the trip you and Martha just took to Aruba.'

He was silent. So I continued, 'Hard to compete with free, you know?'

He was still silent. I thought for a moment that the phone had gone dead.

Then Brian said, 'FedEx me a fresh set of docs, will you? I'll have 'em inked and on your desk by close of business Friday.'

I was stunned. 'Hey, thanks, Bri – that's great. You rock.'

'Don't mention it,' he said quietly.

'I appreciate everything you've done –'

'Really,' he said, a note of hostility entering his voice. 'I mean it. Don't mention it.'

The phone rang again. It was a private caller, which meant it might have been Kate. I picked it up.

'These are the voyages of the Starship *Enterprise*,' said a voice I immediately recognized.

'Graham,' I said, 'how's it going?'

'J-man. Where you been?'

Graham Runkel was a world-class stoner who lived in Central Square, Cambridge, in a first-floor apartment that smelled like bong water. We went to high school together in Worcester, and when I was younger and irresponsible, I'd from time to time buy a nickel bag of marijuana from him. Less and less often in recent years, though, but once in a while I'd stop by his apartment – the Den of Iniquity, he called it – and smoke a joint with him. Kate disapproved, of course, thought it was juvenile behavior, which it was. Ganja could do things to your brain. A couple of years ago, Graham had canceled his subscription to *High Times* because he'd become convinced that the magazine was in fact owned and operated by the Drug Enforcement Administration to lure and entrap unsuspecting pot heads. He once confided to me after a few bong hits that the DEA put a tiny digital tracking device in the binding of each issue, which they located by means of an extensive satellite system.

Graham was a man of many talents. He was always rebuilding engines, working on his 1971 VW Beetle in the backyard of his apartment building. He worked in a record store that sold only vinyl. He was also a 'Trekker,' a fan of the original *Star Trek* TV series, which to him was the height of culture. Only the original series – Classic *Trek*, as they called it; everything else was an abomination, he thought. He knew all the plot lines by heart and all the character names, even the minor, nonrecurring characters. He once told me that his first big crush had been on Lieutenant Uhura. He went to a lot of *Star Trek* conventions, and he'd turned a scale model of the Starship *Enterprise* into a bong.

Graham had also done jail time, not unlike some of my other buddies from the old neighborhood. In his early twenties he went through a rough patch and broke into a couple of houses and apartments, trying to pay back a marijuana deal, and he got caught.

Basically, Graham had ended up where I might have ended up if my parents hadn't been so insistent I go to college. His parents considered college a waste of money and refused to pay for it. He got pissed off and dropped out of high school at the beginning of senior year.

'Sorry, man,' I said. 'It's been real crazy at work.'

'Haven't heard from you in weeks, man. Weeks. Come on over to the Den of Iniquity – we'll do a spliff, get baked, and I'll show you what I've done to the Love Bug. El Huevito.'

'I'm awful sorry, Graham,' I said. 'Another time, okay?'

Around noon, Festino appeared in my office door. 'You hear about Teflon Trevor?' There was a look of unmistakable glee on his face.

'What?'

He snickered. 'He had an appointment with the CEO of the Pavilion Group in Natick to do a meet-and-greet, a handshake kind of thing, and ink the deal. CEO's the kind of guy you don't keep waiting five seconds, you know? Real control freak. So what happens? One of the tires on Trevor's Porsche blows out on the Pike. He missed the meeting, and the CEO was totally pissed.'

'So? We've all had car trouble. So he calls Pavilion on his cell and tells them, and they reschedule. Big deal. It happens.'

'That's the beauty part, Tigger. His cell phone died too. Couldn't make a call. So basically the CEO and everyone else is sitting around waiting for Trevor and he never shows up.' He squeezed out a dab of hand cleaner and looked up at me with a smile.

'Hate when that happens,' I said. I told him about how I'd just turned the Lockwood deal around, about playing the Aruba card. You could see Festino looking at me in a whole new way.

'*You* did that, Tigger?' he said.

'What's that supposed to mean?'

'No, I just mean – wow, I'm impressed, that's all. Never thought you had it in you.'

'There's a lot about me you don't know,' I said mysteriously.

After Festino left, I called Kurt.

'Good work,' he said.

'Thanks, man,' I said.

'No worries.'

I clicked on my Entronics e-mail in-box. 'Listen,' I said. 'A job just opened up here. Corporate Security officer. It says they prefer recent military experience. Experience with handguns. You've got experience with handguns, right?'

'Too much,' he said.

'You interested? Pay's not bad. Better than driving a tow truck, I'll bet.'

'What does it say about background check?'

I looked at the screen. 'It says, "Must be able to pass full criminal, drug, and employment background check."'

'There you go,' he said. 'They see the DD and they stop reading the application.'

'Not if you explain the circumstances.'

'You don't get that chance,' Kurt said. 'But I appreciate the thought, man.'

'I know the Director of Corporate Security,' I said. 'Dennis Scanlon. Good guy. He likes me. I could tell him about you.'

'Not that easy, buddy.'

'Worth a try, don't you think? Wait till I tell him about the softball game. We need to make you a legal Entronics employee. He'll get it.'

'He's looking for a Corporate Security officer, not a pitcher.'

'You saying you're not qualified?'

'Qualified isn't the point, bud.'

'Let me make a call for you,' I said. 'I'll do it right now.'

'I appreciate it.'

'Hey,' I said, 'it's the least I can do.'

I picked up the phone and called Dennis Scanlon, the Director of Corporate Security, and told him briefly about Kurt. How he was in Special Forces, was a nice guy, seemed smart. Got a dishonorable discharge, but not for any bad reason.

Scanlon was immediately interested. He said he loved military types.

11

I had nothing against my smarmy brother-in-law, Craig Glazer, and his social-climbing wife, Susie; but my heart really squeezed for their poor, brilliant, maladjusted eight-year-old son, Ethan.

Let's start with the kid's name. Ethan is what you name a kid who you fully expect, even before he's born, to get beat up on the playground, his lunch money stolen, his glasses snapped in two, and his face pushed into the dirt. Then there's the fact that Susie and Craig were at once overprotective of their son, in their high-strung way, and totally uninterested in him. They seemed to spend as little time with him as possible. When Ethan wasn't being beat up in his fancy private school, or whatever they did to nerds in private schools, he was being raised at home, in isolation from other kids who might have helped drag him into the world of normalcy, by his nanny, a Filipino woman named Corazon. As a result, they were raising a smart and creative and messed-up little boy, and I felt for him. I always hated it when kids like that got picked on.

They say life is high school with money, right? You've probably known people like me in school. I was never the jerk who beat you up and took your lunch money. I wasn't the quarterback of the football team who stole your girl. I wasn't jock enough to make it on any varsity team. I wasn't the brain who did your homework for you, and I sure wasn't one of the rich kids. But there was another guy, remember?

If you were the nerd with the wrong sneakers and the too-tight jeans in the Dungeons & Dragons Club, odds were I didn't hang with you; but unlike most of your classmates, I didn't mock you either. I just said hi and smiled at you when you walked down the hallway. If the bullies started picking on you, I was the one who tried to defuse the situation by pointing out that we'd better start being nice to you, because in ten years, after you founded a behemoth software company, we'd all be working for you.

So despite my feelings for Craig Glazer, his son and I bonded. I much preferred conversing with Ethan, visiting his weird little world of medieval torture chambers – his current obsession – than listening to Craig tell me about how his new pilot blew everyone away at the 'upfronts' in New York.

On the way home I stopped at a Borders Books superstore located in a mall that also had a Kmart and a Sports Authority. I wanted to pick up a present for poor little Ethan. I parked the car and tried once again to call Kate. The last three times I'd gotten our voice mail. I knew she'd left work early today so she could be home when her sister and Craig showed up. I couldn't figure out why she wasn't answering the phone, but maybe she was out shopping or something.

This time, though, she answered. 'Hey, babe,' she said in a boisterous voice. 'Are you on your way back?

Craig and Susie just got here.'

'Oh, great,' I said, heavy on the sarcasm. 'I can't wait.'

She got it but she was having none of it. 'They can't wait to see you too,' she said. I could hear laughter in the background and the tinkling of glasses. 'We're making dinner.'

'We?'

'Don't sound so worried!' she said. A loud guffaw that sounded like Craig. 'Susie just got certified in CPR.'

More laughter in the background.

'I got some really great Porterhouse steaks from John Dewar's,' she said. 'Inch and a half thick.'

'Nice,' I said. 'So, listen. I had my talk with Gordy.'

'No, I'm just going to *crack* the peppercorns a little,' she said to someone. *'Au poivre.'* And to me: 'Go well?'

'He reamed me out,' I said.

'Oh, God.'

'It was a nightmare, Kate. But then I found out something about that guy at Lockwood – ?'

'Can't talk now, babe, I'm sorry. Come on home. We're all famished. We'll talk at home.'

Annoyed, I clicked off and went in to the bookstore. I browsed quickly around the children's section, moved on to teens, and found two possibilities. Ethan, like most boys, had gone through a dinosaur phase and a planets phase, but then he'd taken a sharp left turn into an obsession with the Middle Ages. And I don't mean King Arthur and Merlin and the Knights of the Round Table and the Sword in the Stone. It was instruments of medieval torture that floated his boat. You had to wonder about his parents' marriage.

So here I was, Uncle Jason, the enabler. I went back and forth between a book on the Tower of London and one on the Aztecs, and the Aztecs won out. Better illustrations and more gruesome.

On the way to the cash register I passed by the Business Self-Help section, and a book caught my eye. It was called *Business Is War!* The book jacket had a greenish camouflage look to it.

I remembered Gordy mocking Mark Simkins: *Candy-ass crapola.*

This wasn't candy-ass. This book promised to teach the businessman 'proven, effective secrets of military leadership.' It looked promising.

I thought of Kurt and the way he'd helped me turn around the Lockwood account with one hardball phone call.

Then I found another book, face out on the shelf, called *Victory Secrets of Attila the Hun,* and then another one, called *Patton on Leadership,* and *The Green Beret Manager,* and pretty soon I was holding a tower of hardcover books and CDs.

I gulped at the cash register – hardcover books cost a lot, and CDs cost even more, but I justified it as an investment in my future – and asked them to gift-wrap the Aztec book for Ethan.

The adults were gathered in our cramped kitchen, and young Ethan was nowhere to be found. They were laughing loudly and drinking from grotesquely large martini glasses, and having such a good time that they didn't notice me enter. Even though Susie was four years older, she and Katie looked exactly like each other. Susie's eyelids were a bit heavier, and her mouth tilted down just a bit. Also, the passage of time as well as life in the lap of luxury seemed to have changed her a bit too. Susie had more fine lines around her eyes and forehead than Katie, no doubt from all that time on the beaches of St. Barths. Her hair also looked like it was cut and highlighted once a week at some eight-hundred-dollar-a-visit Beverly Hills salon.

My brother-in-law, Craig, was gesturing with his free hand. 'Concrete,' he was saying. 'Forget granite. Granite is so eighties.'

'Concrete?' I said as I walked into the kitchen and kissed my wife. 'My boss keeps trying to fit me for concrete boots. I can't figure it out.'

Polite chuckles. Craig was once a *Jeopardy!* contestant, so officially he knows everything. He doesn't like to talk about the fact that he wiped out on the easiest question in *Jeopardy!* history – the answer was 'potato' – and his entire winnings were a year's supply of Turtle Wax.

'Hey, Jason,' Susie said, giving me a sisterly peck on the cheek and a half hug. 'Ethan's so excited to see you I think he's going to jump out of his skin.'

'Jason!' exclaimed Craig like we were old buddies. He threw his bony arms around me. He seemed to get skinnier every time I saw him. He was wearing a pair of brand-new-looking blue jeans and an untucked Hawaiian print shirt and white Converse All Stars. I also noticed he'd shaved his head. Obviously the minoxidil wasn't working. He used to have a big mop of curly hair that was thinning on top and made him look like Bozo the Clown. Also, he had new eyeglasses. For years, when he was writing experimental short stories for literary magazines, he wore horn-rimmed spectacles.

When he hit it rich, he went through a contact-lens phase until he discovered he had dry eyes. Then he started wearing whatever glasses were cutting-edge. For a couple of years in a row he wore different versions of nineteen-fifties geek frames. Now he was back to horn-rimmed specs.

'New glasses,' I said. 'Or old?'

'New. Johnny picked them out for me.' I happened to know he and Susie had recently vacationed in St. Vincent and the Grenadines with Johnny Depp. Kate had clipped out the article from *People* magazine and showed it to me.

'Johnny?' I said, just to make him say it. 'Carson? Isn't he dead?'

'Depp,' Craig said, with a fake-bashful shrug. 'Hey, a little too much of the good life, huh?' He patted my stomach, and I almost lost it. 'A week at the Ashram, you'll drop that weight easy. Hiking, Bikram yoga, twelve hundred calories a day – it's a boot camp for celebs. You'll love it.'

Kate saw me revving up to say something I might regret, so she quickly interrupted me. 'Let me get you a martini.' She hoisted a silver martini shaker and poured into one of the giant glasses.

'I didn't even know we had martini glasses,' I said. 'From Grammy Spencer?'

'From Craig and Susie,' Kate said. 'Aren't they special?'

'Special,' I agreed.

'They're Austrian,' said Craig. 'The same glassworks that make those amazing Bordeaux glasses.'

'Careful,' Kate said, handing me a glass. 'Hundred dollars a stem.'

'Oh, there's plenty more where they came from,' said Craig.

'Did you notice Susie's brooch?' Kate said.

I had noticed a big ugly gaudy misshapen thing on Susie's blouse but I thought the polite thing to do was not to embarrass her by pointing it out. 'Is it a starfish?' I asked.

'You like it?' Susie said.

Yep, it was a gold starfish covered in sapphires and rubies and must have cost a fortune. I've never understood why women like pins and brooches so much anyway. But this was a doozy.

'Oh, Suze, it's *fabulous*,' Kate said. 'Where'd you get it?'

'Craig got it for me,' Susie said. 'Was it Harry Winston or Tiffany's?'

'Tiffany's,' Craig said. 'I saw it and thought it was *so Susie* that I had to get it.'

'Jean Schlumberger,' Susie said. 'I would never have spent that kind of money on a piece of jewelry. And it wasn't even my birthday or our anniversary or any special occasion.'

'Every day I'm married to you is a special occasion,' Craig said, and he put his arm around her, and she gave him a kiss, and I wanted to puke.

I also had to change the subject as quickly as possible, because I couldn't take any more, so I said, 'Why were you guys talking about concrete?'

'They want us to put in new countertops,' said Kate. She gave me a quick, conspiratorial look.

'We just got rid of our granite countertops in our Marin County place after Steven had us over,' said Craig.

This time I didn't ask whether he meant Steven Spielberg or Steven Segal. 'Yeah, I've always wanted my kitchen to look like some socialist worker's communal flat in East Berlin,' I said.

Craig flashed his Lumineer smile. He looked at me with kindly condescension, as if I were some Fresh Air Fund kid. 'How's the corporate world?'

'It's okay,' I said, nodding. 'Gets crazy sometimes, but it's okay.'

'Hey, your boss, Dick Hardy, invited me to the Entronics Invitational last year at Pebble Beach. Nice guy. Man, I got to golf with Tiger Woods and Vijay Singh – that was a blast.'

I got his point. He was a buddy of the CEO of my company, whom I'd never even met, and he got to hang with all the celebs because, well, he was a celeb. I couldn't imagine Craig golfing. 'Neat' was all I said.

'I could put in a word for you with Dick,' Craig said.

'Don't waste your time. He doesn't even know who I am.'

'It's cool. I'll just tell him to make sure you're taken care of.'

'Thanks, but no thanks, Craig. I appreciate the thought, though.'

'You work hard, man. I really admire that. I get paid all this insane money for basically playing, but you really work your ass off. Doesn't he, Katie?'

'Oh, he does,' said Kate.

'I don't think I could do what you do,' Craig went on. 'The crap you've got to put up with, huh?'

'You have no idea,' I said.

*

I couldn't take it anymore, so I told them I wanted to change out of my work clothes. Instead, I looked for Ethan and found him in the tiny guest room upstairs, which was supposed to be the future baby's room. He was lying on his stomach on the blue wall-to-wall carpet reading a book, and he looked up when I entered.

'Hey, Uncle Jason,' he said. Ethan had a lisp – something else for his classmates to make fun of him about, like he needed anything more – and glasses.

'Heya, buddy,' I said, sitting down next to him. I handed him the gift-wrapped book. 'You probably don't need another book, right?'

'Thanks,' he said, sitting up and tearing right into it. 'Oh, this is an excellent one,' he said.

'You have it already.'

He nodded solemnly. 'I think it's the finest in the series.'

'I was debating between this one and one on the Tower of London.'

'This was a good choice. I needed another copy anyway, for the Marin house.'

'Okay, good. But tell me something, Ethan. I'm still not clear on why the Aztecs were so into human sacrifice.'

'That's kind of complicated.'

'I bet you can explain it to me.'

'Well, it was sort of to keep the whole universe moving. They believed that there was this kind of spirit in the human bloodstream, but mostly in the heart? And you had to keep giving it to the gods or the universe would just stop.'

'I see. That makes sense.'

'So when things were going really bad they just did more human sacrifice.'

'That happens where I work, too.'

He cocked his head. 'Oh yeah?'

'Sort of.'

'The Aztecs cooked and skinned and ate humans, too.'

'That we don't do.'

'You want to see a picture of the Chair of Spikes?'

'Definitely,' I said, 'but we should probably go downstairs and have dinner, don't you think?'

He stuck out his lower lip and shook his head slowly. 'We don't have to, you know. We can just tell them to bring it up to us. That's what I do a lot.'

'Come on,' I said, getting to my feet and lifting him up. 'We'll both go. Keep each other company.'

'I'll stay up here,' Ethan said.

The adults had switched to red wine, a Bordeaux that Craig had brought. I'm sure it was extremely expensive, though it tasted like dirty sneakers. I could smell steaks in the broiler. Susie was talking about a famous TV star who was in rehab, but Craig interrupted her to say to me, 'Couldn't take any more torture, huh?'

'He's great,' I said. 'He told me that when things got really bad the Aztecs sacrificed more humans.'

'Yeah, well,' he said. 'He'll talk your ear off. Hope he hasn't discouraged you guys from having kids of your own. They don't all turn out like Ethan.'

'He's a good kid,' I said.

'And we love him to pieces,' Craig said in a rote voice, like a disclaimer in a drug ad. 'So, I want to hear about your work life. I'm serious.'

104

'Oh, it's boring,' I said. 'No celebs.'

'I want to hear about it,' Craig said. 'I'm serious. I need to know what regular people's work life is like, especially if I'm going to write about it. I consider it research.'

I looked at him and mentally went through about a dozen really nasty and sarcastic replies, but luckily my cell phone went off. I forgot I'd still had it clipped onto my belt.

'There you go,' Craig said. 'That's got to be the office, right?' He looked from his wife to Kate. 'His boss or something. Something has to be done *right now*. God, I love the way they crack the whip in the corporate world.'

I got up and went into the living room and answered the cell. 'Hey,' a voice said. I immediately recognized Kurt.

'How's it going?' I said, happy to be yanked away from Craig's klieg lights.

'I catch you during dinner?'

'Not at all,' I said.

'Thanks for talking to the Corporate Security guy. I downloaded the job application and filled out the form and e-mailed it back, and I got a call from the guy. He wants me to come in for an interview tomorrow afternoon.'

'You're good to go,' I said. 'He must be seriously interested in you.'

'Or desperate, I figure. Hey, so maybe I can grab you for a few minutes in the morning, talk on the phone. Get your take on Entronics and what the security problems are, all that. I like to be prepared.'

'How's right now?' I said.

12

We met at a place in Harvard Square called Charlie's Kitchen, where they have this excellent double-cheeseburger special. I hadn't eaten much at dinner: Craig had pretty much killed my appetite, plus Kate had overcooked the steaks. Too many martinis. She didn't look too happy at first about my abandoning her little dinner party, but I told her a work crisis had arisen, and that seemed to satisfy her. In fact, she seemed a little relieved, because she could see where the dinner was going, and it wasn't pretty.

I didn't recognize him at first, because his goatee and mullet were gone. He'd gotten a haircut. His salt-and-pepper hair was cut short, but not military short. It was parted on the side, looked stylish. He was a good-looking guy, I realized, and now he looked like a successful business executive, only he was wearing jeans and a sweatshirt.

Kurt just ordered his regular, a glass of ice water. He said that when he was in Iraq and Afghanistan, fresh, clean cold water was a luxury. You drank the water there, he said, you'd get the shits for days. Now he drank it whenever he could.

He said he'd already eaten supper. When my plate

arrived – a big old double cheeseburger and a mountain of fries with a plastic tankard of watery beer – Kurt took one look and scowled. 'You shouldn't eat that shit,' he said.

'You sound like my wife.'

'Don't take this the wrong way, but you might want to think about losing a little weight. You'll feel better.'

Him, too? 'I feel fine.'

'You don't work out, do you?'

'Who has time?'

'You make time.'

'I make time to sleep late,' I said.

'We got to get you to the gym, do some cardio and some free weights. Don't you belong to a gym?'

'Yeah,' I said, 'I pay like a hundred bucks a month for a membership at CorpFit, so I figure I don't actually have to go there.'

'CorpFit? That's one of those pussy smoothie-bar Evian-water places, right?'

'Since I've never gone, I really wouldn't know.'

'Nah. I got to take you to a real gym. Where I go.'

'Sure,' I said, hoping he'd forget we ever talked about working out, but he didn't seem like the kind of guy who forgot anything. I took a look at my mug of beer and called the waiter over and ordered a Diet Coke.

'You still driving that rental?' Kurt said.

'Yeah.'

'When are you getting your car back?'

'I think they said middle of next week.'

'That's too long. Let me give them a call.'

'That'd be great.'

'You have your Entronics ID with you?'

I took it out and put it on the table. He examined it closely. 'Man, do you know how easy it is to counterfeit one of these babies?'

'Never thought about it.'

'I wonder if your security chief ever thought about it.'

'You don't want to piss him off,' I said, tucking into the burger. 'You have a résumé?'

'I can throw one together.'

'In the right format and everything?'

'I don't know.'

'Tell you what. E-mail me what you've got, and I'll go over it, make sure it's in good shape.'

'Hey, that would be awesome.'

'No problem. Now, if I had to predict, I'd say that Scanlon is a tough interview. Though he'll probably ask you the standards, like, 'What's your greatest weakness?' And, 'Tell me about a time when you took the initiative to solve a problem.' Like that. How you work on a team.'

'Sounds like I can handle that,' he said.

'Make sure you get there on time. Early, in fact.'

'I'm a military guy, remember? We're all about punctuality.'

'You're not going to dress like that for the interview, are you?'

'Any idea how many uniform inspections I had to endure?' he said. 'Don't worry about me. There's no corporation in the world more uptight than the U.S. military. But I want to know some details about your access control system.'

'All I know is, you wave this card at one of the boxes and you go in.'

He asked me a bunch more questions, and I told him what little I knew. 'Your wife doesn't mind you staying out late?' he asked.

'I wear the pants in the household,' I told him with a straight face. 'Fact is, I think she was glad to get rid of me.'

'You still duking it out with that guy Trevor for the promotion?'

'Yeah.' I told him about my 'interview' with Gordy. 'He's not going to give it to me, though. I can tell. He's just yanking my chain.'

'Why do you say that?'

'He says I don't have the killer instinct. And Trevor's a superstar. His numbers are always good, but they're especially good this year. He's just a top goddamned salesman. There's also Brett Gleason. He's kind of a lunk, but he has that animal aggressiveness that Gordy likes. Gordy says it's going to be one of us three, but I'd put money on Trevor. He's got a big demonstration before the big swinging dicks at Fidelity Investments on Monday, and if our monitors win the shoot-out – which they will – then he lands Fidelity. Which is huge. Means he wins. And I'm screwed.'

'Look, I don't know anything about how things work in business, but believe me, I've been in my share of situations that looked hopeless. And the one thing I do know for sure is that war's unpredictable. It's volatile. Complex. Generates confusion. That's why they talk about the "fog of war." You often can't believe what you see, and you can never be certain about your enemy's plans and capabilities.'

'What does that have to do with getting a promotion?'

'I'm saying the only way to guarantee a loss is if you don't fight. You've got to go into every battle knowing you can win.' He took a long swig of ice water. 'Make sense?'

13

In the morning I slipped out of bed quietly at six, before the alarm went off. After years of getting up at six, my body was programmed. I could hear Kate's labored breathing, from too much booze last night. I went downstairs to make coffee, bracing myself to encounter Craig, me precaffeine and thus vulnerable, in case he was an early riser. Then I remembered that six in the morning was three in the morning California time, and he was likely to still be asleep, especially after a late night.

The kitchen and dining room were littered with the detritus of the dinner, dishes and serving platters and silverware heaped everywhere. Kate and Susie had grown up with housekeepers picking up after them, and Susie still had someone who cooked meals and cleaned up afterward. Kate . . . well, Kate sometimes lived as if she did. Not as if I had the right to complain about it, since I don't have that excuse. I just hate doing dishes and am a slob by nature. A different excuse.

Wineglasses and martini glasses and Grammy Spencer's cordial glasses cluttered the kitchen counters, and I couldn't find the coffeemaker. Finally, I located it and put some coffee up to brew, accidentally spilling some of the ground coffee onto the green Corian countertop. Concrete, over my dead body.

I heard a clinking sound, and I turned around. There at the kitchen table, concealed behind a tall stack of pots and pans, was little Ethan. He looked small and frail and like the eight-year-old he was, not the scarily precocious kid he normally seemed to be. He was eating Froot Loops from a giant soup tureen he must have found in the china cabinet. The spoon he was using was a sterling silver soup ladle.

'Morning, Ethan,' I said, quietly so as not to wake the slumbering party animals upstairs.

Ethan didn't reply.

'Hey there, buddy,' I said, a bit louder.

'Sorry, Uncle Jason,' Ethan replied. 'I'm not really a morning person.'

'Yeah, well, me neither.' I went up to him, about to muss his hair, but stopped myself when I remembered how much he disliked people mussing his hair. Come to think of it, I never liked that much either. Still don't. I gave him a pat on the back and cleared myself a place, pushing aside a stack of Grammy Spencer's blue Spode china plates, slick with congealed grease from the overcooked steaks. 'You mind if I share some of those Froot Loops?'

Ethan shrugged. 'I don't care. It's yours anyway.'

Kate must have bought them for Ethan when she went shopping yesterday. Her husband gets burlap flakes and twigs. I made a note to register a complaint later. I got a regular cereal bowl from the kitchen cabinet and poured out a generous heap of the carnival-colored little Os and doused it with some of the

112

contraband whole milk from Ethan's carton. I hoped there'd be some left after our guests were gone.

I went out to the porch to get the morning papers. We got two – the *Boston Globe* for Kate, and the *Boston Herald* for me, the one my dad always read. When I returned to the kitchen, Ethan said: 'Mommy said you went out last night to avoid Daddy.'

I laughed hollowly. 'I had to go out on business.'

He nodded as if he saw right through me. He jammed an immense spoonful of cereal into his little mouth. The ladle barely fit. 'Daddy can be annoying,' he said. 'If I could drive, I wouldn't be home very much either.'

Ricky Festino intercepted me as I was about to enter my office. 'They're here,' he said.

'Who?'

'The body disposal team. The cleaners. Mr. Wolf from *Pulp Fiction*.'

'Ricky, it's too early, and I have no idea what you're talking about.'

I switched on my office lights.

Festino grabbed my shoulder. 'The *merger integration team*, asshole. The chain-saw consultants. They've been here since before I got in. Six guys, four of them from McKinsey, and two guys from Tokyo. They've got clipboards and calculators and handhelds and goddamned digital *cameras*. They just came from Royal Meister headquarters in Texas, and let me tell you, they left a trail of bodies in Dallas. I heard about it from a buddy there, called me last night, warned me.'

'Slow down,' I said. 'They're probably just here to figure out how to make the two organizations mesh.'

'Boy, are you living in fantasyland.' I noticed he was sweating already. His blue button-down shirt was soaked through under his arms. 'They're looking for *redundancies*, dude. Identifying *non-value-adding activities*. That means me. Even my wife says I don't add value.'

'Ricky.'

'They say who stays and who goes. This is like corporate *Survivor,* only the losers don't get to go on *Jay Leno.*' He took the little bottle of hand cleaner out of his pocket and began juggling it nervously.

'How long are they here for?' I asked.

'I don't know, maybe a week. My buddy in Dallas told me that they spent a lot of time pulling up everyone's performance reviews. The top twenty percent got invited to keep their jobs. Everyone else is deadwood to be lopped off.'

I closed my office door. 'I'll do what I can to protect you,' I said.

'If you're here,' he said.

'Why shouldn't I be here?' I said.

'Because Gordy hates you?'

'Gordy hates everyone.'

'Except his butt boy, Trevor. If I still have a job and that douche bag becomes my boss, I swear I'm going to go Columbine. Come in here with an Uzi and do my own "performance review."'

'I think you've had too much caffeine,' I said.

The day was long and exhausting. Rumors of impending disaster had begun to run through the halls.

At the end of the day, as I rode the elevator down to the lobby, the other passengers and I watched the flat-screen monitor mounted on the elevator wall. It showed sports news (the Red Sox were a half game ahead of the Yankees in the American League East standings), news headlines (another suicide bombing in Iraq), and selected stock quotes (Entronics was down a buck). The word of the day was 'sapient.' Today's 'celebrity' birthdays were Cher and Honoré de Balzac. A lot of the guys find the elevator TV thing really annoying, but I don't mind it. It takes my mind off the fact that I'm in a sealed steel coffin dangling from cables that might snap at any moment.

When the elevator doors opened at the lobby, I was surprised to see Kurt standing there, talking to the Corporate Security Director, Dennis Scanlon. Kurt was wearing a navy blue suit, white shirt, and striped silver rep tie, and he looked like a vice president. Clipped to his left lapel was a blue temporary Entronics badge. The Corporate Security area was off the lobby of the building – I guess because that's where the Command Center and all the other security facilities were.

'Hey, man,' I said. 'Why are you still here? I thought your interview was this morning.'

'It was.' He smiled.

'Meet our new Corporate Security officer,' said Scanlon. He was a small, froglike man with no neck and a squat body.

'Really?' I said. 'That's great. Smart hire.'

'We're all excited to have him join us,' Scanlon said. 'Kurt's already made some very shrewd suggestions for security improvements – he really knows the technology.'

Kurt shrugged modestly.

Scanlon excused himself, and Kurt and I stood there

for a few seconds. 'So that was fast work,' I said.

'I start Monday. There's an orientation and a boat-load of paperwork to fill out, all that crap. But hey, it's a real job.'

'That's really great,' I said.

'Listen, man, thank you.'

'For what?'

'I mean it. I owe you one. You don't know me very well, but one thing you'll learn is, I never forget a favor.'

I joined Kate in bed after checking my e-mail one last time for the night. She was wearing her usual bedtime attire – extra-large sweatpants and extra-large T-shirt – and watching TV. During a commercial break, she said, 'I'm sorry I didn't get a chance last night to ask you about your interview with Gordy.'

'That's all right. It went okay. As okay as an inter-view with Gordy could go. He basically taunted and threatened me and tried to pump me up and deflate me all at the same time.'

She rolled her eyes. 'What a jerk. You think you're going to get the job?'

'Who knows. Probably not. I told you, Trevor's more the Gordy type – aggressive and ruthless. Gordy sees me as a wimp. A nice guy, but a wimp.'

A really annoying commercial came on, and she pressed the mute button. 'If it doesn't happen, it doesn't happen. At least you tried.'

'That's how I figure.'

'As long as you let him know you want it.'

'I did.'

'But do you really?'

'Want it? Yeah, I think I do. It'll be more work and more stress, but I think if you keep your head down around there, you don't go anywhere.'

'I think that's right.'

'My dad always used to say that the nail that sticks up gets hammered down.'

'You're not your dad.'

'No. He worked in a factory all day and hated it.' I was lost in thought for a moment, remembering my dad's hunched shoulders at the supper table, the missing fingertips on his right hand. His long silences, the defeated look in his eyes. Like he was resigned to whatever crap life handed him. Sometimes he reminded me of a dog whose owner beat him every day and cowered whenever anyone came near and just wanted to be left alone. But he was a good guy, my dad. He didn't let me get away with cutting school, and he made sure I did my homework, and he didn't want me to live the same life as him, and only now was I beginning to realize how much I owed the old man.

'Jason? You know, you're really good with Ethan. I love the way you are with him. I think you're the only adult who pays him any attention. And I really appreciate it.'

'I like the poor kid. I really do. He's kind of warped, I know, but deep down – I think he knows his parents are jerks.'

She nodded, gave a sad smile. 'You identify with him, maybe?'

'Me? He's the polar opposite of me when I was a kid. I was Mister Outgoing.'

'I mean, you were an only child with parents who weren't around much.'

'My parents weren't around much because they worked their asses off. Craig and Susie are too busy going to Majorca with Bobby De Niro. They don't want to be around their son.'

'I know. It's not fair.'

'Not fair?' I looked at her.

There were tears in her eyes. 'We'd give anything to have a baby, and they're lucky enough to have one and they ignore him or treat him like . . .' She shook her head. 'Ironic, isn't it?'

'Am I allowed to tell them what I think about the way they're raising Ethan?'

'No. It'll just piss them off, and they'll say, what do you know, you don't have a kid. And it won't make a difference anyway. Besides, the way you connect with Ethan – that's what'll really make a difference in the kid's life.'

'But it would still be fun to tell Craig off.'

She smiled but shook her head again.

'Hey,' I said, 'I got Kurt a job at Entronics.'

'Kurt.'

'Kurt Semko. The Special Forces guy I met.'

'Right, Kurt. The tow truck driver. What kind of job?'

'Corporate security.'

'Security guard?'

'No, the security guards in the building are rent-a-cops, contracted out. This is to do the inside stuff – loss prevention, monitoring the comings and goings, whatever . . .'

'You don't really know what they do, do you?'

'I have no idea. But the security director was thrilled to hire him.'

'Well, then, you did a good thing for everyone. It's win-win, right?'

'Yeah,' I said. 'It's win-win.'

14

The next morning I unwrapped the CD box of *Business Is War!* and popped the first disk into the CD player in the Geo Metro. The narrator sounded like George C. Scott as Patton. He was barking out orders about 'your battle plan' and 'the chain of command' and saying, 'highly trained and cohesive units with good leadership suffer the fewest casualties.'

I was so totally pumped from listening to Old Blood and Guts, the four-star general, as I imagined the narrator – though he was probably, in reality, a paunchy little dweeb with thick glasses who hadn't been able to make it in AM radio – that I was ready to barge into Gordy's office and just demand the promotion. I was ready to kick ass and take names.

But by the time I got to the office, I'd come to my senses. Besides, I had to drive to Revere to demo a thirty-six-inch screen for the Wonderland Greyhound Park – the dog track. Though I didn't think the guys who go to the dog track would care about the difference between a regular old TV monitor and a plasma flat panel. I didn't return from Revere until mid-afternoon, which was just as well. Gordy tends to be in a better mood after lunch.

I dragged Festino into my office and had him read over a couple of contracts I was hammering out. No one was better than Festino at deconstructing a contract. The problem was, he didn't sign too many of them. He reminded me of how Ethan, when he was a couple of years old, had memorized this potty-training DVD his parents constantly played for him. Ethan had every word and song memorized. He became an expert in potty theory. But for years he refused to use the potty. Festino was like that. He was a genius at contracts but couldn't land one.

'Uh, Houston, we have a problem,' Festino said. 'Paperwork says "FOB destination," but they need it shipped to Florida, right? No way in hell the equipment's going to get to their loading dock before close of business.'

'Crap. You're right.'

'Plus, I don't think we want responsibility for the equipment in transit.'

'No way. But they're going to flip if I tell 'em to change the paperwork.'

'Not a problem. Call 'em, tell 'em to authorize an override, change it to "FOB origin." That way they get the equipment six weeks earlier – remind 'em that "FOB origin" orders go out the door first.'

'Yeah,' I said. 'Good work, man. You're right.'

I was on my way to see Gordy when I noticed Trevor leaving Joan Tureck's office. He looked uncharacteristically grim.

'How's it going there, Trevor?' I said.

'Great,' he said in a flat voice. 'Just great.'

Before I had a chance to express to him my deepest, most heartfelt condolences over his standing up the

CEO of one of America's largest movie-theater chains, he was gone, depriving me of the opportunity, and Joan was beckoning me into her office with a flick of her left hand.

I was immediately on alert. Trevor had looked like he'd been kicked in the family jewels. I suspected Joan had been the bearer of bad news and that I might be next in line.

'Sit down, Jason,' she said. 'Congratulations on the Lockwood deal. I never thought you were going to close it, but I guess we should never underestimate you.'

I nodded, smiled modestly. 'Sometimes you just have to say the right words, and it all falls into place,' I said. 'I figure that ought to demonstrate my meat-eating credentials to Gordy.'

'Dick Hardy already put out the press release on the Lockwood deal,' she said. 'I assume you saw it.'

'Not yet.'

Joan got up and closed her office door. She turned to face me. She heaved a long, loud sigh. Not a good sigh. The circles under her eyes were darker than I'd ever seen them before. She went back to her desk. 'Gordy's not going to move me into Crawford's position,' she said wearily.

'What do you mean?'

'There's something about me Gordy doesn't like.'

'There's something about *everyone* that Gordy doesn't like. Plus there's the fact that you're a woman.'

'And not one whose pants he wants to get into.'

'Call me naïve, but isn't that illegal?'

'Yeah, you're naïve, Jason. Anyway, it's an age-old tradition, using consolidation as an excuse to shed the employees you don't like.'

'He can't be that blatant.'

'Of course not. Gordy's smart. There's always a way to justify laying someone off. I didn't make my number because you guys didn't make yours last quarter. The merger team thinks I'm an unnecessary layer of management anyway. Fat to be trimmed. They've decided to get rid of the AM job entirely. So Gordy's just going to fill Crawford's DVP slot. You or Trevor or Brett. Meaning that whoever gets the nod is going to be under a lot of pressure. That's an awfully big job now.'

'He wants to lay you off?' Now I felt really bad. Here I was, angling for a promotion, and she was losing her job. 'I'm so sorry.' Then the unworthy thought came into my head: I'd just asked her to speak up for me, and she had corporate cooties. Would it rub off on me?

'It's fine, really it is,' she said. 'I've been in talks with FoodMark for a while.'

'That's the company that runs food courts in shopping malls?' I tried to say it neutrally, but I guess I didn't succeed at hiding what I thought.

Her smile was wan and a little embarrassed. 'It's not a bad place, and it's a lot less pressure than this job. Plus, Sheila and I have been wanting to travel more. Enjoy life together. It's just as well, as it turns out. Plasma displays or burritos, what's the difference?'

I didn't want to express my condolences, but congratulations didn't seem in order either. What the hell do you say? 'I guess it's all good, then.'

'Well,' she said. 'Did I ever tell you I'm a vegetarian?'

'Maybe that's the real reason,' I said, a halfhearted attempt at black humor. I thought of Kate's steaks a couple of nights ago, which were unappetizing charred slabs, enough to turn anyone into a strict vegan.

'Maybe,' she said with a rueful smile. 'Whatever. But you might want to go easy on Trevor Allard today. He's had a tough break.'

'What happened?'

'He just lost the biggest deal of his life.'

'You're talking about Pavilion?'

She nodded, compressed her lips.

'All for missing one appointment because of a flat tire?'

'Once would have been acceptable. But not twice.'

'Twice?'

'This morning he was on his way to the rescheduled meeting with Watkins, the CEO of Pavilion. Well, guess what? His Porsche died on the road again.'

'You're kidding.'

'I wish. Electrical system malfunctioned. A real freak coincidence, his car dying two days in a row. He hasn't even had a chance to get his cell phone replaced, so he couldn't call Watkins's office in time. And that was it. They've signed with Toshiba.'

'Jesus!' I said. 'Just like that?'

'The deal was already factored into next quarter's numbers as committed business. Which is a disaster for all of us, especially with the integration team poking around in every corner. All of *you*, I should say, since I'm out of here. Though I'm sure you're more focused on what this does for your chances at the promotion.'

'No, not at all,' I protested lamely.

'The tables seem to have turned. Now it looks like you drive a bigger piece of the number than either one of them.'

'Temporarily, yeah.'

'Gordy's all about momentum, and right now it's on your side. Let me just say one thing, though. I know how much you want this job. But be careful what you ask for. You never know what you might be stepping into.'

Ten minutes later I was checking my e-mail, still feeling dazed, when I noticed Brett Gleason standing in my office doorway.

Whatever he wanted, it wasn't good. 'Hey, Brett,' I said. 'I thought you had a presentation at Bank of America.'

'I lost the directions,' he said.

'To Bank of America? They're on Federal Street, you know that.'

'Lot of floors. Lot of offices.'

'Can't you just call your contact?'

'Guy's new and he's not listed on their website, and besides, I don't remember his last name.'

'You don't have the guy's number?' Why, I wondered, was he in my office? Gleason talked to me as little as possible, and he sure never asked my help on anything.

'That's gone too.'

'What do you mean, gone?'

'You think it's funny?'

'I'm not laughing, Brett. What are you talking about?'

'The Blue Screen of Death.'

'You had a disk crash or something?'

'Permanent and fatal error. Someone screwed with my computer.' He gave me a sidelong look. 'Which also

125

wiped out my Palm Pilot when I hot-synced it this morning. All my contacts, all my records – they're all gone. The IT dweebs say it's totally unrecoverable. Some prank, huh?' He turned to leave.

I thought, but didn't say, that if Brett had printed out his schedule, he wouldn't have had this problem, but I kept my mouth shut. 'You don't seriously think someone did this to you, Brett, do you?' I said to Gleason's back.

But he kept going.

An instant message popped up on my computer screen. It was Gordy, and he wanted to see me immediately.

15

Gordy was wearing a crisp white button-down shirt with a big blue KG monogram on the pocket. He didn't shake my hand as I entered. He stayed seated behind his desk.

'You locked in Lockwood,' he said.

'That's right.'

'Booya.'

'Thanks.'

'Don't know how you finally got 'em to sign on the dotted line, but I'm impressed. We needed the deal. Bad. Especially the way Allard and Gleason've been dropping balls lately.'

'Have they? I'm sorry to hear that.'

'Please,' Gordy said. 'Christ. Practice your bullshit on someone who doesn't know better. Gleason blew off a presentation at Bank of America. Gave them some lame excuse about his computer getting wiped out or something. He's roadkill, far as I'm concerned. And now Trevor.' He shook his head. 'Fact is, I like golf as much as the next guy' – he gestured toward his putter – 'but you don't blow off a seventy-million-dollar client for nine holes at the Myopia Hunt Club.'

'You're kidding,' I said, truly surprised. That didn't sound like Trevor at all.

'I wish,' said Gordy. 'He doesn't know I know it, but I got the lowdown from Watkins at the Pavilion Group. I tried to turn it around, but Watkins wasn't having any of it.'

'Trevor was playing *golf*?'

'He figured he'd get away with it. Stood up Watkins two days in a row claiming car trouble. One day he says he's got a flat, the next day the alternator goes or something, and both days he says his cell phone isn't working.'

'Yeah, but all that really happened,' I said.

'Uh-uh. And you know where the idiot calls Watkins's office from? Right from the links. Number came up on the secretary's caller ID.' He shook his head, disgusted. 'I just can't defend that. Of course he denies it, but . . . Well, anyway, I'm inclined to give Allard another chance. He's a true meat-eater. But I got something for you.'

'Tell me.'

'Who's that guy from NEC that everyone likes?'

'You mean Jim Letasky? The guy who owns the SignNetwork account?'

'Yeah, him. I want to land SignNetwork. Sounds like the only way is to get Letasky on our team. Think you're high-test enough to recruit him? Steal him away?'

'From NEC? He lives in Chicago, got a wife and kids, plus he probably already makes good money.'

'Sounds like you're giving up before you even start,' Gordy said. 'I thought you wanted Crawford's job.'

'No, it's just – that won't be easy. But I'll try.'

'Try? How about, "Done, Gordy"?'

'Done, Gordy,' I said.

I wasted no time trying to reach James Letasky. I found his office phone number on the NEC website, but I wanted to call him at home – the more discreet approach, I figured. Letasky's home number was unlisted, unfortunately. So I waited until Gordy had gone out for a meeting, and I stopped by his secretary's cubicle. She kept his massive database of names and contacts, and I thought she might know how to get hold of Letasky's home phone.

'Jim Letasky?' Melanie said. 'Sure. Easy.'

'You sound like you know the guy.'

She shook her head. She jutted out her lower lip as she tapped at her keyboard, lightning fast. 'Here you go.'

'How'd you do that?'

'Magic.'

'You have all the NEC salesmen's home phone numbers?'

'Naw. Kent's been trying to recruit Letasky for years. I'm always sending his wife flowers.' She looked innocent. She had no idea that her boss was pretending he barely knew who Letasky was. 'But Letasky's unmovable. You want the name of her favorite florist? I have it here, too.'

'No thanks, Mel,' I said. 'I'm not going to be sending flowers.'

16

After work, I drove to Willkie Auto Body to pick up my Acura. On the way, I listened some more to Old Blood and Guts. He was growling something about how 'The only way to survive an ambush is to return fire immediately and run right through the enemy shooters, forcing your enemy to take cover.'

I left the Geo Metro at the body shop, to be picked up by Enterprise Rent-A-Car. Luckily I checked the trunk, where I'd almost left the bag of corporate self-help books.

There's one upside to getting into a car accident: When you get your car back from the shop it looks brand-new. The Acura looked like I'd just driven it off the lot. When I popped the General into the CD player, he sounded even more commanding on my Acura's surround-sound system.

Then I called Kurt Semko on the cell phone and told him I was maybe five miles from his house – he'd told me he rented a house in Holliston – and I had a present for him. He said, sure, come on, stop by.

I found it easily. He lived in a suburban development, in a small raised ranch, red brick, white clapboard, black shutters, like you'd see in every single suburb in America. It was very small, and it was well cared for, recently painted. What was I expecting, an old Quonset hut, maybe?

I parked in the driveway, which was jet-black and obviously recently sealed. I took the stack of books from the trunk and rang Kurt's doorbell. I'd finished reading them, and besides, I thought Kurt needed them more than me.

He came to the door in a white T-shirt.

'Welcome to the Fortress of Solitude.' He opened the screen door for me. 'I'm upgrading the electrical service.'

'You're doing it yourself?'

He nodded. 'It's a rental, but I got tired of the circuit breakers tripping all the time. Hundred amps just doesn't cut it. Plus the wiring's old. So I'm putting in a four-hundred-amp service panel. Figured I'd get rid of the old aluminum branch circuit wiring while I'm at it.'

He noticed the stack of books in my arms. 'Those for me?'

'Well, yeah,' I said.

He scanned the stack. '*Dog Eat Dog: Surviving the Business World,*' he read. '*The Take No Prisoners Guide to the Corporation.* What's all this?'

'Some books I thought you might find useful,' I said, setting them down on the hall table. 'Now that you're working in the corporate world.'

'*Team Secrets of the Navy SEALs: The Elite Military Force's Leadership Principles for Business,*' he said. He seemed amused. '*Corporate Warrior.* This is all military, chief. I don't need to read about it. Seen enough.'

131

I felt like an idiot. Here was a guy who knew all this stuff from real-world experience, and I was giving him a bunch of books for corporate armchair warriors. Plus, what if he was one of those guys who never read books? 'Yeah, but, see, they're all about how to apply what you already know to a world you don't.'

He nodded and said, 'I see. Got it.'

'Check 'em out,' I said. 'See what you think.'

'I will, chief. I will. I'm all about self-improvement.'

'Cool. Hey, so, listen. I need a favor.'

'Name it. Come on in. I'll get you a drink. Show you some of my war trophies.'

His house was just as neat inside as it was outside. Clean and orderly and plain. Almost a temporary look to it. His refrigerator had nothing in it except bottles of Poland Spring water, Gatorade, and protein shakes. I wouldn't be getting a Budweiser.

'Gatorade?'

'Water's fine,' I said.

He tossed me a little bottle of water, took one for himself, and we went to his bare living room – a couch, a recliner, an old TV – and sat down.

I told him a little about the race for the divisional vice president job, how Gleason had blown off an important presentation at Bank of America and Trevor had lost the Pavilion deal. But Trevor was doing a demo at Fidelity on Monday, I said. That would seal the deal. He'd be back in Gordy's good graces.

Then I told him about how Gordy wanted me to recruit Jim Letasky from NEC. 'It's sort of like "Bring me the broomstick of the Wicked Witch of the West,"' I said.

'How so?'

'An impossible assignment. He's setting me up to fail. So he can give the promotion to Trevor.'

'Why're you so sure you're gonna fail?'

'Because I found out from Gordy's secretary that Gordy's tried a bunch of times before, and the guy lives in Chicago with his wife and kids, and he has no reason to move to Boston and start a new job with Entronics.'

'You senior enough to recruit the guy?'

'Technically, I guess. I'm a district manager. But I've met the guy, and we like each other.'

'Know him well?'

'No, that's the thing. Not well at all. I've done the usual research, made a bunch of calls, but I haven't come up with anything I can really sink my teeth into. You don't happen to know anyone in NEC corporate security, do you?'

'Sorry.' He smiled. 'Why, you want a backgrounder on him?'

'Is that even something you can do?'

'All you gotta know is where to look.'

'Think you could find out what his exact compensation package is at NEC?'

'Betcha I can do a lot more than that.'

'That would be awesome.'

'Give me a couple days. I'll see what I can throw together. Actionable intelligence, we used to call it.'

'Thanks, man.'

He shrugged. 'No thanks required. You put it on the line for me, bro.'

'Me?'

'With Scanlon, I mean. You vouched for me.'

'That? That's nothing.'

'It's not nothing, Jason,' he said. 'It's not nothing.'

'Well, happy to do it. So what kind of war trophies do you have?'

He got up and opened the door to what looked like a spare bedroom. It smelled of gunpowder and other things, acrid and musty at the same time. Arranged on a long bench in neat rows were some strange-looking weapons. He picked up an old rifle with a smooth wooden stock. 'Check this out. A World-War-II-vintage Mauser K98. Standard-issue infantry weapon in the *Wehrmacht*. Bought it off an Iraqi farmer who claimed he shot down one of our Apache helicopters with it.' He chuckled. 'Chopper didn't have a scratch.'

'Does it work?'

'No idea. I wouldn't want to try it.' He picked up a pistol, showed it to me. He seemed to want me to handle it, but I just looked. 'Looks like a Beretta Model 1934, right?'

'Absolutely,' I said with a straight face. 'No question.'

'But check out the slide markings.' He held it close to me. 'Made in Pakistan, see? In the hand workshops of Darra Adam Khel.'

'Who?'

'That's a town between Peshawar and Kohat. Famous for making exact replicas of every gun in the world. Armourers to the Pashtun – the Taliban warriors in Stan.'

'Stan?'

'What we called Afghanistan. You can tell it's a Darra special from how poorly the slide stamping is aligned. See?'

'It's a fake?'

'Amazing what you can do with unlimited time, a box of files, and nine sons. And check this out.' He showed me a black rectangle with a bullet hole in the middle of it. 'This is a SAPI plate. Small arms protection insert.'

'Either it's used or it's defective.'

'Saved my life. I'm standing in a tank turret on Highway One in Iraq, and suddenly I'm thrown forward. Sniper got me. Luckily I'd put this in my flak vest. You can see how the bullet pierced it. Even cut through my clothes. Gave me a nasty bruise. Missed my spine, though.'

'You were allowed to take all this stuff back with you?'

'Lot of guys did.'

'Legally?'

He gave a throaty laugh.

'Any of it work?'

'Most of them are replicas. Fakes. Not reliable. You wouldn't want to use them. They could blow up in your face.'

I noticed a tray of tubes, like artist's oil paints. I picked one of the tubes up. It was labeled LIQUID METAL EMBRITTLEMENT AGENT (LME) – MERCURY/ INDIUM AMALGAM. It said UNITED STATES ARMY on it. I was about to ask him what it was when he said, 'You know how to use a gun?'

'Point and shoot, right?'

'Uh, not exactly. Snipers study for years.'

'Morons who live in trailers married to their cousins seem to be able to use them without much training.'

'You know about recoil?'

'Sure. The gun bucks back. I've seen *Bad Boys* like

135

twenty times. Everything I know I learned at the movies.'

'You want to learn how to shoot a gun? I know a guy, owns a firing range not too far.'

'Not my thing.'

'You should, you know. Every guy should learn how to use a gun. This day and age. You've got a wife to protect.'

'When the terrorists come for us, I'll call you.'

'Seriously.'

'No, thanks. Not interested. I'm kinda scared of guns. No offense.'

'None taken.'

'Why do I get a feeling you miss being in the Special Forces?'

'Changed my life, bro.'

'How so?'

'Lousy home life.'

'Where'd you grow up?'

'Grand Rapids. Michigan.'

'Nice town. I've done business with Steelcase.'

'Not the nice part of Grand Rapids. Wrong side of the tracks.'

'Sounds like my neighborhood in Worcester.'

He nodded. 'But I was always in some kind of trouble. Never thought I'd amount to anything. Even when I got drafted by the Tigers, I figured I'd never make the majors. Not good enough. Then I joined the army, and I'm finally good at something. Lot of guys volunteer for Special Forces, but most don't make it through. When I passed the Q Course, I knew I was hot shit. Two-thirds of our class didn't make it.'

'The what course?'

'Q Course. Qualification Course. It's all about weeding

136

guys out – it's constant torture, twenty-four hours a day. They let you have an hour of sleep, and then they wake you up at 2:00 A.M. to go to the hand-to-hand combat pit. Every time a guy quits, they play "Another One Bites the Dust" on the loudspeakers, no matter what time of day or night.'

'I think I know where Gordy gets his management techniques.'

'You have no idea, man. The last part of the course is called Robin Sage, where they throw you into the middle of five thousand square miles of North Carolina forest to do land nav – land navigation. Not allowed to go on roads. You got to live off nuts and berries, and at the beginning they throw you some animal – a rabbit or a chicken – and that's your protein. At the end of the week, you've got to hand in the hind legs. The guys who make it to the end are the ones who just don't give up. That's me.'

'Sounds like Outward Bound.'

He made a *pfft* sound. 'Then if you're lucky, you get to go to one of the real assholes of the universe like Afghanistan or Iraq. If you're really lucky, like me, both.'

'Fun.'

'Yep. You're in Iraq, in the middle of a sandstorm that just won't end, the desert's frickin' *cold* at night, which you'd never expect, your hands are so numb you can't make coffee. Your rations have been cut to one meal a day. There's not enough water to bathe or shave. Or you're in some damned camp in Basra, with sand fleas crawling all over you and biting, and there's mosquitoes carrying malaria, and you're getting red welts all over, and no matter how much insecticide you spray on yourself and in the air it doesn't make a damned bit of difference.'

I nodded, silent for a while. 'Man,' I finally said. 'You're going to find your job kind of boring.'

He shrugged. 'Hey, it's nice to have a real job, finally. Make some money. I can buy a car now. Scanlon wants me to get one, for client meetings and all that. Might even get a new Harley. Save up to buy a house. And maybe someday I'll meet some chick and decide to get married again.'

'Didn't work out last time, huh?'

'Didn't even last a year. Not sure I'm cut out for marriage. Most of the guys in SF are divorced. You want a family, Special Forces isn't for you. So what do *you* want?'

'What do I want?'

'I mean, in life. At work.'

'Red Sox season tickets. Peace on earth.'

'You want kids?'

'Sure.'

'When?'

I shrugged, half smiled. 'We'll see.'

'Ah,' he said. 'Big issue for you.'

'Not an issue.'

'Yeah, it is. You and your wife are struggling with it. Or you're trying, and it's not happening. I can tell from your face.'

'You got a crystal ball in that room too?'

'Seriously. You don't want to talk about it – that's cool – but I can read it in your face. You know what a "tell" is?'

'Poker, right? Little signals that tell you if some-one's bluffing.'

138

'Exactly. Most people aren't comfortable with lying. So when they're bluffing, they smile. Or they get stone-faced. Or they scratch their noses. Some of us in SF took classes in facial expression and threat assessment with this famous psychologist. To learn how to detect deception. Sometimes you want to know if a guy's going for his gun or just pulling out a stick of Wrigley's.'

'I can always tell when Gordy's lying,' I said.

'Oh yeah?'

'Yep. He moves his lips.'

'Yeah, yeah.' He didn't laugh. 'So you want kids. You want a bigger house, a fancier car. More toys.'

'Don't forget about world peace. And the Sox tickets.'

'You want to run Entronics?'

'Last I looked, I wasn't Japanese.'

'You want to run some company, though.'

'Thought's crossed my mind. Usually when I'm half-way through a six-pack.'

He nodded. 'You're an ambitious guy.'

'My wife thinks I'm about as ambitious as a box turtle.'

'She underestimates you.'

'Maybe.'

'Well, I don't, man. Said it before and I'll say it again. I never forget a favor. You'll see.'

17

Saturday morning I called Jim Letasky at home.

He was surprised to hear from me. We talked a bit. I congratulated him on snagging the Albertson's deal away from us, then I got to the point.

'Gordy put you up to this?' Letasky said.

'We've had our eye on you for a while,' I said.

'My wife loves Chicago.'

'She'll love Boston more.'

'I'm flattered,' he said. 'Really. But I already turned down a job offer from Gordy twice already. Three times, come to think of it. No offense, but I love it here. I love my job.'

'You ever get up to Boston on business?' I said.

'All the time,' he said. 'Once a week. It's part of my territory.'

We agreed to meet in a couple of days when he was in Boston. He didn't want to meet at the Entronics headquarters, where he'd see people he knew, and the word would get back to NEC. We arranged to meet for breakfast at his hotel.

Early Monday morning Kurt took me to his gym in Somerville. No beautiful women in Lycra bodysuits working out on brand-new elliptical trainers here. No smoothie bar with bottles of Fiji water.

This was a serious weight lifter's gym that stank of sweat and leather and adrenaline. The floor was ancient splintery planks. There were racks for speed bags, there were medicine balls and heavy bags and double-end bags, and there was a boxing ring in the center of the room. Guys were jumping rope. They all seemed to know Kurt and like him. The toilet had an old-fashioned wooden cistern up above, and you pulled a chain to flush it. There was a NO SPITTING sign. The locker room was gross.

But I loved it. It was real, far more real than CorpFit or any of the other 'fitness clubs' I'd belonged to and almost never gone to. There were a couple of old treadmills and stair climbers, and racks of free weights.

We were both on the bikes warming up, Kurt and I, at five-thirty in the morning. Ten or fifteen minutes of hard pedaling to get our blood pumping, Kurt insisted, before we went through the floor workout. Kurt was wearing a black Everlast muscle T. The guy had huge biceps, and delts that bulged out of his sleeveless shirt like grapefruit.

We talked a bit while we worked out. He told me he was going to initiate an upgrade of the building's closed-circuit camera system to digital. 'All the recordings will be digital,' he said. 'Internet-based, too. Then I gotta do something about our access control system.'

'But we all have those proximity badges,' I said.

'So do the cleaning people. They can get into any office. And how much do you think it costs to bribe one of those illegal aliens to get their card? A hundred bucks, maybe? We gotta go biometric. Thumbprint or fingerprint readers.'

'You really think Scanlon's going to sign on to that?'

'Not yet. He's in favor, but it costs a bundle.'

'Scanlon talk to Gordy about it?'

'Gordy? Nah, Scanlon says it has to get approved at Dick Hardy's level. He wants to wait a few months. See, no one wants to spend on security unless there's a problem. Money flows only when blood flows.'

'You're new,' I said. 'You probably shouldn't twist Scanlon's arm too hard.'

'I'm not gonna twist his arm at all. You gotta know when to fight and when to retreat.' He smiled. 'One of the first things you learn in the box. It's in those books you gave me, too.'

'The box?'

'Sorry. In country.'

'Ah. Makes sense.' I was short of breath and trying to economize my words.

'Hey, I love those corporate warfare books. I get it, man. I really get it.'

'Yeah,' I panted. 'Probably in a way . . . most corporate executives don't.'

'Roger that. All these bogus corporate warriors with all their bullshit about killing the competition. It's funny.' He jumped off the bike. 'Ready for abs?'

After we'd showered and changed, Kurt handed me a folder. I stood outside on the street in the early morning sunlight, the cars roaring by, and read through it.

I had no idea how he'd done it, but he'd managed to get the exact dollar figure of Jim Letasky's take-home for the last four years – salary, commission, and bonuses. He had the amount of Letasky's mortgage, the monthly payment, the rate, and the balance remaining, plus what he'd paid for his house, in Evanston, and what it was worth now.

His car payments. The names of his wife and three kids. The fact that Letasky was born and raised in Amarillo, Texas. Kurt had noted that Letasky's wife didn't work – outside the home, as they say – and that his three kids were in private school, and what that cost. His checking account balance, how much of a balance he kept on his credit cards, what the major expenditures were. It was scary how much Kurt had found out.

'How'd you get all this?' I said as we walked to his motorcycle.

Kurt smiled. 'That's NTK, man.'

'Huh?'

'Need-to-know basis. And all *you* need to know is, you always wanna have better intel than the enemy.'

Since it was Kurt's first day on the job, I offered to take him out to lunch to celebrate. But he was tied up with all sorts of paperwork and orientation sessions and the like. When Trevor Allard returned to the office from Fidelity, around noon – earlier than I'd expected – I strolled over to his cubicle, and said, as casually as I could, 'How'd it go?'

We didn't like each other very much, but we were good at reading each other, the way a couple of wolves size each other up in a few seconds. There was nothing outwardly competitive about the way I asked, but he got what I was really asking: *Did you land the deal? You going to be my boss now?*

143

He looked at me blankly.

'The demo,' I reminded him. 'This morning. At Fidelity.'

'Yeah,' he said.

'You were demo'ing the sixty-one-inch, right?'

He nodded, watching me the whole while, his nostrils flaring. 'The demo flopped.'

'Flopped?'

'Mm-hmm. The monitor wouldn't even turn on. Total dud.'

'You're kidding.'

'No, Jason, I'm not kidding.' His voice was cold and hard. 'I'm not kidding at all.'

'Of course. Jeez, I'm sorry. So what happened – you lose Fidelity?'

He nodded again, watching my face closely. 'Naturally. No one wants to spend ten thousand bucks per unit on a bunch of plasmas that are questionable. So, yep, I lost 'em.'

'Crap. And you forecast Fidelity as a "commit," right.' That meant as close to a sure thing as you could get in this world.

He compressed his lips. 'So here's the thing, Jason. Me and Brett, we've had a run of real bad luck recently. My car gets a flat tire, then some kind of electrical problem. Brett's computer gets wiped out. Now I somehow get a bad monitor, after having it tested. Both of us lose major deals as a result.'

'Yeah?'

'What do Brett and I have in common? We're both in the running for Crawford's job. Against you. And nothing happens to you. So I can't help but wonder how and why this is all happening.'

144

'You're looking for a reason? An explanation? I mean, it sucks, and I'm sorry about it, but you guys have both been unlucky lately. That's all.'

Maybe it wasn't just a matter of bad luck. Two competitive guys, Gleason and Allard. Rivals for a job that paid a lot more and put them on the management track. Was it possible that they'd been sabotaging each other? Guys could be like that. Even buddies like those two. Scorpions in a bottle. Maybe it was like a frat hazing? Stranger things happened in high-pressure companies like ours. I made a mental note to start backing everything up, all my files, and taking copies home.

'Unlucky,' he repeated. His nostrils flared again. 'See, I've always been the kind of guy who has great luck.'

'Oh, I get it now. You've been dropping deals all over the place, but it's *my* fault. That's sad. Listen to me, Trevor. You make your own luck.'

I was about to let loose – I was really fed up – when there was a scream from down the hall. We looked at each other in puzzlement.

Another scream, female, and then someone else shouted, and we both went to see what the matter was.

A small crowd had gathered outside the Plasma Lab. The woman who'd screamed, a young admin, was screaming even louder and clutching the doorjamb as if to keep from sinking to the floor.

'What is it?' I said. 'What happened?'

'Meryl kept knocking and knocking, and Phil didn't answer, so she opened the door to see if he was in,' said Kevin Taminek, the manager for inside sales. 'I

145

mean, he's always there, and it's late morning. And *Jesus*.'

Gordy came up, short of breath, shouted, 'What goes on *here*?'

'Somebody call Security,' said another guy, who did inside sales with Taminek. 'Or the police. Or both.'

'Oh, good God almighty,' Gordy said, his voice loud and trembling.

I came a few feet closer so I could see what they were all looking at, and I gasped.

Philip Rifkin was dangling in midair, hanging from the ceiling.

His eyes were open, bulging. He wasn't wearing his glasses. His mouth was partly open, and the tip of his tongue protruded. His face was dark, bluish. A black cord cut deeply into his neck, knotted at the back of his head. I recognized it as component cable, which he kept in giant spools. A chair was tipped over a few feet away. I could see that he'd removed one of the drop ceiling panels and had tied the other end of the cable around a steel joist.

'My God!' Trevor said, turning away, gagging.

'Jesus,' I breathed, 'he hanged himself.'

'Call Security!' Gordy shouted. He grabbed the door handle and pulled it shut. 'And get the hell out of here, all of you. Back to work.'

18

My muscles were burning, but Kurt wouldn't let me stop. He had me running up and down the steps of Harvard Stadium. He called it the 'Stairway to Heaven.'

'Time for a rest,' I said.

'Nope. Keep going. Body relaxed. Swing those arms all the way back, right up to your shoulders.'

'I'm dying here. My muscles feel like they're on fire.'

'Lactic acid. Outstanding.'

'Isn't that bad?'

'Keep moving.'

'You're not even winded.'

'It takes a lot to get me winded.'

'All right,' I said, 'you win. I surrender. I confess.'

'Two more.'

When we were done, he made us fast-walk along the banks of the Charles River as a way to cool down. I thought a Starbucks Frappuccino would work better.

'Was it as good for you as it was for me?' I said, still gasping.

'Pain is just weakness leaving the body,' Kurt said, punching me lightly on the shoulder. 'So you guys had an ugly incident up there yesterday, I hear. Someone took a swing, huh?'

'Horrible,' I said, shaking my head, panting.

'Scanlon told me he used a wire or something.'

'Yeah. Component cable.'

'Sad.'

'Scanlon tell you – if Rifkin left a note?'

Kurt shrugged. 'No idea.'

We walked for a few minutes until I was able to talk almost normally. 'Trevor thinks I'm trying to wrongfoot him. Screw him over. You know that big demonstration he had? In front of Fidelity – one of our sixty-one-inch plasmas? Thing was dead when he switched it on. Of course he lost the account.'

'Bad for him, good for you.'

'Maybe. But he thinks I sabotaged the monitor.'

'Did you?'

'Come on. Not exactly my style. Plus, I wouldn't know how to do it even if I wanted to.'

'Couldn't the monitor have gone bad on the truck?'

'Sure. There's all kinds of ways a plasma monitor can go out of whack. Couple of months ago Circuit City said six of our flat-panel TVs came in dead. It turned out some dimwit janitor at our Rochester warehouse had been cleaning the toilets with some mixture of toilet-bowl cleaner and Clorox. Didn't know it releases chlorine gas. Which corrodes the microchips or the printed circuits or something – totally fried the monitors. So it could have been anything.'

'All you can do is ignore the guy. No one's going to take his accusations seriously, right? It just sounds like he's trying to make excuses.'

I nodded. Walked for a bit. 'I'm going to have to miss our workout Thursday morning,' I said. 'I'm having breakfast with Letasky.'

148

'Gonna make him an offer he can't refuse, huh?'

'Do my best. Thanks to you.'

'Glad to help. Anything I can do, just ask.'

I paused. 'Listen, I read through the file you gave me. That intel is going to be a huge help. Huge.'

He shrugged modestly.

'And I really appreciate all the work you did to get it for me. Some of it – well, I don't want to know how you got hold of it, but – you need to be really careful with that stuff. Some of that crosses the line. And if either of us is caught with it, we could get in some serious trouble.'

He was silent. The morning was starting to warm up, and his tank top was starting to soak through. My T-shirt was already dripping wet.

A minute went by in silence, then another minute. There was a flock of geese waddling along the river-bank by the Lars Anderson Bridge. A pair of early morning joggers, a man and a woman.

'You're the one who asked me to get a backgrounder on Letasky,' he said, sounding almost defensive.

'I know I did. You're right. But I shouldn't have. I'm just uncomfortable with this.'

Another minute of silence. A car roared by along Storrow Drive.

'So I guess you're not interested in another tidbit about James Letasky that just came in.'

I stared down at the sidewalk. Exhaled slowly. I wanted to say yes, but couldn't quite bring myself to do so.

Kurt went on, without waiting for a reply. 'Last couple of years the Letasky family's spent their vacations camping. Wisconsin, Indiana, Michigan, places

149

like that. But the place James and his wife really love is Martha's Vineyard. That's where they honeymooned. They keep wanting to go back, but it's too far from Chicago.'

'Interesting,' I said. Martha's Vineyard was a lot closer to Boston than to Chicago. 'How did you –' I saw Kurt's expression, and stopped. 'Right. NTK.'

Kurt looked at his watch. 'We both got to get to work,' he said.

'You playing softball tonight?'

'Wouldn't miss it,' Kurt said.

19

The hotshot from NEC, Jim Letasky, was a plump, round-faced guy in his midthirties with blond hair cut in a pudding-basin, Franciscan friar haircut. He had a ready smile and couldn't have been more charismatic and winning. He was blunt and straightforward – no mind games, no coyness – and I liked that. He knew we wanted to hire him, and he knew why, and he made no secret of the fact that he wasn't much interested. Still, he hadn't slammed the door shut, since after all he was sitting here at breakfast with me at the Hyatt Regency on Memorial Drive in Cambridge.

We exchanged the usual chitchat about the business, and I congratulated him again on the Albertson's deal, and he was suitably modest about it. I pried a little about his connection at that middleman company, SignNetwork, but he got a little evasive. Trade secrets and all that. We talked about Amarillo, Texas, his hometown, and I told him about my weakness for Big Red soda, which he loved too.

When he'd finished his third cup of coffee, Letasky said, 'Jason, it's always great to see you, but can we speak frankly? Entronics can't afford me.'

'Top talent costs,' I said.

'You don't know what I make.'

I tried not to smile. 'Your comp package is only one small part of what we can offer you,' I said.

He laughed. 'Not too small a part, I hope,' he said.

I told him what we'd offer. It was exactly twenty-five percent higher than he made at NEC, and it didn't require him to bust his balls as much. I knew from his private complaints to his boss – Kurt's dossier even included some of Letasky's private e-mails – that he was trying to cut back on the travel, spend more time with his kids. Given the kind of numbers Letasky drove, and our bonus structure, Entronics would still end up ahead.

'See, we want our salesguys to have a life,' I said. That was so bogus, I couldn't believe the words were tumbling out of my mouth. 'The way the package is structured, you can make a lot more than you make now by working significantly fewer hours. I mean, you'd still be logging the miles and all, don't get me wrong, but this way you get to watch your kids grow up. You get to go to Kenny's hockey practice and the twins' ballet recitals.'

'How do you know – ?' he began.

'I've done my homework. I'm telling you, my orders are not to let you get up from this table until you say yes.'

He blinked, momentarily silenced.

'These are precious years in your kids' lives,' I said. Just about word-for-word what he'd e-mailed his boss, in fact. 'And they go fast. Sure, you're the bread-winner, but do you really want to get home every night too late to tuck them in? I want you to think about what you're missing.'

'I've thought about it,' he conceded in a small voice.

'See, you can make a better living and also be there for your wife and kids. Wouldn't it be nice to be able to spend three weeks in the Grand Tetons instead of one?' That one hit home, I knew. He'd e-mailed that to his boss too.

'Yeah,' he said, his brows jutting up, the smile gone from his face. 'It would.'

'And why should you spend forty-five minutes commuting to work? That's time you could be spending with your kids. Helping them with their homework.'

'We've got a great house.'

'Have you ever seen Wellesley?' I said. 'Didn't Gail go to school there?' Gail was his wife, and she'd gone to Wellesley College. 'It's a fifteen-minute drive from Framingham, a straight shot down 135.'

'It's that close?'

'For what you could get for your house in Evanston, you could be living in this house.' I took out a photo that I'd printed out from a Wellesley real estate website that morning. 'Over two hundred years old. An old farmhouse that's been added to over the years. Nice, huh?'

He stared at the photo. 'Man.'

'Cliff Road is the most exclusive neighborhood in Wellesley. See the size of that property? Your kids can play in the yard, and you and Gail don't have to worry about the cars. There's a great Montessori school not too far away – don't the twins go to a Montessori school?'

He exhaled. 'The hassle of moving,' he began.

I slid another piece of paper across the table at him.

'This is the relocation and signing bonus we're prepared to offer you.'

He read the number and blinked twice. 'It says the offer expires today.'

'I want you to have time to talk this over with Gail. But I don't want you using this as leverage within NEC to negotiate a better package.'

'They'd never match this,' he said. I really liked his honesty. It was refreshing. 'It wouldn't do any good.'

'You're not the top performer there. Here, you would be. So we're willing to pay.'

'I have until five o'clock today to decide?'

'Boston time,' I said. 'That's four o'clock Chicago time.'

'Wow, man. I don't – this is so sudden.'

'You've thought about it for quite a while,' I said. I knew he'd just turned down an offer from Panasonic. 'Sometimes you just have to close your eyes and jump.'

He looked at me, but his eyes were focused on some point in the middle distance. I could see he was thinking hard.

'Plus, do you know how close we are to the Vineyard?' I said. 'A hop, skip, and a jump. Ever been there? Your family would love it.'

I suggested he go back up to his hotel room and call his wife. I told him I'd wait down in the lobby, making calls and doing e-mail on my BlackBerry. I told him I had all the time in the world, which wasn't true.

Forty-five minutes later he returned to the lobby.

Gordy's jaw dropped. I mean, you hear the expression, but how often do you ever really see someone's jaw drop? Gordy's mouth came open, and for a few seconds he was speechless.

'Holy shit,' he said. He kept looking at Jim Letasky's signature on the agreement, and then back at my face. 'How the hell did you do that?'

'You approved the package,' I said.

'I've offered him damn good packages before. What did you promise him?' he said suspiciously.

'Nothing you don't know about. I guess we just finally broke down his resistance.'

'Well,' he said, 'good job.' He put both hands on my shoulders and squeezed hard. 'I don't know how you did it, but I'm impressed.'

He did not look happy.

20

When I got back to my office after lunch on Friday, there was a voice mail from Gordy. He wanted me to come by his office at three o'clock.

I called right back, talked to Melanie, and confirmed.

Managed to get through an hour and a half of calls and paperwork, all the while replaying Gordy's message in my head, trying to read his inscrutable voice, figure out whether it was bad news or good.

At a few minutes before three I walked down the hall to his office.

'Booya,' Gordy said. He actually stood when I entered his office. Next to him stood Yoshi Tanaka, eyes dead behind thick lenses. 'The better man won. Our new Vice President of Sales. Congratulations.'

Gordy extended a hand and gave what seemed to me a pretty damned grudging shake. His giant gold monogrammed cuff links glittered. Yoshi didn't shake my hand. He bowed, ever so slightly. He didn't know how to do handshakes, but then again, I didn't know how to bow. Neither man smiled. Yoshi apparently didn't know how to do that either, but Gordy struck me as unusually subdued, as if someone had a gun to his back.

'Thank you,' I said.

'Sit down,' Gordy said. We all took our places.

'I wish I could say this is a tribute to your own success,' Gordy said, 'but that's only part of it. You've had some good wins. Some *big* wins. You really seem to be getting your shit together. Getting Letasky was a major coup, and I frankly didn't think you could pull it off. But the main thing is, I can't have a bumbler in this job. I need someone totally reliable. Not like Gleason, spacing out on appointments. Even Trevor, dropping the ball on Fidelity. Playing golf and blowing off Pavilion.'

'Well, I look forward to the challenge,' I said, which, when I heard the words come out of my mouth, almost made me barf.

'And challenge it will be,' said Gordy. 'You have no idea. You'll be doing Joan's job *and* Crawford's job now. Anyway, I think Yoshi-san wants to say a few words.'

Tanaka bowed his head solemnly. 'My most congratulation – to you.'

'Thank you.'

'You have very – imposu – job to do.'

'What kind of job?'

'Imposu – impo – sent.'

'Important, yes.'

'Not good time for our – business.'

I nodded.

'Very – hard time.'

'I understand.'

'I think you not know how hard time,' Tanaka said quietly.

157

'Thank you, Yoshi-san,' said Gordy. 'Now I'd like to discuss salary specifics with Steadman. Yoshi-san, maybe you could give us a little privacy.'

Tanaka rose, tipped his head in a parting bow, and walked out.

'Could you close the door?' Gordy called out. 'Thank you, Yoshi-san.'

I was determined to seize the initiative, not let Gordy see me as a wimp. Kurt would be proud. 'I have a pretty good sense of what my salary requirements are –' I began.

'Your *requirements*,' Gordy spit out. 'Give me a break. We're not negotiating. Your package is take-it-or-leave-it. I just said that to get the Jap out of the room.'

I met his eyes and nodded, waiting. No more Mister Nice Guy, I guess.

He told me what it was, and I tried not to smile. It was more than I'd expected. A lot more.

'You weren't my top choice, I think you know that,' Gordy said.

Now I understand why Yoshi was there. He was the enforcer, making sure Tokyo's will was done, or at least making sure Gordy remembered who called the shots. Gordy must have hated that – a guy who ostensibly worked for him, who barely spoke English, telling him what to do.

'I hope to prove you wrong,' I said.

He stared malevolently. 'I already told you there's shit raining down on us from the MegaTower in Tokyo. Well, let me tell you who's doing the shitting. You know the name Hideo Nakamura, I assume.'

'Sure.' A couple of weeks ago a press release was

e-mailed around that the president and CEO of Entronics, a guy named something-Ikehara, had been 'promoted' and was being replaced by this guy Nakamura. No one knew anything about Nakamura – that was way up the stratosphere. But the word was that the old guy, Ikehara, had become what the Japanese call a *madogiwa-zoku,* a 'window-watcher.' Basically that means getting put out to pasture. In Japan, no one gets fired; instead, you get humiliated by being put on the payroll with nothing to do except stare out the window. They literally give you a desk by the window, which, in Japan, isn't a good thing the way it is here. In Japan, a corner office means you're on corporate death row.

'I flew down to Santa Clara to meet this guy Nakamura, and he's real polished. Real smooth. Speaks good English. Loves golf and Scotch. But this guy's an executioner. Might as well been wearing the black hood and carrying a noose. They put him in because the very top guys in the MegaTower are real unhappy. They don't like our numbers. That's why they bought Royal Meister's U.S. business – because they want to extend their reach into the U.S. market.'

'I see.'

'So we gotta show Nakamura what we're made of. Can you do that?'

'I can.'

'Can you incent the guys to work harder? Crack the whip?'

'I can.'

'Can you pull a rabbit out of your hat?'

I almost said, *I'll do my best.* Or, *I'll sure as hell try.* But I said, 'You know it.'

159

'I'm going to expect a lot out of you. I'll be riding you mercilessly. Now, get out of here. We've got to prepare for the weekly conference call.'

I stood up.

He stuck out his hand. 'I hope I haven't made a mistake,' he said.

I tried not to smile. 'You haven't,' I said.

Melanie smiled at me as I left. 'Say hi to Bob,' I said.

'Thanks. Hi to Kate.'

I made my way to my office. Coming out of the men's room was Cal Taylor. He gave me a lopsided grin and wiped his mouth with the back of his hand. I knew he'd just had a little midafternoon cheer – his cubicle was too public. 'Hey there,' Cal said, weaving toward me.

'Hey, Cal,' I said cheerfully, and kept walking.

'You look like the cat that got the cream,' he said. Even soused, which he was most of the time, he was scary perceptive.

I chuckled politely and gave him a friendly wave, and smiled all the way to my office. There I shut the door and pumped my fists into the air.

I called Kate's cell. 'Hey, babe,' I said. 'You at work?'

'I'm just sitting here at Starbucks, having coffee with Claudia.' Claudia had gone to prep school and college with Kate, had an immense trust fund, and apparently did nothing but go out with her friends. She didn't understand why Kate insisted on working at the foundation.

'I just saw Gordy.' I kept my voice neutral, a blank.

'And? You don't sound so good. You didn't get it?'

'I got it.'

160

'What?'

'I got the promotion,' I said, my voice louder. 'You're talking to a vice president. I want some deference.'

She let out a loud squeal.

'Oh, my God. Jason! That's so wonderful!'

'Do you know what this means? It's a huge boost in salary. *Serious* bonus.'

'We've got to celebrate,' she said. 'Let's go out to dinner. I'll make reservations at Hamersley's.'

'I'm kind of wiped out,' I said. 'It's been a long day.'

'All right, baby. We'll do something at home.'

The word got around pretty quickly. The reactions from the Band of Brothers were interesting and not entirely unexpected. Ricky Festino could not have been happier for mc. He acted like I'd just been elected President of the United States instead of picked as some VP of sales. Brett Gleason did something totally out of character for him, which was to acknowledge my existence by saying 'Have a good weekend.' Which was frankly kind of big of him, since he'd just been beat out of the job he wanted. Trevor Allard ignored me, which was basically what I thought he'd do, and which gave me endless satisfaction, because he was obviously really pissed off.

Everything felt good now. In the elevator, on the screen, the word of the day happened to be 'felicitation,' which sounded like a positive thing. Entronics stock was up. Everyone in the elevator looked and smelled good.

I stopped in at Corporate Security on my way out of the lobby and found Kurt at his cubicle. I told him the good news.

'No way,' he said. 'You're it? You're the man?'

'Yep.'

He stood up, gave me a manly hug. 'You rock. You got your stripes, man. Bravo Zulu.'

'Huh?'

'Army talk. Congrats, bro.'

21

In the car on the way to the Atrium Mall in Chestnut Hill, I listened to some more of Old Blood and Guts. 'When you're downrange and you come under attack,' he barked, 'you're gonna have to act immediately. The enemy can shoot you in the back when you're running away just as easily as he can shoot you in the front running toward him. In the time it takes you to read this paragraph, one of your team members will die. So you've got to give an order, and fast. Don't hesitate. Just make a *goddamned decision*!'

I was half listening, half daydreaming about my new job. How happy Kate was going to be, now that I was finally making money. We could move. Buy a house she liked for once.

I took the escalator up to Tiffany's and asked to see the brooches. I'd never been inside Tiffany's before, believe it or not, and I discovered that their jewelry isn't organized by category, like necklaces in one case and earrings in the other, but by where you can afford to shop. On one side of the store are the things that regular well-off people can afford, mostly sterling silver and semiprecious stones. On the other side of the store are the gold and diamonds, where you don't dare to tread unless you run your own hedge fund.

When I described which brooch I was looking for, the saleswoman escorted me over to the wrong side of the store, the high-rent district. I gulped. Then she went behind a glass case and took out the starfish and put it on a black velvet square and cooed over it.

'That's it,' I said. I turned it over, pretending to look at the back but really trying to get a look at the price tag, and when I saw it, I gulped again. This was more than I'd spent on Kate's diamond engagement ring. But I reminded myself that I'd just gotten a sizable salary increase, and I'd be getting a handsome bonus, so I put it on my Visa and asked her to gift-wrap it.

By the time I got home I was feeling pretty good about life. I'd just been promoted, and there was a tiny robin's-egg blue Tiffany's bag on the passenger seat next to me. Granted, the car was an Acura, and not a new one, but still. I was *good,* damn it, and I worked for a great company. I was a meat-eater.

Kate ran to meet me at the door. She was wearing a white T-shirt and jeans, looked and smelled great. She threw her arms around me, kissed me right on the lips, and I kissed her back, and kept going. I was immediately aroused.

When you've been married for a while, that kind of spontaneous combustion doesn't happen all that often, but I felt this surge of testosterone. I felt like the conquering hero returning home for some nookie. I was Og, Cro-Magnon man, returning to his woman in the cave, having speared a woolly mammoth.

I dropped my briefcase and the blue Tiffany's bag to the carpet and slipped my hands under the waist-

164

band of her jeans. I felt her silky-smooth warm skin and began kneading her butt.

She gave a throaty giggle, pulled back. 'What's the special occasion?' she said.

'Every day I'm married to you is a special occasion,' I said, and I went back to kissing her.

I moved us into the living room, pushed her back onto Grammy Spencer's rock-hard, chintz-covered couch. The floor would have been more comfortable.

'Jase,' she said. 'Wow.'

'We're allowed to do this without a plastic specimen cup, you know,' I said as I started to peel off her T-shirt.

'Wait,' she said. 'Wait.' She wriggled free, went over to close the drapes so the neighbors didn't get a free show and their little children wouldn't have therapy bills for decades.

When she came back, I finished taking off her T-shirt. I hadn't looked closely at her breasts in such a long time that I got as excited as I'd been the first time we did it. 'You're a beautiful woman, anyone ever tell you that?' I said, and I unzipped her jeans. She was already aroused, I was surprised to see.

'Should – think we should move to the bedroom?' she said.

'Nope,' I said, stroking her down there.

Just then my BlackBerry buzzed – it was clipped to my belt, somewhere in the heap on the floor – but I ignored it. I got on top of her and, without any more foreplay, slid into her slipperiness with delicious ease.

'Jase,' she said. 'Wow.'

*

'Stay there,' she said afterward.

She ran to the bathroom and peed, and then went into the kitchen, where I could hear the refrigerator being opened and glasses clinking, and a couple of minutes later she emerged with a tray. She carried it over to the couch, naked, and set it down on the coffee table. It was a bottle of Krug champagne and two champagne flutes and a mound of black caviar in a silver bowl with a couple of tortoiseshell caviar spoons and little round blini. Also, a flat rectangular package wrapped in fancy paper.

I hate caviar, but it's not like we had it very often, and she must have forgotten.

I said, with all the excitement I could muster, 'Caviar!'

'Could you do the honors?' She handed me the cold champagne bottle. I used to think that when you opened a bottle of champagne you wanted a loud festive pop and a big geyser. Kate taught me that that really wasn't the way it was done. I stripped off the lead foil and twisted off the wire cage and eased the cork out expertly, turning the bottle as I did it. The cork came out with a quiet burp. No geyser. I poured it into the flutes slowly, let the bubbles settle, and poured in some more. Then I handed her a glass and we clinked.

'Wait,' she said as I put my flute to my lips. 'A toast.'

'To the classics,' I said. 'Champagne and caviar and sex.'

'No,' she said with a laugh. 'To love and desire – the spirit's wings to great deeds. Goethe.'

'I haven't done any great deeds.'

'As Balzac said, "There's no such thing as a great talent without great willpower."'

I clinked her glass again, and said, 'Behind every great man is a great woman.'

'Rolling her eyes,' Kate said. 'And sticking out her tongue.' She smiled. 'Honey, do you realize what you've accomplished? How you've turned your whole career around?'

I nodded, couldn't look at her. My dad had a job. I have a *career*.

And if she only knew what kind of help I was getting.

'Vice president. I'm so proud of you.'

'Aw, shucks,' I said.

'You really kick ass when you put your mind to it.'

'Well, you're the one who gave me the push. The jump start.'

'Sweetie.' She took the package from the tray and handed it to me. *'Un petit cadeau.'*

'Moi?' I said. 'Hold on.' I got up and picked up the Tiffany's bag from the floor where it had fallen. I handed it to her. 'Swap.'

'Tiffany's? Jason, you are so bad.'

'Go ahead. You first.'

'No, you. It's just a little nothing.'

I tore off the wrapping paper as she said, 'Something new to listen to on the way to work.'

It was a CD of a book called *You're the Boss Now – So Now What? A Ten Point Plan.*

'Oh, nice,' I said. I made it sound convincing. 'Thanks.' I wasn't going to tell her I'd already moved on to harder drugs – the four-star general.

I knew that my world was alien to her, and basically

boring, and she didn't quite get it. But if she was going to be married to a Yanomami warrior, why not a chieftain? So she'd make sure I had my face paint on right, at least. She didn't really get into what I did all day, but damn it, she was going to make sure my buzzard-feather headdress was on straight.

'Hit the ground running,' she said. 'And something to carry it in.' She reached under the sofa and pulled out a much larger box.

'Wait, I know what it is,' I said.

'You do not.'

'I do. It's one of those Yanomami blowguns. With the poison darts. Right?'

She gave me her great, sexy knowing smile. I loved that smile. It always melted me.

I unwrapped the box. It was a beautiful briefcase in chestnut leather with brass fittings. It had to cost a fortune. 'Jesus,' I said. 'Amazing.'

'It's made by Swaine Adeney Briggs and Sons of St. James's. London. Claudia helped me pick it out. She says it's the Rolls-Royce of attaché cases.'

'And maybe someday a Rolls-Royce to put it in,' I said. 'Babe, this is incredibly sweet of you. 'Your turn.'

Her eyes shone, wide with excitement, as she carefully undid the blue paper and then opened the box. Then I saw the light in her eyes go dim.

'What's the matter?'

She turned the gold, jewel-encrusted starfish over suspiciously, as if searching for the price tag the way I did at the store. 'I don't believe it,' she said, tonelessly. 'My God.'

'Don't you recognize it?'

168

'Sure. It's just that I –'

'Susie won't mind if you have one, too.'

'No, I don't imagine she'd – Jason, how much did this cost?'

'We can afford it.'

'Are you sure?'

'I'm sure,' I said. 'I just got my stripes.'

'Your stripes?'

'Army talk,' I said.

She took a sip of champagne and then turned back to the coffee table. She spread some of the vile, oily black eggs on a cracker and offered it to me with a sweet smile. 'Sevruga?'

PART TWO

PART TWO

22

We found out Kate was pregnant two weeks later. She'd gone back to the IVF clinic with greater dread than usual to start going through the whole gruesome process all over again, the shots and the thermometers and the cold stirrups and the high hopes that would probably be dashed. They gave her the usual blood work, all this stuff I never quite understood about levels of some hormone that told the docs when her next ovulation would be. But I didn't have to understand it. I just did what they told me to do, went in when they told me to and did my heroic duty. The next day Dr. DiMarco called Kate to tell her that an interesting complication had arisen, and there might not be a need for an IVF cycle after all. He seemed a little miffed, Kate told me. We'd gotten pregnant the old-fashioned way. That wasn't supposed to happen.

I had a secret theory, which I'd never tell Kate. I think she got pregnant because things had started to break my way. Call me crazy, but you know how some parents try for years to have a baby, then as soon as they adopt, boom, they get pregnant? Their biological roadblock gets blown away just by the decision to adopt. The relief, maybe. There are studies, too, about how men who feel good about themselves tend to be more fertile. At least I think I read something about this.

Then again, it's possible that she got pregnant just because we'd finally had real sex, after months of my doing it into a plastic cup in a lab.

Whatever the reason, we were both elated. Kate insisted that we couldn't tell anyone until we heard the heartbeat, around seven or eight weeks. Only then would she tell her father – her mother had died long before I met Kate – and her sister and all her friends. Both my parents were dead – smokers, the two of them, so they went early – and I didn't have any brothers or sisters to tell anyway.

I'd always had lots of friends, but you get married, and you start going out only with other married people, and the guys aren't allowed to go out without their wives unless they're wearing an electronic ankle bracelet, and then they have kids, and after a while you don't have so many pals. There were some friends from college I still stayed in touch with. A couple of my frat brothers. But I wasn't going to tell anyone until we heard the heartbeat.

Telling people wasn't the main thing to me anyway. What was important was that I was in love with the most beautiful woman in the world, and we were having a baby, and I was starting to feel really positive about my work. It was all good.

At the twelve-week point, I started telling the guys at work. Gordy could not have been less interested. He had four kids and avoided them as much as possible. He liked to brag about how little he saw his family. It was a macho thing to him.

Festino shook my hand and even momentarily forgot about the Purell. 'Congratulations on the death of your sex life, Tigger,' he said.

'Not totally dead yet,' I said.

'Yeah, well, just wait. Babies themselves are the best form of birth control. You'll see.'

'If you say so.'

'Oh, yeah. My wife and I do it doggie-style. I sit up and beg, and she rolls over and plays dead.'

I pantomimed a Borscht Belt rimshot in the air. 'Thank you, you're a wonderful audience, I'm here all week,' I said. 'Try the veal chop, it's great.'

'Wait till you've got the Barney song stuck in your head,' Festino said. 'Earworm from hell. Or till the only TV show you're allowed to watch anymore is *The Wiggles*. And when you go out to dinner, it's Chuck E. Cheese's at five o'clock. So when are you going to do an amnio?'

'Amnio?'

'You know, that test for birth defects.'

'Boy, you do look on the dark side, don't you?' I said. 'Kate's not close to thirty-five.'

'It's like what doctors always say. Prepare for the worst and all that.'

It seemed like a kind of personal question, but mostly I was surprised that Festino cared. 'It's "Hope for the best and prepare for the worst,"' I said. 'You left out the first part.'

'I was just cutting to the chase,' Festino said.

The pregnancy was the biggest thing to happen to us in the first couple of months after my promotion, but it wasn't the only big thing. We moved out of the little

175

house in Belmont and into a town house in Cambridge. We still couldn't swing one of those houses on Brattle Street she'd been fantasizing about, but we bought a beautiful Victorian on Hilliard Street, just off Brattle, that had been renovated a few years ago by a Harvard professor who'd just been lured away to Princeton. There were things we wanted to change – the carpet on the steep stairs to the second floor was badly frayed, for instance – but we figured we'd get around to it sometime.

We probably underpriced the Belmont house, since Kate couldn't wait to move to Cambridge. It sold within two days of our putting it on the market. So we were in our new house within two months. I hadn't seen her happier in years, and that made me happy.

In the driveway – no garages in this fancy part of Cambridge, believe it or not – sat our two brand-new cars. I'd traded in my totally rebuilt Acura for a new Mercedes SLK 55 AMG Roadster, and Kate reluctantly traded in her tired old Nissan Maxima for a Lexus SUV hybrid, only because it was, she said, far more fuel-efficient and less polluting. My Mercedes just looked sweet.

It was all happening fast – maybe too fast.

Just about every morning I worked out with Kurt now, at his gym or at Harvard Stadium or running along the Charles River. Kurt had become my personal trainer. He told me I had to lose the paunch, had to become lean and mean, and once I started feeling better about myself physically, everything would follow.

He was right, of course. I dropped ten pounds in a couple of weeks, and after a couple of months I was down thirty pounds. I had to buy new clothes, which Kate was delighted about. She saw it as an opportunity to upgrade my wardrobe, get me out of those Men's Warehouse suits and into some suits from Louis of Boston in confusing European sizes with unpronounceable names of Italian designers inside.

Kurt had strong feelings about how I ate – i.e., I was poisoning myself – and he had me eating high-protein and low-fat and only 'good' carbs. Lots of fish and vegetables and stuff. I cut way back on the eggplant parmesan subs and the olive loaf sandwiches at lunch. I stopped visiting my stoner friend Graham, cut out the weed entirely, because Kurt had convinced me that it was a vile habit, that I needed to keep all my faculties sharp. Sound mind, sound body, all that.

He insisted I take the stairs at work at least once a week instead of the elevator. *Twenty floors?* I squawked. *You're out of your mind!* One morning I tried it, and I had to change my shirt as soon as I got to my office. But after a while climbing (or descending) twenty flights wasn't all that brutal. When you have an elevator phobia, you'll put up with a lot of pain to avoid being trapped in the vertical coffin.

Kate was thrilled about my Extreme Makeover. She was determined to eat healthy throughout her pregnancy, and now I was along for the ride. She'd never met this guy Kurt, but she liked what he was doing for me.

She didn't know the half, of course.

In my new, bigger office, I put up all these framed, military-themed, corporate motivational posters. One was a photo of a sniper in camouflage fatigues and camo face paint lying on the ground aiming his weapon at us. It said, in big letters, BRAVERY, and then: 'It takes an extraordinary person to face danger and maintain composure.' Another one showed some guys on a tank and the words, 'AUTHORITY: It is the strongest who prevail.' I had FORTITUDE and PATIENCE too. Hokey? Sure. But just looking at them got me pumped.

At work, especially, things just started clicking into place for me. It was as if every pitch I swung at was a home run, every putt dropped, every three-pointer swished, nothing but net. I had a hot hand. One good thing led to another.

Even buying the new Mercedes led to a major sales coup.

One morning I was sitting in the plush waiting room of the Harry Belkin Mercedes dealership in Allston, waiting for my new car to be prepped. I sat there for a good hour on a leather sofa, drinking a cappuccino from an automatic machine, watching *Live with Regis and Kelly* on their surround-sound TV.

And then I thought: how come they don't have Entronics plasma screens in here, running features and ads on the latest Mercedes models? You know, beauty shots. Mercedes would pay for it. Then I started thinking, the Harry Belkin Company was the largest auto dealership in New England. They had BMW dealerships, and Porsche dealerships, and Maybach dealerships. Lots of others, too. Why not suggest the idea? Hell, supermarkets were doing it – why not high-end auto dealerships?

I did some research online and identified the right guy to talk to. He was the Senior Vice President for Marketing, and his name was Fred Naseem. I called him, pitched my idea, and he was immediately intrigued. Of course, the price was a concern, but isn't it always? I pulled out my entire arsenal of tried-and-true sales tricks. I told him about how much added revenue the supermarket chains were generating using plasma screens to advertise at checkout lines. Waiting rooms are just like checkout lines, I told him. Everyone hates to wait. It's a waste of time. But people like to be informed, to get new information. And be entertained. So entertain them and educate them – and sell them on the most exciting features of your new-model cars. Then I broke down the costs for him, only of course I never called it a 'cost' or a 'price' but an 'investment.' Broke it right down to dollars per day invested versus what they'd generate. It was a no-brainer. Then I did the classic 'yes-set' close – giving him a series of tic-down questions to which I knew he had to answer 'yes.' Your customers are discerning, aren't they? I'll bet they appreciate the amenities you provide for them in the waiting room, like the coffee and the bagels, don't they? They'd think the Entronics monitors looked cool up on the wall, don't you think? Boom boom boom. Yes yes yes. Then: Is it accurate to say that your boss, Harry Belkin, would like to increase the average revenue generated in each of your auto dealerships? Well, what's he gonna say? No? Then I moved in for the kill. Asked the Big Question: Are you ready to start making the additional profits that the Entronics monitors will surely generate for you?

The Big Yes.

When he wavered at the very end, as customers often do, I hit him with a couple of legendary closing tricks I'd picked up from my Mark Simkins CDs. I think it was the set called *The Mark Simkins College of Advanced Closing*. The sharp-angle close, where you maneuver them into making a demand you know you can meet. I told him that for this much inventory, delivery would probably be six months off. Well, now that he was all hot and bothered about getting those flat-screens into his dealerships, he wanted it all and he wanted it now. He wanted delivery in half that time. Three months.

That I could do. I could have done two months if he'd insisted. But I wanted him to demand something I could do. As soon as I agreed, I knew he as good as owned it.

Then I threw in the old 'wrong conclusion' close. You say something you know is wrong so they have to correct you.

'So, that's six hundred thirty-six-inch monitors and another twelve hundred fifty-nine-inchers, right?'

'No, no, no,' Freddy Naseem said. 'The other way around. Six hundred fifty-nine-inchers and twelve hundred of the thirty-six.'

'Ah,' I said. 'My mistake. Got it.'

He was mine. I loved the irony of selling to a guy who worked in auto sales. No one was safe.

He was stoked. In fact, this became his idea – that's how I knew I had traction. He talked to Harry Belkin himself, called me back and said that Mr. Belkin was sold on the idea, and now it was only a matter of negotiating the price.

Sometimes I amaze myself.

A day later he called me back. 'Jason,' he said, all excited. 'I have some numbers for you, and I hope you have some numbers for me.' He told me how many plasma displays they wanted – huge ones for the walls of their forty-six dealerships, smaller ceiling-mounted ones. I didn't get it. The number was a lot higher. And then he explained: it wasn't just the BMW and Mercedes dealerships. It was the Hyundai and Kia dealerships too. Cadillac. Dodge. Everything.

I was almost at a loss for words. For me, this is unusual.

When I recovered, I said, 'Let me put some numbers together for you and circle back to you tomorrow. I'm not going to waste your time. I'm going to get you the best price I can get.'

Everything seemed to be falling my way.

Except Gordy. He was still Gordy. The biggest drawback to my new job was that it was all Gordy all the time. He had me coming in at 7:00 A.M. and would regularly storm into my office with one complaint or another. He'd IM me, sounding urgent, summon me to his office, and it would turn out to be nothing. Notes for a presentation he wanted me to look at. A spreadsheet. Whatever trivial thing he happened to think was important at that second.

I did my share of complaining about him to Kate. She listened patiently. One night I came home after work and she handed me a white plastic bag from a bookstore. It held CDs for me to play to and from work: *How to Work for Bullies* and *Tyrants at the Office* and *Since Strangling Isn't an Option*.

'Gordy's not leaving,' she said. 'You're just going to have to learn to deal with him.'

'Strangling,' I said. 'Now, there's an idea.'

'Sweetie,' she said, 'how come you never ask me about *my* day?'

181

She was right; I rarely did, and now I felt intensely guilty. 'Because I'm a guy?'

'Jason.'

'Sorry. How was your day?'

When the Harry Belkin deal seemed to be far enough along, I stopped in to see Gordy and tell him the good news. He nodded, asked a few questions, didn't seem all that interested. He handed me the monthly expense reports and told me to go over them. 'Two months,' he said. 'Two months till the end of Q2.' Entronics operated on the Japanese fiscal year, which sometimes got confusing.

I glimpsed at the expense report, and said, 'Jesus, the Band of Brothers spends a lot on T&E, huh?' That's Travel & Entertainment – hotels, travel, meals.

'See?' he said. 'It's crazy. I've been meaning to crack down on abuses of corporate credit cards for some time. But now that I've got one throat to choke, I want *you* to come up with a new T&E policy.'

He wanted me to be the bad guy. *Why not you?* I thought. *Everyone hates you already.*

'Got it,' I said.

'One more thing. Time to rank 'n' yank.'

I knew what he meant – stack-rank everybody and fire the underperformers – but was he saying he wanted *me* to do it?

'You're kidding.'

'No one said it was gonna be easy. You and I get to rate our guys on a five-point scale, and then you're gonna get rid of the underperformers. Up 'n' out.'

'The underperformers?' I said, wanting to hear him say it aloud.

182

'The C players get fired.'

'Bottom ten percent?'

'No,' he said with a fierce stare. 'Bottom third.'

'*Third?*'

'We can't afford 'em anymore. This is a Darwinian struggle. Only the toughest survive. I want Tokyo to see an immediate change in our numbers.'

'How immediate are we talking about?'

He stared at me for a few seconds, then got up and shut his office door. He sat back down, folded his arms.

'So here's how it's going down, Steadman, and don't you breathe a *word* of this to any of your Band of Brothers. By the end of the second quarter – that's barely two months from now – Dick Hardy and the boys in the MegaTower are going to be making a decision. It's either gonna be us or the Royal Meister sales force. Framingham or Dallas. Not both.'

'They're going to winnow out all but the top performers,' I said, nodding. 'Consolidation. Survival of the fittest.'

He gave his shark's smile. 'You still don't get it, do you? They're not cherry-picking. One lives, the other dies. It's a bake-off. The one with the best numbers gets to survive. The other office gets shut down. A "soft quarter" is not going to be shrugged off anymore. It's a goddamned death sentence. We have another quarter like this one and everyone in this building gets their walking papers. Now, ready for the bad news?'

'That was the good news?'

'It's all riding on you, buddy. You've got to pull a goddamned rabbit out of your hat in the next couple of months or everyone in the Entronics Framingham office, including you and your so-called Band of Brothers, gets shot. It's all up to you. You cannot afford a single misstep.'

'Don't you think we should let everyone know the stakes?' I said.

'No way, Steadman. Scared salesmen can't sell. Clients can see the flop sweat. They smell the panic. Bad enough with all the rumors flying around the halls, the turmoil we've been seeing. So this is our little secret. You and me. You're working directly for me now. And if you screw up, I'm gonna have to get my résumé printed up too. The difference is, I'm eminently employable. You, on the other hand, will be black-balled from here to Tokyo. I will personally see to it.'

I wanted to say something about how the flop sweat wasn't good for managers either, but I stayed silent.

'You know,' Gordy said, 'I didn't want to give you this job at first. But now I'm glad I did. You know why?'

I tried to swallow, but my mouth had gone dry. 'Why's that, Gordy?'

'Because I like Trevor a lot more than I like you, and I wouldn't wish this on him.'

On the way out of Gordy's office, I passed Cal Taylor in the hallway. He'd just come from the rest-room, and he was looking a little loopy. Ten in the morning, poor guy.

'Hey there, boss,' he said. 'Something wrong?'

'Wrong? No, nothing's wrong.'

'You look like you just ate a bad clam,' Cal said.

You have no idea, I thought.

23

For the rest of the morning, I went over the T&E expenses and began to devise the tough new policy that Gordy wanted. I thought of this as my 'no more Mister Nice Guy' memo. It was pretty hard-line, I have to admit. No more flying business class: economy all the way, unless you used your own frequent-flyer miles to upgrade. No more fancy hotels: now the limit was a hundred and seventy-five bucks a night. All business trips had to be scheduled at least seven days in advance, because it was cheaper; any last-minute trips had to be authorized in advance, by me. I lowered the per diem to fifty bucks a day, which was pretty harsh, but dealable, I thought. You couldn't write off any meals beyond that unless you were taking a customer. And no more taking customers out for drinks unless there was food too. We spent way too much on off-site meetings, so I cut down on those too. A lot of money had been dumped on catering lunch meetings at the office, but no more. Now you had to bring your own lunch.

I did some number-crunching and figured out how much this new policy would save the company, and I e-mailed the memo to Gordy.

Right after lunch, he called and said, 'I love it.'

I took a break, returned a bunch of calls, then I read over my memo again. Tried to soften the language a bit so that it didn't sound quite so hard-ass. Then I e-mailed it to Franny to read over and double-check for typos and such.

Franny – Frances Barber – was the secretary I'd been assigned. She'd been with the company for over twenty years, and her only flaw was that she went out for a cigarette break every half hour. She sat in the cubicle outside my new office. Franny had a real no-nonsense look, a tight mouth with vertical lines above her upper lip. She was forty-five but looked ten years older, wore a strong, unpleasant perfume that smelled like bug spray, and was pretty fearsome if you didn't know her. But we hit it off right away. She even began to reveal a bone-dry sense of humor, though it took a while.

She buzzed me on the intercom and said, 'A Mister Sulu for you?' She sounded uncertain. Her voice was so cigarette-destroyed it was deeper than mine. 'Though he doesn't exactly *sound* Japanese. He sounds more like a surfer.'

Obviously she didn't know Classic *Trek*. 'Graham,' I said as I picked up. 'Long time.'

'You sound kinda spun out.'

'Insane around here.'

'You been avoiding me, J-man? I'm starting to feel like a Klingon.'

'I'm sorry, Graham. I'm – well, I'm on this new regimen now.'

'*Regimen?* It's Kate, isn't it? She finally won.'

'It's a lot of things. Kate's pregnant, did you hear?'

186

'Hey, congratulations! Right? Or condolences. Which is it?'

'I'll take the congratulations.'

'A baby Steadman. Blows my mind. Too weird. The pitter-patter of little Tribble feet, huh?'

'Tribbles didn't have feet,' I said.

'You got me,' Graham said. 'And I call myself a Trekker. Well, lemme cut to the chase. I've got some stellar shit here. Some killer White Widow.'

'That some kind of heroin?'

He answered in a Jamaican accent: 'Ganja, mon. The only true worth is what comes from the earth, mon.' He added, 'And not just any ganja, dawg. We're talking Cannabis Cup first prize. Indica/Sativa mix, but more toward Sativa. A very energetic, social buzz. A legend, J-man.'

'I don't think so.'

'Come on over to Central Square, I'll roll us a big doobie or fire up the Starship *Enterprise,* and we'll go for a ride in the Love Bug.'

'I told you, Graham,' I said firmly. 'I don't do that anymore.'

'Dude. You've never done White Widow.'

'I'm sorry, Graham. It's just – things have changed.'

'This 'cuz of Little Jason coming along? The old ball-and-chain put her spike heel down?'

'Come on, man. It's not that.'

His voice got small. 'Okay, man, I think I get it. You're a vice president, now, right? Says that on your company's website. You got your own secretary, and a big fancy house. Guess you got to put a little distance between where you come from and where you are now, that it?'

187

'Does that sound like me, Graham?'

'I don't know,' he said. 'Not sure I even know who you are anymore.'

'That's way harsh. Don't do the guilt number on me, come on.'

'I call it like I see it, dude. Always did.'

'Cut me a little slack, will you? I'm over my head at work. As soon as I can, we'll go out. Dinner's on me. Okay?'

'Yeah,' Graham said sullenly. 'I'll wait for your call.'

'Graham –' I said, but he'd hung up, and now I felt bad.

Franny came into my office. 'Uh, Jason,' she said, standing at the door awkwardly, adjusting her glasses. 'You sure you really want to send this out?'

'Why not?'

'Because I was just starting to like you, and I don't know if I'll like the next guy as much.'

I smiled. 'Gordy approved it,' I said.

'Sure he did,' Franny said, and she gave a little nervous laugh that turned into a smoker's hack. 'Had you put it in your name so you'd catch the flak, not him.'

'It's a dirty job, but someone's got to do it,' I said, turning back to my computer.

'If you'll excuse me, I have to go out for a smoke and buy a bulletproof vest,' Franny said, and she went back to her cubicle.

I looked the memo over one more time. It was harsh. It was guaranteed to be unpopular, which meant it would make its author unpopular. It was something Gordy should have done himself, not me. It could only end badly.

I clicked send.

Then the shit hit the fan.

Rick Festino came flying into my office maybe five minutes later. 'What the hell's this?' he said. He wasn't holding or pointing to anything.

'What's what?' I said blandly.

'You know damned well what. This T&E shit.'

'Come on, Rick. Everyone's abusing the system, and we're trying to cut costs –'

'Jason. Hello? It's me you're talking to. You don't have to bullshit me. We're buddies.'

'It's not bullshit, Rick.'

'You just nailed the ninety-six theses to the door, and to me it looks more like Gordy than Jason Steadman. What the hell are you doing?'

'I always thought it was ninety-five theses,' I said.

He stared at me. 'Did Gordy make you put your name on this?'

I shook my head. 'He approved it, but it was my work.'

'You trying to get assassinated? It's not safe out there.'

'This is the way it's going to be,' I said. 'The new normal.'

'The beatings will continue until morale improves, huh? This is Captain Queeg stuff.'

'Captain who?'

'You never saw *The Caine Mutiny*?'

'I saw *Mutiny on the Bounty*.'

'Yeah, well, whatever. That's what you're going to be facing. You think Trevor and Gleason and all those guys are going to put up with staying at Motel Six and taking their clients to Applebee's?'

'I didn't say anything about Motel Six or Applebee's. Come on.' He was exaggerating, but it wasn't much better.

'The guys aren't going to put up with this.'

'They're not going to have a choice.'

'Don't be so sure, kid,' Festino said.

I was getting ready to leave for the day – Kate wanted to go shopping for baby stuff, which was the last thing I felt like doing – when Trevor Allard stopped me in the middle of the cubicle farm on his way out.

'Nice memo,' he said.

I nodded.

'Brilliant strategy, taking away perks like that. That's the way to hang on to your top talent.'

'You planning to take another job?' I said.

'I don't need to. I just have to wait for you to fall on your face. Which seems to be happening even sooner than I hoped.'

'There's no "I" in team, Trevor,' I said.

'Yeah. But there's a "Me" in Messiah.'

On the drive over to BabyWorld, I was lost in thought about the damn memo I'd just sent out. Everyone was now calling it the Queeg Memo. Guys who didn't even know who Queeg was were calling it the Queeg Memo. I wondered whether Gordy expected an immediate, enraged reaction like this. No wonder he wanted me to be the bad guy.

'Jason,' Kate said, interrupting my train of thought.

I looked over at her. She sounded somber. Her hair was pulled back in an elastic band. Her angular face had begun to fill out, her complexion was getting rosy.

190

Pregnancy became her. 'What's wrong, babe?'

'I tripped on the stairs again.'

'What happened? You okay?'

'I'm fine, but I'm pregnant, remember? I have to be really careful.'

'That's right.'

'The carpeting is worn through in places. It's a real trip hazard.'

'Okay.' I wasn't in the mood to talk about home improvements. I wanted to talk Gordy and Trevor and the Queeg Memo, but I knew she wasn't interested.

'What does that mean, "Okay"? Can you do something about it?'

'What do I look like, the *This Old House* guy? Call someone, Kate.'

'Who?'

'Kate,' I said, 'how the hell do I know?'

She stared at me for a few seconds, eyes cold. I was staring at the road, but I could feel her eyes on me. Then she shook her head sorrowfully. 'Thanks for your help,' she said.

'Look, I'm sorry. I'm just preoccupied with –'

'More important things. I know.'

'It's Gordy again.'

'What a shock. Well, I hope you can keep your mind off your job long enough to pick out your baby's crib.'

Sometimes I didn't get my wife at all. One day she wanted me to be Napoleon Bonaparte. The next day she wanted me to be Mister Mom.

Had to be the hormones. But I sure as hell wasn't going to say anything.

*

BabyWorld was supremely annoying. It was a giant fluorescent-lit warehouse stocked with only baby things, from low-end to high. Its slogan was 'Isn't your baby worth the best?' That was reason enough to walk out, but Kate was set on stocking the nursery. Plus, there was this creepy music playing over and over, their theme song, little kids' voices and a xylophone. I started getting a headache.

She rolled through the departments like an Abrams tank, picking out a changing table, and a contoured changing pad, and a mobile that had farmyard animals dangling from it and played classical music, to help develop the baby's cognitive skills.

Meanwhile, I kept furtively checking my Black-Berry and my cell phone. My cell phone said no service – another reason to hate BabyWorld – while my BlackBerry kept receiving messages. Different service providers, I guess that was the reason. There were a lot of e-mails on my BlackBerry complaining about the Queeg Memo.

Kate was showing me a Bellini crib. 'Sally Wynter bought this one for Anderson,' she said, 'and she thinks it's the best.' She heard my BlackBerry buzz, and she threw me an exasperated look. 'Are you here, or are you at work?'

I'd have rather been anywhere else. 'Sorry,' I said. I switched the BlackBerry alert mode to silent, so she wouldn't hear it anymore. 'Does that come already assembled?'

'It says some assembly required. I don't think it's all that complicated.'

'If you went to MIT,' I said.

We moved into a diaper-rich environment, tall stacks

of Huggies and Pampers, floor-to-ceiling, a bewildering assortment. This was more confusing than the sanitary napkin section of CVS, where Kate had sent me once. I'd fled screaming in terror.

'I can't decide between the Diaper Genie and the Diaper Champ,' she said. 'This one uses regular garbage bags.'

'But this one seems to make diaper link sausages,' I said. 'That's kind of cool.' You get your kicks where you can.

We moved on to small electronics. She grabbed a box off the shelf and dropped it into our shopping cart. 'This is so genius,' she said. 'It's a backseat baby monitor.'

'For the car?'

'You plug it into the cigarette lighter, and the camera goes on the back of the headrest, and the monitor goes on the dashboard. So you can keep a watch on baby without turning around.'

That's what I need, I thought. More distractions while I'm driving. 'Cool,' I said.

'Here's a video monitoring system,' she said, grabbing another box from the shelf and showing it to me. 'See that little portable video monitor you can carry around with you? So the baby's never out of sight. Plus, there's infrared for night viewing.'

Jesus, I thought, this baby's going to be under more intensive surveillance than Patrick McGoohan in that old TV show *The Prisoner*.

'Great idea,' I said.

'Oh, here we are,' Kate said. 'The best part of all.' I followed her into the baby carriage department, where she immediately glommed on to a big, scary, black carriage with big wheels, antique-looking and forbidding. It seemed like something out of *Rosemary's Baby*.

'God, Jason, will you look at this Silver Cross Balmoral pram?' she said. 'It's so unbelievably elegant, isn't it?'

'What's that movie where the baby buggy rolls down all those steps?'

'*Potemkin,*' she said with an annoyed headshake.

I took a look at the price tag. 'Does that say twenty-eight hundred, or do I need reading glasses already?'

'Is that how much it is?'

'Maybe it's in Italian lire.'

'They don't use lire anymore. It's euros now.'

'Two thousand eight hundred dollars?'

'Forget it,' Kate said. 'That's crazy. Sorry.'

'Whatever you want, Kate.'

'For way less money, there's the Stokke Xplory,' she said. 'The baby rides higher off the ground. It encourages parent-child bonding. Not much storage space underneath, though. But it's pretty macho-looking, don't you think? That telescoping handle?' I saw her cast a longing glance at the Silver Cross Balmoral pram when she thought I wasn't looking.

'It's macho, all right,' I said. I sneaked a glance at my BlackBerry and saw an e-mail from Gordy. Its subject line was URGENT!

'Of course, there's always the Bugaboo Frog.'

I clicked onto the message and read, 'I tried to call your cell but no answer. Call me IMMEDIATELY.'

'Doesn't it remind you of a mountain bike?' Kate was saying.

'What? A mountain bike?'

'I've been hearing a lot about the Bebe Confort Lite Chassis,' Kate said. 'It's a little more than the Bugaboo, but still a fraction of the price of the Silver Cross.'

'I've got to make a call,' I said.

'Can't it wait?'

'It's important.'

'This is important too.'

'Gordy's been trying to reach me, and he says it's urgent. I'm sorry. This shouldn't take more than a minute.'

I turned and hurried through the aisles to the parking lot, where I picked up a cell phone signal. I punched out Gordy's cell number, got a number wrong, and tried again.

'What the hell are you doing?' Gordy barked when he picked up.

'Shopping for baby stuff.'

'This goddamned T&E memo of yours. What the hell's that all about?'

'Gordy, you approved it before I sent it out.'

He hesitated only for a second. 'I didn't get into the weeds. I left that to you.'

'Is there a problem?'

'Is there a *problem*? Trevor just came into my office and told me how the entire sales force is on the verge of revolt.'

'Trevor?' I said. Goddamned Trevor was going to Gordy behind my back now, was that it? 'Trevor doesn't speak for the "entire sales force,"' I said.

'Well, I got news for you. We just lost Forsythe over this.'

'What do you mean, we "lost" Forsythe?'

'It was the last straw for the guy. Apparently he had a standing offer from our old friend Crawford at Sony, and guess what? Late this afternoon he called and accepted their offer. Why? Because of your damned crackdown. You have the guys eating in Denny's and staying at fleabag motels, and now we just lost our star performer.'

My crackdown?

'Now who's next? Gleason? Allard? All because of what the guys are calling the Queeg Memo.'

'What do you want me to do?'

'I've taken care of it,' Gordy said. 'I just sent out an e-mail revoking your new policy. Told them there was a miscommunication.'

I gritted my teeth. *God damn him.* 'So what about Forsythe?' I said. 'Is he still leaving?'

But Gordy had hung up.

I walked across BabyWorld, the goddamned xylophone and the kids' voices grating on me like fingernails on a blackboard. Kate was staring at me as I approached.

'Everything okay?' she said. 'You look like you just got kicked in the stomach.'

'The balls, more like it. Kate, there's all kinds of shit going down at work.'

'Well, I'm ready to check out anyway. But you shouldn't have come tonight. You should have stayed at work.'

'What's that supposed to mean?'

'You're totally distracted with your job. You're not required to go shopping with me, Jase.'

'I wanted to do this,' I said.

'You make it sound like an assignment.'

196

'That's not fair. We're buying baby stuff. I think it's important for us to do it together.'

'Yeah, but you're not exactly here, are you? Your head is back at the office.'

'And I always thought you loved me for my body.'

'Jason.'

She pushed the cart toward the checkout line, and I followed her. Both of us were silent, stewing in our own juices. We stood there in line. Finally, I said, 'Why don't you go get the tag for the *Rosemary's Baby* carriage?'

'The Silver Cross Balmoral pram?' Kate said. 'But that's crazy expensive.'

'It's the one you want. It's the one we'll get.'

'Jason, we don't need to spend that kind of money on a baby carriage.'

'Come on, Kate. It would be downright irresponsible to put our baby in a carriage that doesn't have shock absorbers and side-impact bars.' I broke off. 'Look, I want to do this right. Baby Steadman's going to travel in style. It does come with power steering, right?'

When the cashier rang everything up, I stared at the bill for a few seconds in disbelief. If my father had seen how much we were spending on baby stuff, he'd have had a heart attack in his Barcalounger right in front of the TV set.

I whipped out my gold MasterCard bravely. 'I am oppressed by the debt of the capitalist society,' I said.

24

As soon as Doug Forsythe got in the next morning, I strolled by his cubicle and tapped him on the shoulder.

'Got a minute?' I said.

He looked up at me and said, 'Sure thing, boss.' He knew what this was about and didn't bother to hide it.

He followed me to my office.

'Doug, let me ask you something. Did you just accept an offer from Sony?'

He paused, but only for a second. 'Verbally, yeah,' he said. 'I won't lie to you. Crawford made me a killer offer.'

Verbally, he was careful to say. Meaning maybe there was some wiggle room.

'You've been here eight years. Are you unhappy?'

'Unhappy? No, not at all. God, no.'

'Then why've you been talking to Crawford?'

He shrugged and opened his palms. 'He made an offer.'

'He wouldn't make an offer unless he knew you were considering a move.'

Forsythe paused again. 'Look, Jason, I don't even know if I'm going to be here a year from now.'

'You're crazy, Doug. You're bulletproof. With numbers like yours, you don't have a worry in the world.'

'I'm not talking about me personally. I mean all of us.'

'I don't follow.'

'Well, that expenses memo – that really put the fear of God into a lot of us guys. Like, Entronics must really be in rough shape.'

'We're not in rough shape,' I said. 'We just need to be more competitive. Cut costs. A lot of our travel expenses are frankly out of line. Anyway, Gordy over-ruled me on that.' I was tempted to tell the truth – that Gordy had made me his flak-catcher, told me to do it, then backed down when the shit hit the fan – but I decided to just suck it up.

'I know,' Forsythe said. 'But I get a feeling that's just the tip of the old iceberg.'

'How so?'

He lowered his voice. 'I've heard talk, is all.'

'What kind of talk?'

'About how Entronics is planning to get rid of its entire Visual Systems sales force. Now that they have Royal Meister's, they don't need us.'

'Where did you hear that?'

'I've heard it,' he said.

'That's ridiculous.'

'It's not true?' He looked right at me now.

I shook my head. Lying like a kid caught with his hand stuck in the cookie jar. 'Totally not true,' I said.

'Really?' He sounded genuinely perplexed.

'You don't want to move to New Jersey,' I said.

'I was born and raised in Rutherford.'

'I don't mean it like that,' I said quickly. 'Now, obviously we'll match any offer Sony makes you. We don't want to lose you, you know that.'

'I do.'

'Come on, Doug,' I said. 'We need you here. Entronics is your home,' I said.

He didn't reply.

'So forget those rumors,' I said. 'You can't listen to nutty rumors like that.'

He blinked, nodded slowly.

'So I'll see you at the game tonight,' I said. 'Right?'

I was finally on my way out of the office around six when my phone rang. The calls that come after five are often from people trying to avoid talking to a human being. They want to get voice mail. We call this playing dodgeball. Actually, it's harder and harder to play dodgeball these days, what with cell phones and e-mail, so when someone tries it, it's pretty obvious.

Franny was still in, and I heard her say, 'One moment, Mr. Naseem. You're in luck. You just caught him on his way out.'

I said, 'I'll take it,' and I went back to my desk. This could be it, I thought. We'd gone back and forth on numbers, and the last time we talked, Freddy Naseem told me he was close to having sign-off from Mr. Belkin himself. This would be the biggest deal I'd closed in six months.

'Hey, Freddy,' I said. 'How're we doing?'

'Jason,' he said, and I could tell from his voice that it wasn't good news. 'There's been a little complication.'

'Don't worry about it,' I said. 'I can work with you.'

He paused. 'No, you see . . . I just got some bad

news.'

'Okay.' This was not what I wanted to hear.

'I've just been informed that we're buying the plasmas from Panasonic.'

'What?' I blurted out. Then, calmer: 'You weren't even talking to Panasonic.'

'I'm afraid we didn't have a choice. Mr. Belkin liked your idea so much he's decided not to wait, but to start installing the flat-screens in three of our dealerships in two weeks.'

'Two weeks? But three months is what we agreed on –'

'And Panasonic has the inventory to deliver next week. So I really had no choice.'

We couldn't possibly turn around hundreds of plasma monitors in a month, let alone a week. Panasonic must have had a lot of overstock in their Northeast warehouse.

'But – but it was my idea!' I sputtered. I immediately wished I hadn't said that. It made me sound like a pouting ten-year-old. 'Will you at least give me the chance to see if I can scrape some inventory together?'

'I think things have progressed beyond that point.' He sounded stiff and formal.

'Freddy,' I said, 'you have to give me the chance to see what I can do. Given that I suggested the idea to you in the first place.'

'My hands are tied. Sometimes Mr. Belkin makes decisions without consulting me. He's the boss. And you know what they say. "The boss may not always be right, but he's always the boss."' He laughed hollowly.

'Freddy –'

'I'm sorry, Jason. I'm terribly sorry.'

*

I went to see Gordy to see if he could pull any strings, make some swaps, maybe free up a few hundred flat-screen monitors.

Melanie had gone home, but Gordy was still in his office, on the phone. He was standing, staring at his PictureScreen windows. The ocean waves were crashing against the crystalline white sand. It was strange: In the window by Melanie's cubicle I could see the fading summer daylight, and just a few feet away was the dazzling artificial midday sunshine of Gordy's PictureScreen windows. His imaginary world.

I waited for a few minutes. He happened to turn around, saw me. Didn't acknowledge me. He guffawed, made large wheeling gestures with his hands. Finally, he hung up, and I went in.

He had a triumphant look on his face. 'Booya, Steadman. *Booya!* That was Hardy. Sent me a Hardy-gram *and* called. *And* invited me to go for a sail on his new yacht.'

'What's the occasion?'

'He flipped when I told him about my Harry Belkin idea, Steadman. Putting plasmas in forty-six auto dealerships – I love it.'

I nodded. I didn't say thank you, because he wasn't complimenting me. He was congratulating himself, since this had somehow become his idea.

He pointed a stubby finger at me. 'See, this is what Hardy calls bowling alley positioning, okay? Aim the bowling ball right, and the first pin knocks down all the rest of them.'

'I don't follow.'

'It's a wedge. Once Harry Belkin signs on, then we've got every other auto dealership in the country saying, "How come I didn't think of this? Give me some too." God, it's brilliant.'

'Brilliant,' I said. I wanted to get out of his office and go home.

'What's the latest on that?'

'I'll – I still have to follow up on that,' I said.

'For Christ's sake, close it, man. *Close* it. I don't want to lose it. You lock that one down, and get a couple more big contracts, and we're safe. How's the Chicago Presbyterian deal coming?'

'I think I'm close to nailing it.'

'How about Atlanta airport? You get that, it's huge. *Huge!*'

'Working on that one too.' The Atlanta airport wanted to replace all the monitors used in their flight information display system, which meant hundreds and hundreds of screens.

'And?'

'I don't know yet. Too early.'

'I want you to do anything to land Atlanta, understand?'

'I get it,' I said. 'I'm all over it. Listen, I want –'

'You talk to Doug Forsythe?' He tugged on his lapels and straightened his tie.

'I think that's a lost cause, Gordy. He's already made a verbal commitment –'

'A *what*? A lost cause? Can you translate that for me, please? I don't speak that language. That's not in my vocabulary. Now, if you're on the G Team, you don't accept defeat. You make sure Forsythe doesn't walk. Are we clear?'

'Yes, Gordy.'

'Are you on the G Team or not?'

'Yes, Gordy,' I said. 'I'm on the G Team.'

25

I drove home too fast, angry and confused. Freddy Naseem had screwed me over, and so had Gordy, and now the deal he'd stolen credit for had fallen through. Maybe there was an irony here, but I didn't appreciate it. I was too pissed off.

On the CD player, General Patton was talking about 'the predator mind-set.' He growled, 'It's just like the animal kingdom. Ninety percent of us are prey. The other ten percent are predators. Which are you?'

When I got home I noticed an almost-new-looking black Mustang parked in our narrow brick-topped driveway. Kurt's. He'd bought it from his friend who owned the auto body shop.

I hurried into the house, wondering why he was here.

Kurt was sitting in our living room, the formal room we never used, talking to Kate. The two of them were laughing about something. Kate had set out Grammy Spencer's tea tray with butter cookies.

'Well, hello,' I said. 'Sorry I'm late,' I said to Kate. 'Lot happening at the office.'

'Jason,' Kate said, 'you never told me Kurt's a handyman too.'

'Amateur,' Kurt said.

'Hey, Kurt. What a surprise, huh?'

'Hey, bro. I had to meet with a vendor in Cambridge. I finally got approval for the biometric fingerprint verification system, and I had to finalize some details. I figured since I was in your neck of the woods, I'd give you a lift to the softball game.'

'Okay, sure,' I said.

'Though I saw your new Mercedes out front. Nice wheels. Bling for the king, huh?'

'Will you take a look at the stairs?' Kate said to me. 'Take a look at what Kurt did.'

'Come on,' Kurt said. 'It's no big deal.'

I followed her to the staircase that led to the second floor. The junky oatmeal-colored carpet had been removed, exposing handsome wood. The old carpet lay in a neat pile, cut up into rectangular sections, next to discarded strips of wood with sharp-looking tacks sticking out from them, also neatly stacked. A crowbar and a utility knife lay on the floor nearby.

'Can you believe how beautiful that wood is?' Kate said. 'You'd never know it, with that gross carpet covering it up.'

'Wasn't safe,' Kurt said. 'You could break your neck. With Kate pregnant and all, you've really got to take care of stuff like that.'

'Very kind of you,' I said.

'I'm thinking you should install a runner,' Kurt said.

'Oh, but I love the wood,' Kate said.

'Still see it, either side,' Kurt said. 'Maybe one of those Axminster oriental rug deals. Good thick padding under it. Safer that way.'

'And how about brass carpet rods?' Kate said, excited.

'Easy,' Kurt said.

'Speak for yourself,' I said, a little peevish. 'I had no idea you knew how to do this. You can kill people *and* remove old carpeting.'

Kurt ignored the dig. Or maybe it wasn't a dig to him. 'Taking it out's the easy part,' he said with a modest chuckle. 'Worked for a contractor after high school, did a lot of odd jobs.'

'Could you do that, do you think?' Kate said. 'The runner and the carpet rods and everything? We'd pay you, of course. We insist.'

'Don't worry about it,' Kurt said. 'Your husband here got me my job. I owe him.'

'You don't owe me anything,' I said.

'Kurt thinks we have way too many things plugged into that power strip thingy in the living room.'

'Electrical hazard,' Kurt said. 'You need another outlet on that wall. Easy to put in.'

'You're an electrician too?' Kate said.

'You don't have to be a master electrician to put in an electrical outlet. That's easy.'

'He just rewired his entire house,' I said, 'and it's not even his house.'

'God,' Kate said to Kurt, 'is there anything you *can't* do?'

Kurt drove his Mustang fast and skillfully. I was impressed. Most drivers who haven't grown up around Boston get intimidated by the aggressiveness of the native Boston driver. Kurt, who'd grown up in Michigan, handled the traffic like a native.

We sat in silence for a good ten minutes, and then

Kurt said, 'Hey, man, did I piss you off?'

'Piss me off? Why do you say that?'

'At your house. Like you were ticked off I was there when you got home.'

'No,' I said in that terse, male way where the tone says it all – you know, *what the hell you talkin' about*?

'Just trying to help you there, bud. With the stairs. I figured, I know how to fix stuff, and you're a busy executive.'

'Don't worry about it,' I said. 'I mean, I appreciate it. Kate did too. You were right – she's pregnant, and we've got to be careful about stuff like that.'

'All right. Just so long as we're cool.'

'Yeah, sure. I just had a bad day at work.' I told him about my big auto-dealership brainstorm and how Gordy had stolen credit for it, and how Harry Belkin had decided to go with Panasonic instead.

'He's a snake,' Kurt said.

'Who, Gordy?'

'Both of those guys. Gordy we know about. But the Harry Belkin guy – if he's gonna change the terms of the deal, doesn't he at least have to give you the chance to bid on it? Since it was your idea?'

'He should have. But I'd already told him we couldn't deliver the stuff for a couple of months. That's standard. Panasonic must have had excess inventory. You know, it's like when you go test-drive a car and you totally fall in love with it, and then the salesman says, sorry, the waiting list is two months long. And you go, *two months? I want it today!* Well, Panasonic must have said, "This is your lucky day. We happen to have some right here in our warehouse. You can have 'em today!"'

'That's not right. That really sucks.'

'Yes, it does.'

'You've gotta do something about that, man.'

'There's nothing to do. That's the problem. We're at least a month out – we have to get inventory from Tokyo.'

'Don't sit back and take it, bro. Go after it.'

'How? What am I supposed to do, take out one of your replica handguns and put it up to Freddy Naseem's forehead?'

'My point is, sometimes the quiet, behind-the-scenes approach is the best way. Like the time when we were in Stan and we found this air base near Kandahar, with a big old Russian chopper. One of our local informants told us some of the top Taliban commanders used the helicopter to head up to their secret headquarters in the mountains. I figured, well, we could just nuke the thing, or we could be clever. So we waited till four in the morning, when there was only one TB sentry on duty.'

'TB?'

'Taliban, sorry. I snuck up behind him, garroted him to kill him silently. Then we got inside the base and painted some LME on the tail section near the rear rotor, and the rotor blades. Totally invisible.'

'LME?'

'Liquid metal embrittlement agent. Remember that tube you were looking at in my war trophy collection?'

'I think so.'

'Very cool stuff. Classified technology. A mix of some liquid metal, like mercury, with some other metal. Copper powder or indium or whatever. Paint it on steel, and it forms a chemical reaction. Turns steel as brittle as a cracker.'

209

'Neat.'

'So the Taliban guys probably did the routine pre-flight check for bombs and shit, but they didn't see anything, right? That night, there's this big crash, and the helicopter just flew apart in the air. Six Taliban generals turned into corned beef hash. Better than just blowing up an empty helicopter, right?'

'What's that got to do with Entronics?'

'My point is that sometimes it's the covert stuff that's the real force multiplier. That's what wins the battle. Not the guns and bombs and mortar rounds.'

'I'd rather you didn't garrote Freddy Naseem. Not good for the corporate image.'

'Forget Freddy Naseem. I'm just saying, there comes a time for behind-the-scenes action.'

'Like what?'

'I don't know. I'd need to know more. But I'm here to help, whatever it is.'

I shook my head. 'I don't do underhanded stuff.'

'What about getting inside dope on Brian Borque at Lockwood Hotels? Or Jim Letasky?'

I hesitated. 'I feel kind of funny about it, to be honest.'

'And you don't think Panasonic was being . . . underhanded, as you put it, for snagging the Harry Belkin deal?'

'Yeah, they were. But I don't believe in tit for tat. I don't want to be a snake.'

'Let me ask you this. Kill a guy in an alley somewhere, it's murder, right? But kill a guy in the middle of a battlefield, it's heroism. What's the difference?'

'Simple,' I said. 'One's war, the other's not.'

'I thought business is war.' Kurt grinned. 'It's in all

210

those books you gave me. I read 'em cover to cover.'

'It's a figure of speech.'

'Funny,' he said. 'I missed that part.'

That night we played EMC, a giant computer-storage company headquartered in Hopkinton, and once again we won. The guys from EMC must have gotten the word that we were a totally transformed team, so they came to play, as if they'd had a practice before showing up. We were short one player, unfortunately. Doug Forsythe never showed up, which wasn't a good sign.

My own softball game had improved, for some reason. When I stepped up to the plate, I didn't flinch at the pitch anymore. I swung harder and with greater confidence. I felt more relaxed at the plate, and I began hitting them deep. My fielding was better too.

But a couple of times, Trevor Allard deliberately threw the ball by me and around me, deliberately cutting me off, as if I couldn't be trusted with the ball. The one time he threw the ball to me was when I wasn't prepared – I was half turned away – and he almost took off my ear.

After the game, Kurt and I walked to the parking lot. Trevor was in his Porsche, blasting that Kanye West song, 'Gold Digger,' as I passed by – *He got that ambition, baby, look in his eyes* – and it didn't seem to be a coincidence.

I told Kurt I wanted to head right home if he didn't mind giving me a lift.

'So you don't want to go out with the guys?' Kurt said.

'Nah. Long day. Plus, I told Kate I'd be home. These days she doesn't like me staying out as late.'

'Pregnant women need to feel protected,' Kurt said. 'Primitive instinct. Listen to me – like I know. She's a nice chick. Pretty, too.'

'And mine.'

'Things okay on the home front?'

'Not bad,' I said.

'It's a tough gig, marriage.'

I nodded.

'Important to take care of the home front,' he said. 'If the home front isn't in good shape, everything else suffers.'

'Yeah.'

'Hey, so what happened to Doug Forsythe tonight?' Kurt said.

'I think we're about to lose him to Sony.'

'Because of your hard-ass memo?'

'That may have been the last straw. Gordy's obsessed with me trying to keep him. I twisted Doug's arm, pleaded with him, but no go. There's only so much I can do. The guy obviously wants to leave. And I can't totally blame him. Gordy's no fun to work for.'

'I'll bet there's a Gordy in every company.'

'I'd hate to believe that,' I said. 'But what do I know? I've only worked for one company.'

'Listen,' Kurt said. 'It's none of my business, but you can't let Trevor disrespect you.'

'It's just a game.'

'Nothing's just a game,' Kurt said. 'If he thinks he can get away with that kind of disrespect on the ball field, it's just going to carry over to the workplace.'

'It's no big deal.'

'Yes, it is,' Kurt said. 'It's a big deal. And it's unsat.'

26

It was seven-thirty in the morning, and Gordy was on his third giant mug of coffee. Gordy overcaffeinated was not a pretty sight. He was bouncing off the walls.

'Rank 'n' yank time,' he said, like he was a camp counselor and it was time for the white-water rafting. 'Gotta tell ya, your performance reviews of some of these guys were awful generous. Don't forget, I know these guys pretty well.' He turned to face me slowly.

I said nothing. He was right. I'd been generous in my assessments. I'd also given a boost to some of the outliers, like Festino and Taylor. I didn't want to give Gordy any ammunition he didn't need.

'Time for Taylor and Festino to hit the road,' he said.

So what was the point of the 'performance review' exercise he'd just put me through? Rank everyone one to five on all sorts of things, when only one number counted?

'Cal Taylor's two years from retirement,' I said.

'He retired years ago. He just didn't tell anyone.'

'Festino just needs some more hands-on guidance.'

'Festino's a big boy. We've been floating him for years. Gave the guy extra tutoring after school. Held his hand.'

'What about moving him to Inside Sales?'

'Why, so he can botch that too? Taminek's been handling Inside Sales just fine. Festino's been on life support for too long. Shoulda finished law school. Now it's time to yank the feeding tube. Topgrade him out of here.'

'Gordy,' I said, 'the guy's a family man with a mortgage and a kid in private school.'

'You don't understand. I wasn't asking your advice.'

'I can't do this, Gordy.'

He stared at me. 'Why does that not surprise me? Why do I get the feeling you're not cut out for the G Team?'

I'd never fired anyone before, and I had to start with a sixty-three-year-old man.

Cal Taylor cried in my office.

I didn't know how to deal with that. I pushed a box of Kleenex across the desk at him and assured him that this was nothing personal. Though in one sense it was entirely personal. It was all about his inability to crawl out of the Jack Daniel's bottle long enough to get on the phone and deal with the constant rejection that all of us salespeople face every day.

I won't say it was more painful to me than it was to him. But it was pretty bad. He sat there in front of me wearing his cheap gray summerweight suit that he wore year-round and had probably bought in a burst of deluded optimism during the Lyndon Johnson administration. His shirt collar was frayed. His white hair was Brylcreemed back, his nicotine-yellowed mustache neatly trimmed. His smoker's hack was worse than ever.

214

And he wept.

Entronics had a 'termination script' you had to use whenever you fired anyone. No ad-libbing allowed. After me, he'd have to go to HR and then outplacement counseling. They'd tell him about his health benefits and how long he'd continue to get his salary. Then a Corporate Security officer would escort him out of the building. That was the final indignity. Forty years with the company, and they shooed you out like you were a shoplifter.

And when the deed was done, he stood up, and said, 'What about you?'

'Me?'

He looked at me with injured eyes. 'You happy? Being Gordy's hatchet man? His chief executioner officer?'

That didn't require an answer, so I didn't give him one. I felt as if I'd been kicked in the balls. I could only imagine how he felt. I closed my office door and sank down in my desk chair and watched him walk, slope-shouldered, across the expanse of the cube farm to his cubicle.

Through the gaps in the venetian blinds, I could see him talking to Forsythe and Harnett. My phone rang, and I let Franny get it. She intercommed me and asked if I wanted to take a call from Barry Ulasewicz at Chicago Presbyterian Hospital, and I told her I was in a meeting. She knew I wasn't on the phone or with anyone, and she said, 'You okay?'

'I'll be fine, thanks,' I said. 'I just need a couple of minutes.'

Someone had brought Taylor a stack of white cardboard cartons and was setting them up for him. A few

215

people gathered around his cubicle as he began putting his belongings in boxes. Trevor was shooting baleful glances in my direction.

It was like a pantomime of bereavement: I could see but not hear. The word had spread like ripples on the surface of a pond. People came up to him and said brief, consoling things, then walked rapidly away. Others were passing by and making broad gestures but not slowing their stride. It's funny the way people act around someone who's been fired. Getting terminated is sort of like having a serious communicable disease; for every one who stopped to share his sadness there were two who didn't want to get too close and catch it. Or didn't want to seem to be in league with poor Cal Taylor, conspiring with him. They wanted to demonstrate their neutrality.

As I picked up my phone to ask Festino to come in, there was a knock at the door.

It was Festino.

27

'Steadman,' Festino said. 'Tell me you didn't just shoot Cal Taylor.'

'Sit down, Ricky,' I said.

'I don't *believe* this. Is it the body snatchers? The merger integration team? That who gave the orders?'

I wanted to say, *It wasn't my idea,* but that was too weaselly. Though true. I said, 'Have a seat, Ricky.'

He did. 'How come Gordy didn't do it, huh? I figured he'd want to do it himself. He enjoys that kind of thing.'

I didn't reply.

'I gotta tell you, as your friend, that I don't like what's happening to you. You've gone over to the dark side.'

'Ricky,' I tried to interrupt.

But he was on a roll. 'First there's that ridiculous Queeg Memo. Now you're Gordy's executioner. This is not good. I'm telling you this as your buddy.'

'Ricky, stop talking for a second.'

'So Taylor's the first to swim with the fishes, huh? The first guy voted off the island? Who's next, me?'

I looked at him for a couple of seconds before looking away.

'You're kidding, right? Don't kid a kidder, Jason.'

'The lower thirty percent are being let go, Ricky,' I said softly.

I could see the blood drain from his face. He shook his head. 'Who's going to go over your contracts if I'm gone?' he said in a small voice.

'I'm really sorry.'

'Jason,' he said, a note of wheedling entering his voice, 'I've got a family to feed.'

'I know. I really hate this.'

'No, you don't know. Entronics covers my wife's and kids' health plans.'

'You won't just be cut off, Ricky. Your benefits will be continued for up to eighteen months.'

'I've got school *tuition* to pay, Jason. You know what that school costs me? It's like thirty thousand bucks a *year*.'

'You can –'

'They don't give financial aid. Not to guys like me, anyway.'

'The public schools are great where you live, Ricky.'

'Not for a kid with Down's syndrome, Steadman.' His eyes were fierce, and they were moist.

I couldn't talk for a couple of seconds. 'I had no idea, Ricky.'

'Is this your decision, Jason?'

'Gordy's,' I said at last, feeling like the coward I was.

'And you're just following orders. Like Nuremberg.'

'Pretty much,' I said. 'I'm so sorry. I know how much this sucks.'

'Who can I appeal this to? Gordy? I'll talk to Gordy if you think it'll help.'

'It won't help, Ricky. He's made up his mind.'

'You can talk to him for me, then. Right? You're his golden boy now. He'll listen to you.'

I was silent.

'Jason, please.'

I was silent. I was dying inside.

'You of all people,' he said. He stood up slowly and went to the door.

'Ricky,' I said. He stopped, his back to me, his hand on the knob.

'Let me talk to Gordy,' I said.

Melanie stopped me outside Gordy's office. 'He's on the phone with Hardy,' she said.

'I'll come back.'

She glanced through Gordy's venetian blinds. 'His body language tells me he's almost off.'

Melanie and I talked for a bit about her husband, Bob's, plan to go in with some guys to buy a franchise for a Chilean sandwich place that was really popular in downtown Boston. I didn't know how he'd scrape together the money. Bob worked for an insurance company.

Finally, Gordy was off the phone, and I went in.

'I need to talk to you about Festino,' I said.

'Guy freaks out on you, you call Security. He could do that, you know. Go off the deep end. I can see it in him.'

'No, it's not that.' I told him about Festino's child and the special school, which we'd all assumed was some hoity-toity prep school where the boys wore little blue blazers and beanies.

Gordy's eyes grew beady. I stared at his pompadour, because I couldn't look into his eyes. It seemed

219

puffier than usual. He looked like he'd had his hair colored recently. 'I really don't give a shit,' he said.

'We can't do it.'

'You think this is a charity? Some frickin' social services agency?'

'I won't do it,' I said. 'I won't fire Festino. I can't do it to the guy.'

He tipped his head to one side, looked curious. 'You're *refusing*?'

I swallowed and hoped it wasn't audible. I had the feeling I was about to cross some kind of office Rubicon. 'Yeah,' I said.

A long, long silence. His stare was unrelenting. Then he said, slowly and deliberately, 'Okay. For now. But after TechComm, you and me are going to have a talk.'

TechComm was the huge trade show, where we always threw a swanky dinner for our biggest customers. Last year it was in Las Vegas. This year it was in Miami. Gordy was always the master of ceremonies at the dinner, and he liked to keep the theme a secret until we got there. 'I don't want any disruptions before TechComm.'

'Sure,' I said.

'You know something? I don't think you have what it takes.'

For once I didn't answer.

28

I wanted to get out of the office on time today. Kurt had Red Sox tickets. I had to get home and change out of my suit and kiss Kate and get over to Fenway Park by seven.

I was packing up my fancy leather briefcase when I saw Doug Forsythe standing at my office door.

'Hey, Doug,' I said. 'Come on in.'

'Got a sec?'

'Of course.'

He sat down slowly, with a tentative look about him. 'You know, what you said yesterday? I really took it to heart.'

I nodded. I had no idea what he was getting at.

'I've been thinking. And – you're right. Entronics is my home.'

I was stunned. 'Really? Hey, that's great.'

I noticed an instant message pop up on my computer screen. It was from Gordy. CALL ME NOW, it said.

'Yeah,' he said. 'I just think it's the right thing.'

'Doug, I'm so happy to hear that. Everyone's going to be psyched that you're staying.'

Another IM. WHERE THE HELL ARE YOU? GET OVER HERE!

I swiveled around to the keyboard, typed, IN MEET-
ING, GIVE ME A MINUTE.

'Yeah, well,' he said. He didn't sound happy, that
was the strange thing. 'I guess it's for the best.'

'Doug,' I said, 'say it like you mean it.'

'I mean it. It's the right thing. So . . . So that's it.'

'You want us to match Sony's offer,' I said, taking a
stab at it. 'And I told you we would. Forward the
e-mail to me, or the letter, and I'll get right to it.'

He inhaled slowly, deeply. 'No need,' he said. 'I
don't want to hold you guys up for more money.'

No salesguy in the history of Western civilization
has ever said that. Or at least said it and meant it. I
was immediately on alert. What was going on?

'Doug,' I said, 'I gave you a promise. Now, don't
make me beg.'

Forsythe stood up. 'Really, it's fine,' he said. 'Here I
am, and here I'll stay. I'm fine with it. I'm cool, I really
am.'

He left, and I sat there for a few seconds, baffled. I
turned back to the screen and saw another IM from
Gordy. NOW! it said. WHAT THE HELL??!!

I IM'd back: ON MY WAY.

As I escorted Forsythe out of my office, I noticed
Trevor Allard in his cubicle, darkly watching me. The
background on his computer desktop was a photo of
his beloved Porsche Carrera. I wondered how much
Trevor knew about Forsythe's job offer, how much
he'd been urging Forsythe out of here, pouring poison
in his ear. And what he knew about Forsythe's decision to stay.

*

Gordy was leaning all the way back in his office chair, arms folded behind his back, beaming like a lunatic.

'What took you so long?' he said.

'Doug Forsythe just came into my office,' I said. 'He's staying.'

'Oh, is *that* right?' he said archly. 'Now, I wonder why *that* is.'

'What are you talking about, Gordy?'

'All of a sudden Forsythe's lost interest in defecting to Sony? Like all of a *sudden*?'

'It's strange,' I said.

'I wonder why that could be,' he said. 'What in the world would make a high-test guy like Doug Forsythe back out of a job offer that's at least thirty percent better than what he's doing here, huh?'

'Didn't want to move to New Jersey?'

'Did he ask you to match Sony's offer?'

'No, in fact.'

'You didn't think that was bizarre?'

'Yeah, it was.'

'You ask to see Sony's offer?'

'What are you saying, Forsythe made the whole thing up or something?'

'Oh no. He's not a devious guy.'

'Then what?'

He tipped his chair all the way forward, planted his elbows on his desk, and said triumphantly, '*The god-damned offer dried up.*'

'Dried up?'

'Sony pulled it.'

'That's impossible.'

'I kid you not. I just got a call from a buddy of mine at Sony. Something happened. Some hiccup. Somewhere way up in the hierarchy, someone got cold feet about Doug Forsythe. Higher than Crawford's level, I suspect. He was notified early this afternoon that they were revoking the offer.'

'But why?'

He shook his head. 'No idea. No one knows. Something must have come up. I have no idea what. But it's over and done with. Forsythe returns to the mothership.' He cackled. 'Love it when shit like this happens.'

I wasn't really listening to General Patton on my *Business Is War!* CD as I drove home. I was remembering Cal Taylor being escorted out of the building by a security guy, not Kurt. Thinking about Festino. About Doug Forsythe, wondering why Sony had revoked the offer, which was unheard of.

The narrator was saying, 'A sand tiger shark usually produces only one pup during breeding season. Why? Because in his mother's womb, the biggest shark devours his brothers and sisters. Or take the spotted hyena. They're born with fully erupted front teeth, and if two littermates are of the same sex, one will kill the other at birth. The golden eagle lays two eggs, but often the stronger chick eats the weaker sibling within the first few weeks after hatching. Why? *Survival of the fittest!*'

I switched it off.

By the time I got home I was fairly calm. I entered the house very quietly. Kate had taken to coming home early and taking a late-afternoon nap in the front sitting room. Her morning sickness had gone away, but she was getting tired a lot.

The floor of the entry foyer was antique travertine,

and it echoed when you walked on it. So I took off my shoes and went past the sitting room in my stockinged feet. The air-conditioning was on full blast.

'You're home early.' Kate was sitting on Grammy Spencer's hard sofa. Finally, Grammy Spencer's furniture looked at home.

I came up and kissed her. She was reading a book, a black paperback of Alice Munro stories. 'Hey, babe. How're you feeling?' She had changed out of her work outfit into her sweats. I slipped my hand under her T-shirt and caressed her tummy.

'I don't know. A little funny.'

'Funny?' I said, alarmed.

'No, just queasy. Heartburn. The usual.'

'Oh. Okay.'

'Hey, Jason, can we talk?'

'Uh, sure.' *Can we have a talk* is up there with *We've found a lump* as the scariest words in the English language.

She patted the sofa next to her. 'Want to have a seat?'

I sat down. 'What's up?' I sneaked a glance at my watch. I figured I had ten minutes max to get into my jeans and Red Sox jersey so I could make it to Fenway in time.

'Listen, honey, I want to apologize. I've been giving you a hard time about working so hard, and I think I'm not being fair.'

'Don't worry about it,' I said. 'Apology accepted.' I didn't want to sound too abrupt, but I couldn't get sandbagged into a deep talk.

'I know how hard Gordy has you working, and I just want you to know I appreciate it. I was out of line at BabyWorld.'

'No worries,' I said.

'"No worries"?' she repeated. 'Since when do you say that?'

'Who knows?'

'I mean, look at this place.' She spread her arms wide. 'This house is gorgeous, and it's all because of you. Because of your hard work. It's all you. And I never forget that.'

'Thanks,' I said. I stood up and kissed her again. 'Gotta go.'

'Where're you going?'

'Fenway,' I said. 'I told you.'

'You did?'

'I thought I did. I'm pretty sure I did.'

'With Kurt?'

'Yeah,' I said. 'I've got to go change.'

When I came back downstairs, Kate was in the kitchen making herself a Boca burger and some broccoli. Voluntarily, too.

I kissed her good-bye, and she said, 'Aren't you going to ask me how my day was?'

'I'm sorry. How *was* your day?'

'It was incredible. Marie had an opening at this gallery in the South End, and I went there as a representative of the foundation. And she showed up with three of her kids – she doesn't have any child care or any relatives here. So I offered to watch the kids while she talked to the *Boston Globe* art critic.'

'*You* took care of three kids?'

She nodded. 'For an hour.'

'Oh, my God.'

'I know what you're thinking. Like, it was a disaster, right?'

'It wasn't?'

'At first it was. The first ten minutes or so I thought I was going to lose my mind. But then – I don't know, I did it. It actually was okay. I was pretty good, even. And I realized, you know – I can do this, Jase. I can do this.'

There were tears in her eyes, and there were tears in mine, too. I kissed her, and said, 'I'm sorry I've got to go.'

'Go,' she said.

29

There was the usual crowd around Fenway Park, the scalpers asking if I needed a ticket or had one to sell, the guys hawking Italian sausages and hot dogs and programs. I found Kurt standing at the turnstiles near Gate A, as we'd arranged. I was surprised to see that he had his arm around a woman's waist.

She had brassy red hair, a cascade of frizzy curls, and she wore a peach tank top that was tight on her enormous boobs. She had a tiny waist and a great ass, which was well displayed by a pair of short shorts, almost hot pants. She had heavy eye shadow and big eyelashes and bright red lipstick.

Once I got over my raw animal excitement at the sight of this chick, I was immediately disappointed. This was not the sort of woman I expected Kurt to be going out with. He'd never mentioned any girlfriend, and you don't bring just anybody to a Red Sox game. The tickets are too hard to get.

'Hey, chief,' he said, reaching out for me with his left hand, touching my shoulder.

'Sorry I'm late,' I said.

'They haven't thrown out the first pitch yet,' he said. 'Jason, I'd like you to meet Leslie.'

'Hi, Leslie,' I said. We shook hands. She had very long red fingernails. She smiled, and I smiled, and we looked at each other for a couple of seconds, not knowing what to say.

'Let's rock 'n' roll,' Kurt said.

I walked alongside them through the cavernous underbelly of the ballpark, looking for our section. I felt like a third wheel.

When we got to the stairs at our section, Leslie announced she had to use the little girls' room. That's what she called it. We were going to miss the first pitch for sure.

'She's cute,' I said, when Leslie had gone off to the little girls' room.

'Yep.'

'What's Leslie's last name?'

He shrugged. 'Ask her.'

'How long have you been going out with her?'

He glanced at his watch. 'About eighteen hours. Met her in a bar last night.'

'I think I'm going to get a steak-and-cheese sub. You want one?'

'You don't want to eat that shit,' Kurt said. 'Look at all the progress you're making. You don't want that crap in your body.'

'How about a Fenway Frank?' Those are the hot dogs they sell at the ballpark. One of the secrets you learn if you go to Fenway a lot is that if you prefer your hot dog cooked, you don't buy it in the stands, where they often give it to you lukewarm or even cold. Yuck.

'Not for me, thanks.'

I'd lost my appetite. 'How's work going?'

'Good,' he said. 'Been doing some background investigations and some badge-replacement. Had to drive out to Westwood today. Routine stuff. Though I did have to open an investigation on someone.'

'Oh yeah? Who?'

'Can't say. No one you know. Guy's fencing LCD monitors. Selling them on eBay. I had to put in an additional camera and pull the guy's hard drive.'

'You gonna catch him?'

'Count on it. And the biometric fingerprint readers are in, so everyone's going to have to stop down at Corporate Security over the next couple of days and give us a fingerprint.' He looked at me. 'You're not sleeping. What's up?'

'I'm sleeping.'

'Not enough. Problems on the home front?'

'Not really,' I said. 'It's Gordy.'

'Guy's such a broke dick,' he said. 'He's like a one-man Q Course.'

'Yeah, but the difference is, Gordy isn't trying to make me into a better soldier.'

'True. He's trying to wash you out for real. Guy has it in for you. Gotta do something about that.'

'What do you mean, he has it in for me? You know something?'

He paused just long enough for me to tell that he really did know something after all. 'One of my responsibilities is to monitor e-mail.'

'You guys do that?'

'Have to. Scan for key words and stuff.'

'But you're looking at his e-mail for other reasons,' I said.

He blinked.

'You shouldn't do that.'

'Part of my job,' he said.

'What does he say about me?'

'You're obviously a threat. We gotta do something about the guy.'

'You're not answering my question.'

'Clearly. See, what Gordy doesn't understand is that his job isn't quite so secure as he thinks.'

'What does that mean?'

'The Japanese don't like his style. His profanity. His crudeness.'

'I don't know about that,' I said. 'As long as he gets results, they're happy with him. And he gets results. So he's safe.'

He shook his head. 'He's a racist. Hates the Japanese. And the Japanese don't like that. I've been doing some reading. The Japanese admire the strong-willed American manager style. But they won't tolerate anti-Japanese racism. Believe me, the second he shows his racism in public, he's gone. So fast your head will spin.'

'He's too smart for that.'

'Maybe,' Kurt said.

Then Leslie walked up in a toxic cloud of cheap perfume. She put her arm around Kurt, grabbing his butt.

'Let's find our seats,' he said.

I've been to Fenway scores of times, maybe a hundred times, but I never fail to feel a thrill when I walk up the steps and the field appears before me suddenly, brilliant green glittering in the sun or the lights, the red dirt, the throngs.

We had amazing seats, right behind the Red Sox dugout, two rows from the field. We could watch the ESPN cameramen changing lenses and stuff, the blond on-air talent applying her lipstick.

Leslie didn't know too much about baseball and wanted Kurt to explain the game to her. He said he'd do it later.

'One bit of good news today,' I said to Kurt in a low voice as we watched the game. 'Doug Forsythe decided to stay.'

'Oh yeah?'

This is the thing about baseball: There's a lot of downtime when you can talk. 'Yeah. Something happened to his Sony offer. Someone got cold feet – the offer was withdrawn. Never heard of that happening before.'

'Kurt,' said Leslie, 'I don't think I even know what your sign is.'

'My sign?' Kurt said, turning to her. 'My sign is "Do Not Disturb."'

We'd been talking so much we missed a great play, so we both looked up at the enormous electronic scoreboard, where they run the video instant replays.

'I can't even see what happened,' Kurt said.

'It's a lousy screen,' I said.

'We must have something better than that.' He meant Entronics, and it was interesting that he was saying 'we' already.

'Oh, God, yeah. That's an old RGB LED large-format video display. Got to be six or seven years old, but the technology moves fast. We've got a large-format HD video screen that's crystal clear.'

'Well?'

232

'Well what?'

'I know the assistant equipment manager. You can talk to him. He'll know who to talk to.'

'About replacing the scoreboard? Interesting.'

'Right.'

'Great idea, man.'

'I've got a million of 'em.'

Suddenly the Sox hit a grand slam, and everyone jumped to their feet.

'What just happened?' Leslie asked. 'Was that good or bad?'

30

I got to the office right at seven, feeling invigorated and a little mellow after a particularly tough workout at Kurt's gym. I plowed through paperwork and reports, played a little dodgeball myself by leaving phone messages for people I didn't want to talk to. Of the thirty or so sales cycles I was involved in, the two biggest by far – now that Freddy Naseem had screwed me over on the Harry Belkin deal – were the Chicago Presbyterian Hospital project and, giant among giants, the Atlanta airport. I sent off some e-mails on those. Did some research into the other big auto dealerships around the country. Man, there were some big ones out there. AutoNation, out of Fort Lauderdale, and United Auto Group, out of Secaucus, New Jersey, both made Harry Belkin look like your neighborhood chop shop. Belkin was like number fourteen on the list of megadealers. The damn thing was, I'd put in so much work on the deal and gotten so close.

And the Red Sox scoreboard thing had really got under my skin. The more I looked into it, the more intrigued I got. The scoreboard at Fenway was basic-ally a twenty-four-foot-by-thirty-one-foot video screen that used light-emitting diode technology – that's LEDs to you. Lots and lots of little pixels spaced about an inch apart, each pixel made up of a bunch of little LEDs that contain a chemical compound that turns different colors when you pass electricity through it. The whole thing's run by a digitized video driver. From a distance it looks great, like a giant TV screen. From a distance.

They've got these electronic digital signs all over the world by now. My online research told me that the biggest one was in central Berlin, on the Kurfürstendamm. There's the big Coca-Cola sign in Times Square, in New York, and the NASDAQ sign, and there's another big one on top of the Reuters building in London and in Piccadilly Circus, and of course they've got them all over Las Vegas.

What's cool about these signs is that, with a few keystrokes of a computer, you can change the display entirely. Not like the old billboard days when guys had to go up there and tear down the old poster and paste up the new one. Now it could be done in seconds.

They're cool, but they're also kind of grainy, kind of coarse. You can see the little colored dots. The technology was developed a decade ago. Entronics didn't do these huge outdoor displays. The technology was too specialized, and besides, our LCD and plasma displays had never been bright enough to use outdoors.

But not anymore. Now we had something even brighter, even better. We had the new flexible OLED PictureScreen in prototype, like the ones in the windows of Gordy's office. It was high-definition, low-glare, weather-safe, and it was way better than anything else out there.

Fenway Park was only the beginning. Fenway was

the first bowling pin. Once I got an Entronics Picture-Screen above center field in Boston, I could start getting them in other baseball parks, then football stadiums. Then Times Square and Piccadilly Circus and the Kurfürstendamm and Las Vegas. Movie trailers on outdoor billboards. Rock concerts. The Tour de France. Formula One. The Cannes Film Festival.

The *Vatican*. They had those huge projection TVs around St. Peter's Square so people could watch the Pope celebrate mass, or the Pope's funeral, or whatever. Shouldn't the Vatican, with all their gold, have the best technology out there?

How come, I wondered, no one at the top of Entronics in Tokyo had thought of this? It was a true brainstorm. It was *huge*.

And why stop at outdoor signs? Why not indoor billboards too – airports, shopping malls, big retail stores, company lobbies . . .

Sometimes I amaze even myself.

So in a state of total delirium, I wrote up a business plan, an outline of how Entronics PictureScreens could take over the world. I did quick-and-dirty research into the drawbacks to the existing technologies. I found out who the biggest companies were that provided electronic digital signs around the world, since we'd have to deal with them – we didn't have the infrastructure to put the stuff together ourselves. This was truly a killer application.

And by nine o'clock, I finished a draft of a memo that, I was convinced, would transform Entronics, save our division, and catapult me to the top of the company. Well, not the top. Not Tokyo – since I'm not Japanese. But close.

Now what? Now what should I do with it? Give it to Gordy so he could swipe it and claim credit? But I couldn't just shoot it off via e-mail to the MegaTower in Tokyo. The company didn't work that way.

I looked up as someone passed my office, a scrawny Japanese man with aviator glasses.

Yoshi Tanaka.

The spy, the ambassador, the conduit to the higher-ups in Tokyo.

Yoshi was my ticket. He was the guy I'd have to talk to. I waved at him, beckoned him into my office.

'Jason-san,' he said. 'Hello.'

'Say, Yoshi, I've got this killer idea I want to run by you, see what you think.

He furrowed his brow. I told him about the memo I'd written. How much revenue I thought this concept could generate for the company. We'd already developed the technology – the sunk costs were already budgeted. There'd be no additional R&D. 'See, we don't need to bolt small panels together anymore to make a huge one,' I said. 'Our PictureScreen's going to make the existing LED display technology look like JumboTron out of 1985. The revenue potential is immense.' The more I talked, the better it sounded.

Then I saw Yoshi's blank stare of utter incomprehension. The man hadn't understood a word I was saying. I'd just wasted five minutes gassing on and on.

I might as well have been speaking . . . well, English.

After lunch I stopped down at Corporate Security and spent about thirty seconds putting my index finger in a biometric reader so the machine could learn my fingerprint. When I came back up, I went to Gordy's office and told him I needed a few minutes of his time to tell him about an idea I had.

I'd realized I was going to have to get Gordy's sign-off on my big electronic billboard idea, like it or not. Without his endorsement, the concept wasn't going anywhere.

He leaned back in his chair, arms folded behind his back in his smuggest 'impress me' mode.

I told him. I handed him a hard copy of my business plan.

'Oh, so now you're going into product marketing,' he said. 'We're in sales, remember? Looking to move to Santa Clara? Or Tokyo?'

'We're allowed to originate ideas.'

'Don't waste your time.'

I felt deflated. 'Why is it a waste of time?'

'Believe me, that idea's so old it's got whiskers and liver spots. That came up at the last product-planning meeting in Tokyo, and the Jap engineers said it wouldn't fly.'

'Why not?'

'Not enough candelas or something to use outside.'

'I've been over the PictureScreen technical specs, and it's as bright as an LED.'

'It's a glare issue.'

'There's no glare. That was the whole breakthrough.'

'Look, Jason. Forget it, okay? I'm not an engineer. But it's not going to work.'

'You don't think it's worth e-mailing Tokyo?'

'Jason,' he said patiently. He drummed his fingers on top of the business plan. 'I'm a change agent. I'm a Six Sigma black belt. I was schooled in the change acceleration process, okay? But I know when to give

238

up the fight, and that's something you've got to learn.'

I hesitated. I was crestfallen. 'Okay,' I said. I got up and reached for my business plan, but Gordy picked it off his desk, scrunched it up in his fist, and deposited it in his trash can.

'Now here's what I want your mind on. TechComm. From the second we all arrive in Miami, a couple of days from now, I want you schmoozing our resellers and channel partners. And remember, first night of TechComm is the big Entronics dinner for all the sales guys and our biggest customers, and I'm the emcee. So I want you in full battle mode. Okay? Stick to your knitting. We got a division to save.'

31

Kurt's black Mustang was parked in my driveway.

I entered quietly. I felt suspicious, but also guilty about feeling that way. Kate and Kurt were sitting in the living room talking. They didn't hear me come in.

'It's too much,' she was saying. 'It's eating him up. It's all he wants to talk about, Gordy and the Band of Brothers.'

Kurt mumbled something, and Kate said, 'But Gordy's just going to stand in his way, don't you think? If he's going to climb any higher in that company, it's not going to be with Gordy's help.'

'My ears are burning,' I said.

That jolted the two of them. 'Jason!' Kate said.

'Sorry to interrupt your conversation.'

Kurt turned around in his chair. Grammy Spencer's chintz-covered easy chair. Much more comfortable than her Victorian sofa.

'Notice anything?' Kate said.

'Besides the fact that my wife and my friend seem to be conducting an affair?'

'The walls, silly.'

I looked at the living room walls, and all I saw were the framed paintings Kate had collected over the years from artists the Meyer Foundation funded.

'You got a new painting?' They all looked pretty much the same to me.

'You don't notice they're all hanging straight, finally?'

'Oh, right. Yes, very straight.'

'Kurt,' she announced.

Kurt shook his head modestly. 'I always like to use two hangers on each frame – that brass kind with the three brads.'

'Me, too,' I said.

'And I used a level. Hard to get 'em straight without a level.'

'I've always thought so,' I said.

'And Kurt fixed that dripping faucet in the bathroom that's always driving us crazy,' Kate said.

'It never bothered me,' I said. Kurt did this and Kurt did that. I wanted to barf.

'Just needed a new washer and O-ring,' Kurt said. 'A little plumber's grease and an adjustable wrench.'

'Very kind of you, Kurt,' I said. 'You just happen to carry plumber's grease and adjustable wrenches and O-rings around with you in your briefcase?'

'Jason,' Kate said.

'I keep a bunch of tools in a storage unit back of my buddy's auto body shop,' Kurt said. 'Just stopped over there on the way over. No big deal.'

'You had to see a vendor in Cambridge again?'

He nodded. 'Figured I'd just stop by and say hi, and Kate put me to work.'

I shot Kate a dirty look. 'Are we still going to the movies tonight, Kate?' I said.

Kurt got the message and said good-bye. Then Kate began the incredibly long and involved process of getting ready to go out – there's always a 'quick shower,' and about forty-five minutes of blow-drying her hair, and then the makeup, which she applies as if she's about to walk down the red carpet to the Kodak Theatre to get an Oscar. Then the inevitable, frantic race to get to the movie on time. Of course, the more I hounded her to hurry up, the slower she went.

So I sat in the bedroom, impatiently watching her do her makeup. 'Hey, Kate,' I said.

'Mm?' She was lining her lips with that pencil-looking thing.

'I don't want you to exploit Kurt anymore.'

'*Exploit* him? What are you talking about?' She stopped in midstroke, turned around.

'You're treating him like your servant. Every time he comes over here, you put him to work fixing something.'

'Oh, come on, Jason, he *volunteers.* Anyway, does he *look* like he resents it? I think it makes him feel useful. Needed.'

'Uh-huh. Well, it strikes me as a little – I don't know, entitled.'

'*Entitled?*'

'Like you're the lady of the manor, and he's some peasant.'

'Or maybe I'm Lady Chatterley and he's the gamekeeper, is that it?' she said sarcastically.

I shrugged. I didn't get the reference.

'Do I detect a note of jealousy?'

'Come on,' I said. 'Don't be ridiculous.'

'You are jealous, aren't you?'

'Jesus, Kate. Of what?'

'I don't know. Maybe you're jealous of the fact that he's so handy, such a regular *guy.*'

'A regular guy,' I repeated. 'And I'm – what? Thurston Howell the Third? My dad worked in a sheet-metal plant, for God's sake.'

She shook her head, snorted softly. 'When you told me he was Special Forces, I was expecting something, I don't know, *different*. Crude, maybe. Rough around the edges. But he's awfully considerate.' She let out a low giggle. 'Plus, he's not unattractive.'

'"Not unattractive"? What's that supposed to mean?'

'Oh, you know what I mean. Not – not what I expected, that's all. Don't be jealous, sweetie. *You're* my husband.'

'Yeah, and he's, what? Now he's like your – your Yohimbe warrior with the blowgun and the machete?'

'Yanomami.'

'Whatever.'

'Well, sometimes a machete is just the tool you need,' she said.

I sulked for a while in the car, but by the time we got there I'd cooled off.

My wife likes films that have subtitles. I like movies that have cars that crash through plate-glass windows. Her all-time favorite movie is *Closely Watched Trains*. She likes them slow and contemplative, preferably in Czech or Polish, captioned in Serbo-Croatian.

Whereas my all-time favorite movie is *Terminator 2*.

I like movies, not films. My requirements are simple: big explosions and car chases and gratuitous violence and unnecessary flashes of female nudity.

So naturally we'd gone to a foreign-film theater that evening in Kendall Square in Cambridge to see a film set in Argentina about a young priest in a coma who's in love with a quadriplegic dancer. Or maybe I should say, she watched it while I snuck glances at my BlackBerry, which I hid from her behind the popcorn bucket. The guy I was dealing with at Chicago Presbyterian, the Assistant Vice President for Communications, had once again changed his specs for the plasma screens he wanted in their one hundred operating rooms and wanted me to reprice the whole proposal. The facilities manager at the Hartsfield-Jackson Atlanta International Airport said that he'd just been told by Pioneer that *their* plasma displays had a higher resolution and a better greyscale performance than Entronics and wanted to know if that was true. I was damned if I was going to lose this deal to Pioneer.

And an e-mail from Freddy Naseem. He wanted me to give him a call.

What the hell could that be about?

'Did you like it?' Kate said, as we walked to the car. You had to take your parking ticket to get it validated in one place, then pay for it somewhere else. It was a system apparently designed in the Soviet Union.

'Yeah,' I said. 'It was moving.'

I figured that would make her happy, but she said, 'Which part?'

'Most of it, really,' I said.

'What was it about?'

'What was what about?'

'The movie. What was the plot?'

'Is this a quiz?'

'Yeah,' she said. 'What was the story?'

'Come on, Katie.' I beeped the Mercedes open and went around to the passenger's side and opened the door for her.

'No, I'm serious,' she said. 'I don't think you watched any of it. You spent the whole time on your BlackBerry. Which really pissed off everyone around us, by the way.'

'I glanced at it a couple times, Kate.' She stood there, refusing to get in. 'There's some stuff I really needed to check on.'

'This is a night off,' she said. 'You've got to stop.'

'I thought you said you understood this came with the job. Didn't we talk about this? Come on, get in.'

She stood there, arms folded. She was starting to show already. You could see the swell in her belly underneath her cotton dress. 'You need an intervention or something. You're out of control.'

'You're never going to live like you did when you were a kid, you know. Not as long as you're married to me.'

'Jason, that's enough.' She looked around as if to see who might be listening. 'My God, I feel like I've created a monster.'

32

In the morning I called Freddy Naseem at eight-thirty on the dot, when I knew he always got in.

'Jason,' he said, sounding overjoyed to hear from me. 'Did you ever find out how quickly you'd be able to get us the plasma monitors?'

'But I thought you were all set with Panasonic. You said they could get the screens to you within a week. Did something change?'

He paused. 'They got us all the monitors yesterday. But there was just one little problem. None of them worked.'

'*None* of them?'

'Every single one – dead as a doornail. Panasonic is blaming some glitch at their Westwood warehouse. They say there was a gas leak of some sort – chlorine gas, I think. Apparently chlorine gas destroys the microchips or some such thing. And hundreds of flat-screen TVs and monitors in that warehouse were ruined. The problem is, they won't be able to replace the product for a few months at least, and Harry Belkin is desperate to have them in.'

I answered slowly. My mind was reeling. 'Well,' I said, 'you've come to the right place.'

*

I found Kurt in the company Command Center on the ground floor adjacent to the main entrance. I'd had to page him, and when I told him I needed to see him right away, he told me to meet him there.

The Command Center was lined with banks of Entronics closed-circuit TV monitors and a big curved console around the room where guys wearing microfleece pullovers – the air was cold here because of all the computers – sat tapping at keyboards or shooting the breeze with one another. You could see on the monitors every entrance to the building, every computer room and common area; you could see people coming in and out and walking around. It was amazing, and a little creepy, how much of the company you could see from here.

Kurt was standing with folded arms talking to one of the guys in fleece. He was wearing a blue shirt and rep tie and looked very much in charge. The guys in fleece were, I knew, contract security officers, so Kurt really was their boss.

'Bro,' he said when he saw me. He looked concerned. 'What's up?'

'We gotta talk,' I said, grabbing him by the shoulder.

His eyes grew hard. 'Let's talk.'

'In private,' I said. I led the way out of the Command Center to the hall and found an unoccupied break room. It was littered with old copies of the *Herald* and a Dunkin' Donuts carton and discarded cardboard coffee cups, and it smelled like someone had been sneaking a smoke.

'I just got a call from Freddy Naseem.'

'The guy from Harry Belkin.'

247

'Right. He told me that all the Panasonic monitors arrived dead, so he wants to do business with us.'

'Hey, that's great news. Big win for you.'

I stared at him. 'There was a chlorine-gas leak at Panasonic's Westwood facility. Fried the printed circuits in the monitors.'

'You asking me to do something for you?'

'I think you already did,' I said quietly.

He blinked. His face was unreadable. He turned away, studying the empty Dunkin' Donuts box. Then he said, 'You got the deal back, didn't you?'

My stomach sank. He'd done it.

If he'd done that, then was there really any question that he'd done the things Trevor accused me of? Trevor's car trouble. The plasma screen that conked out at Trevor's presentation to Fidelity. Gleason's Blue Screen of Death.

Doug Forsythe's job offer drying up.

What else had he done?

'This isn't the way I wanted it, Kurt.'

'Panasonic snaked you. That's unsat.'

'Do you realize what kind of deep shit we'd both be in if anyone connected us to what happened?'

Now he looked annoyed. 'I know how to cover my tracks, bro.'

'You can't do this,' I said. 'Maybe sabotage is acceptable in the Special Forces, but not in the business world.'

He stared right back at me. 'And I expected a little gratitude.'

'No, Kurt. Don't ever do this again. Are we clear? I don't want any more of your help.'

He shrugged, but his eyes were cold. 'You don't understand, do you? I take care of my friends. That's what I do. That's who I am. Like the Marines say, no better friend, no worse enemy.'

'Yeah, well,' I said, 'I'm glad I'm not your enemy.'

33

I had a midmorning flight to Miami, out of Logan, so I didn't go in to work. I decided to sleep late. Late being relative, of course. Kate snuggled right up against me in bed, which was nice, until I suddenly noticed the time. It was almost eight. I bolted out of bed to finish the packing I'd started the night before.

'Hey, Kate,' I said, 'aren't you going to work?'

She mumbled something into the pillow.

'What?'

'I said, I don't feel well.'

'What's the matter?'

'Cramps.'

Alarmed, I went to her side of the bed. 'Down – there?'

'Yeah.'

'Is that normal?'

'I don't know. I've never been pregnant before.'

'Call Dr. DiMarco.'

'It's not a big deal.'

'Call him anyway.'

She paged him while I nervously bustled about packing, brushed my teeth, took a shower, shaved. When I came out of the bathroom, she was asleep.

'Did he call back?'

She turned over. 'He said not to worry. Said call him if there's spotting or bleeding.'

'Will you call me on my cell?'

'Don't worry about it, sweetie. I'll call if there's anything. How long are you going to be gone for?'

'TechComm lasts three days. Think of all the foreign movies you can watch on Bravo while I'm gone.'

Just about all of the Band of Brothers was aboard the Delta flight to Miami. Everyone but Gordy sat in economy. Gordy was in business class. Not sitting in first class was his money-saving gesture.

I had an aisle seat, several rows away from any of the other guys, and I was enjoying the fact that there were empty seats on either side. Until a woman sidled past me, holding a screaming baby. She started speaking Spanish to the infant, who wouldn't stop crying. Then she poked a finger into the baby's diaper, unwrapped it, and began changing the wriggling creature on her lap, right there. The smell of baby poop was overpowering.

I thought: Good God almighty, is this what's in store for me? Changing diapers on airplanes?

When the mother finished changing the diaper, she scrunched up the old one, reclosed the Velcro tabs to tighten the poop package, then jammed the soiled diaper into the seat pocket in front of her.

Behind me, some of the Entronics guys were getting a little rowdy, like frat boys. I turned around for a quick look. They were laughing loudly as some guy, whose face I couldn't see, was showing them something in a magazine. Trevor waved the guy over, said something, and both of them exploded in guffaws. The guy punched Trevor lightly on the shoulder and turned around and I could see it was Kurt.

At that moment he saw me and walked down the aisle. 'This seat taken?' he asked.

'Hey, Kurt,' I said warily. 'What are you doing here?'

'My job. Booth security. Mind if I sit down?'

'Sure, but it might be someone's seat.'

'It is. It's mine,' he said, squeezing past me. He turned to the Spanish woman with the baby. *'Buenos días, señora,'* he said in what sounded to me like an awfully good Spanish accent. She said something back. Then he turned back to me. 'Cuban,' he whispered. He sniffed the air, caught the diaper aroma. 'That you?' He was trying to defuse the tension by cracking a joke.

I smiled to say I got it but it wasn't funny.

'So, you still don't want my help?'

I nodded.

'That include information I happened to come across that concerns you?'

I hesitated. Inhaled slowly, then let out my breath even more slowly. I couldn't let him keep doing this. It was wrong, and I knew it.

But the lure was overpowering. 'All right,' I said. 'Let's hear it.'

He unzipped a nylon portfolio and took out a brown file folder and handed it to me.

'What's this?' I said.

He spoke quietly. 'You know that big idea you came up with at Fenway?'

'The billboard thing?'

'Take a look.'

I hesitated, then opened the folder. It held printouts of e-mails between Gordy and Dick Hardy, the CEO of Entronics USA.

'I guess our CEO was in Tokyo for the Global Executive Summary. But he's coming to TechComm.'

'He never misses it.' I read through the e-mails. Gordy was all excited about a 'major idea' he'd come up with, a 'disruptive' application of existing technology that could transform Entronics' position in the global market. Digital signage! He used some of the exact phrases I'd used: 'The sunk costs are already budgeted.' And: 'It will put Entronics on the map in the digital signage industry.' And: 'PictureScreen will make existing LED display technology look like JumboTron in 1985.'

'This pisses me off,' I said.

'I thought it might. That broke dick's not going to get away with screwing you over again.'

'What are you talking about?'

'I'm not talking.'

'What are you *thinking* about?'

'Nothing. When you're in combat, you don't have time to think. You just act.'

'No,' I said. 'No favors.'

He was silent.

'I mean it,' I said.

He remained silent.

'Come on, Kurt. No more. Please.'

34

The hotel was a big fancy Westin attached to the convention center. Our rooms all had balconies overlooking Miami and Biscayne Bay. I'd forgotten how much I liked Miami, even though the heat was oppressive in the summer, and I wondered why I didn't live here.

I worked out in the hotel fitness center and had a late room-service lunch while I did e-mail and returned calls. I checked in with Kate at home and asked how she was feeling, and she said the cramps had gone away so she was a lot better.

TechComm, I should explain, is the big trade show for the audiovisual industry, which is just about as geeky as it sounds. Twenty-five thousand people from eighty countries attend, all of them connected in some way to a multibillion-dollar industry that's populated by the guys from the Dungeons & Dragons Club in high school. Understand that the highlight of the whole show is not the awards banquet but the 'Projection Shoot-out', a big demo of LCD projectors, okay?

At five, I dressed in Miami casual, which meant a nice golf shirt and a pair of pressed chinos, and went down to the big opening reception in Ballrooms B and C. It was the kickoff to the convention. When I got there, I saw that the whole Band of Brothers, plus Gordy, were dressed pretty much the same way as me. There was bad music and decent hors d'oeuvres and drinks. People were getting their badges and program guides and figuring out which seminars and panel discussions they wanted to go to when they weren't on booth duty. 'Principles of AV Design'? 'Fundamentals of Video Conferencing'? The hot one seemed to be 'The Future of Digital Cinema.'

Snatches of conversation wafted by me: '. . . Native resolution of nineteen-twenty-by-ten-eighty . . . that four million pixels makes HD video look *soft* . . . unstable signal environments . . . totally seamless playback . . .' Festino told me that NEC was giving away a Corvette and wondered whether we could enter the drawing. Then he said, 'Hey, look. It's Mister Big.'

Dick Hardy entered the party like Jay Gatsby. He was a big, trim man with a big head, a ruddy face, a strong jaw. He looked like a CEO out of Central Casting, which is probably why our Japanese overlords named him to the job. He was wearing a blue blazer over some kind of white linen T-shirt.

Gordy spotted him and rushed over, gave him a bear hug. Since Hardy was a lot taller than Gordy, the hug was comic – Gordy's arms grabbed Hardy around the belly.

Nerdy or not, TechComm is pretty damned cool. Everywhere the next morning you could see huge screens and displays, multimedia shows of light and sound. Video walls twelve feet high playing movie trailers and commercials. One booth was a virtual-reality simulation of a Renaissance palace you could walk into, all done by hologram. It was magic. The future was on display. People in the rental and staging business were checking out the latest audio-mixing consoles. One company was showing off its wireless digital video broadcast system for the home. Another one was inviting people to try its wireless phone conference system. Yet another had outdoor digital touchscreens.

We had the PictureScreen on display, mounted into a big picture window, along with our biggest and best plasma and LCD displays and our six newest, lightest, and brightest LCD projectors for schools and businesses. I manned the booth a little, greeting walk-bys, but most of the time I was in meetings with big customers. I did two lunches. Kurt and a couple of guys from our facilities department had gotten here early to set up the booth and get it wired and move boxes, and Kurt had spent much of the day hovering nearby, keeping watch on the equipment and especially the unguarded area behind the booth. He'd gotten pretty popular among the Band of Brothers, I noticed.

I didn't see Gordy much. He and Dick Hardy had a long meeting with some folks from Bank of America. I was perfectly civil to him, of course. He was a scumbag. What else was new? During a break between meetings, Gordy stopped by our booth, glad-handed a little, and took me aside.

'Booya on that Belkin dealership deal,' he said, an arm around my shoulder. 'You see the press release Dick Hardy just sent out?'

'Already?'

'Hardy doesn't waste time. Entronics stock is already trading higher on the New York Stock Exchange.'

'Because of that one deal? That's got to be a pimple on Entronics' ass.'

'It's all about momentum. Who's up, who's down. Good timing, too, Entronics announcing the deal at TechComm. Love it. *Love it!*'

'Good timing,' I agreed.

'You know something, Steadman? I'm starting to think I might have underestimated you after all. When we get back, we should get together one of these nights, you and me and the ladies, huh?'

'That sounds like a lot of fun,' I said with a straight face.

Later on, I did the booth crawl, checking out the competitors. People were grabbing freebies all over the place, swag like messenger bags and beach towels and Frisbees. I stopped at the booth of one company that did rotating video displays and weatherproof, 360-degree outdoor LED displays. I'd removed my badge so they'd think I was just another end user. At the booth of a company that sold huge indoor/outdoor LED video screens, assembled from smaller modular panels, I really dug deep, asking a bunch of questions about pixel pitch and color correction. Questions that probably made me seem smart, like the number of nits, which is a unit of brightness, and the pixel uniformity technology. But I wasn't trying to impress them. I really wanted to know what the competition was up to. They told me their video screens had been used in Sting and Metallica and Red Hot Chili Peppers concerts.

I checked out the booth of a company called AirView Systems, which sold flight information display systems to airports. They were one of our biggest competitors for the Atlanta airport contract, so I wanted to see what they did. AirView wasn't a big company, so all the top officers were there schmoozing. I shook hands with the CFO, Steve Bingham, a handsome guy in his fifties with silver anchorman hair, a lean face, deep-set eyes.

Then I stopped at the Royal Meister booth, which was larger than ours, and even more decked out with plasmas and LCDs and projectors. The young guy who was manning the booth was all over me, since he thought I was a potential customer. He handed me his business card, wanted to show us the latest and greatest. He could have been me five years ago. He asked for my business card, and I patted my pockets and told him I must have left them back at my hotel room and turned to get the hell out of there, hoping he wouldn't see me at the Entronics booth when *he* did his booth crawl.

'Let me introduce you to our new Senior Vice President of Sales,' he said.

'Thanks, but I've got to get to a seminar.'

'Are you sure?' a woman said. 'I always like to say hello to prospects.'

I didn't recognize her at first. Her mousy brown hair was the color of honey. She'd put highlights in her hair too. She was wearing makeup for the first time.

'Joan,' I said, startled. 'Fancy meeting you here.'

'Jason,' Joan Tureck said, extending her hand to shake. 'I don't see an exhibitor badge – you're no longer with Entronics?'

'No, I – I think I misplaced the badge,' I said.

'Along with his business card,' said the young sales guy, now visibly ticked off.

258

'But I thought you were with FoodMark.'

'This position opened up suddenly, and I couldn't resist. Meister wanted someone with an intimate understanding of the visual systems space, and I happened to be available. Being a carnivore wasn't a requirement.'

It made perfect sense that Royal Meister had hired Joan Tureck. In the big battle between divisions, with two megacorporations duking it out over which sales force lived and which died, she was a huge asset. She knew where all the bodies were buried at Entronics. She knew where all our fault lines were, all our weaknesses and soft spots.

'You – you look great,' I said.

'It's Dallas,' she shrugged.

'So you've got the equivalent of Gordy's job,' I said.

'I wish that were all there was to it. Most of my job these days is taken up with planning for the integration.'

'Meaning what's going to happen to your sales force?'

She smiled again. 'More like what's going to happen to *your* sales force.'

'You look like the cat that got the cream, Joan.' Old Cal Taylor's line.

'Strictly two percent. You know me.'

'I thought you hated Dallas.'

'Sheila grew up in Austin, you know. So it's not so bad. They've invented something called air-conditioning.'

'They have great steak houses in Dallas.'

'I'm still a vegan.' Her smile faded. 'I heard about Phil Rifkin. That was a shock.'

I nodded.

'He was such a nice guy. Brilliant. A little strange, sure, but he never struck me as suicidal.'

'I never thought so either.'

'Very peculiar. And very sad.'

I nodded.

'I saw the press release Dick Hardy put out. I guess Gordy landed a major deal at the Harry Belkin auto dealerships.'

I nodded again. 'That was news to me, too,' I said. 'I thought *I'd* done it, but hey, what do I know?'

She drew closer and walked with me out of the booth. 'Jason, can I give you some unsolicited advice?'

'Of course.'

'I've always liked you. You know that.'

I nodded.

'Get out now, while you can. Before you and all the rest of you are out on the street. It's much easier to look for a job when you already have one.'

'It's not a sure thing, Joan,' I said weakly.

'I'm telling you as a friend, Jason. Call me a rat, but I know a sinking ship when I see one.'

I didn't reply, just looked at her for a few seconds.

'We'll stay in touch,' she said.

35

When the show was closing for the day, I stopped back in to check in on my guys and see who they'd connected with. Festino had the Purell out and was furiously trying to kill the microbes he'd picked up from the disease-ridden hands of hundreds of customers. Kurt was at work securing the equipment for the night.

'Coming to the big dinner?' I asked Kurt, as he secured the equipment.

'Oh, I wouldn't miss it,' he said.

As I walked back to my room to shower and change into a suit, I saw Trevor Allard standing by the elevator banks. 'How's it going, Trevor?' I said.

He turned to me. 'Interesting,' he said. 'It's always nice to run into old friends.'

'Who'd you see?'

The elevator binged, and we got on, the only ones.

'A buddy of mine from Panasonic,' he said.

'Oh, yeah?'

'Mm-hmm.' The elevator doors closed.

'He told me you got the Harry Belkin contract because a whole shipment of Panasonic plasmas were DOA.'

I nodded. I was feeling the usual anxiety, being inside the steel coffin, but now I felt a dread of a different sort. 'It's weird,' I said.

'Very weird. Bad for Panasonic. But good for you.'

'And Entronics.'

'Sure enough. Your deal, of course. A huge win for you. Good bit of luck, huh?'

I shrugged. 'Hey,' I said, 'you make your own luck.' *Or someone makes it for you.*

'Really got me thinking,' Trevor said carefully. We were both watching the elevator buttons. No elevator TV here, unfortunately. What would the word of the day be? *Imputation? Insinuation?* 'Took me down memory lane. Reminded me of Fidelity. I had a bum monitor, too, remember?'

'We've been through that, Trevor.'

'Yep. I lost Fidelity over it. Then there was that car trouble I had a few months ago – I lost Pavilion, remember? Then there was Brett Gleason's Blue Screen of Death.'

'You're still harping on this nonsense?'

'Bad things happen to your adversaries, don't they? There seems to be a real pattern here.'

The elevator binged again, and we'd arrived at our floor.

'Right,' I said. 'And even paranoids have enemies.'

'I'm not dropping this, Jason,' he said as he turned right and I turned left to go to our rooms. 'Brett and I are going to dig deep. I know you're behind all this stuff, and I'm going to find out the truth. I promise you.'

36

I called Kate, took a shower, and changed into a suit and tie for dinner. Entronics had taken over one of the Westin ballrooms. Gordy had, as usual, kept the theme of the dinner a secret.

His TechComm dinners were always blowout extravaganzas. The year before, the theme had been *The Apprentice*, and he got to be Donald Trump, of course. The year before that was *Survivor*. Everyone got bandanas and was forced to eat a bowl of 'dirt,' made of crumbled Oreos and gummy worms. He always gave an over-the-top, borderline-insane talk, a cross between that self-help guru Tony Robbins and Mr. Pink from *Reservoir Dogs*.

We were all wondering what it would be this year.

When I walked in I saw that the whole place had been decorated, at what had to be enormous expense, to look like a boxing arena. Projected on the walls – using Entronics projectors, no doubt – were all sorts of vintage fight posters, the kind that usually came in mustard yellow with big red-and-white crudely printed letters and monochrome photos of the fighters. There were posters for JERSEY JOE WALCOTT VS. ROCKY MARCIANO and CASSIUS CLAY VS. DONNIE

Fleeman and Sugar Ray Forsythe vs. Henry
Armstrong.

In the middle of the room was a boxing ring. I'm
serious. Gordy had actually had a boxing ring brought
in – he must have rented it somewhere in Miami –
steel frame and corner posts, covered ropes, canvas
floor, wooden stepladder to climb in, even the stools
in opposite corners. There was a black steel ring gong
mounted on a freestanding wooden post nearby. It sat
there in the middle of the banquet hall, surrounded by
dining tables.

It looked incredibly stupid.

Kurt saw me enter and came right up to me. 'This
must have cost a couple of bucks, huh?'

'What's going on?'

'You'll see. Gordy asked my advice. I should be
flattered.'

'Advice on what.'

'You'll see.'

'Where's Gordy?'

'Probably backstage having a last hit of courage.
He asked me to go get his Scotch bottle.'

I found my assigned seat, at a table close to the
boxing ring. Each of the Band of Brothers was seated,
one or two to a table, with important customers.

I just had time to introduce myself to a guy from
SignNetwork before the lights went down and a pair
of spotlights swung around and stopped at the blue
velvet stage curtains at the front of the room. A loud
trumpet fanfare blared from loudspeakers: the theme
from the movie *Rocky*.

The curtains parted and two burly guys burst
through carrying a throne. On it sat Gordy, wearing a

shiny red boxing robe with gold trim and hood, and shiny red boxing gloves. He was wearing black high-top Converse sneakers. The throne was labeled 'CHAMP.' In front of them scurried a young woman, flinging rose petals from a basket. Gordy was beaming and punching the air.

The burly guys carried Gordy down a path cleared between the dining tables, while the woman threw rose petals just ahead of them, and 'Gonna Fly Now' blared from the speakers.

There was tittering, and some outright laughter, from the tables. People didn't know what to make of it all.

The guys set the throne down next to the boxing ring, and Gordy rose to his feet, gloves way up in the air, as the music faded.

'Yo, Adrian!' he shouted. The rose-petal woman now busied herself clipping a wireless lapel mike to his robe.

There was laughter. People were starting to roll with it. I still couldn't believe Gordy was doing this, but he was known to do strange routines at our annual kickoffs.

He turned around to show off the back of his robe. It said ITALIAN STALLION in gold block letters. It even had a white patch sewn on the top that said SHAM-ROCK MEATS INC., just like in the first *Rocky* movie.

He turned back around and lifted his robe coquettishly to give us a peek of his stars-and-stripes boxing trunks.

'Wrong movie,' Trevor shouted from his table over to one side. 'That's *Rocky III*!'

'Yeah, yeah,' Gordy said, beaming.

'I thought you're Irish!' shouted Forsythe, getting into it.

'Honorary Italian,' he said. 'My wife's Italian. Where's my drink?' He found his bottle of Talisker 18 on a little table next to the ring, glugged some into a glass, and took a swig before stepping into the ring. He made a hand gesture, and the rose-petal woman hit the ring gong with a striking hammer. He bowed, and there was applause.

'Booya!' he shouted.

'Booya,' some of the guys replied.

'*Booya!*' he yelled, louder.

'*Booya!*' everyone shouted back.

He pulled down the hood but left the robe on – probably a wise decision, given his physique. 'We at Entronics are going to go the distance for you,' he shouted. There was a high-pitched squeal of feedback.

'Yeah!' Trevor shouted back, and he was joined by a bunch of the other guys. I clapped and tried not to roll my eyes.

'We're going all fifteen rounds!' Gordy shouted.

The rose-petal woman was standing at a long table next to the ring, cracking eggs into glasses. There was a pile of egg cartons on the table. I knew what was coming up. There were probably twenty-eight glasses lined up, and she was cracking three eggs into each glass.

Gordy took another gulp of his Scotch. 'When your back is to the wall and it's do or die, you look within yourself to find the spirit of a hero,' he said. 'Like Rocky Balboa, we think of ourselves as the underdog. Rocky had Apollo Creed. Well, we have NEC and Mitsubishi. Rocky had Mr. T – we have Hitachi. Rocky

266

had Tommy Gunn – we have Panasonic. Rocky had Ivan Drago – we have Sony!'

Raucous cheers from the Band of Brothers, and from some of the channel partners and distributors now too.

'We say, "Be a thinker, not a stinker!"' Gordy said. 'We're here to make your dreams a reality! Now, I'm not going to get down and do one-arm pushups for you.'

'Aww, come on!' Taminek shouted. 'Do it!'

'Come on, Gordy!' Trevor shouted.

'I'll spare you,' he said. 'Because this is not about Gordy. It's about the *team*.' His words seemed to be a little slurred. 'The G Team! We're all team players. And we're gonna show you now what we mean. Jason, where are you?'

'Right here,' I said, my stomach sinking.

'Get up here, sparring partner!'

I stood up. Was he going to ask me to box him in the ring? Good God. Get me the hell out of here. 'Hey, Gordy,' I said.

'Come on,' he said, waving me toward him with his left glove.

I approached the ring, and the rose-petal girl came up to me with a glass of raw eggs.

'Drink it down, Jason,' Gordy said.

I could hear cheering and laughter.

I held the glass of eggs, looked at it, smiled like a good sport. I held it up for everyone to see, and I shook my head. 'I've got high cholesterol,' I said.

'Aww,' said Trevor, and he was joined by Forsythe and Taminek and then the others.

'Come on, Tigger,' said Festino.

'You're all fired,' I said.

'Drink up,' Gordy commanded.

I lifted the glass to my mouth and poured it down my throat and began swallowing. The eggs slid down in a gooey, viscous string. I felt sick, but I kept going. When I handed the empty glass to the rose-petal girl, a cheer arose.

'All *right*!' Gordy said. He tapped my head with a glove. 'Who's next? Where's Forsythe? Where's Festino?'

'I don't want to get salmonella,' Festino said.

I returned to my table, looking around for the nearest restroom in case I had to hurl.

'Pussy,' Gordy slurred. 'Trevor, show 'em a real man.'

'I want to see Jason chug another glass.' Trevor laughed.

Gordy began weaving around the canvas like a real punch-drunk fighter, and I could tell he wasn't faking it. He was drunk. 'See, thing is, wanna know why we invited you all?' he said. 'All you customers? Think we invited you because we like spending time with you? Hell, no.'

There was laughter. Trevor sat down, relieved that the moment had passed.

'We want every frickin' last one of you to standardize on Entronics,' Gordy said. 'Know why?' He held up his gloves, punched the air. 'Because I want the whole G Team to be as rich as me.'

Some of the Band of Brothers guffawed loudly. So did a few of the customers, only not quite as loudly. Some, however, were not smiling.

'You know what kind of car Gordy drives?' he said. 'A Hummer. Not a Geo Metro. Not a goddamned Toyota. Not a Japmobile. A Hummer. Know what kind of

268

watch Gordy wears? A Rolex. Not a stinking Seiko. It ain't made in Japan. Where's Yoshi Tanaka?'

'Not here,' someone said.

'Yoshi-*san*,' Gordy said with a sarcastic twist. 'Not here. Good. Fact, I b'lieve none of our Japanese expatriates are here. Prob'ly too busy filing their secret informant reports on us. Sending *microdots* back to Tokyo. Goddamned spies.'

There was laughter, but now it was the nervous kind.

'Japs don't trust us,' Gordy went on, 'but we show them, don' we? Don' we, guys?'

There was rustling, the clinking of forks as the guests quietly ate their salads.

'They're slow-kill, those Japs,' he said. 'Passive-aggressive. Let the dust pile up in the corner. Never tell you what the hell they're thinking, those Japs. Inscrutable assholes.'

'Gordy,' Trevor called out. 'Take a seat.'

Gordy was leaning on the ropes now. 'Think it's easy working for a bunch of slant eyes who want you to fail just because you're a white guy?' he said. His words were more and more slurred, getting indistinct. 'The G Team,' he said.

Trevor got up, and I did too. 'Come on, Gordy,' he called out. 'Jesus,' Trevor muttered, 'he's plastered.' We walked over to the ring, and so did Kurt and Forsythe. Gordy was leaning against the ropes, canting all the way over. He looked up and saw us approaching. His eyes were bleary and bloodshot. 'The hell away from me,' he said.

We grabbed him, and he struggled for a few seconds, but not very hard. I heard him mumble, 'Wha' happens in Miami stays in . . . Miami . . .' before he passed out.

As we carried Gordy out of the banquet room, I saw Dick Hardy standing against a wall, his arms folded, his face a dark mask of fury.

PART THREE

37

The first thing I did was to get rid of the Caribbean. I had them remove all the PictureScreens from my new office. I wanted to be able to see out of the windows, even if all I could see was the parking lot.

Everything Gordy used to do I wanted to do the opposite. After all, I was the anti-Gordy. That's why Dick Hardy had named me the new VP of Sales.

That and the fact that Entronics was desperate to fill the slot as fast as possible. They wanted to put the Gordy debacle behind them.

Gordy's drunken rampage was all over the Internet the next day. The message boards on Yahoo were filled with stories of the *Rocky* show, the glasses of raw eggs, the Rolex and the Hummer, and especially the anti-Japanese slurs. Gordy, who was well-known in the small world of high-tech sales, had become a celebrity.

And in Tokyo, the top officers of Entronics were beyond embarrassed. They were livid. They'd been willing to accept Gordy's private bigotry, but the moment he began spouting publicly, he had to be shot.

The Entronics Public Relations Manager in Santa Clara put out a press release saying that 'Kent Gordon has left Entronics for personal and family reasons.'

I got a slew of congratulatory phone calls and e-mails – from friends I hadn't heard from in years, from people who were probably positioning themselves for a job with Entronics, not knowing there might not be any jobs at all soon. Joan Tureck sent me a very nice e-mail congratulating me and adding, ominously, 'Good luck. That most of all. You'll need it.'

The second thing I did was to call in Yoshi Tanaka and let him know that things were going to be different from now on. Unlike my predecessor, I wanted to work with him. I wanted his input. I wanted to know what he thought. I wanted to know what he thought the guys in Tokyo thought. I spoke slowly, used simple words.

I won't say Yoshi smiled at me – his facial muscles apparently didn't have that ability – but he nodded solemnly and thanked me. I think he understood what I was saying, though I couldn't be sure.

The third thing I did was ask Dick Hardy to make a stopover in Boston on his way from New York to Santa Clara. I called all my troops together in our biggest conference room to meet Mister Big and give them a rousing, inspirational speech. I told them my door was always open. I told them they should feel free to come to me with any complaints, that although I expected nothing but the best efforts from them, I wasn't going to ream them out for telling me when something wasn't going right, that I was here to help. I announced a small increase in incentive pay and bonuses. This turned out to be a bit more popular with the Band of Brothers than the Queeg Memo.

Dick Hardy stood next to me in the front of the room, wearing a navy-blue suit and crisp white shirt and blue-and-silver-striped rep tie and looking very much the CEO, with his big square jaw and his silver hair combed straight back and the heavy dark pouches under his intense, icy blue eyes. He shook everyone's hands as they filed in, and said, 'Good to know you' to each one as if he really meant it. He told them they were the 'lifeblood' of Entronics Visual Systems and that he had 'complete confidence' in me.

Hardy clapped me on both shoulders when we had a few private moments after the staff rally. 'It's been a rough ride,' he said soulfully. 'But if anyone can steady the keel, it's you.' He loved sailing metaphors. He looked directly into my eyes, and said, 'Remember: You can't control the wind. You can only control the sail.'

'Yes, sir.'

'I take heart in your string of successes, though.'

'I've had a nice run of luck,' I said.

He shook his head solemnly. 'As one of my vice presidents, you're going to get sick of hearing me say it, but I firmly believe you create your own luck.'

And the fourth thing I did was to promote Trevor Allard to my old job. Why? It's complicated. I think partly it was to make amends to him. I didn't like the guy, but if it hadn't been for Kurt, Trevor would probably have been in Gordy's office, not me.

Partly it was because I knew he'd be good at the job, like it or not. And partly, I admit, it was that old saying, 'Keep your friends close and your enemies closer.'

So now I had to work with him. I don't know who it was most uncomfortable for, him or me. I assigned Gordy's old assistant, Melanie, to Trevor, which might not have been considerate to her – it was a big step down in prestige – but I knew I could trust her to keep her eyes on him, since she liked me. Plus, she was used to working for jerks. I kept Franny, who'd been around forever and knew how things worked better than anyone else.

And, finally, I told Kurt that I really didn't need his help anymore. I didn't want his inside information; I didn't want him misusing Corporate Security that way. I sure as hell didn't want anyone finding out.

Kurt's reaction was muted. It was clear that his feelings were hurt, although he wasn't the type to ever say so.

I broke it to him early one morning at the gym in Somerville while I was lifting and he was spotting. 'I can't risk it,' I said. On the third set, I wimped out on the sixth rep, my arms trembling, going into muscle failure, and for the first time he didn't help me finish the set. He also stopped spotting me. He just watched me struggle to raise the bar high enough to replace it in the stand.

I didn't make it, and the bar came crashing down on my chest. I groaned. Then he lifted it up and out of my way. 'You're afraid you're going to get caught?' he said. 'That it?'

'No,' I said. 'Because it's wrong. It creeps me out.'

'Look who's suddenly got religion.'

'Come on,' I said, sitting up, feeling a stabbing pain in my rib cage when I breathed. 'I've always been . . . uncomfortable about it.'

'But you haven't stopped me.'

'Like I could.'

'Not when you really needed my help. You didn't

refuse to read Gordy's e-mails to Hardy, did you? And believe me, there's going to be times when you need me again.'

'Maybe,' I said. 'But I'm just going to have to do without your help.'

'Now's when you need me more than ever. You're running the sales force of a major division of Entronics. You can't afford to make a wrong move. You need to know everything that's going on. IFF, we call it.'

'IFF?'

'Identify Friend from Foe. Basic procedure. So you shoot your enemies and not your friends. One of the things you learn downrange. Sometimes, when you're outside the official battle lines, it's hard to tell the good guys from the bad guys. Lots of companies hire competitive intelligence firms, you know.'

'Not like this.'

'No,' he admitted. 'They're not as good. Not as thorough. Like, for example, you need to know what Yoshi Tanaka's really up to. He's the key player here. He's incredibly powerful. You want to stay on his good side.'

'I assume he's working for the top guys, not for me. His loyalty lies in Tokyo. As long as I keep that in mind, I'm fine.'

'You think that's all you need to know about Yoshi? What if I told you I'd captured a couple of e-mails he's sent to Tokyo in the last couple of days? Encrypted, of course – 512-bit public-key encryption – but Corporate Security is required to hold one of the keys. Written in Japanese, but I know a Japanese chick. Tell me you don't want to know what he's saying about you.' He smiled.

I hesitated, but only for a second. 'No,' I said. 'I don't.'

'And your buddy Trevor?'

I shook my head. I was tempted to tell him about Trevor's suspicions, but I decided not to. 'No,' I said. 'No more.'

His smile looked a little sardonic now. 'Up to you, boss.'

Dick Hardy checked in on me fairly often, by phone or by e-mail. I felt a little like a teenager who'd just been given a learner's permit and the keys to Dad's car, and every night Dad checked it over for dings. He went over projections for the third quarter, wanted to make sure they were on target, wanted to see if I could jack them up a bit, wanted to know the status of every major deal. Wanted to make sure I was riding my guys hard enough.

'You can't let up, even for a second,' he said on the phone several times. 'This is it. This is the big time. Everything's riding on this. *Everything*.'

I told him I understood. I told him I appreciated his faith in me, and he wouldn't be disappointed.

I wasn't sure I believed it myself.

I was in the restroom taking a pee when Trevor Allard came in. He nodded at me and went to the urinal at the far end of the row.

He waited for me to talk first, and I waited for him. I was his direct boss now.

I was perfectly willing to be civil to the guy, but I wasn't going to extend myself. That was his job. Let him suck up a little.

We each stared at the walls vacantly, which is what

278

guys do when they urinate. We're animals that way.

When I'd finished, I went to the sink to wash my hands, and after I'd dried them and wadded up the paper towel, Trevor spoke.

'How's it going, Jason?' His voice echoed.

'Good, Trevor,' I said. 'You?'

'Fine.'

I was Jason now, no longer Steadman. That was a start.

He zipped up, washed his hands, dried them. Then he turned to face me. He spoke softly, quickly. 'Brett Gleason went to Corporate Security to ask for copies of the surveillance tapes – the AVI files, actually – for the night and day before his computer got wiped out. And guess what happened to them?'

'Why are we still talking about this?' I said.

'They're gone, Jason. Erased.'

I shrugged. 'I don't know anything about it.'

'Would you like to guess who the last person was to access those files? Just a couple of weeks ago? Whose name do you think was on the log?'

I said nothing.

'A guy in Corporate Security named Kurt Semko. Our pitcher. Your asshole buddy.'

I shrugged, shook my head.

'So you know what it looks like to me? It looks like you're abusing Corporate Security to get revenge on people you don't like. You're using this guy to do your dirty work, Jason.'

'Bullshit. I don't think Kurt was even working here when Brett's computer crashed. And I wouldn't know the first thing about how to wipe out a computer. You're full of it.'

'Yeah, I bet it was really hard to get Kurt in here before he got his own employee badge. If you think you can get away with using Corporate Security as your personal goon squad, you've got your head up your ass.'

'That's ridiculous.'

'A lot of the guys are taken in by you. Your whole Easy Ed act. But I see right through you. Like when I had car trouble two days in a row, made me lose the Pavilion deal. You think I didn't follow up on that? You think I didn't call and apologize and tell them what happened? And you know what they told me?'

I said nothing.

'They said I called them from a golf club. Like I was playing golf, blowing them off. Well, I know someone who's a member at Myopia, and I asked around. And the lady who runs the pro shop told me some guy in a leather Harley jacket came in that morning and asked to use the phone. Right around the time Pavilion got that call. She remembers because he didn't look like a member.'

'Trevor, I don't know what you're talking about.'

'Of course not. What do they call that – plausible deniability? Well, stay tuned, Jason. There's more to come. A lot more.'

38

Kate wanted to celebrate my latest promotion, but this time she wanted to throw a dinner party for the occasion. She'd hired a caterer, the same one who'd catered several of her friends' parties.

I didn't want to celebrate this promotion. The circumstances were too unpleasant. But it seemed important to Kate. I think she wanted to show off to her friends that I was finally a success. So I said okay.

If a caterer had come to our old house for a dinner, she'd have run screaming after seeing our kitchen. But the kitchen in our Hilliard Street house was spacious and newly renovated – not concrete, but French tile countertops and island, fairly modern appliances. The caterer and her all-female staff set to work in the kitchen, preparing the grilled fillet of beef in an herbed crust with chanterelle Madeira sauce and Muscovado glazed carrots.

Or maybe it was grilled beef in a Muscovado sauce and Madeira glazed carrots. Whatever.

Meanwhile, Kate and I were upstairs getting dressed. I'd brought her a half glass of cold white wine. She liked to have a little wine before people came over, and her obstetrician had told her that a little wine was not a problem. After all, he said, look at all those French and Italian women who drink wine throughout their pregnancies. French and Italian kids come out just fine. If you overlook the fact they can't speak English.

She sat on Grammy Spencer's chaise lounge and watched me undress. 'You know, you've got a great body.'

'Are you putting the moves on me, woman?'

'You do. Look at how you've slimmed down. You've got pecs and delts and all that. You're a very sexy guy.'

'Well, thanks.'

'And don't say I look great too. I'm fat. I have fat ankles.'

'Pregnancy becomes you. You're beautiful.' And yes, you have fat ankles now, but it's okay. I was never really an ankle man.

'Are you excited about the baby?' She asked that every forty-eight hours.

'Of course I'm excited.' I'm terrified. I'm dreading it. When the baby was just hypothetical, no one was more enthusiastic than me. But I was the Senior Vice President of Sales of Entronics USA, and in a few months, I'd have a newborn and be totally sleep-deprived, and I didn't know how I'd get through. Or I'd be out of a job, and then what?

'I'm scared,' she said. 'I'm terrified.'

I came up to her and kissed her. 'Sure you are. So am I. It's like you've got this thing growing inside you that's going to take us over when it pops out. Like *Alien*.'

'I wish you hadn't said that.'

'Sorry. Maybe it's like – it's like you're jumping out

282

of a C-141 Starlifter over Iraq. You don't know if your parachute's going to malfunction or if you're going to get shot at on the way down.'

'Yep, that sounds like Kurt,' she said.

I shrugged, embarrassed. 'He's got some great stories. He's done some amazing stuff.'

'Stuff you'd never want to do.'

'That too. And . . . some stuff he shouldn't do.'

'Hmm?'

'He reads people's e-mail, for one thing.'

'Whose? Yours?'

'Gordy's.'

'Fine. Anyway, they say you really shouldn't send anything in an e-mail that you wouldn't put on a post-card. Isn't Corporate Security supposed to monitor e-mail?'

I nodded. 'I guess.'

'He's really loyal to you, Jason. He's a really good friend to you.'

'Maybe too good a friend.'

'What's that supposed to mean? He'd do anything for you.'

I was quiet for several seconds. *Yeah, 'anything' is right.* The 'backgrounders' – the inside information he'd gotten me on Brian Borque of Lockwood Hotels and on Jim Letasky – that was borderline acceptable, as far as I was concerned. It made me uncomfortable. But what he'd done to all the Panasonic monitors: That was some kind of lunacy. A felony, probably, given the value of the equipment he'd destroyed. But worse, it was evidence of a strange violent streak, a brazenness. He was dangerous.

And what about Gordy's drunken tirade? Gordy

had asked Kurt to get him the Talisker bottle. Did Kurt spike it with something?

That broke dick's not going to get away with screwing you over again, he'd said.

Well, Kurt was right. That was the end of Gordy.

Kurt had boosted me up the corporate ladder, a fact that I never wanted to tell Kate. But now he was out of control. He had to be stopped.

Trevor was digging, and in time he'd unearth proof that Kurt had done some of these things. And I'd be implicated too. I'd go down. It would end my career.

And that I couldn't afford. Not with this house, this mortgage, car payments, and a baby on the way.

I'd made a terrible mistake getting him a job in the first place. Now I'd have to make things right. I'd have to talk to Dennis Scanlon, Kurt's boss, and lay it all out.

Kurt had to be fired. There really was no choice.

I took a deep breath, weighing how much to tell Kate.

But then she cocked her head. 'I think I hear the doorbell. Can you go down and let them in?'

39

In the morning I flew to Chicago with one of our junior sales reps, Wayne Fallon, for a quick morning meeting to try to nail down the big hospital contract. I met in a conference room of Chicago Presbyterian with the Assistant Vice President for Communications, a guy named Barry Ulasewicz. He was a top administrator who was in charge of the hospital's media services – everything from photography to satellite teleconferencing to their TV studio. We'd been going back and forth on prices and delivery dates for months now. He wanted fifty-inch plasmas for their one hundred operating rooms, plasmas and projectors for more than a hundred conference rooms, and a bunch more for their waiting rooms and lobbies. Wayne was there to observe, mostly, and he watched the jousting match between me and Ulasewicz with fascination.

I didn't like the guy, but that wasn't important. Just so long as he liked me. And he seemed to. We started at ten in the morning and met with a parade of administrators and techies. He even brought in the CEO of the hospital for a grip-and-grin.

Around one in the afternoon, when I was feeling squeezed out like a lemon and was in desperate need of lunch and a caffeine fix, Ulasewicz suddenly pulled out a proposal he'd gotten from Royal Meister that was identical in every way except for the prices, which were about ten percent lower. I'd given him the lowest price I could get away with – really cut to the bone – and this pissed me off. He yanked the RFP out with a theatrical flourish, like some cheesy actor in a bad dinner theater doing Hercule Poirot or something.

And he expected me to cave. Because I'd put in months and months, and flown to Chicago, and I thought it was a lock. I'd almost caught the mechanical bunny rabbit. Ulasewicz figured that at this point I'd do anything to save the deal.

But he didn't realize that I had flow. I once read an article on the Internet by some guy with an unpronounceable name about something he called 'flow.' It's the way a painter gets so absorbed in his canvas that he loses track of time. The way a musician disappears into the piece she's playing. Happens to athletes and surgeons and chess players. You're in this state of ecstasy where everything comes together, you've got the juice, you're in the zone. The good neurotransmitters are flooding your synapses.

That's what had happened to me. I was in the zone. I had flow.

And I was doing it on my own, without Kurt's poisoned candy.

I calmly looked over the Royal Meister proposal. It was full of tangled and hidden clauses, all kinds of smoke and mirrors. The delivery dates were estimates. The prices could change due to fluctuations in the euro. I don't know who wrote this contract, but it was brilliant.

I pointed this out to Ulasewicz, and he began to argue.

And then I stood up, shook his hand, and packed up my leather portfolio.

'Barry,' I said, 'we're not going to waste any more of your time. I see where this is headed. Obviously you prefer the uncertainty of Meister's terms, and you don't mind their higher failure rate. You don't mind the fact that you'll probably end up paying more for an inferior product that you won't get when you want it and that won't get replaced if anything goes wrong. And that's okay. So I want to thank you for considering Entronics, and I wish you the best of luck.'

And I picked up our contracts and left the room. I was able to sneak a glimpse of Barry Ulasewicz's stunned expression, which almost made it all worth it. Wayne grabbed me in the elevator, panic-stricken, and said, 'We just lost it. We just lost the deal, Jason. Don't you think you should have negotiated? That's what he wanted to do, I think.'

I shook my head. 'Just be patient,' I said.

By the time we got down to the parking garage, my cell phone was ringing. I looked at Wayne and smiled. His look of panic had changed to wide-eyed admiration.

I flew back home with executed copies of the agreement.

40

I went straight from the airport to the office.

There was a Hardygram waiting for me in my e-mail – 'Great job in Chicago!' Dick Hardy wrote. Joan Tureck congratulated me, too, which was gracious of her, considering that I'd outsold her.

A little *too* gracious, I thought. The graciousness of a victor, maybe.

I considered, then rejected, e-mailing Dennis Scanlon. I knew Kurt was able to read my e-mail and everyone else's. I didn't want to take that chance. Instead, I called Scanlon. Got him on the second try. I asked him to come to my office.

Dennis Scanlon always reminded me of Mr. Toad of Toad Hall. His shirt and tie were so tight around his neck that I worried he was going to lose circulation and pass out in front of me. He was sweaty and eager to please and had a funny sort of speech impediment.

I told him I wanted to speak in absolute confidence, and then I told him that I had some concerns about one of his employees, Kurt Semko.

'But – weren't you the one who recommended him?' he said.

'I think frankly I may have made a mistake,' I said. 'I didn't know him well enough.'

He ran a hand over his damp face. 'Can you give me any specifics? As to your concerns, I mean. Has he been causing problems of any sort?'

I folded my hands and hunched forward. 'I've been hearing complaints about Kurt from some of my employees. Little pranks he's pulled. Harassment.'

'Pranks? Not good-natured pranks, I'm assuming.'

'Bad stuff. Destructive.'

'Can you give me specifics?'

I could give him all sorts of specifics. Many of them just allegations. But did I really want Scanlon investigating whether Kurt had tampered with Brett Gleason's computer? How far did I want to go with this? Should I tell Scanlon about all the e-mails Kurt had accessed?

No. Any or all of it could come back to bite me in the ass. Kurt would fight it. Might even say that I'd asked him to get me information – after all, it only benefited me, not him. I couldn't take that chance.

'I don't know all the details,' I said. 'But it's my strong feeling – and, again, it's of the utmost importance that this conversation remain strictly confidential – that Kurt should be let go.'

Scanlon nodded for a long time. 'Are you willing to file a complaint report?'

I hesitated, but only for a second. 'Not with my name on it, no. I think that would get too complicated. Especially given the fact that I mistakenly recommended him in the first place.'

He nodded some more. 'I can't just let him go for no reason. You know that. You've got to paper the file. Would any of your employees be willing to file complaints with me, then?'

'I'd rather not ask them. Plus, I don't think anyone would want to stick their necks out. You understand, I'm sure.'

'You sound like you know something.'

'I've heard things, yes.'

'He says you and he are good friends.'

'It's complicated.'

'Listen, Jason. Kurt is one of the best hires I've ever made. The fellow can do anything.'

'I understand.'

'I don't want to lose him. But I also don't want any of my employees causing trouble up here. So I'll look into this.'

'That's all I ask,' I said.

I called Kate at work and was told she'd taken the day off. I called her at home, and woke her up.

'You still have cramps?' I said.

'Yeah. I thought I should stay home.'

'What did DiMarco say?'

'Just lie down until they pass.'

'Is it – anything? Anything serious?'

'No,' she said. 'He says it's normal. Just take it easy.'

'Good idea. I wanted to remind you that I have a business dinner tonight.'

'Oh, right. The hospital people?'

'Airport. Atlanta airport. But whatever.'

'Atlanta airport in Boston? I don't understand.'

'It's boring,' I said. 'Trade show.'

It was the big Information Display trade show at the Bayside Expo Center. I didn't have to work the show, thank God – I'm sure it would have been a regular laff riot – but some of my guys did. When I heard the Atlanta folks were going to be in town for the Information Display show, I invited them all out for dinner, told them it would be a great opportunity to 'celebrate' our agreement. Translation: I wanted to try to nail down the huge Atlanta airport deal.

A man can hope.

'Where are you taking them?'

'I don't know the name of it. Some fancy restaurant in the South End that Franny likes. But if you need to reach me, I'll have my cell with me.'

'I'm not going to bother you.'

'In case there's a problem. Don't hesitate, babe.'

I hung up the phone, and then I noticed that Kurt was standing in the doorway to my office.

'Missed you at the gym this morning,' Kurt said.

'Had to fly to Chicago early.'

'So, you were talking to Scanlon.'

I nodded. 'A background check that HR doesn't seem to be able to do.'

'You can always ask me, you know.'

'Thought it might be better to separate the business from the personal.'

'I think that's a good idea,' he said, closing the door. 'So if you have a problem with my work, you should take it up with me. Not with my boss.'

I swallowed. 'I don't have a problem with your work.'

'Really? Then why're you trying to get me fired?'

I looked at him for a few seconds. 'What makes you say that?'

He advanced into my office. Stood directly in front of my desk. 'My suggestion to you – my *strong feeling*' – his eyebrows shot up, and he began speaking archly – 'and, again, it's of the *utmost importance that this conversation remain strictly confidential . . .*' He smiled. '. . . Is that if you have issues with me, you take them up with me. *Mano a mano*. But don't sneak around. Don't go behind my back. Because I will find out. And you will regret it.' His stare was icy. 'Are we clear?'

I was freaked out: He knew what I'd said to Scanlon, word for word.

I didn't know how, but it had to be some surveillance device he'd placed in my office. He sure had the technology.

Now I wondered what else he'd heard me say in the office. I'd been concerned about Scanlon being indiscreet, saying something to Kurt. But I realized that Kurt didn't need to hear it secondhand.

And now that he knew I was trying to have him terminated, there was going to be trouble between us. Things could never go back to the way they used to be.

In the car on the way to South End, my phone rang. I was back to my bad habits, using the cell phone in the car, but I had no choice. I had to be reachable at all times.

It was Dick Hardy. 'What's your take on the Atlanta airport?' he said.

'I'm feeling good about it.'

'Then *I'm* feeling good about it. If this comes through, this may do it. This may save the division.'

292

'All I can do is my best.'

'I'm counting on it, Jason. Everything's riding on this. Everything.'

I handed my keys to the valet and entered the restaurant with a nonchalant grin plastered on my face. Unfortunately, it was one of those restaurants with an open kitchen, which always made me nervous, maybe because I was subconsciously afraid I'd have to do the dishes after we ate.

Jim Letasky was already at the table, studying a file. We were fifteen minutes early. I'd invited Jim Letasky to join me at dinner. I wanted to bring him in on the biggest deal I had going. I needed his wattage. He'd gotten us a table far away from other people, and he'd tipped the waiter to leave us alone as much as possible, because this was a business dinner.

I had an ulterior motive, too, but he was a smart fellow, and he'd figured it out.

'I know why you wanted me here,' he said.

'Besides the fact that you're great at what you do?'

'Because you're afraid that our main competition is NEC.'

'Who, me?'

'I've just spent nine years telling the world how much better NEC's products are than anyone else's, and now –'

'Now you've found God.'

'I feel bad about it, you know.'

'Not too bad, I hope.'

'Not *too* bad. It is war, after all.'

'That's the attitude.' I looked over the wine list, trying to figure out which wines to order. My Queeg Memo had instructed all Entronics salespeople to make sure they always ordered the wine at a customer dinner and not leave it to the customer.

'But listen, Jason. I think you're wrong about NEC.'

'Don't tell me we're going head-to-head with Royal Meister again?'

He shook his head, squeezed lime into his Pellegrino water. 'I dug deep into the Hartsfield-Jackson Atlanta International Airport website. There's a company called AirView Systems, based in Atlanta.'

I nodded. 'I met the CFO at TechComm. Guy named Steve Bingham.' I remembered the silver anchorman hair, the deep-set eyes.

'Biggest provider of flight information display systems. They put in the system for Atlanta last time. So my big question is, how come the airport isn't going with them again? Why change horses in midstream?'

'Maybe that horse was too expensive.'

'AirView just sold them a bunch of portable LED signs.'

'News to me. All I know is, they've been negotiating hard.'

'You've been negotiating directly with Duffy, right?'

'You do your homework,' I said. Tom Duffy was the Aviation General Manager of the airport. Mister Big. Lorna Evers, our other dinner guest, was the Deputy Procurement Officer for the City of Atlanta in the Aviation Division.

'The workday starts the night before.'

I smiled. 'Duffy's the decision maker. Lorna I've never met, but she's basically a rubber stamp.'

'They're not just in this for a free dinner, right?'

'I think they want to close the deal.'

'I'm not so sure.'

'The power of negative thinking,' I said, and then I saw our two dinner guests enter the restaurant. 'Let's knock 'em dead, Letasky.'

Lorna Evers was a buxom blonde of that indeterminate age that could have been early fifties or maybe hard-living forties. She'd also obviously had work done: Her eyes had a slight Asian tilt to them. She had big bee-stung, cosmetically enhanced lips – trout pout, I think it's called. Her face was a deeply tanned mask. When she smiled, only her overstuffed lips moved. Someone had overdone the Botox and the collagen injections.

'So you're the new Gordy,' she said, adjusting the gold silk scarf around her neck.

'You could say that.'

'Don't let this man have any Scotch,' she said, and she threw back her head and gave a raucous, open-mouthed laugh. Her eyes didn't move.

Tom Duffy was an affable, moon-faced, burly man with a double chin and a gray crew cut. He wore a bow tie and a loose navy blazer. He laughed quietly.

'Nice to meet you,' she said, extending a hand. Her fingernails were pink and dangerously long. 'So there's been a hell of a lot of turnover at Entronics, I hear.'

'I just joined Entronics from NEC,' Letasky said. 'I figured it was time to join the championship team.'

Score one for Letasky. Give this man a raise.

'I'm talking about layoffs,' she said, settling into her chair. I held it for her. Not that I'm such a gentleman, but I wanted to make sure she sat so that she and Duffy couldn't make eye contact without our seeing it. A basic sales meeting trick. Duffy sat where we wanted him to as well. 'You guys going to be there next year?'

'Entronics was founded in 1902,' I said. 'Back when it was called Osaka Telephone and Telegraph. I think it'll be around long after we're gone.'

'Is it true you guys had a suicide there not too long ago?'

'A tragedy,' I said. 'Phil Rifkin was one of our finest employees.'

'Entronics must be a stressful place to work,' she said.

'Not at all,' I lied. 'You just never can know what's going on in someone's personal life.'

'Well, I'll tell you what's going on in *my* personal life,' said Lorna. 'Thirst. I need a glass of wine.'

'Let's order,' I said, reaching for the long leather wine list.

But Lorna was quicker. She grabbed the menu – there was only one, unfortunately – and flipped it open.

'Warm evening like this, I like to get a nice crisp white,' Duffy said.

Lorna was peering at the list through black reading glasses. 'And I was thinking of a Pauillac. How about the Lafite Rothschild?'

I almost gulped. That was four hundred dollars a bottle, and this woman looked like she was a serious wine guzzler.

'Great idea,' Letasky said, giving me a quick look that said, I think, that for the millions we're going to make on this deal, forget about the wine bill.

Lorna waved the waiter over and ordered the Pauillac and an expensive Montrachet for Duffy and a couple of bottles of Pellegrino for the table.

'So, Atlanta airport is one of the busiest in the country,' Letasky said.

'The busiest in the world, in fact,' Duffy said.

'Not O'Hare?'

'Nope. And we've got the flight records to prove it. We had thirteen thousand more flights than O'Hare this year, January to June. We serve three million more passengers.'

Lorna's cell rang, and she picked it up and began talking loudly. A waiter came over and whispered in her ear, and she glared at him, then snapped it closed with visible annoyance.

'They insist all guests turn off their phones,' she announced. 'As if anyone can hear a cell phone ring in this place. I'm going positively *deaf*.'

I reached down and turned mine off, trying to be subtle about it.

After dinner – Lorna ordered a lobster dish with truffles, the most expensive thing on the menu, of course, and Duffy ordered the Statler chicken – I excused myself to go to the john.

Letasky joined me in there a minute or so later.

'At the risk of stating the obvious,' he said, standing at the other urinal, 'I think Tom Duffy has been deballed.'

'You know what a "tell" is in poker?'

'Sure. Why?'

'People take classes in how to read facial micro-expressions,' I said. 'And you know what?'

'What?'

'You don't need any of that junk to see that every move she makes, Duffy mirrors. She's the decision maker. Not Duffy.'

'You think they're sleeping together or something?'

'No way. I can tell.'

'I've seen stranger couples. This is not looking good, this dinner.'

'We're getting jerked around,' I said. 'This woman changes the whole equation, damn it. I had Duffy hooked until she showed up.'

'You think she has another candidate?'

'I'll tell you this much – she didn't listen to a word I said.'

'She nodded a lot when you were talking.'

'Women do that. They nod to show they're listening. It doesn't mean anything.'

'You're right. You think it's time for a little brinksmanship?' I'd told him about Chicago.

'No,' I said. 'She's not ours. We get up from the table, and the deal goes to Hitachi or whatever.'

'AirView Systems.'

The restroom door opened, and Duffy entered.

'All yours,' I said, going to the sink.

By the time dinner was over, the conversation had rambled everywhere but flight information display systems. We'd gone through three bottles of the Pauillac, and Lorna had had a great time. I silently cursed her and her immobile face.

We said good night, and I got my car from the valet and popped my phone into the hands-free cradle and turned it on.

There were six voice mail messages.

Kate's voice was weak. 'Jason, I'm – I'm bleeding.'

I went cold all over.

The next four messages were from Kate, too. She

was sounding weaker and more desperate. There was a lot of blood, she said. She needed help.

'Where are you?' she said. 'Will you call me back? Please?'

The sixth message was a male voice. Kurt's.

'Jason,' he said. 'I'm with Kate at the Children's Hospital emergency room. Just drove her over here. Call me on my cell. Or just get over here. Now.'

41

I rushed into the emergency room, saw Kurt sitting in the waiting room, his face stony.

'Where is she?' I said.

'Trauma room.' He pointed, off there somewhere. 'She's okay. Lost a lot of blood.'

The big dinner was sitting heavy in my stomach. The wooziness from all the wine was gone, replaced by fear and adrenaline.

'Did we lose the baby?' I couldn't believe I was saying the words.

He shook his head. 'Talk to the nurse. I think it's okay.'

'Thank God.'

His eyes were fierce. 'Why the hell didn't you tell her where you were?'

'I –' I began. What, I didn't know the name of the restaurant? 'She has my cell phone number.'

'Yeah, and you should have left it on. You've got a pregnant wife, for Christ's sake. You're out at dinner and you turn off your phone because you don't want to screw up a *sale*? That's messed up, man.' He shook his head.

I felt a rush of contradictory emotions. Gratitude

that he'd brought her here. Anger at his indignation – where did he get off being so righteous? Massive guilt. Relief that Kate was okay. Relief that we hadn't lost the baby. 'I had to turn it off.'

'You're lucky I was there.'

'She called you?'

'I called the house. Good thing too.'

'Mr. Steadman?' An ER nurse approached Kurt. She wore blue scrubs, had silver hair, clear blue eyes. She looked to be in her late fifties and had a reassuring air of authority. 'Your wife is fine. She came in anemic, but we're replacing the lost blood.'

'I'm the husband,' I said.

'Oh,' the nurse said, turning to me. 'Sorry. She's, what, sixteen weeks pregnant?'

'Right.' I noticed she hadn't used the past tense. She *is* pregnant. Not *was*.

'Would you prefer to speak in private, Mr. Steadman?'

'No, it's all right.' I glanced at Kurt. 'He's a friend.'

'Okay. She has something called placenta previa, where the placenta covers the cervix. Do you need me to explain?' She spoke in a calm, almost hypnotic voice. She had a working-class Boston accent, sounded like my mom.

'I think I get it,' I said.

'Her pregnancy is considered high-risk. She's going to have to stay in the hospital for a couple of days, in the high-risk maternity ward, then stay in bed for the remainder of the pregnancy. On bed rest. That means lying on her side as much as possible, using bedpans. After a while she'll be able to sit up and take the occasional car ride. But she can't exert herself. There's a risk of preterm delivery. At this stage of the pregnancy, the fetus wouldn't make it.'

'What's the risk to my wife?'

'Only ten percent of women diagnosed with placenta previa still have it when they deliver. There's a pretty good chance the placenta will start to move away from the cervix on its own. She should be fine.' The nurse crossed her fingers.

The fetus. It was a baby, dammit. 'How's the baby?'

'The fetal heartbeat is normal. That means the fetus wasn't distressed by all the loss of blood.'

I nodded.

'Did she have any cramping before this? Any bleeding?'

'I don't think there was any bleeding. But she had cramps.'

'Did she see her obstetrician?'

'He just told her to take it easy.'

'I see. When did you last have sexual intercourse?'

It's stupid, but I became aware of Kurt's eyes on me. Of all the ridiculous things to get defensive about at a time like this. 'A while,' I said. 'Probably a month. Can I see her?'

Kurt stayed out in the waiting room while I went in to see Kate.

She looked pale, circles under her eyes. Looked sad. She was hooked up to a couple of IVs, one with blood and one with clear fluid, and a cardiac monitor and a fetal monitor.

'Baby,' I said. I put a hand on her forehead, stroked her face, her hair. 'How are you feeling?'

'Tired. I almost passed out. There was blood every-

302

where.'

I nodded. 'They said you're going to be okay. The baby's going to be okay.'

'There was a surgeon in here who said I have to stay here for a while.'

'Just a couple of days.'

'I'm going to have to stay in bed until I deliver.'

'I know. But you're okay, and the baby's okay.'

'I guess that means I'm taking an early pregnancy leave.'

'The foundation will get by without you.'

'That's what I'm afraid of.' She smiled a little, an attempt at a joke.

'I'm sorry I had my cell phone turned off. The restaurant made me do it, but I should have left it on anyway. Or called you with the number of the restaurant.'

'It's okay. I called Claudia, but she's in New York, and I called Sally and Amy, and I couldn't reach either one of them, and then I was about to call an ambulance, but then Kurt called, thank God.'

'Thank God.'

'What a good friend that guy is, huh?'

No better friend, he'd said. *No* worse enemy.

I nodded but didn't reply.

42

I spent the night in Kate's hospital room on a couch. In the morning, aching all over and exhausted, I drove home, retrieved some things she wanted, and brought them to the hospital. Not until noon did I get to work.

I found a message on my cell phone from Jim Letasky, but when I called him back, there was no answer on his cell or at his office. I called Festino and asked him to locate Letasky for me. Festino said Letasky was out of the building at a presentation but wanted to talk to me about something important.

When I got into the office, I checked my e-mail while listening to my voice mail on speaker, and I was surprised to hear a message from Kurt.

'Hey,' he said. 'Let me know the latest on Kate, man, okay?'

Now I felt really weird, totally conflicted, about Kurt. I owed him in a big way for taking Kate to the hospital, but that didn't change how I felt about him, fundamentally, or what I knew I had to do. He had to leave the company. But I was beginning to feel that he deserved better than my going behind his back again to get him fired. At the very least, he deserved to hear it from me face-to-face. Scanlon hadn't called back, and I doubt he'd seriously 'looked into' firing Kurt.

So I decided to tell Kurt, man-to-man, that he had to leave Entronics. I'd help him find a good job somewhere else. But his career at Entronics was over.

As I picked up the phone to call Kurt, the phone rang.

'How's she doing?' Kurt said.

'Better. Still on fluids.'

'I shouldn't have yelled at you about not answering your cell,' he said.

'No, you're right. I shouldn't have turned it off. Screw protocol. And Kurt – I never thanked you.'

'No need.'

'Well, thanks, man. I owe you one.'

'You keeping score?'

Every chance I got I went on the Internet and researched placenta previa. Some of the websites made it seem like not a big deal. Some of them made it sound awfully dire. I didn't know which one to believe.

Letasky appeared in my doorway, dressed in a suit and tie.

'You have your browser open?'

'Yeah?'

'Go to the City of Atlanta website.'

I typed in the web address.

'Now go to Departments, and then Procurement. Got it?'

'What is it, Jim? You gonna torture me?'

'No, I want you to see it. You see "Aviation RFPs/Bids"?'

It came up on the screen: The deal I once thought was ours. In red letters it said APPARENT LOW BIDDER

305

AirView Systems Corporation and Contract Award Pending. The contact name was Lorna Evers.

My stomach sank. 'Crap. You mean those bastards let us take them to dinner, and all the while this was up on their website?'

'Just appeared this morning.'

I sank down in my chair. 'Shit. We needed this. I thought we had it.'

'You didn't have a chance,' Letasky said. 'We didn't have a chance. The fix was in.'

The fix was in. Every salesman's favorite complaint. That along with *They never return my calls.* 'You have no idea how badly we needed this. So is this it? The deal's done?'

'Officially and formally it's tentative. "Under consideration," meaning it just requires sign-off at the highest levels. But yeah, it looks like it's done.'

'We tried,' I said. 'Tried our best.'

'Not always good enough,' Letasky said.

An e-mail popped up in my in-box from Dick Hardy. The subject line was: ATLANTA. The message contained one word: 'Well?'

I e-mailed back, 'Still working it. Not optimistic.'

On his way out of the office, Letasky stopped for a few seconds and turned back. 'Oh, listen. Trevor invited me to play basketball with him on Thursday nights, and if Gail lets me, I'll probably do it.'

'Okay,' I said, not sure what he was getting at.

'I just wanted you to know. It's not like I'm choosing up sides or anything.'

'Sides? Trevor's my second-line manager. We're not on opposite sides.'

'Okay.' Letasky nodded, humoring me. 'It's just

that – well, you know, maybe it's none of my business, and maybe I should keep my mouth shut, being new and all. But, well, did anyone ever tell you that Trevor sometimes . . . says stuff about you?'

'I'm sorry to hear that.'

'Not always very nice. Kinda bad-mouths you, sometimes. He says you can be ruthless – that you do stuff to your rivals.'

I shook my head, smiled sadly.

'I just thought you should know,' he said.

'Well, that's too bad. But I appreciate your telling me.'

After Letasky had left, I stared for a long time at the City of Atlanta website. Then I picked up the phone and called Kurt.

'I need your help,' I said. *Dear God,* I thought, *now you're really mucking things up.* 'Just one more time.'

43

At the hospital that night we got the word that Kate was okay to go home in the morning. Which worked for me, because I was in serious need of a chiropractor after spending the nights on the soft couch in her room. I told Kate I wanted to hire a private nurse to help her out at home, since she was supposed to get out of bed as little as possible, but she told me I was being ridiculous, she didn't need a nurse.

She looked at me out of the corner of her eye. 'Susie wants to visit. You know, make sure I'm okay.'

I nodded. 'Good. I don't want you home alone.'

'She's flying over from Nantucket.' Craig and Susie had taken a house in Nantucket for August and September, as usual.

'It'll be nice to see Susie and Ethan again,' I said. I'd enjoy seeing Ethan, in fact. 'Craig, not so much.' Christ, I thought, wasn't there some legal limit on the number of times I had to see Craig?

'Craig isn't coming. He's back in L.A. She's bringing Ethan. It really would be good for Ethan to spend more time with you.'

'It would be good for Ethan to be taken away from them and placed in foster care.'

'Jason.'

'Anyway, I don't have much time to hang out with him, you know that.'

'I know.'

'Well, I'm glad she's coming.' Without Craig.

Kurt called me on my cell phone as I was drifting off to sleep.

'How long does this trade show go on?' he asked.

'The one at Bayside?'

'Right. The one your friends from Atlanta are attending.'

'Two more days. Why?'

'I came across something interesting. Called in some favors with an SF guy in Marietta, Georgia, who knows people in Atlanta.'

'Interesting how?'

'Let's talk in the morning when I have something more concrete.'

In the morning, they did an amnio on Kate to make sure everything was okay. The nurse asked us if we wanted to know the sex of the baby, and Kate quickly said no, so the nurse said they'd send the results without mentioning sex.

Then I signed Kate out of the hospital, and one of the nurses brought her down to the main entrance in a wheelchair and I drove her home. I skipped my morning workout and instead spent a few hours being a good husband, getting her set up in bed with a commode right next to her so she wouldn't have to get up to relieve herself. I made sure the phone and the TV remote were within reach on the bedside table. I set up one of those Airport gizmos, which wasn't as hard as I feared, so she could easily use her laptop in bed, lying on her side. I put a tall stack of books on the table too. For Christmas last year I'd bought her a hardcover set of Russian novels in a 'hot new translation,' as Kate put it. *Anna Karenina* and *The Brothers Karamazov* and *Crime and Punishment* and *The Double* and *The Gambler,* and a bunch more. One of them had been an Oprah Book Club selection. Her idea, obviously; to me, that's worse than getting socks for Christmas. She often talked about how she wished she had time to read all of Dostoyevsky. Now was her chance. She'd grabbed *The Brothers Karamazov* greedily and dived right in.

I arrived at the office late, and among my many voice-mail messages was one from Kurt inviting me to lunch. I called him back and said, 'Thanks, man, but I'm just going to grab a sandwich and work at my desk. You know, the old crumbs-in-the-keyboard –'

'I've made reservations at a really nice Japanese restaurant in Boston,' Kurt interrupted. 'One o'clock.'

I didn't even know Kurt liked Japanese food, and I didn't quite get his insistence. 'Another time would be great.'

'This is not optional,' Kurt said. 'We've had a lucky break. Meet me at Kansai at one.'

'I'll give you a ride.'

'That's okay. I'm in the city already. Took the morning off work.'

I'd worked for a Japanese-owned company for years, but I'd never really gotten into Japanese food. Too healthy, maybe. Too minimalist.

'So what's this about?' I said.

'You'll see. Are you hungry?'

310

'Not so much.'

'Me either. No worries.'

We were shown to a low black-lacquered table where we had to remove our shoes and sit on tatami mats on the floor. There was a hot plate on the table with a big bowl on it boiling away, a big hunk of kelp floating in some murky water.

'Need to use the bathroom?' he said.

'No, thanks, Dad.'

'Why don't you anyway?'

'This going to be a long lunch?'

'Men's room is down the hall on the left. But you might want to keep going down the row to the last booth on your right.'

'And?'

'Go ahead.'

I shrugged and went down the hall to the last booth on the right. A rice-paper screen provided privacy, but by shifting over a few inches I was able to see in at an angle.

What I saw in there almost took the top of my head off.

Lorna Evers, the Deputy Procurement Officer for the City of Atlanta, was enjoying a romantic luncheon with a man with silver anchorman hair and deep-set eyes. Steve Bingham, the CFO of AirView Systems.

The company that had just won the Atlanta airport contract that we should have gotten.

They were sitting next to each other on one side of the table, sucking face, and Lorna's hand was expertly kneading the man's crotch. On the table in front of them, untouched, was a platter of paper-thin, blood-red slices of raw beef.

It took a lot of willpower to keep from knocking over the shoji screen and telling Lorna Evers what I thought of her procurement process. I went back to our table.

Kurt watched me approach, eyebrows raised.

'How'd you know?' I asked, stony.

'Told you, I know a guy in Marietta. Who knows a P.I. in Atlanta. Who deals a lot with the City of Atlanta. So I did a little prep work in Lorna's hotel room.'

'God*dammit*. She's the goddamned deputy procurement officer. The city's got to have all kinds of laws against this.'

'Code of ethics, sections 2-812 and 2-813,' Kurt said. 'Thought you'd want to know some specifics. Miss Lorna can not only lose her job but also get locked up for six months. I also don't think her husband would be too happy about it.'

'She's married?'

'So is Steve Bingham. Steve has five kids too.'

I stood up. 'Excuse me. I want to say hi to Lorna.'

I made my way back to her booth and barged right in to the gap between the rice-paper screens. The two were going at it hot and heavy, and they looked up, embarrassed.

'Oh, hey, Lorna,' I said. 'Great place, huh?'

'J-Jason?'

'I hear the hand roll's excellent.'

'You – what are you – ?'

'Aren't you going to introduce me to your friend?' I said. 'Steve, right? Steve Bingham, from AirView? I think we met at TechComm.'

Steve Bingham's deep crimson blush contrasted interestingly with his silver hair. He crossed his legs to

312

conceal the obvious bulge in his trousers. 'We've met?' he said, and cleared his throat.

'TechComm can be a zoo,' I said. 'You meet so many people. But you two are obviously well acquainted.'

'Jason –' Lorna said in a pleading tone.

'Awful sorry to interrupt,' I said. 'I'll call you on your cell later on.' And I gave her a little wink.

As it turned out, I didn't have to call Lorna. She called me an hour or so later. She'd found some 'discrepancies' in AirView's bid, she said, and had decided to award the contract to me.

I should have been elated, but instead I felt sullied. This was not how I'd hoped to win the biggest deal in my career.

The Hardygram came a few minutes after I e-mailed him the good news, sent from his BlackBerry. In all caps, he wrote:

YOU DID IT!

He called shortly thereafter, almost giddy with excitement, to tell me that he was almost certain I'd saved our division from the chopping block.

'Great,' I said. 'I'm glad.'

'Boy, are you low-key about this,' Hardy said, his voice booming. 'You're a modest fellow, aren't you?'

'Sometimes,' I said.

'Well, the press release is going out over the Internet any minute now. Hedge fund managers are starting to look at Entronics stock differently now. They know what a big deal this is. Even if you don't.'

I stopped home to change and check on Kate. She was lying on her side in bed, tapping away on her laptop.

313

She was researching placenta previa, too, but apparently she'd only found the scary websites. I told her about the less scary ones, and how the nurse had said that if she took it easy everything would probably be okay.

She nodded, considering. 'I'm not worried,' she said. 'You're right. If you go by the odds, I'll be fine.' She placed a hand on her belly. 'And baby'll be fine too.'

'Right,' I said. I tried to sound upbeat and authoritative.

'So I'm not going to worry about it.'

'Exactly.'

'Worrying won't do me any good.'

'Right.'

'Right.' She took a breath. 'This morning I e-mailed some JPEGs of Marie Bastien's work to the director of the Franz Koerner Gallery in New York.'

It took me a minute to remember who Marie Bastien was. 'The quilts,' I said.

'The director's a friend of Claudia's.'

'Convenient.'

'Yeah, well, if you've got the connections, use them, I figure. I'm not going to say a word to Marie, of course. But if they're interested, this could be just the breakthrough she needs. You look bored.'

'I'm not bored.'

'I didn't ask you about your day. I'm sorry. How was your day?'

I told her that I'd just probably saved the division by winning the Atlanta airport contract, but I didn't tell her how. She responded with a pretty convincing imitation of enthusiasm. Then she said, 'The cable's not working.'

'That's a bummer. Did you call the cable company?'

'Obviously,' she said, peevishly. 'They said we have a signal. Which is not true. They said if we want the box replaced, they can get someone out here in a couple of days. I really don't want to wait. I'm under house arrest here.'

'Well, at least you've got the Internet.' We had high-speed DSL through the phone company.

'I know. But I want to watch TV. Is that so much to ask? Can you *please* take a look at the cable?'

'Kate, I have no idea how to fix a cable box.'

'It might just be the wiring.'

'I'm not a cable guy. It all looks like a bowl of spaghetti back there to me.' I paused a second and couldn't resist adding, 'Why don't you call Kurt? He can fix anything.'

'Good idea,' she said, not getting my little dig. Or maybe she did and she didn't want to 'dignify it,' as she liked to say. Not that my digs ever needed dignifying. She turned back to her laptop. 'You know that actress who was in the movie we saw last night?' She now had two accounts with an Internet movie-rental company so she could rent twelve DVDs at a time. She'd been renting a lot of indie films. I believe they all starred Parker Posey. 'Did you know she was in *Fast Times at Ridgemont High*?'

'News to me.'

'And did you know the director grew up in Malden? He used to write for *Major Dad*.'

'I think maybe you've been spending too much time on the Internet,' I said. I noticed that her bookmark in *The Brothers Karamazov* was still only about a milli-meter of the way into the book. 'How's the Brothers K?

315

A real page-turner, I see. Can't put it down if you don't pick it up.'

'That's the thing about bed rest,' she said. 'You have all the time in the world, but you lose the ability to concentrate. So I just go on the Internet and look something up, and that leads to something else and something else, and I just click and click and click and pretty soon I'm lost in cyberspace. I thought you have a game tonight.'

'I do, but I'm staying here with you.'

'For what? Don't be silly. If I need to reach you, I know how. Just keep your cell on this time.'

Kurt was really pitching lights-out that night, as the radio announcers say. But what was really amazing was how many long balls Trevor hit. He was good, and he usually hit a home run in each game. This evening, though, every time he stepped up to the plate, the balls just exploded off his bat, each flying easily three hundred feet. Trevor himself seemed amazed at how well he was playing. I figured his confidence was stoked by the possibility of bringing me down. He was playing better than Kurt.

The Metadyne guys weren't great, weren't terrible. This was a company that made testing equipment for semiconductor chips, which is as exciting as it sounds, so softball was the high point of their week, but they weren't enjoying this game.

In the fourth inning, Trevor slugged another one, and his bat went flying out of his hands, slamming against the dirt with a loud metallic ping, and then something bizarre happened.

The end of his bat had popped off. The end cap had

separated from the barrel and rolled a good distance away into the infield. A bunch of the players laughed, even Trevor. The ball was gone. One of the outfielders gamely gave chase. Another one of the Metadyne players picked up the end cap as Trevor ran the bases.

He looked at it curiously, weighed it in his hand. 'Man,' he said. 'Heavy. Look at this!'

He took it over to another one of the Metadyne players, who I remembered was an electrical engineer. The engineer weighed it in his palm just like the other guy had done. 'Oh, man, someone put, like, lead fishing weights and hot melt inside this cap. Unbelievable.' Then he walked over to the decapitated metal bat and picked it up. He looked inside, then waved some of his teammates over.

'Hey,' one of them shouted. 'This bat is juiced!'

Trevor, running triumphantly home, nowhere near out of breath, looked to see what the commotion was.

'You doctored the bat,' another one of the Metadyne guys shouted.

'What?' Trevor said, loping over to where they were all inspecting his bat.

Our own team had left the benches to see what the fuss was about.

'The inside of this bat's been machined, or lathed, or something,' the engineer was saying. 'Like maybe with one of those Dremel tools. You can even see the shavings – graphite or resin, I think. And check out this lead tape inside the end of it.'

'Hey, I didn't do that!' Trevor protested. 'I wouldn't even know how.'

'Nah,' said another Metadyne guy with an adenoidal, buzz-saw voice, 'he sent it to one of those bat doctors.'

'No way!' Trevor shouted.

'It's a forfeit,' the engineer said. 'The game gets forfeited. That's the rules.'

'No wonder these Entronics guys are suddenly on a winning streak,' said the buzz-saw-voiced guy. 'They're cheating.'

The Metadyne team insisted on doing a visual inspection of all the rest of our bats, and all they found were the usual scratches and dings. Only Trevor's bat had been doctored. Apparently thinning the walls with a lathe to make it springier, and weighting the end, increased what the Metadyne engineer called the trampoline effect, making the bat really hot.

But Trevor was not going down without a fight. He stood there in his cargo shorts and his LIFE IS GOOD T-shirt and his pukka shells and his brand-new white Adidas and his backwards faded Red Sox cap, and he protested that he'd never in his life cheated at sports, that he'd never do such a thing, that he wouldn't even know how to begin.

It was hard to tell how many of the guys believed him. I overheard Festino say to Letasky, 'For a company softball game? Now *that's* competitive.' Letasky, ever the diplomat, pretended he hadn't heard. He was playing basketball with Trevor and Gleason on Thursday, he'd told me. He was being very careful not to take sides, as he'd put it.

'Either the thing came that way,' Trevor said, 'or . . .'

He looked at Kurt. 'This bastard did it.' His voice rose. 'He set me up again.' Now he pointed to me, then to Kurt. 'Both of these guys. It's like a goddamned

318

reign of terror around here, have you guys noticed?'

Kurt gave him a puzzled look, shrugged, then headed off toward the parking lot. I followed him.

'How come?' I said when we were out of earshot of our teammates.

'You don't think I did that, do you?'

'Yes. I do.'

But Trevor had caught up with us, walking along-side us, speaking quickly, in clipped tones. 'You're an interesting guy,' he said, addressing Kurt. 'A man of many secrets.'

'That right?' Kurt said blandly, not letting up his pace. It was twilight, and the sodium lamps in the park-ing lot were sickly yellow. The cars cast long shadows.

'I did a little research on you,' Trevor said. 'I found this Special Forces website, and I posted a notice. I asked if anyone knew a Kurt Semko.'

Kurt gave Trevor a sidelong glance. 'You discov-ered that I don't exist, right? I'm a mirage. I'm in the Witness Protection program.'

I was looking back and forth between the two of them, watching this verbal tennis match, bewildered.

'And someone posted an answer the next day. I didn't know you had a dishonorable discharge from the army, Kurt. Did you know that, Jason? You vouched for him. You recommended him.'

'Trevor, that's enough,' I said.

'But did you know *why*, Jason?'

I didn't answer.

'How much do you know about the – what's the term they used? – "sick shit" Kurt got into in Iraq, Jason?'

I shook my head.

319

'Now I see why your friend is so willing to do your dirty work,' Trevor said. 'Why he's so willing to be your instrument in your little reign of terror. Because you got him a job he never would have gotten if anyone did a little digging.' He looked at Kurt. 'You can threaten me all you want. You can try to sabotage me. But in the end, both of you are going down.'

Kurt stopped, came close to Trevor. He grabbed Trevor by the T-shirt and pulled him close.

Trevor drew breath. 'Go ahead, hit me. I'll see to it you don't have a job to go to tomorrow morning.'

'Kurt,' I said.

Kurt lowered his head, moved right in so their faces were almost touching. He was just about the same height but much broader and much more powerful-looking. 'I have another secret I want to share with you,' he said in a low, guttural voice.

Trevor watched him, wincing, waiting for the blow. 'Go ahead.'

'I killed Kennedy,' Kurt said, letting go of Trevor's T-shirt abruptly. Trevor's shoulders slumped. The fabric of his LIFE IS GOOD T-shirt remained bunched.

'Trevor,' Kurt said, 'are you sure?'

'Am I sure of what?'

'Your shirt, I mean.' He pointed at Trevor's T-shirt. His index finger circled the LIFE IS GOOD logo. 'Are you sure life is good, Trevor? Because I wouldn't be so sure if I were you.'

44

When I got home, Kate was still awake. She was clicking away on her laptop, surfing a tsunami of trivia on
the Internet, digging deep into movie adaptations of
Jane Austen novels.

'Aren't you the one who said that watching movie
versions of Jane Austen's novels was like hearing a
Beethoven symphony played on a harmonica?' I said.

'Did we ever rent *Clueless*? You might be into that
one. It's Jane Austen's *Emma,* but it's set in a Beverly
Hills high school and it stars Alicia Silverstone.'

'You know they're remaking *Pride and Prejudice*
with Vin Diesel as that guy?'

'Mister *Darcy*? No way!' She was appalled.

'Way. In the first scene, Vin drives his Hummer
through the plate-glass window of this English manor
house.'

She glared at me. 'I asked Kurt to take a look at the
cable,' she said. 'As you suggested.'

'That's nice.'

'He's coming over tomorrow after work. I also
invited him to stay for dinner.'

'For dinner?'

'Yeah, is that a big deal? You're always saying I

exploit him – I thought it was only right to invite him to break bread with us. Or papadams, at least. Maybe you can pick up some Indian, or Thai, or something.'

'I thought your sister's coming tomorrow.'

'I thought she and Kurt might enjoy meeting each other. Ethan would definitely love Kurt. Is that okay?'

'Sure,' I said. 'Why wouldn't it be okay?' I could think of a couple of reasons, like she was still spending too much time with Kurt. Or like I couldn't see Kurt and St. Barths Susie having a whole lot to talk about.

Or like he scared me.

'Um, Kate, I think we need to talk.'

'Isn't that my line?'

'It's about Kurt.'

I told her what I should have told her before.

'How come you never said anything?' she said.

'I don't know,' I said after a long pause. 'Maybe because I was embarrassed.'

'*Embarrassed?* About what?'

'Because if it wasn't for him I wouldn't be here.'

'I don't believe that. Maybe he gave you a leg up, but it's you who's doing the job so incredibly well.'

'I think maybe I was afraid that if I told you, you'd want me to just – shut up and go along. Put up with it.'

'Why in the world would I want that?'

'Because of *this*.' I waved around the room, just as she'd once done, indicating the whole house. 'As long as Kurt was helping me up the greasy pole, I knew we'd have this. And I know how much this house means to you.'

322

She blinked and shrugged. Then I saw the tears at the corner of her eyes.

More softly, I said, 'And I knew that as soon as I went up against him, I'd be putting all this in jeopardy.'

She bowed her head, and a few tears dripped to the bedsheets. 'So what?' she said, her voice muffled.

'So what? Because I know how important this house was to you.'

She shook her head. Her teardrops were making big damp splotches. 'You think that's what I care about?'

I was silent.

She looked up. Her eyes were red. 'Look, I grew up in a huge house with servants and a pool and tennis court and horseback-riding lessons and ballet classes and winters in Bermuda and spring vacations in Europe and summers on the beach. And all of a sudden, poof, it was gone. We lost the house, the Cape house, I got yanked out of school . . . It was really hard to lose all that. And yeah, I miss it, I won't lie to you. But that's not what I'm about.'

'Hey, correct me if I'm wrong here, but aren't you the one who was looking at houses on Realtor.com?'

'Guilty. Okay? Did I want our kids to grow up in a house that has room to run around in, and a yard, and all that? Sure. Did it have to be this nice? Of course not. I love this place, I won't deny that. But I'd give it up in a second if we had to.'

'Please.'

'I didn't marry you because I thought you'd make me rich again. I married you because you were *real*. All those phonies I went out with, mouthing all that crap about Derrida and Levi-Strauss, and then all of a sudden I meet this guy who's got no pretense, no phoniness, and I loved it.'

'Levi-Strauss,' I began.

'The anthropologist, not the jeans,' she said, shaking her head, knowing I was about to poke fun at her. 'And I loved your energy. Your drive, your ambition, whatever you want to call it. But then you started to lose it.'

I nodded.

'You can see how you've changed, can't you? The confidence? You're not settling anymore. I admire you so much, you know that?'

Tears were running down her cheeks. I flicked my eyes at her, looked down. I felt like a jerk.

'Because you know something? When I was born, I was handed the keys. And you had to earn them.'

'Huh?'

'I was given everything, all the advantages, all the connections. And what have I done with them? Nothing.'

'Look what you're doing for the Haitian quilt lady,' I said.

'Yeah,' she said miserably. 'Once in a while I help out some poor artist. That's true. But you – look at where you've come from. What you've achieved on your own.'

'With the help –'

'No,' she said fiercely. '*Without* Kurt. *That's* what makes me happy. Not all the toys we can afford to buy now. Like that ridiculous starfish.'

'That Tiffany's thing?'

'I hate it. I'm sorry, but I do.'

I groaned. 'No wonder you never wear it. Do you

have any idea how much –' I stopped. 'Thanks for telling me now. It's kinda late to return it.'

'Jason, it's not me,' she said gently. 'It's glitzy and showy and . . . hideous. It's Susie, not me.'

'You went gaga over it when you saw it on her.'

'I was just trying to make her feel good. You think I want to compete with Susie on everything? I don't want her husband and I don't want her kid and I hate the way they treat him and I don't want her stupid glitzy social-climbing life. You think I'm like my sister? Ever notice she's got a thousand dollars' worth of cosmetics in her travel bag? I use stuff from CVS. We're just worlds apart. Always have been.'

Maybe I underestimated her even more than she ever underestimated me.

'Oh, I'm sorry,' she said. 'I've hurt your feelings.'

'The brooch? Nah, I can deal. Actually, I'm just glad I don't have to look at the thing.'

She laughed, relieved, through her tears. 'You really think it's too late to return it?'

'They won't be happy about it, but hey, I'm in sales. I'm sure I can persuade them to take it back.'

'What am I going to do about tomorrow?' she said. 'I can't uninvite Kurt, can I?'

I shook my head. 'Better not to, I think.'

'I think it's better for him to think everything's normal.'

'Whatever normal is with him.'

'Well,' she said, 'until you do whatever you do about him – and you need to do *something* – I just think it's better to stay on his good side.'

325

45

Thursday afternoon Kate called me to ask me to pick up some Thai food for dinner. 'Susie loves Thai food,' she said.

'Why don't you ask Susie to pick it up?'

'She doesn't have a car, you know that.'

'Oh, right. Is Kurt there now?'

'He just left. He already fixed the cable box, but he's coming back around seven.'

'I'll be home at six-forty-five,' I said.

On the way home I picked up a book on medieval torture that I was fairly certain Ethan didn't have. I was long past feeling guilty about aiding and abetting Ethan's twisted obsessions. I also stopped at a cell phone store and bought a new cell phone, keeping the same phone number. I had no idea if it was even possible to bug a cell phone, but if so, I'd have to assume that Kurt had bugged mine.

I kissed and hugged Susie, who was making herbal tea for Kate in the kitchen. She was so deeply tanned she looked like she'd applied walnut stain. 'Enjoying Nantucket?' I said. 'You've really been out in the sun.'

'Me? Please. Clarins self-tanner. I hate the sun.'

'And where's Ethan?'

'Upstairs reading.' She noticed the gift-wrapped book. 'Is that for him?'

'The latest from the Torture-Book-of-the-Month Club.'

'Oh. Um, he's not into torture anymore.'

'Hey, well, that's good news.'

'Well, it's not really an improvement,' she started to say, but Ethan had appeared in the kitchen doorway.

I went up to the kid and gave him a hug. 'I bought you a book, but I guess I'm behind the curve. I hear you're not interested in medieval torture these days.'

'I've become interested in cannibalism,' he said.

'Oh,' I said. 'Well, I bet that makes for some fascinating dinner conversation.'

'I told him he should look into vampires,' Susie said, with an edge of hysteria. 'There's lots of books on vampires. Lots of excellent novels.'

'Vampires are for teenage girls,' Ethan said. 'Did you know the Fore tribe in Papua New Guinea used to eat the brains of their deceased relatives, and that's why they got this fatal disease called kuru?'

'That'll teach you not to eat your relatives' brains,' I said, wagging my forefinger sternly.

'Who's this friend who's coming over for dinner?' Susie asked.

'He's – he's an interesting guy,' I said. I looked at my watch. 'He's late.'

'Is that dinner?' Ethan asked, pointing at the oil-stained paper bags I'd just brought in.

'Yep,' I said. 'Thai food.'

'I hate Thai food. Is there any sushi?'

327

'No sushi,' I said. 'Sorry.'

'Mom, can I have Froot Loops for dinner?'

'Kurt's late,' I said to Kate. 'Should we just start eating?'

'Let's wait a bit longer.'

I'd set up the Thai food in a kind of buffet on a table in the dining room. Kate was lying back on Grammy Spencer's couch. She was now allowed to sit up, even get out of bed, so long as she lay down as much as possible.

She was tapping at the keyboard of her laptop. 'Hey, you're not going to believe this,' she said. 'I just got an e-mail from the director of the Koerner gallery in New York. She loves Marie's works. I mean, *loves* it. She compares her to Faith Ringgold – just like I told you! She thinks Marie's going to be up there with Romare Bearden and Jacob Lawrence, and she's throwing around names like Philomé Obin and Hector Hyppolite!'

'That's wonderful,' I said.

At seven-forty-five I tried Kurt's cell, but there was no answer. I took out his business card from my wallet and got his office number and tried it, but there was no answer there either. I'd never called him on his home phone, just his cell, but I looked in the phone book, just in case. No Kurt Semko listed.

By eight, Susie and Kate and I started in on the skewers of chicken satay. At eight-thirty, the doorbell rang.

Kurt's hair was wet, and he smelled like soap and looked like he'd just gotten out of a shower. 'Sorry, man,' he said. 'I must have fallen asleep.'

'Turned off your cell? After giving me all that grief?'

'Didn't have it with me. Sorry.'

'I hope you don't mind we ate already.'

'No worries. Can I join you anyway?'

'Of course.'

Ethan came down from his bedroom and said hello. 'Are you a soldier?' he said.

'Was,' said Kurt.

'Do you know that when Napoleon's army retreated from Russia they got so hungry they ate their own horses? And then they resorted to cannibalism?'

Kurt glanced at me quickly, then said, 'Oh, sure. That also happened to the German soldiers during World War II. Battle of Stalingrad. Ran out of food, so they started eating their fellow soldiers. Dead ones, I mean. Talk about your military snafus.'

'That wasn't in my book,' Ethan said. 'I'm going to have to look into that. Soldiers and cannibalism.'

He followed me into the living room, where Kurt kissed Kate on the cheek. I didn't know they were on kissing terms already, but I didn't say anything. He shook Susie's hand. 'How's the cable TV?' he asked Kate.

'You know,' Kate said, 'I've noticed the reception is even better than it used to be. I mean, it's digital cable, and it's supposed to be perfect, but the analog channels were always a little fuzzy. Now they're as good as the digital ones. Oh, there's one satay skewer left – sorry – but there's plenty of pad thai.'

I thought I heard my cell phone ringing in my study upstairs, but I ignored it.

Kurt took a paper plate and shoveled on pad thai, vegetables in garlic sauce, fried rice, beef salad. 'I don't know who wired the cable for you, but I changed the

329

RF connection to S-video, and it's way better. Now you're taking advantage of the plasma.'

'I see,' Kate said. 'Thank you.'

'Plus, I replaced the old four-way splitter with a powered signal amplifier/splitter – makes a big difference. Also the analog-to-digital converter hardware in this cable box was lousy – I went over to the cable company and swapped this out for a new box. They never tell you, but they have a much better one now. And I put in some nice silver-coated video cables. Really upgrades the picture.'

'You're starting to sound like Phil Rifkin, may he rest in peace,' I said.

'How do you know all this stuff?' Susie marveled.

'Did a lot of the electronics in the Special Forces.'

'How are you at PowerPoint?' I asked.

'You were in the Special Forces?' Susie said. 'Like, the Green Berets?'

'No one calls it that anymore,' Kurt said.

'The guys who looked for Osama bin Laden in Afghanistan?'

'Not me, but some of the SF guys, yeah.'

'Is it true you guys had him surrounded in Tora Bora but you had no orders to capture him so you had to stand by and watch as Russian helicopters landed and spirited him away to Pakistan?'

'Not to my knowledge,' Kurt said.

It definitely was my cell phone, and it was ringing again, a second or third attempt.

'He doesn't have anything to drink,' Kate said. 'Jason, could you go to the kitchen and get him a beer? We have Sam Adams, do you like that?'

'Just water. Tap's fine.'

330

I went down the hall to the kitchen, and the wall phone rang.

'Jason? Jason – it's Jim Letasky.' He sounded out of breath.

'Oh, hey, Jim,' I said, a little surprised that he was calling me at home. 'Was that you on my cell just now?'

'Jason – oh, Jesus. Oh, my God.'

'What is it?'

'It's – my God. My God.' He was breathing hard.

'What *is* it, Jim? You okay?'

'I was at this – this high-school gym in Waltham, I guess? Where Trevor and Brett play basketball? And – and –'

'And *what*? Something happen? Everything all right?'

'Oh, *Christ*. Jason, there was an accident.' He was crying. 'Car accident. They're – dead.'

'Dead? Who's dead?'

'Trevor and Brett. He – Trevor was driving his Porsche real hard, and I guess he lost control – oh, man. This guy saw it happen. They went into the median strip and hit a guardrail and flipped over. The cops came and everything and . . .'

I felt unsteady. My knees buckled, and I sank to the kitchen floor, the phone receiver flying out of my hand, dangling on its cord.

After a minute or so of sitting there, in a state of shock, I got up unsteadily and hung up the phone. I sat on a kitchen chair staring into space, my mind racing. I must have sat there for five, maybe ten minutes.

Then I was jolted by Kurt's voice. He stood in the kitchen doorway. 'Hey, bro,' he said, peering at me curiously. 'You okay?'

I looked up at him. 'Trevor and Gleason were in a car accident,' I said. 'Trevor's car went out of control.' I paused. 'They were both killed.'

Kurt seemed to take this in for a couple of seconds. Then his eyes widened. 'You're kidding me. This just happen?'

'They were on their way to basketball. Trevor was driving his Porsche. Car hit a guardrail and rolled over.'

'Oh, shit. Unbelievable.' His eyes were on mine. He didn't glance away, nothing like that.

It felt like there was an icicle in my stomach, in my bowels. I shuddered.

That CD I'd listened to in the car about nonverbal communication. Kurt had recommended it to me. It was all about reading people's faces to look for tiny changes in the facial muscles, little subconscious gestures we all make.

Even practiced liars.

It was the delay in Kurt's reaction, a quick tightening of the muscles around the eyes. The way he lifted his chin, tilted his head back almost imperceptibly. A couple of rapid blinks.

He already knew.

'Huh,' I said.

Kurt folded his arms. 'What?'

I smiled. A forced smile, but still a smile. 'Couldn't happen to a nicer couple of guys.'

Kurt watched my face, didn't react.

I breathed in, breathed out. Kept the smile on. 'Sometimes fate just lends a hand,' I said. 'Kicks in when you need a little cosmic help.'

Kurt didn't react.

'Couldn't ask for a more convenient car accident.'

Kurt was watching my face, I could see that. Watching closely. His eyes narrowed ever so slightly.

He was reading me. Assessing me. Trying to determine whether I meant it. Whether I was really that cold-blooded.

Whether I was trying to manipulate him.

I relaxed my face. Didn't want him to think I was trying to read him back. I looked down, wiped a hand across my forehead, brushed back my hair. Like I was deep in thought. 'Let's face it,' I said. 'The guy was a cockroach, right? Both of them were.'

Kurt grunted. The kind of grunt that says you don't agree, you don't disagree.

'They could have caused me some serious problems,' I said.

After a pause, Kurt said, 'Might have.'

'You watch out for me,' I said. 'I appreciate that.'

'I don't get what you're saying,' Kurt said. I couldn't read his expression.

'Are you absolutely positive,' I said very quietly, 'that no one can ever find out?'

I didn't look at him. I looked down, studied the tile. Waited.

'Find out what?' he said.

I looked around the kitchen, as if checking to make sure no one was within earshot.

I looked up, saw the set of his mouth, a glint in his eyes. Not quite a smile, not a smirk. But something. An unspoken satisfaction. Irony, maybe.

'How'd you do it?' I said, even more quietly. Looked at the floor, then back up at him.

Five, ten seconds.

'You did something to his car, didn't you?' I said. My stomach was flooded with something sour.

A bitter taste in my mouth. I felt something acidic rise.

'I don't know what you're talking about,' Kurt said.

I lunged for the kitchen sink and vomited.

Heaved, retched until there was nothing left in my stomach, and then kept going. The taste of acid and copper pennies in my mouth. Pinpoints of light hovered around my head. I felt as if I was going to pass out.

I could see Kurt standing beside me, his face looming grotesquely large. 'You okay?'

Another wave of nausea hit me, propelling my head forward, down toward the sink. Nothing left in my stomach. Dry heaves.

I gripped the edge of the counter, the tile cold in my hands. Slowly I turned to face him, my face hot, everything around me too bright, tiny lights dancing in my peripheral vision. The stench of vomit rose up to assault my nostrils. I could smell undigested pad thai.

'You killed them,' I said. 'You goddamn *killed* them.'

Something hardened in Kurt's expression.

'You're upset,' he said. 'Lot of pressure on you, obviously. Now this.'

'*You killed them.* You did something to Trevor's Porsche. You knew they'd both be in it on their basketball night. You knew he likes to drive it hard. My God.'

Kurt's eyes went flat, dead. 'That's enough,' he said. 'You've crossed the line there, buddy. Throwing wild accusations around like that. The only people who talk to me like that –'

'Are you *denying* it?' I shouted.

'Will you chill, please? Throttle back, huh? And keep your voice down. Now, you're going to have to stop with the crazy shit. I don't like to be accused of something I didn't do. Upset or not, I don't care. You're going to have to hold it together. Calm down. Get hold of yourself. Because you don't want to be talking to me like that. I really don't like it.'

I just looked at him, didn't know what to say.

'Friends don't talk to me like that,' he said, an opaque look in his eyes. 'And you don't want me as your enemy. Believe me. You don't want me as an enemy.'

Then he turned around slowly, and without saying another word he walked out of the house.

46

Should I have told Kate right then and there?

Maybe so. But I knew how upset she'd be when I told her my suspicions.

Neither one of us wanted to jeopardize the pregnancy. Maybe it was too late in the pregnancy for stress to cause her to lose the baby – I had no idea – but I wasn't going to take that chance.

Kurt had denied it, of course. But I knew.

At some point soon I'd have to tell her. Or she'd find it out. But I wanted to get myself together, tell her in the right way. Calmly, reasoned. Having thought everything through. Sounding in control, a protector.

'Was that you throwing up?' she said.

'Yeah.'

'Do you think the food was bad?' Susie said. 'Like the chicken or something? I thought it might have tasted funny.'

'No, the food's fine. Just a case of nerves, I guess.'

'Stress,' Susie said. 'Craig throws up every time he has to present a pilot to the network execs.'

'Yeah?' I said, wishing she'd leave already.

'Where's Kurt?' Kate asked.

'He had to take off.'

'Did you guys have a fight or something? I thought I heard an argument.' She looked at me closely.

'No big deal. Yeah, we sort of had it out on something at work. Nothing important. Can I put the food away?'

'Jason, you look really upset. What happened? Who was that on the phone?'

'Really,' I said. 'Nothing important.'

'Well, in the meantime, I just called Marie and told her about the gallery. And do you know what she said to me? She said something in Creole, I don't really remember how it goes, but it means something like, You must remember the rain that made your corn grow. That was her way of saying she owed it all to me. Isn't that just the sweetest?'

'I'm proud of you, baby. You did a good thing.'

'You don't look right, Jason,' she said. 'Are you sure everything's all right?'

'Everything's fine,' I said.

I barely slept.

I got up at my usual, ridiculously early, five in the morning, my body trained to grab a cup of coffee and head out to Kurt's gym. But then, as I slipped silently out of bed, I remembered.

I made coffee and checked e-mail in my study. Wrote an e-mail to all employees of the Framingham office telling them the news. Was it 'sad' news or 'tragic'? I finally decided to open with 'It is my sad duty this morning to tell you of the tragic deaths of Trevor Allard and Brett Gleason . . .'

At around six, I went down to get the *Herald* and the *Globe* from the front porch. I scanned them quickly, looking for articles on the accident, but I found nothing. The *Herald* lived to report that sort of thing – the print equivalent of 'if it bleeds, it leads': two young men, top employees of one of the largest corporations in the world. A Porsche spinning out of control, both occupants killed. But the news hadn't made it into either paper yet.

I drove to the office in silence – no books on tape, no General Patton, no music, no talk radio – and thought.

When I got to the office – the first one there – I opened my Internet browser and Googled 'Massachusetts State Police' and 'homicide' to see if any of the names that turned up were familiar. The first thing that came up was the Massachusetts State Police web page with a welcome message from a scary-looking dude in full state trooper dress uniform, a colonel who I guessed was the superintendent of the state police. On the right was a column of 'News & Updates,' and the first line jumped out at me: WALTHAM FATAL. I clicked on the hyperlink. A press release came right up, headed, *State Police Respond to a Single-Car Fatal Crash in Waltham.*

Trevor's name in boldface, and Gleason's. Phrases: 'pronounced deceased at the scene' and 'traveling north on Interstate 95 in Waltham south of Exit 26.'

It said, 'Preliminary information collected in the investigation by Trooper Sean McAfee indicates that a 2005 Porsche 911 Carrera 4S veered off the road into the median and struck the guardrail and an abutment before rolling over. The vehicle was towed by J & A Towing.' It said, 'The cause of the crash remains under investigation with the assistance of the State Police Collision Analysis and Reconstruction Section and the State Police Crime Scene Services Section.' And: 'Though the crash remains under investigation,

338

speed is believed to be a factor in the crash.' And: 'No further information is available for public disclosure. Please do not contact the barracks directly.'

Man, everything and everyone has a website these days. I was amazed that the news was already public. When I Googled Trooper Sean McAfee, nothing came up. But it wouldn't be hard to find his phone number by calling the state police.

And then what? What did I have besides suspicion? Was I going to call Trooper McAfee and tell him that I thought my colleague and friend Kurt Semko had done something to the Porsche to cause the crash? He'd ask why I thought so, what reason I had to suspect Mr. Semko.

No, that would be stupid. The crash was under investigation. Maybe they'd find something in the wreck of the Porsche that would tell them what really happened. Until I had something concrete, though, there was no sense in dropping the dime.

I didn't know what Kurt would do if he heard that I'd reported my suspicions to the cops, but I could imagine it wouldn't be good.

Still, I had to do something. I'd come to my senses. It had taken me too long to realize that Kurt was a dangerous man, that he was out of control, that I had to stop him. He'd helped me in all sorts of ways, big and small. Maybe in ways I wasn't even aware of. And I'd silently gone along with the things he'd done for me, even though I knew they were wrong.

Ambition only went so far, though. *Should* only go so far, anyway. I'd crossed a line, yes. I wanted to do the right thing.

But what?

47

The guys started gathering in my office around nine – first Letasky, then Festino and Forsythe, until I had a small crowd. Whether or not they liked Trevor Allard or Brett Gleason, they'd worked with the two, seen them every day, bantered with them in the break room, talked sports and women and cars and business, and they were all in shock. They spoke quietly, trying to puzzle out what had happened. Letasky told them what he'd heard from the basketball team member who'd been driving behind the Porsche – how the highway curved to the right but the Porsche drove straight into the guardrail and then a concrete bridge-support column, and then the car had flipped over. The emergency medical technicians who arrived and realized that no ambulance was needed: Both men were dead. How the left lane was closed down for hours.

'Was Trevor drunk or something?' Forsythe asked. 'I don't remember Trevor as a big drinker.'

No one knew, of course.

'The pathologist usually tests for blood alcohol,' Festino said. 'That's what you see on, like, *CSI*, anyway.'

'I doubt it,' Letasky said. 'I mean, I didn't know Trevor as well as you guys, and I barely knew Gleason at all, but they were on their way to play basketball. They weren't going to get plowed before a game. After, maybe. Not before.'

'Gleason was a big drinker,' Festino said. 'Big party animal.'

'But still,' said Letasky.

There was nodding all around. Allard couldn't have been drunk; it didn't figure.

'I know he drove fast,' Forsythe said. 'Really fast. But he knew how to drive. How could he lose control of the car? It didn't rain last night, right?'

Letasky shook his head.

'An oil slick or something?' Forsythe asked.

'I took 95,' Letasky said, 'and there wasn't any kind of oil slick that I saw.'

'Ever meet his wife?' asked the youngest sales rep, Detwiler.

'A real hot babe,' Festino said. 'Blonde, big tits. What you'd expect Trevor to marry.' He looked around, saw the disapproving looks. 'Sorry.'

'They didn't have any kids, thank God,' Letasky said.

'Thank God,' I said. I'd been listening, not talking. I didn't want to risk letting them know my suspicions.

'Mechanical defect or something?' said Detwiler.

Letasky inhaled. 'I suppose anything's possible.'

'Mrs. Allard's going to have one hell of a lawsuit against Porsche,' Festino said.

As the guys filed out a few minutes later – everyone had calls to make – Festino lingered behind.

'Say,' he said tentatively. 'About Trevor?'

341

'Yeah?' I said.

'I know you're not supposed to speak ill of the dead, but I hated the asshole. You know that. I assume you did, too.'

I didn't answer.

'But – I don't know – maybe he wasn't so bad. Gleason, too. Though he was even harder to like.'

I just nodded.

'And, well – I know it's probably in bad taste, but have you decided who you're going to assign their accounts to?'

News travels fast in the age of e-mail. Just before lunchtime I got an e-mail from Joan Tureck in Dallas:

> **I'm so sorry to hear about Trevor Allard and Brett Gleason. I can scarcely believe it. If I were at all superstitious, I'd say Entronics is cursed.**

Maybe she had a point.

At lunchtime, I found a pay phone in the employee cafeteria. It's hardly ever used – not in an office building where everyone has desk phones and cell phones.

I'd decided to call the cops.

What I really wanted to do was to call some anonymous crime tip line. But amazingly enough, the Massachusetts State Police didn't seem to have one. On their website I found tip lines for terrorism, arson, fugitives from justice, auto theft, charity scams. Even an Oxycontin tip line. But nothing for plain old murder.

So I called the state trooper whose name was on the online press release. Trooper Sean McAfee, the one who was in charge of investigating the collision, was out of the Concord barracks of the state police. Troop

342

A headquarters. Though I doubted he was doing anything but the most pro forma investigation.

I didn't want this call tracked back to me, though. The police, I assumed, can trace just about any call these days, including cell phones. If they were going to trace the call, at least they'd get no further than a pay phone in the employee cafeteria of the Entronics building in Framingham.

'This is Sergeant McAfee,' said a rough voice, Southie vowels.

No one was anywhere nearby – this was an alcove off the cafeteria by a service door – but I still didn't dare speak loudly. Yet I wanted to sound confident, sure of myself. 'Sergeant McAfee,' I said in my best cold-calling voice, 'you're investigating a collision that took place last night on I-95 in Waltham? The Porsche?'

Suspicious: 'Yeah?'

'I have some information about it.'

'Who's this?'

I was prepared for that. 'I'm a friend of the driver's.'

'Name?'

My name? Name of the driver? 'I'm afraid I can't give my name.'

'What's your information?'

'I think something might have been done to the Porsche.'

Long pause. 'Why do you think that?'

'Because the driver had an enemy.'

'An enemy. You think someone forced him off the road, that it?'

'No.'

'Then you think someone monkeyed around with the car?'

'That's what I think.'

'Sir, if you have information that might be material to this investigation, you should do yourself and the deceased a favor and come in to talk to me.'

'I can't do that.'

'I'm happy to come out to Framingham,' he said.

He knew where the call was coming from.

'I can't meet with you.'

The cop began to sound exasperated. He raised his voice. 'Sir, without more information, like a name of this "enemy" you're talking about, I don't have enough to work with. The crime scene techs did a whole investigation of the scene last night, the forensic mapping, the whole nine yards. And there's no tire marks, no skid marks or yaw marks, nothing that tells us anything except the driver drove straight into the guard-rail. Far as we're concerned, it's a single-car fatal, driver error. Now, if you got something that'll change our minds, you should give us what you got. Otherwise, forget it.'

I wasn't expecting the cop to get belligerent on me. I wondered whether he was trying to shame me into cooperating, or whether he really just didn't give a shit.

'I just think,' I said very quietly, 'that you should have your guys look very closely at the car. I'll bet you find evidence of sabotage.'

'Look closely at the car?' the cop shot back. 'Sir, the car was totaled, and then it caught fire. There's not a hell of a lot left of the car, okay? I doubt anyone's going to find anything.'

'His name's Kurt Semko,' I said quickly, and I hung up the phone.

As I walked out of the alcove and back to the cafeteria, I saw Kurt, sitting with a couple of guys from Security. They were talking loudly, and laughing, but Kurt was watching me.

48

The intercom buzzed, and Franny said, 'It's Mr. Hardy.'

'Jason,' came the big mellifluous voice, 'please forgive this short notice, but I need you to fly out to L.A. tomorrow. I've set up a meeting, and I want you there.'

He paused. I groaned inwardly, said, 'Gotcha.'

'With Nakamura-san,' he added.

'Nakamura-san? Hideo Nakamura?' Did I misunderstand him? Hideo Nakamura was the chairman of the board of the Entronics Corporation. He was like the great Oz. No one had ever seen him. Just Gordy, once.

'You got it. The great man himself. He's flying in from New York, en route to Tokyo. I persuaded him to make a quick stopover in Santa Clara, receive a personal briefing from my best-and-brightest. See for himself how you've turned around sales.'

'Just – me?'

'You and two of the other top VPs. I want to knock his socks off.'

'Yes, sir,' I said. 'Can do.'

'I had to do a good deal of arm-twisting to get him to make a stop. He comes to the U.S. once or twice a year, if that, you know.'

'Wow.'

'I think he'll be impressed with you. I know he'll be impressed with what you've done.'

'Should I prepare an agenda?'

'Of course. Nakamura-san loves PowerPoint. Do a brief PowerPoint presentation. Five or six bullet points, no more. Very macro. The ten-thousand-foot view. Performance of your division, key achievements, key struggles. He always likes his employees to acknowledge their struggles.'

'Gotcha.'

'Arrive by ten-thirty at the boardroom here at Santa Clara. I'll go over your PowerPoint first. Nakamura-san and his entourage will arrive at precisely eleven o'clock, and will leave at precisely twelve o'clock. One hour. Chop chop.'

'Gotcha.'

'Leave plenty of time for delays. It is imperative that you be on time. *Imperative.* Nakamura-san is extraordinarily punctual.'

'Gotcha. It's too late to make an evening flight, but I'm sure there are plenty of early-morning ones.'

'Remember to bring your business cards. Your *meishi,* as they call it. Present it to him with both hands, holding it at the corners. When he gives you yours, accept it with both hands and study it carefully. And whatever you do, don't put it in your pocket.'

'Don't worry,' I said. 'I know the rituals. I'll be there.'

'On time,' Hardy said.

'Early,' I said.

'And afterward, if you have time, come out for a sail with me on the *Samurai.*'

347

'The *Samurai*?'

'My new eighty-foot Lazzara. It's a real beauty. You'll love it.'

While Franny set to work on getting me a flight, I canceled my next day's appointments, and called Kate to tell her my change in plans. I told her I'd fly back home tomorrow, after the big presentation. Then I started crunching numbers and composing a rough draft of my PowerPoint slides for Franny to make up.

A little while later she stopped in. 'This is a tough one. It's too late to make the six or seven o'clock flights tonight,' she said. 'There's an 8:20 P.M. to San Jose, but that's full. Overbooked, in fact. San Francisco, Oakland, same thing.'

'How about the corporate jet?'

'In your dreams, honey.' The corporate jet lived in New York or Tokyo and wasn't for the likes of me. She knew I was kidding.

'What about flying out in the morning?'

'There's only one flight that'll get you there with enough time. U.S. Air's six-thirty into San Francisco. Arrives nine fifty-two. It'll be close. Santa Clara is thirty-one miles away, so I'll rent you a car. The usual Rolls-Royce?'

The woman was developing a sense of humor. 'I think a Bentley this time.'

She went back out to her cubicle to call our corporate travel company, while I went out, the corporate hunter-gatherer, in search of numbers to crunch.

When I got back, twenty minutes or so later, Franny said, 'Kurt was here.'

348

'Oh?'

'Put something on your desk. He said he'll stop by later. He had something important to discuss, he said.'

I felt a prickle of tension. Kurt had no business-related reason to come by. It couldn't be good.

There was nothing on my desk.

My cell phone rang. I looked around my desk for it, couldn't find it. It rang again, sounding muffled and distant. It was coming from my fancy English briefcase. I didn't remember leaving it in my briefcase, but I was a little scattered these days.

I lifted the briefcase from the floor next to my desk, opened it –

And something exploded.

There was a loud pop, a great whoosh, and something hit my face, a whole scattering of something, momentarily blinding me. I leapt backwards and out of the way.

'Jesus!' I shouted.

I swept small, hard particles off my face, out of my eyes. Looked at what came off in my hands: tiny, colorful bits of plastic and silver foil in the shape of parasols and stars. My desk was covered with the stuff.

Confetti.

I heard low, hoarse laughter. Kurt was standing there, laughing helplessly. Franny had run in, her hands to her face, terrified.

'Happy birthday,' Kurt said. 'Excuse me.'

He nudged Franny out of the door and closed the door behind her.

'It's not my birthday,' I said.

'Had this been an actual emergency, you'd be pink mist.'

'What the hell was that?'

'Look for yourself. Hobby store stuff. Model rocket motor, electrically initiated. A microswitch from Radio Shack. A clothespin, a couple of thumb-tacks, some rosin-core solder, and a nine-volt battery. Fortu-nately for you, the rocket motor was stuck in a bag of confetti. But let's say instead of a rocket motor, I used an electric blasting cap. And let's say instead of a bag of confetti I used some C-4 plastic explosive. Granted, can't get that stuff at Radio Shack, but some of us know where to get it, right?' He winked. 'My point getting through here? One day you open the trunk of your car, maybe. Kablooey. And it's not going to be confetti.'

'What do you want, Kurt?'

'I got a heads-up from a buddy of mine on the state police.'

I shrugged.

'Said someone called in with an anonymous tip. About the death of Trevor Allard. From a pay phone. The one off the cafeteria.'

Jesus. I blinked, shrugged again.

'The caller mentioned my name.'

I prayed nothing in my face gave me away.

'My buddy said, "What the hell's going on, you piss someone off, Kurt? Someone trying to smear dirt on you?"'

'What are you talking to me for?'

Kurt drew close. 'Let me tell you something,' he said, almost under his breath. 'I've got a lot of friends in a lot of places. Anyone you talk to in the cops, guaranteed I'll hear about it within a couple hours. Who the *hell* you think you're playing with?'

I tried to look right into his eyes, but they were too intense, too menacing. I looked down at my desk, shook my head.

'You don't want to be my enemy, bro. Haven't you figured that out yet?'

'Because you kill your enemies. Right? Why haven't you killed me yet? I don't understand.'

'You're not my enemy, Jason. If you were, you wouldn't be here.'

'So I guess that makes me your friend.'

'Has anyone ever done more for you than me?'

I was struck speechless for a few seconds. 'You're serious, aren't you?'

'I hope you don't think you got where you are today on your own. You owe it all to me. We both know that.'

'Yep,' I said. 'I really have no talents or intelligence of my own. I'm just your puppet.'

'Talent without drive gets you nowhere, friend. I changed your life.'

'You were just willing to play dirty, Kurt. I should have cut you off long ago, but I was weak. I'm not weak anymore.'

'Because you think you don't need me. That's all. But we were a team. Look at how well we worked together. Anything in your way – any obstacles – they just vanished, didn't they?'

'You were out of control,' I said.

'And you don't know what a pawn you are. You have no idea. "Save the division"? That's a laugh. Ask the merger integration team from McKinsey if they're here to save the Framingham office or sell the building. Amazing what you can find if you look. I found job security. Just by uncovering Dick Hardy's Hush-mail account. Interesting stuff there.'

I shook my head. What was he getting at? What did he have on Dick Hardy?

'Gordy was just waiting for the right opportunity to get rid of you, you know. You were a threat to him.'

'So you got him drunk, that it?'

'Drunk? That wasn't just booze, friend. Roofies, for one thing.'

'Roofies?'

'Rohypnol. The forget-me drug. Betcha Gordy didn't remember any of it the next day. A cocktail. A drop of DMT – Dimethyltryptamine, a psychedelic. Plus a little upper. And he lost his inhibitions. Showed his true colors. Like Napoleon said, "Never interrupt your enemy when he's making a mistake."'

'You're a goddamned lunatic.'

'Does this mean you're not going to make me your kid's godfather? Don't tell me you didn't know what I was doing. You knew all along. You *wanted* me to do what I did. You just didn't want to acknowledge it. Don't ask, don't tell. Where's your gratitude?'

'You didn't kill Trevor and Gleason because of me. You killed them because they were uncovering what you'd done. They could have landed you in serious trouble.'

'I could have handled it,' Kurt said. 'Everything I did, I did for you. Aren't you the guy who's always talking about killing the competition?' He chuckled. 'Hey, it's like your books say. The *Take No Prisoners Guide to Business*? What do you think "take no pris-oners" means? You don't take any enemy prisoners because you kill them instead. No Havahart traps in

the field, Jason. What part of this do you not understand? So my advice to you is to keep your goddamned mouth shut. Because everything you do, I'm
watching. Everywhere you go. Every call you make.
It's like that Police song, right? "Every Breath You
Take"? I'm listening. I'm watching. There is *nothing*'
– he bared his lower teeth like some sort of rabid
animal – 'nothing you can do that I won't find out
about. You've got a lot to lose.'

He winked. 'You know who I mean.'

The bottom of my stomach dropped. I knew he
meant Kate.

'And after all I've done for you,' he said, and turned.
'You disappoint me.'

'Any idea when I can get started on the PowerPoint
slides?' Franny asked. 'I've got three teenage sons
who'll burn down the house if I don't get dinner on
the table.'

'You'd better tell 'em to get takeout,' I said. 'Gonna
be a late night.'

I could barely concentrate on the PowerPoint slides.
Next to Kurt's threat, they seemed a pointless distraction.

I didn't get out of the office until almost nine, but
before I left I did a quick search for the Special Forces
website that Trevor had mentioned. The one where
he'd posted a question about Kurt, and someone had
answered.

The search didn't take long. I just put 'Kurt Semko'
and 'Special Forces' in Google and immediately found
it. It was a Special Forces 'teamhouse,' some kind of a
Listserv for former members of the Special Forces and

their friends and family. In one area of the site was the 'guest book,' where Trevor had posted his question, and I found the reply, from someone named Scolaro with a Hotmail address.

I clicked on the address and wrote Scolaro an e-mail. 'What kind of "sick shit" did he get into?' I wrote. 'Guy lives next door and I want to know.' I put down an AOL address I rarely used, the initials of my college and year of graduation. No name.

It felt like putting a message into a bottle and hurling it into the ocean. Who knew what I'd get back, if anything – and when, if ever.

My phone had been ringing, but I'd shut off the ringer so I could concentrate, and asked Franny to answer, and only put the call through if it was Kate or Dick Hardy. She didn't put any calls through.

I closed my office door and said good night to Franny, who was eating a grilled chicken Caesar salad she'd had delivered. A PowerPoint slide was on her big Entronics monitor.

'You like?' she said. 'I can do a Teal Taffy double fade, if you want.'

'Nothing fancy,' I said. 'Bare bones. Nakamura is probably a "just-the-facts, ma'am" kind of guy.'

'Flash? Swish? Wipes?'

'No thanks.'

'Oh, and you got a call, but I didn't disturb you for it. Well, you got a bunch of calls, but one I thought you should know about. From the state police. An investigator named, let me see here, Ray Kenyon. He wanted to talk to you. I said you'd gone home for the day.'

'Great. Thanks.'

An investigator.

'Did he say what it's about?'

'Just left his name and number.' She handed me a message slip. 'You want me to put the call through for you?'

'No, thanks,' I said. I put the message in my pocket. 'I've got to get home. It's late.'

'That's right,' Franny said. 'You have a pregnant wife to buy pickles and ice cream for. I'll e-mail you the presentation when I finish. Good luck tomorrow.'

'I'll need it.'

'You? Why do you think Hardy wants you out there? You're a star.'

'Did I ever tell you I like you, Franny?'

'No, I don't think you ever have.'

'Oh. Franny?'

'Yes?'

'Could you do me a favor?'

'Perhaps.'

'Could you take down all those military posters from my office walls? I'm tired of looking at them.'

49

I got to the airport at 4:45 A.M., almost two hours before my flight was supposed to leave. I left my car in the Terminal B garage and went to one of the E-ticket kiosks. The terminal was dark, almost deserted. I found the one open coffee place, got a large coffee and a bagel and sat down on a plastic bucket seat. I took my laptop out of my old nylon briefcase – I'd left the English briefcase, the one Kurt had tampered with, back in my office – ponied up the eight bucks for WiFi Internet access, and checked my e-mail. Went over the PowerPoint presentation. Rehearsed it silently, although I think a cleaning lady looked at me funny when she heard me talking to myself.

I tried to keep my mind on my presentation and Nakamura-san, not on Kurt's threats. Or on the police detective who'd left a message. Which, if I allowed myself to think about it, would make me far more nervous than presenting to Nakamura-san.

You've got a lot to lose.

You know who I mean.

When I'd arrived home last night, everyone in the house was asleep.

They were all still asleep, naturally, when I left the house at four-thirty in the morning. That was just as well; I might have been tempted to talk to Kate, tell her about Kurt's threats. Which I most definitely didn't want to do.

Because I had no doubt that Kurt had somehow rigged Trevor's car to make it crash.

And I knew he was an extremely dangerous man. Who was no longer my friend.

He'd warned me not to tell anybody my suspicions about Trevor's car. Not in so many words, but he'd made that clear. He knew I'd tried to get him fired.

No, I couldn't prove anything, but his threats alone told me he was guilty. Yet what was I supposed to do when the police detective asked me questions about the car crash? Probably the safe thing to do was to say nothing. To tell the detective I knew nothing about it. Strictly speaking, that was true. I had only suspicions. I *knew* nothing.

Because I didn't doubt that if I talked to the cops, Kurt would find out.

I've got a lot of friends in a lot of places.

An hour later I got into the security line. There were other people already in line, probably all flying to San Francisco. Some businessmen and business-women, probably going to Silicon Valley via San Francisco because they wanted to arrive earlier than the flights to San Jose. Or maybe they didn't want to change planes in Phoenix or Atlanta or Houston. Since I travel a lot, I've got it down to almost a science – BlackBerry and cell phone in my briefcase, the slip-on shoes with no steel shank, all my metal objects in one pocket for quick removal.

The line moved slowly. Most people in line were half-asleep anyway. I felt like a sheep being herded into the pen. Ever since 9/11, traveling has been a nightmare of taking off shoes and putting stuff on moving belts and getting wanded. There was a time when I loved to travel, but no longer, and it wasn't just salesman burnout. It was all the security, which didn't make us any more secure.

I took my laptop out of my briefcase and put it on the conveyor belt, put the briefcase on the belt after it, slipped off my shoes – the lace-up ones were in my overnight bag, since the slip-on ones weren't dressy enough for Nakamura-san – and put them in the gray Rubbermaid tray. I put my keys and coins in the little coin tray, and shuffled through the metal detector. Passed with flying colors, and smiled at the somber guy standing there. A woman asked me to turn my computer on, which I did.

I padded over to the next portal, one of the new explosives detectors they'd just installed. Stood there while I was hit with a blast of air. An electronic voice told me to move on.

And then, a few seconds later, a high-pitched alarm went off.

One of the TSA security agents grabbed my overnight bag as it emerged from the explosives detector. For some reason, my overnight bag had set off the alarm. Another one took me by the elbow, and said, 'Sir, please come with us.'

I was no longer half-awake. The adrenaline had kicked in. 'What's going on?' I said. 'There some kind of problem here?'

'This way, sir.'

People in line stared as I was pulled off to the side, behind a tall panel. 'Hands in front of you, sir,' one of them said.

I put my hands out. 'What is it?' I asked.

No one answered. The other agent passed a metal-detector wand up and down my chest, up the inside of my legs to my crotch and back down the other leg. When he was done, a third guy – a supervisor, I guessed, a thick-necked man with a bad comb-over and over-sized glasses, said, 'Follow me, sir.'

'I have a flight to catch,' I said.

He led me to a small, harshly lit, glassed-in room. 'Sit here, please.'

'Where's my briefcase?' I said.

He asked for my ticket and boarding pass. He wanted to know what my final destination was, and why I was flying to California and back in one day.

Ah. Maybe it was the one-day trip to California that had aroused suspicion in their pea brains. Or the fact that I'd booked the flight the night before. Something like that.

'Am I on some kind of no-fly list?' I said.

The TSA man didn't answer.

'Did you pack your bags yourself?' the man asked, not exactly answering my question.

'No, my valet did. Yes, of course I did.'

'Was your suitcase out of your possession at any time?'

'My overnight bag? What do you mean, out of my possession? Here at the airport, this morning? At *any* time?'

'At any time.'

'I keep it in my office. I travel a lot. Sometimes I

leave my office to go home. What's the problem? Was there something in it?'

He didn't answer. I looked at my watch. 'I'm going to miss my flight,' I said. 'Where's my cell phone?'

'I wouldn't worry about it,' the TSA man said. 'You're not going to be on that flight.'

I wondered how often this man got to really bully passengers around, really scare the shit out of them. Less and less often, I figured, as we moved farther and farther away from 9/11, when traveling in the United States was sort of like moving around Albania.

'Look, I have a really important business meeting. With the chairman of the board of my corporation. The Entronics Corporation.' I looked at my watch, remembered that Franny had said only one flight would get me there in time for Nakamura-san's arrival. 'I need my cell phone.'

'Not possible, sir. All the contents of your briefcase are being swabbed and inspected.'

'Swabbed?'

'Yes, sir.'

'Swabbed for what?'

He didn't answer.

'Are you at least going to get me on the next flight out?'

'We don't have anything to do with the airlines, sir. I would have no idea what other flights there are or when they leave or which flights have availability, if any.'

'Then the least you can do is let me use a phone so I can get myself on the next flight out.'

'I don't think you're going to be on the next flight out, sir.'

360

'What's *that* supposed to mean?' I said raising my voice.

'We're not done with you.'

'You're not done with me? What is this, East Berlin?'

'Sir, if you don't keep your voice down, I can have you arrested.'

'Even when you're arrested you're allowed one phone call.'

'If you want to be arrested, I'd be happy to arrange that.'

He stood up and walked out. Closed the door behind him. I heard it lock. A National Guardsman, crew-cut and bulky and wearing camouflage fatigues, was now standing guard outside the room. What the hell was this?

Another twenty minutes went by. I'd definitely missed my flight. I wondered if another airline had a flight that would get me there close to eleven. Maybe I could floor it and still get to Santa Clara on time. Or just a little late.

I kept looking at my watch, saw the minutes tick by. Another twenty minutes later, a couple of Boston police officers, a man and a woman, came into the room, showed their badges, and asked to see my ticket and boarding pass.

'What's the problem, Officers?' I said. Outwardly I was calm, friendly. Reasonable. Inwardly I wanted to rip their faces off.

'Where are you traveling, Mr. Steadman?' the man said.

'Santa Clara. I just went through all this with the TSA guy.'

'A one-day trip to California?' said the woman.

'My wife's pregnant,' I said. 'I wanted to get back home so she's not left alone. She's confined to bed. A high-risk pregnancy.'

Get it? I wanted to say. Corporate executive, family man, married, wife pregnant. Not exactly the standard profile of an al-Qaeda terrorist.

'Mr. Steadman,' the woman said, 'your suitcase tested positive for the presence of C-4. Plastic explosives.'

'*What?* That's obviously a mistake. Your machine's screwed up.'

'No, sir,' the male officer said. 'The screeners confirmed it by running another test. They took a swab and wiped down the portfolio and ran it through another machine, and that came up positive, too.'

'Well, it's a false positive,' I said. 'I've never touched C-4 in my life. You might want to think about getting your machines checked out.'

'They're not our machines,' the woman said.

'Right. Well, I'm a senior vice president at a major corporation. I'm flying to Santa Clara for a meeting with the chairman of the board. At least I was. You can check all that out. One simple phone call, and you'll be able to confirm what I'm saying. Why don't you do that right now?'

The cops remained stony-faced.

'I think we all know there's been some kind of a mistake. I've read about how those three-million-dollar machines can be set off by the particles in stuff like dry cleaning fluid and hand cream and fertilizers.'

'Are you carrying any fertilizer?'

'Does my PowerPoint presentation count?'

She glowered at me.

'You get my point. Machines make mistakes. Now,

can we all be reasonable here? You have my name and my address and phone number. If you need to reach me for anything, you know where I live. I own a house in Cambridge. With a pregnant wife and a mortgage.'

'Thank you, sir,' the man said, sounding like he was concluding the interview. They both got up and left me there to cool my heels for another half an hour or so before the TSA supervisor with the comb-over came in and told me I was free to go.

It was just after eight in the morning. I ran to the departure gate and found a U.S. Airways agent and asked her when the next flight to San Francisco was. Or San Jose. Or Oakland.

There was an American Airlines flight at 9:10, she said. Arriving at 12:23. I could be in Santa Clara at 1:00. When the extremely punctual, and very pissed off, Nakamura-san would be sitting in first class on his way to Tokyo.

I called Dick Hardy. In California it was a little after five in the morning, and I knew he wouldn't appreciate being awakened at home.

'Steadman,' he said, his voice thick.

'Very sorry to wake you, sir,' I said. 'But I'm not on the flight to San Francisco. I was detained for questioning. Some sort of huge screwup.'

'Well, get on the next one, for God's sake.'

'The next one gets me in at 12:23.'

'Twelve twenty-three? That's too late. Nakamura-san will be long gone. Got to be an earlier flight. He's arriving at eleven o'clock promptly.'

'I know. I know. But there's nothing else.'

Now he was fully awake. 'You're standing up Hideo Nakamura?'

'I don't know what else to do. Unless you can reschedule him –'

'Reschedule *Nakamura-san*? After the way I twisted his arm to get him here for one goddamned hour?'

'Sir, I'm terribly sorry. But all these ridiculous terrorist precautions –'

'God*damn* you, Steadman,' he said, and he hung up.

I walked back to the parking garage, dazed. I'd just blown off my boss and the chairman of the board.

It was unreal, an out-of-body experience.

I kept flashing on the TSA supervisor with the stupid comb-over.

'Did you pack your bags yourself?'

And: *'Was your suitcase out of your possession at any time?'*

Was it out of my possession at any time?

Franny saying, *'Kurt was here.'*

'Oh?'

'Put something on your desk.'

He knew I was flying to Santa Clara, and he'd been in my office recently, rigging up my briefcase with his little toy confetti bomb. I kept my overnight bag in my office closet.

He'd set me up.

The way he'd set the other guys up. Trevor Allard and Brett Gleason were dead.

And now Kurt had turned on me.

50

My day's appointments had been canceled, so I drove straight home, steaming mad. Kate was surprised to see me at home. She seemed somber, depressed, remote. She told me that her sister had taken Ethan to the Museum of Fine Arts to look at the mummies, and I gave her the short version of how airport security had detained me for almost two hours on a bogus suspicion that I was carrying a bomb.

She was barely listening, and normally this was the sort of thing that really got her going. Normally she'd be listening with eyes flashing, indignant along with me, saying things like, 'Oh, you're kidding,' and 'Those bastards.'

Instead she made little pro forma clucks of sympathy, her mind somewhere else far away. She looked haggard. Her eyes were bloodshot. While I was telling her how Dick Hardy had basically exploded, she cut me off. 'You must be so unhappy with me.'

'Now what?' I said. 'What in the world makes you say that?'

Her eyebrows knit together. Her face crumpled. Her eyes got all squinty, and her tears began flowing. 'I sit here all day like – like an invalid – and I just know how sexually – frustrated you must be.'

'Kate,' I said, 'where's all this coming from? You're pregnant. High-risk pregnancy. We both understand that. We're in this together.'

She was crying even harder. She could barely speak. 'You're a senior vice president now. A big shot.' Her words came in ragged clumps, between gasps. 'Women are probably coming on to you all the time.'

I leaned over next to her, took her head in my hands, stroked her hair. The pregnancy, the crazy hormones, all this time in bed. She was going out of her mind. 'Not even in my wet dreams,' I tried to joke. 'Don't worry about it.'

But she reached over to her nightstand and picked something up, held it out to me without looking.

'Why, Jason? How could you?'

I looked. It was a condom, still in its packet. A Durex condom.

'That's not mine,' I said.

She shook her head slowly. 'It was in your suit jacket.'

'That's impossible.'

'You dropped your suit on the bed this morning when you were packing. And when I got up, I felt something in one of your pockets.' Her breathing was uneven. 'And I – you – oh, God, I can't believe you.'

'Baby, it's not mine.'

She twisted her head to look up at me. Her face was all red and blotchy. 'Please don't lie to me. Don't tell me you're carrying someone else's condom around.'

'I didn't put it there, Kate. Believe me. It's not mine.'

She bowed her head. Pushed my hands away. 'How can you do this?' she said. 'How can you *do* this?'

Furious now, I grabbed my BlackBerry from my

suitcoat pocket and hurled it toward her. It landed on the pillow next to her head. 'There you go,' I shouted. 'That's my personal scheduler. Go ahead, look through it. Maybe you can figure out when the hell I'd even have *time* to have an affair, huh? Huh?'

She stared at me, taken aback.

'Let's see,' I said. 'Ah, yes. How about sneaking in some quickie nookie between my eight-forty-five supply-chain management call and the nine o'clock long-term-strategy staff meeting? Slip in a little horizontal mamba between the ten o'clock end of the staff meeting and the ten-fifteen sales call with Detwiler? Some coochie in the two minutes between the meeting with the systems integrators at the Briefing Center and the forecast review session?'

'Jason.'

'Or maybe a minute and a half of the funky monkey between the eleven-forty-five cross-functional concall and the twelve-fifteen meeting with the order admin, then a quick game of hide-the-salami in the fifteen seconds I have to get to a lunch meeting with the district managers? Kate, do you realize how *insane* this is? Even if I wanted to, which I don't, I don't have a goddamned free *second*! And for you to accuse me of something like this just pisses me off. I can't believe it.'

'He told me, you know. He told me he was worried for us.'

'Who?'

'Kurt. He said – said he probably shouldn't say anything – wasn't his business, he said – but he wondered if maybe you were having an affair.' Her words were muffled, and I had to listen hard to understand.

'Kurt,' I said. '*Kurt* said this. When did he say this to you?'

'I don't know. A couple of weeks ago.'

'Don't you understand what he's doing? That just fits right in to the pattern of everything else.'

She glanced at me, shaking her head, a disgusted look on her face. 'This isn't about Kurt, whatever his flaws,' she said. 'We have bigger problems than Kurt.'

'No, Kate. You don't know about Kurt. You don't know what he did.'

'You told me.'

'No,' I said. 'There's more.'

I told her everything now.

Her disbelief slowly melted. Maybe it's more accurate to say it turned into disbelief of another kind.

'Are you leaving anything out?'

'Nothing.'

'Jason, you've got to talk to the police. No anonymous calls. Openly. You have nothing to hide. Tell them everything you know. Tell them what you told me.'

'He'll find out.'

'Come *on*, Jason.'

'He knows people all over the place. In the state police, everywhere. He'll find out. He's got everything wired.' I paused. 'And – he threatened me. He said he'll do something to you.'

'He wouldn't. He likes me.'

'We were friends, too, him and me – remember? But he's totally ruthless. He'll do anything to protect himself.'

'That's why you've got to stop him. You can do it. I know you can. Because you *have* to.'

We were both quiet for a few seconds. She looked at me. 'Do you hear a funny sound?'

I smiled. 'No.'

'It sounds like a . . . maraca. Not right now, but I keep hearing something.'

'I don't hear anything. Bathroom fan, maybe?'

'The bathroom fan's not on. Maybe I'm losing my mind. But I want you to call the police. He's got to be arrested.'

I fried some eggs, toasted an English muffin, brought a breakfast tray up to her. Then I went to my study and called Franny and filled her in.

'The detective called again,' she said. 'Sergeant Kenyon. He asked for your cell number, but I wouldn't give it to him. You'd better call him back.'

'I will.'

As I spoke, I was tapping away on my laptop. I pulled up that Special Forces website I'd bookmarked and went to the 'Guestbook' where Trevor had posted his question about Kurt. No other replies had gone up.

'I'll be in soon,' I told Franny, and hung up.

I signed on to AOL, the account I hardly ever used. Six e-mails in the in-box. Five of them were spam.

One was from a Hotmail address. Scolaro. The guy who'd replied to Trevor, said he knew something about Kurt.

I opened it.

I don't know this guy Semko personally. One of my SF brothers does and I asked him. He said Semko got a DD for fragging a team member.

369

DD, I remembered, meant 'dishonorable discharge.'
I hit reply and typed:

Thanks.
Where can I get proof of his DD?

I hit SEND, and was about to sign off, when the little
blue AOL triangle started bouncing. New mail.
It was from Scolaro.

If he got DD he was court-martialed. Army court
documents are public record. Go to the Army Court
of Criminal Appeals website. They're all available
online.

Quickly I typed a reply:

What's your tel #? I'd like to give you a call.

I waited a minute. E-mail is strange – sometimes it
goes through in a couple of seconds; other times the
big pipeline, wherever it is, gets clogged, and mail
won't get through for an hour.
Or maybe he just didn't want to answer.
While I waited, I did a Google search for the Army
Court of Criminal Appeals. The browser cranked
and cranked and eventually popped up with a warning box.
Access Restricted to Military Active Duty, Reserve
or Veterans. Please enter valid military ID or Veterans
Identification card number.
I couldn't get in.
I sat there for a few moments, thinking. Who did I
know who might have a military ID number?
I picked up the phone and called Cal Taylor. 'Cal,' I
said, 'it's Jason Steadman.'

A long, long silence. A TV blared in the background, some game show. 'Yeah,' he said at last.

'I need your help,' I said.

'You're kidding me.'

I entered Cal's ID number, and the website opened.

I scanned it. I didn't know what that guy Scolaro was talking about. I didn't see any court documents. On the menu bar on the left, one of the items was 'Published Army Opinions,' and I clicked on 'By Name.'

A list came right up. Each line began with a last name. Then ARMY and a seven- or eight-digit number – a court case number, maybe? – and the 'United States v.' and the rank and name of a soldier. Staff Sergeant Smith or Colonel Jones or whatever.

The names were listed in alphabetical order. I scrolled down, so fast that the list became a blur, then slowed down a bit.

And came to SEMKO.

'United States vs. Sergeant KURT L. SEMKO.'

My heart raced.

The blue AOL triangle was bouncing. Another e-mail from Scolaro. I double-clicked on it.

No way. Not talking about Semko. Said too much already. I got a wife and kids. Sorry. You're on your own.

I heard Kate's voice from down the hall. 'Jason, there's that maraca sound again.'

'Okay,' I yelled back. 'Be there in a minute.'

A PDF document opened.

UNITED STATES ARMY COURT OF
CRIMINAL APPEALS
UNITED STATES, Appellee

v.

Sergeant First Class KURT M. SEMKO
United States Army Special Forces, Appellant

A lot of names and numbers and legalese. Then:

*A general court-martial composed of officer and
enlisted members convicted appellant, contrary to
his pleas, of signing a false official document with
intent to deceive (three specifications), one specifica-
tion of false swearing, and three specifications of
obstruction of justice. Appellant pled not guilty to
and was acquitted of premeditated murder . . .*

I skimmed it quickly. Kurt had been charged with
the murder of a fellow soldier – a 'fragging,' they called
it – named Sergeant First Class James F. Donadio.
Donadio was described as 'formerly a close friend of
the appellant.' A 'protégé,' some of Kurt's teammates
testified. Until Donadio had reported to their captain
that Kurt had been stealing war trophies – 'retained
illegal weapons' – which was against regulations.

Then Kurt had turned on his former protégé. It was
all there, under 'Background and Facts.' Donadio had
found a cartridge jammed into the barrel of his M4
rifle. The weapon would have blown up if he hadn't
noticed it. Then a 'flash-bang' grenade, normally used
to clear a room, had been rigged up to Donadio's bed
so it exploded one night. Flash-bang grenades made a
loud explosion but caused no injuries.

Another time, a jumpmaster noticed that Donadio's
static-line parachute had been sabotaged. If he hadn't

realized that the pack closing loop had been switched with another line, Donadio would have been badly hurt.

Pranks, I guess you'd say.

Kurt was suspected of all these acts, but there was no evidence. Then one morning, Donadio had opened the door to the Ground Mobility Vehicle he always drove and maintained, and an M-67 fragmentation grenade exploded.

Donadio was killed. No grenade was found to be missing from Kurt's gear, but one was missing from the team's general weapons locker. Everyone on the team had the combination.

All but one of the twelve team members testified against Kurt. But again, the evidence was lacking. The defense argued that Kurt Semko was a highly decorated, much-lauded soldier of documented bravery in combat. He'd won three Purple Hearts.

Kurt was found not guilty of premeditated murder, but found guilty of making false statements to the criminal investigator. He was given a dishonorable discharge but not sentenced to any time.

So that story he'd told about confronting his commanding officer over a 'suicide mission' that killed Jimmy Donadio – he'd made it up. The truth was simpler. He'd fragged a protégé who'd turned against him.

The words on the laptop began to swim. I felt a little light-headed.

'Jason,' Kate called out.

I was stunned but not surprised. It all made perfect sense

But this was exactly what I needed. The state police would see who they were dealing with. There'd be no doubt that Kurt was capable of disabling Trevor's car, killing him and Gleason. No doubt at all.

I hit PRINT. Printed five copies.

Then went down the hall to the bedroom to see what Kate wanted. As I neared the bedroom, Kate began screaming.

51

I ran into the bedroom.

Kate was cowering on the bed, screaming, her hands flailing in the air, gesturing toward the bathroom.

I turned my gaze to the bathroom and saw it.

Undulating, slithering along the baseboard, moving slowly from the bathroom to the bedroom. It must have been six feet long and as thick as my arm. Its scales were large and coarse, yet intricately patterned: black and beige and brown and white with a white diamond pattern. It was rattling and hissing.

I'd never seen a rattlesnake outside the movies, but I knew right away what it was.

Kate screamed.

'It's a rattlesnake,' I said.

'Oh, God, Jason, you have to kill it,' she shouted. 'Get a shovel or something.'

'That's when they bite you. When you try to kill them.'

'Get it *out* of here! Oh, my *God*!'

'I don't want to go near the thing,' I said. I was maybe twenty feet away. Frozen in place, right where I stood. 'When these guys strike, they can move like a hundred, two hundred miles an hour or something.'

'Jason, kill it!'

'Kate,' I said. 'Quiet. Keep your voice down.' The snake had stopped slithering and had begun to double back on itself, forming a loose coil. 'Shit. That's what they do when they strike.' I backed away slowly.

Kate was pulling the sheets and blankets up over her head. '*Get – it – out* of here!' she screamed from under the bedclothes, her voice muffled.

'Kate, shut up!'

The snake was rearing up now, its wide head moving slowly back and forth, two or three feet in the air, exposing a gray belly. It was flicking a long, forked black tongue and rattling its tail. It sounded like an old bathroom ventilation fan, getting faster, louder.

'Don't make a sound,' I said. 'It's scared. When they're scared, they attack.'

'*It's* scared? *It's* scared?'

'Quiet. Now, I want you to get out of bed.'

'No!'

'Come on. Out of bed. Quietly. I want you to get out of here, down to my study, and I'll call someone.'

'Who?'

'Well,' I said. 'Not Kurt.'

From my study I called a company called AAAA Animal Control and Removal Service. A professorial-looking guy showed up half an hour later, carrying a long pair of broad-jawed tongs, a pair of elbow-length gloves, and a flat white cardboard carton, open at both ends, that said SNAKE GUARD on it. When he entered our bedroom, he let out a low whistle.

'Don't see many of those critters around here,' he said.

'It's a rattlesnake, isn't it?' I said.

'Eastern Diamondback. Big mother, too. You see these guys in Florida and North Carolina. Sometimes Louisiana. Not in Massachusetts, though.'

'How'd it get here then?' I asked.

'Who the heck knows? I know people buy exotic snakes over the Internet nowadays. VenomousReptiles.com, places like that.'

The snake had gone back to slithering along the bedroom carpet and was approaching the TV.

'Looking for a place to hide,' the animal control guy said. He watched for a minute longer, and then put on the long red gloves and got about ten feet away from the snake before he put down the cardboard box, right up against the wall, and pushed it closer to the snake with the long blue aluminum tongs.

'They like the close spaces. Looking for shelter. Coupla drops of snake lure inside, but I doubt we need it. Belt and suspenders, I figure. Critter gets stuck on the glue inside.'

I watched as the rattlesnake, sure enough, began undulating slowly toward the box, stopped curiously just before it, then poked its head inside one end.

'Man,' the animal guy said, 'I saw one of these back in Florida when I was a kid. But never up here. Never. Watch him.'

It was slithering into the box.

'Good thing you didn't get too close. This fella bites you, you're gonna die. Most dangerous snake in North America. Largest rattlesnake in the world, matter of fact.'

Then Kate's voice: 'What are you going to do with it?' She was standing at the threshold to the bedroom, a blanket wrapped around her like a cape.

The white box began to move. Shake back and forth. More than half the snake's body was still outside the trap, and it began whipping back and forth, trying to free itself. It wriggled farther into the trap, and now most of the thing seemed to be stuck.

'What are we going to do with it?' the animal guy said. 'Legally, I'm supposed to tell you we dispose of it humanely.'

'And in reality?' Kate said.

'Depends on whose definition of humane. Ours, or the snake's. We got the critter, that's the main thing.' He walked right up to the white box and picked it up. 'Boy, you just never see Eastern Diamondbacks around here. Fact, I can't remember the last time I even saw a venomous snake in this town. Gotta wonder how the heck it got in here.'

'Yeah,' Kate said, heavy on the sarcasm. 'Gotta wonder.'

She got back into bed, but only after I'd checked the bedroom and the bathroom, even lifted the lid to the toilet tank.

Then she read over the court-martial record that I'd printed out.

'Is this enough to get Kurt arrested?'

'I doubt it. But it'll help. It's obviously enough to get him fired, but that's only the first step. A half measure. And what do I do until then? Until I can convince the police to arrest him?'

She nodded. 'He's totally charming and seductive. He likes to feel superior. Narcissists like that, they need to be adored. They crave it. They're like drug addicts. He needs your adulation.'

'The way he got yours, let me remind you.'

'We were both taken in.'

'Well, that's over, and he knows it. It's all out in the open between us now. He knows how I feel.'

'Well, turn the tap back on. The adulation. This is what you're good at. Sell him. Let him think there's more hero worship in the tank, that you've got an endless supply.'

'Why?'

'To neutralize him. Until you get the cops in to arrest him.'

'You make it sound easy,' I said. 'It's not going to be easy at all.'

'Do you have a choice?' she said.

I headed right to Corporate Security to look for Scanlon.

I was mad, and in a hurry, and I didn't have my badge out, so I used the biometric fingerprint reader to get in.

I remembered Kurt's threat: '. . . *Everything you do, I'm watching. Everywhere you go. Every call you make. It's like that Police song, right?*'

As the fingerprint reader beeped to admit me, I suddenly realized how Kurt always knew where I went in the building, and it was so obvious I felt like a moron. My access badge, the fingerprint reader – every time I accessed another part of the building, he probably knew right away.

I found the door with the plaque that said DIRECTOR OF CORPORATE SECURITY. It was closed. I walked up, grabbed the knob, but I was stopped by Scanlon's secretary, who was sitting at a desk perpendicular to the door.

'He's on the phone,' the secretary said.

'Good,' I said, and I turned the knob and barged right into Scanlon's office. Against the sun streaming in from the glass, the security director was only a silhouette. He was on the phone, looking out the window.

'Hey,' I said. In one hand I held a printout of Kurt's court-martial record.

He swiveled around slowly. 'You're looking for the director?' Kurt said, putting the phone down.

I stared in shock.

'Scanlon opted for early retirement,' Kurt said. 'I'm the new Director of Corporate Security. Can I help you?'

When I got to my office, I saw a man sitting at the empty cubicle near Franny's cube that I used as a waiting room for my visitors. He was a black man, maybe fifty, with small ears and a large bullet head. He wore khaki dress slacks and a blue blazer, a blue shirt and solid navy blue tie.

'Jason,' Franny said, turning around in her chair.

'Mr. Steadman,' said the man, rising quickly. I noticed a pair of handcuffs on his belt, and a gun. 'Sergeant Ray Kenyon, Massachusetts State Police. You're a hard one to reach.'

52

He wanted to talk in my office, but I led him instead to an empty conference room.

'I'm investigating a collision involving two of your employees, Trevor Allard and Brett Gleason.'

I nodded. 'A terrible tragedy. They were both friends of mine. Anything I can do to help.'

He smiled. His skin was very dark, and his teeth were incredibly white. Up close he might have been in his midforties. Hard to tell. His head was a cue ball, so shiny it looked waxed. He spoke slowly, like he wasn't the sharpest knife in the drawer, but I could see that his eyes missed nothing.

'How well did you know these two men, Mr. Allard and Mr. Gleason?'

'Fairly well. They worked for me. I can't say they were close friends, but I saw them every day.'

'You all got along?'

'Sure.'

'There was no animosity between and among you all?'

'Animosity?' I wondered who he'd talked to, what he knew about how I'd come to really dislike those two. Had I sent Trevor or Gleason any hostile e-mails?

Not my kind of thing, usually – if I wanted to chew either one of them out, I did it in person. Fortunately. 'Sergeant Kenyon, I don't get why you're asking all these questions. I thought Trevor and Brett died in a car crash.'

'They did. We want to find out why that happened.'

'Are you saying it wasn't just an accident?'

He peered at me for a few seconds. 'What do you think?'

I stared right back, but squinted as if I didn't quite understand.

I knew that whatever I said next would change everything.

If I said I had no suspicions about the crash – well, what if he somehow knew I'd made that damned 'anonymous' call? If so, then he knew I was lying.

But how could anyone prove it had been me who'd used the pay phone next to the cafeteria, and not someone else in the company?

Obviously I wanted the police to investigate the crash – but for me to accuse Kurt openly . . . Well, there was no putting that toothpaste back in the tube. Kurt would find out.

'I've wondered about it,' I said. 'How it could have happened, you know? *Was* there something done to Trevor's car?'

'That's not my department. That's Accident Recon. The CARS unit. Collision Analysis and Reconstruction. They're the experts on all the mechanical stuff. I just do the background investigation. Help them out.'

'They must have found something,' I said. 'If you're here.'

'Well, now,' he said, and I thought he looked pretty

382

darned evasive, 'we work separately, understand. They look at the brake lines and such, and I look at the people.'

'So you're talking to Trevor's and Brett's friends and acquaintances.'

'And coworkers. Which brings me back to my question. Which you didn't answer. Whether there was any tension, any bad feeling, between you and them.'

I shook my head. 'Not that I can recall.'

A ghost of a smile. 'There was, or there wasn't?'

'There wasn't,' I said.

He nodded for what must have been half a minute, exhaling loudly through his nostrils. 'Mr. Steadman, I don't have any reason to dispute what you're saying. I'm just trying to make all the pieces fit, you know? But what you're saying, it doesn't quite dovetail with this.'

He pulled out of his pocket a folded piece of white paper. He unfolded it, put it on the conference table in front of me. The paper looked like it had been folded and refolded dozens of time. It was a photocopy of an e-mail.

From me to Trevor. Dated about a week ago.

I won't put up with your disrespect & your undermining of me anymore. There are ways to get rid of you that don't involve HR.

'That's not me,' I said. 'It doesn't even sound like me.'

'No?'

'I'd never make a threat like that. That's ridiculous. And I'd sure never put it in an e-mail.'

'You wouldn't want a record out there, that it?'

I closed my eyes in frustration. 'I didn't write it. Look, I –'

'Mr. Steadman, have you ever been in Mr. Allard's car?'

I shook my head.

'Did he have a regular parking spot here, at work?'

'Not an assigned spot.'

'You've never touched his car? I mean, placed your hands on it at any point?'

'Place my hands on it? I mean, theoretically, it's possible, but I don't recall ever even touching his car. It's a Porsche, and he's pretty fussy about it. Was, I mean.'

'What about his home? Have you been there?'

'No, never. He never invited me over. We weren't really personal friends.'

'Yet you knew them "fairly well," you said.'

'Yes. But I also said we weren't close friends.'

'You know where he lives?'

'I know he lives – *lived* – in Wellesley. But I've never been to his house.'

'I see. And his home garage – connected to his house. Were you ever there?'

'No. I just told you, I've never been to his house.'

He nodded. Kenyon appeared to be thinking. 'So I'm just wondering, you know, why your fingerprints might have been found in his garage.'

'My fingerprints? That's impossible.'

'Your right index finger, anyway. Doesn't seem to be any doubt about that.'

'Come *on*,' I said. 'You don't even have my fingerprints to compare them against.'

He looked puzzled. 'You didn't give the print of your index finger to your Corporate Security department? For the new biometric reader?'

'Yes. Right. I forgot. I did – we all did. Our forefinger or our thumb. But I never went to Trevor Allard's house or garage.'

His eyes watched me steadily. They were large and a little bloodshot, I noticed. 'See, the problem with fingerprints,' he said quietly, 'is that they don't lie.'

'Doesn't it strike you as maybe a little too convenient?'

'What's too convenient, Mr. Steadman?'

'The one fingerprint you found in Trevor's garage is my right index finger, right? Which is the one print that Corporate Security has in their biometric reader?'

'So?'

'So you tell me – aren't there ways to copy and transfer a fingerprint? You guys believe in coincidence?'

'Coincidence?'

'What do you have? A print from one single finger that happens to be the same as the one print I gave Corporate Security. An e-mail I didn't write –'

'There's all kinds of headers and paths and directories on every e-mail, Mr. Steadman –'

'Which can be forged,' I said.

'Not so easily.'

'It's easy if you work in Corporate Security.'

That shut him up for a second. 'See,' I said, 'we have an employee who's done this sort of thing before.'

'In Corporate Security?'

I swallowed. Nodded. I leaned forward, my eyes on his. 'I want to show you a document,' I said. 'That should give you a sense of who we're dealing with.'

I handed him the court-martial printout. He read through it. He took a lot of notes in his spiral-bound notebook.

And when he'd finished, he said, 'Jesus Christ, your company hired this guy?'

I nodded.

'Don't you do background checks?'

'It's my fault,' I said.

'You didn't hire the guy, did you? Corporate Security hired this wack job, right?'

'Because I vouched for him. I didn't know him well at the time.'

He shook his head, looking disgusted. But I could tell that he was looking at me differently. Something in him had shifted. He seemed to be taking me seriously now.

'This guy Semko,' he said. 'What kind of reason would he have to set you up?'

'It's a long story. Complicated. He and I were friends. I brought him into the company. He has a military background, and he's pretty smart.'

Kenyon's expression had grown very still. He was watching me closely. 'You're friends,' he said.

'We were,' I said. 'He did some things to help me out. Some things he shouldn't have done.'

'Like?'

'Underhanded things. But . . . Look, Detective –'

'Sergeant Kenyon.'

'Sergeant. He's already threatened me. He told me if I said anything to the cops, he'd kill my wife.'

Kenyon raised his eyebrows. 'Did he?'

'If he finds out that I talked to you – I know him. He'll carry out his threat. He'll make it look like an accident. He knows lots of clever ways to kill people.'

'You're talking to me now.'

'I have to trust you. Can I?'

'Trust me how?'

'Not to tell anyone else in the state police that I've spoken with you.'

'I can't promise you that.'

'What?'

'I'm not a priest, Mr. Steadman. This isn't a confessional. I'm a cop. If you committed a crime –'

'I *didn't* commit a crime.'

'Then you have nothing to worry about. I'm also not a reporter for the *Globe*. I don't plan to publish an exposé. Point is, I don't want to give you assurances I can't keep.'

'He knows people in the state police. A lot of people. He has contacts who tell him what's going on.'

Kenyon smiled cryptically, nodded.

'What?' I said. 'You look skeptical.'

'No. In fact, I'm not skeptical. I'm not going to lie to you. I'd like to tell you that kind of thing can't happen, but the truth is – well, I can believe it. We leak like a sieve. Military guys like your friend here, sometimes they know a lot of people on the force.'

'Great,' I said darkly. 'If he finds out I've even talked to you, he'll do something to my wife. He works in Corporate Security – he knows the names of everyone who comes and goes here. You probably signed in at the front desk, right? You wrote Mass. State Police, and your name, right? To see Jason Steadman?'

'It's not like that. I'm here to talk to a lot of people.'

'Okay.'

'I'm going to need to get specifics from you. Like

some of the "underhanded things" this Semko person did. Were any of them targeted at Allard or Gleason?'

I felt a pulse of relief. 'Absolutely.'

He turned a page of his notebook. He asked me questions. I talked, and he took a lot of notes.

'Maybe we can help each other,' he said. He handed me his card. He wrote down another number on the back. 'My direct line, and my cell. If you call me at the DA's office, sometimes my partner, Sanchez, answers my line. You can trust him.'

I shook my head. 'If I call you, I don't want to leave my name. How about if I use a fake name? I'll use –' I thought a moment. 'Josh Gibson.'

His big white smile took over his face. 'Josh Gibson? You're thinking *the* Josh Gibson? Negro Leagues?'

'One of the greatest power hitters of all time,' I said.

'I'll remember,' Kenyon said.

53

I had a lunch presentation to one of our dealers and
Ricky Festino, trying to save a deal he was losing. I
hadn't been on my game – I was too distracted by
Sergeant Kenyon – and I probably shouldn't have
gone.

Right after lunch, instead of returning to the office,
I drove to a Starbucks a few miles from the Entronics
building. I ordered a large cappuccino – I refuse to use
the bogus Starbucks language like 'venti' and 'grande'
– and found a comfortable chair in a corner and
plugged in my laptop. I bought a month's worth of
wireless Internet access, and a few minutes later I'd set
up several e-mail addresses.

I had no doubt that Kurt could pretty much find
out anything I did online while I was at the office. But
it wouldn't be easy for him to discover this Internet
account, and even if he did, it would take him a while.
And at the rate things were happening now, I didn't
need more than a couple of days.

Man, you don't know what a pawn you are, Kurt
had said.

*Ask the merger integration team from McKinsey if
they're here to save the Framingham office or sell the*

building. Amazing what you can find if you look.

Did that mean that the MegaTower had been planning all along to shut down my division? Had that already been decided? If it had – then why had Dick Hardy been pressuring us so hard to perform, to sign up new business?

I didn't get it. What was the logic? Entronics was a few weeks away from closing a massive deal to acquire Royal Meister's U.S. plasma-and-LCD business. Why the hell would anyone in Tokyo care about how their own U.S. business unit did if they were about to close it down?

What piece of the puzzle was I missing?

The answers probably lay in the confidential Entronics strategic-planning documents that concerned the acquisition of the Meister unit and their plans going forward. Most of these documents were probably in Japanese and stored in some inaccessible, compartmented corporate intranet.

But there were other ways.

Like the consulting firm of McKinsey and the merger integration team that had recently been prowling the halls.

I didn't know any of them, but I did know some of their names. And after some quick research on their website, I found the name of the most senior partner on the Entronics account. And then I found the name and e-mail of his executive assistant.

Then, Dick Hardy sent her an e-mail. He used his Hushmail account.

Well, actually, the e-mail came from *rhardy@hushmail.com*.

An account I'd set up. Dick Hardy was e-mailing

from his yacht, see. He'd misplaced the latest draft of the merger integration report, and he needed a copy e-mailed to him at once. To this private address, of course.

I finished my cappuccino and got another coffee, black, and while I waited for McKinsey's reply, I went back to the Army Court of Appeals website and found Kurt's court-martial record. I remembered that the Army's Criminal Investigation Division had done a report on the fragging, in the course of which their investigator had interviewed everyone else on Kurt's Special Forces team.

Everyone on the team but one had told the CID interviewer that they thought Kurt had done the murder. I wrote down the full names of each of the team members. His only defender was named Jeremiah Willkie.

I remembered the night I'd met Kurt, when he took me to that autobody shop owned by a friend and SF buddy of his. He'd asked after the owner, whose name was Jeremiah.

Not too many Jeremiahs in the Special Forces, I figured.

Willkie Auto Body had repaired my Acura. That was the place where Kurt mentioned he kept a storage unit for his tools and such.

I did a quick Google search under Willkie Auto Body and pulled up an interesting fact. Willkie Auto Body was listed as the owner of a towing company called M.E. Walsh Tow. That was the towing company Kurt used to work for, I remembered. He said it was owned by a buddy of his.

Then I began to plug into Google the names of the

other members of Special Forces Operational Detachment Alpha 561. Some of the names, even with middle initials, came up in different locations around the country. That just meant I hadn't narrowed them down enough. Was James W. Kelly now a software developer in Cambridge, England? I didn't think so. An accordionist and composer? A surgeon? A professor of oceanography and meteorology? A full-time blogger?

But a few names were unusual enough for me to be certain I had the right man, and of those, a few even had biographies online. One was a fireman in a small town in Connecticut. Another worked for a security firm in Cincinnati. Another taught military history at a community college in upstate New York.

I found the e-mail addresses of the last two easily. I sipped some more of my coffee, trying to kick my brain into higher gear. I figured they disliked Kurt, since they'd both been called as witnesses at Kurt's court-martial and had testified against him. So I wrote to each of them. Using a third e-mail address, with a fake name, I told them that Kurt Semko had moved in next door and was spending a lot of time with my teenaged daughter, and I wanted to make a discreet inquiry into whether it was true he'd fragged a fellow officer in Iraq.

One of them, the one who worked for the security firm, answered right back.

'Kurt Semko is a discredit to the Special Forces,' he wrote. 'He's a dangerous and unbalanced man. If it were my daughter, I'd keep her away from Semko. No, I'd probably move.'

I thanked him and asked him to give me specifics about what Kurt had done.

I waited, but there was no reply.

Then I checked Dick Hardy's Hushmail account. The executive assistant from McKinsey had replied, with an attachment containing the merger integration team report. I downloaded it.

The McKinsey report went on forever, but everything was in the executive summary up front.

And it was all there.

They weren't evaluating Dallas versus Framingham. They weren't trying to decide which unit got shuttered and which survived.

It was a business case for closing the Framingham office and an action plan for how to do it.

The whole bake-off thing that Gordy and Hardy had talked about – it was a ruse. The McKinsey report never even mentioned it.

We'd all been hoodwinked.

But *why*?

Why the bake-off? Why pit Framingham against Dallas? Why crack the whip so hard?

One of the appendices to the McKinsey report was the confidential term sheet for the Entronics-Meister acquisition. All the secret details were there. Maybe the answer was in the term sheet.

If you knew how to read it.

I didn't, but I knew someone who did.

Fifteen minutes later, Festino entered Starbucks, looked around, and found me in my comfortable chair in the back corner.

'You didn't invite me here for an Iced Caramel Macchiato, I assume,' he said grumpily.

'Go ahead and get one,' I said. 'On your nickel.'

393

'Yes, boss. Hey, thanks for lunch, by the way. We landed the deal.'

'Good to hear,' I said, although I really didn't care at that moment.

He returned after a few minutes with his drink, then pulled up a chair next to mine. 'Jesus, will you look at this seat cushion? Can you imagine how many filthy asses have been on it?' He inspected it suspiciously and sat down slowly, reluctantly. 'So what's this?'

I told him about the fraudulent bake-off.

His mouth came open, and his face reddened. 'Those bastards. The whole thing was a cruel hoax?'

'So it appears.'

'So in a month I'm going to be standing over a Frialator in the back of some McDonald's? They couldn't have told me this in June, when McDonald's was hiring? Hand me your laptop.' He squinted at the screen for a moment. 'How'd you get this?'

'I think they call it "social engineering."'

'From the ghoul squad themselves?'

'The merger integration team? Sort of.'

'Hey, this is the term sheet for the Meister deal. Coolio.'

'Yep.'

'This is supposed to be under lock and key. Double-secret probation. You really *do* know how to get stuff, don't you?'

'Sometimes.'

He was silent a while longer. Then he started muttering words like 'consideration' and 'exchange ratio' and 'closing price,' and he said, 'Man, this is some complex deal. But the boot's less than twenty percent.

394

That's standard.'

'The boot?'

'Cash. Investment banker talk. And there's a soft collar in the deal.'

'Now it's a collar?'

'See, if the price of Entronics stock goes down by closing date, they have to pay Meister more. If Entronics stock goes up, they pay less. A *lot* less, it looks like. Okay, now . . . I have a theory. Let me . . .' He was on the Internet, searching. 'Yes. Here we go. Look at this – since the day the Meister deal was announced, Hardy's given exactly three interviews. In Japanese.'

'In Japanese?'

'I mean, to Japanese newspapers. One in English, to the *Japan Times*. One to *Asahi Shimbun*. Another one to *Nihon Keizai Shimbun*. All of them upbeat, bragging about how Entronics U.S. business in flat-screens is taking off.'

'So?'

'Why do you think he only talked to Japanese journalists?'

'That's simple. Entronics is a Japanese company. He figured his bosses would read the interviews and be impressed.'

'Come on, Jason. His bosses knew the numbers before *Nihon Keizai Shimbun* did. See, when you're going through a merger or acquisition, the SEC's always on your ass about talking to the press. But they can't stop you from talking to foreign journalists in foreign countries. And who reads Japanese newspapers? In addition to Japanese-speakers?'

'I'm not following you.'

'The Japanese offices of some of the biggest American hedge funds, okay? They pick up a morsel of news about Entronics, figuring they got a jump on the rest of the world, and they start buying. Next thing, the program traders kick in. Pretty soon Entronics stock starts jumping.'

'So Dick Hardy was helping Entronics save a bundle on the Meister deal.'

'Exactly.'

'So he lights a fire under us, gets us to sign deals all over the place so we can save our jobs, but in reality all we're doing is helping Entronics do a little bargain shopping.'

'Exactly. Evil, huh?'

'But we don't know whether Dick Hardy did this at the direction of the MegaTower, or whether this was his own idea.'

'Who cares? Either way, he's going to get a gold star,' Festino said. He took out a brand-new miniature bottle of hand sanitizer, unwrapped it, and squeezed out a big dollop onto the palm of his left hand. 'And we get screwed.'

'Aha.'

'You can't do anything about this, you know. In case you were planning something. This is all far, far above your pay grade.' He began feverishly rubbing his hands together. 'Look at the stains on this armrest. It's disgusting. I don't think it's coffee either.'

'Maybe you're right. Maybe there's nothing I can do.'

'Anyway, I always liked McDonald's fries. Even after they stopped frying them in beef tallow. You coming tomorrow night?'

'Tomorrow night?'

'The softball game. Remember? You haven't played in two weeks. And now that I'm coach, it's all on my shoulders. We're down two players.'

'Festino.'

'Sorry. But we are.'

'I'll be there,' I said.

54

I pulled into the Entronics parking lot at just before five-thirty. A black Mustang pulled in the space beside me with a loud squealing of brakes, and Kurt jumped out.

I sat in the car, waited for him to keep going. But he opened my passenger-side door and got in.

'How goes the battle?' he said.

'Tough day. Weirdest thing happened at home. We found a rattlesnake in our bedroom.'

'That right,' he said. 'I didn't even know there were any rattlesnakes in Massachusetts. Live and learn. But I thought you were going to California.'

'Missed the flight,' I said.

'That's a bummer.'

'Yeah, well. It happens. So, congratulations on your promotion.'

He nodded, smiled. 'It's good to be king.'

'I'm impressed. Dick Hardy must think highly of you.'

'Dick Hardy wants me to be happy. He's decided I'm invaluable.'

'You got something on him, huh?' I smiled, nodding, as if I appreciated his cleverness. He could have

398

been a wholesaler bragging to me about some clever way they'd scammed Best Buy into paying for shipping.

'He even invited me on his yacht. Ever been on his yacht?'

'He invited me,' I said. 'But I couldn't make it.'

'It's an eighty-foot Lazzara, I read. A bargain at 2.3 million. But it sure seemed out of his league, given his salary. So I did a little digging. Turns out Hardy has been doing a little stock trading on the side. Set up a Channel Island trust in the name of something called the Samurai Trust. Samurai being the name of his yacht, you see. And the Samurai Trust has been buying and selling out-of-the-money options on Entronics stock on the Australian Stock Exchange. Every time an Entronics press release goes out, every time there's another blip of good news, the Samurai Trust cashes in. Making a fortune. Of course, if there's bad news, he makes money, too, on shorts. Very clever – just about impossible to get caught. And all to pay for his yacht. Man, he could buy ten yachts by now.'

Finally, I understood. Dick Hardy might have been trying to save Entronics a bundle on the Royal Meister deal, but that wasn't his sole motive. He was lining his own pockets at the same time.

'He's a clever guy,' I said.

'Clever enough to do his personal banking business using an encrypted Hushmail account. Not clever enough to realize that whenever he did e-mails on the company computer, I could access his hard disk remotely.'

'Wow. Very cool.'

'Everyone's got a secret. You've got your secrets too. I just happen to know them. And there you are, you and your Band of Brothers, working your butts off to try to save your division. When all you're really doing is paying off his yacht. Or his new house in the Highland Park section of Dallas.'

'Dallas?'

'Choke on that, buddy. Wonder why he's moving to Dallas.'

'You're right. I was a pawn.'

He shrugged.

My shoulders sagged. I looked up, shaking my head regretfully. 'You were just trying to help me out. And I've been taking you for granted. Like an idiot. While Gordy and Hardy were moving me around like a chess piece. You're my only ally.'

He turned to look at me. I couldn't read his face.

It was funny to remember how marginal he looked when I'd first met him, like an old hippie, someone who'd fallen off the grid. The goatee, the bandana, the mullet, the ratty T-shirts. Now he was well dressed and successful looking, in a good suit and tie and conservative shoes.

'I mean it,' I said. 'I really don't give a shit what you did to Trevor and Brett. I freaked out, I admit it. I called the cops – I'm not going to lie to you. That was a stupid thing to do.' I sounded so genuinely contrite that I was beginning to believe it myself. 'I could say I'm sorry, but that's inadequate. You've been a good friend to me. This whole time. I just didn't see it.'

He was staring straight ahead out the windshield.

I fell silent. My old sales guru, Mark Simkins, whose CDs I used to play over and over again, was always talking about the strategic pause. The most important skill in closing, he said, is silence.

So I said nothing. And waited for it to sink in.

God, I hoped Kate's theory was right, that Kurt was a sucker for adulation.

Kurt's eyes flicked toward me, then back toward the windshield.

I compressed my lips. Stared at the steering wheel.

'You talked with that cop,' Kurt said. His voice was softer. 'Kenyon. Did I not warn you to keep your mouth shut?'

'You did. And I did. But the guy showed up at my office. He said he's talking to everyone who worked with Trevor and Brett. So I gave him a whole lot of blather. He asked about you, and I told him that as far as I knew you had a good relationship with those two. That you played softball with them, and they really admired you.'

Kurt nodded. 'That's good,' he said.

It was working. Thank God. Relief flooded my body.

'That's very good. Very smooth. I see why you're so good at closing deals.' He turned, his face a few inches from mine. 'Because you're a goddamned *liar*,' he shouted. His voice was deafening. His spittle sprayed my face. 'I know every goddamned word you said to that cop. "He knows lots of clever ways to kill people," you said.'

No. Had Kenyon talked to somebody on the force who knew Kurt?

'"I have to trust you,"' he went on. '"Can I?" No, asshole, you *can't* trust anyone. You think you can talk anywhere in the building without my knowing?'

Of course. With all the Corporate Security resources he had at his disposal, he had the conference room bugged too.

'Now, I'm not going to say this again. Go behind my back one more time – within the company, to the police, anybody – I will find out. There is nothing you can do that I don't know about. Nothing. And if you step over the line – one millimeter over the line . . .'

'Yeah?' My heart was thrumming, fast and loud.

'A little friendly advice? You think you and your wife live in a safe neighborhood. But break-ins happen all the time in that part of town. Home invasions. Bad guys take stuff. Sometimes they even kill innocent people. Happens. You've got a wife and unborn child, Jason. You want to be real careful.'

55

Graham Runkel's apartment still smelled like a bong, and his 1971 VW bug was still in his backyard. It looked like he was working on it.

'How's the Love Bug?' I said. 'El Huevito.'

'I'm hot-rodding it. Turbo rebuild. Wait right here.'

He came back with a Ziploc bag of marijuana buds. 'The last of the White Widow. A peace offering. Welcome back.'

'Not for me, thanks. I told you, I don't do that anymore.' I handed him a wrapped package.

'What's this?'

'A guilt offering. Because I'm a jerk.'

He tore it open. 'A complete set of *The Prisoner* on DVD? Unfreakingbelievable, Steadman.' He admired the picture of Patrick McGoohan on the front of the box. Back in Worcester, Graham used to come over to my house when my parents were at work, and we'd get high and watch old reruns of the classic British spy show. 'What's the occasion? Is it my birthday? I forget.'

'No,' I said. 'I'm here to ask for your help, and I feel like such an asshole just showing up after all these months that I figured this might make you feel a little less pissed off at me.'

'It certainly goes a long way,' he said. 'But what you really need is the comfort of the White Widow. You're wound tighter than a . . . whatever's wound really tight.' Graham's brown hair was shoulder length and looked dirty. He was wearing his old red T-shirt with yellow McDonald's golden arches on it. It said MARIJUANA and OVER 1 BILLION STONED.

'If you wanted to do something to someone's car so it wiped out while he drove it, what would you do?'

He looked at me funny. 'Wiped out?'

'Crashed.'

'Cut the brake lines? This a quiz?'

'If you cut the brake lines, wouldn't the brakes feel all mushy as soon as you start driving it?'

'What's this about, J-man?'

I gave him a quick overview, told him about Kurt and what I thought he'd done. Graham listened with his bloodshot eyes open wide. This was a guy who believed the DEA put transmitters in every copy of *High Times* magazine, so he was inclined to believe my theory.

'It was a Porsche?' he said.

I nodded. 'Carrera 911. Brand-new. At most, a year old.'

'Was the driver wasted?'

I shook my head.

'Just lost control? No other car involved?'

'Correct.'

'Hmm. Well, yeah, you wouldn't cut the brake lines. The driver would know right away. You wouldn't loosen the lug nuts on the wheels either – the car would start wobbling as soon as it hit the road. But look, man, unless the cops are total bozos, this is the first stuff they'd look for – missing lug nuts, slashed tires, a bolt missing from the steering knuckle, cut brake lines. Shit like that.'

'It's all going to be fairly obvious,' I said.

'Of course, if somebody screwed with the ball joints . . . *man.*'

'What?'

'The driver would just lose control.'

'Screwed with the ball joints? How? Like, cut it? Wouldn't that be obvious?'

'Unless they weren't cut. Shaved down or filed away or something. Weakened somehow. So when the car –'

'Weakened?' I said. 'How do you weaken metal?'

'Shit, I don't know. Lots of ways, I figure.'

'Weaken metal,' I said aloud, but really to myself. I thought of that story Kurt had once told me about how his team had put something from a tube on parts of a Taliban helicopter in Afghanistan. 'I think I know.'

'Okay, man. Good. So why don't we celebrate?' He reached for the bag of marijuana. 'Last call,' he said.

I got home around seven-thirty. Susie and Ethan were finishing up a take-out dinner in the kitchen – I guess they'd found a sushi place that delivered – and Kate was in bed and clicking away in cyberspace.

'Kate, have you been outside at all today?'

'Outside?' She gave me a puzzled look.

'You look like you could use a little fresh air.'

'Fresh air?' Then she saw me putting my index finger over my lips. She nodded. 'Good idea,' she said.

She slipped out of bed, and I lifted her up. It was surprisingly easy, probably because of all of Kurt's strength conditioning. I carried her down the stairs and out of the house. Ethan came out of the kitchen, saw me carrying Kate, and rolled his eyes.

I took her out to our small backyard. 'I'm sorry, but I have to assume that Kurt has our bedroom bugged.'

Her eyes widened. 'No way!'

'I don't know. I just have to assume it. Listen, how long does Susie have that rental in Nantucket?'

She cocked her head. 'Till the end of September, probably. Why, you're thinking maybe we could borrow it for a couple of days? I'm not exactly in the best condition to take a vacation.'

'I'm not talking about a vacation. Do you think it's safe for you to fly over there?'

'Flying's fine. As long as I don't exert myself. But what's this all about?'

'I want Susie and Ethan to go back to Nantucket and take you with them. As soon as possible. Tomorrow morning, first thing.'

She looked at me. A series of expressions played on her face: confusion, skepticism, amusement.

Then realization. 'It's about Kurt, isn't it?' she said.

Susie and Kate and Ethan got in a cab the next morning for Logan Airport and a flight to Nantucket. I went to the office, and at nine o'clock I grabbed a few minutes between meetings. I returned a call from the CEO of the Red Sox, who turned out to be a supernice guy – I guess I was expecting George Steinbrenner with a Boston accent or something – and wanted me to set up a demo of the PictureScreen and get him some numbers. We agreed to meet in a week.

As soon as I hung up, I took the elevator down to the

lobby. Left the Entronics building, drove a few blocks away, took out Sergeant Kenyon's card, and called him from my cell.

The phone was answered in a gruff voice, a Spanish accent: 'State police, Trooper Sanchez.'

Office noise in the background, phones ringing, voices.

I said, 'Sergeant Kenyon, please.'

'Who's calling?'

I paused just a second. 'Josh Gibson.'

In a minute, Kenyon picked up. 'Mr. Gibson,' he said. 'Let me take this in my office.' He put me on hold, then picked up again a few seconds later.

'Well, this is a nice bit of timing,' Kenyon said. 'I was going to call you, give you the news.'

'News?'

'Accident Recon found nothing.'

'They found nothing,' I said. That stopped me in my tracks.

'That's right. No evidence of a crime. No evidence of a crime means no investigation. Means I get assigned to something else.'

'But I know that Kurt – I *know* he did something to the car.'

'If the CARS unit says there's nothing wrong, there isn't a lot I can do.'

'They didn't look hard enough.'

'You may be right. I don't know. They're busy. Lots to do.'

'It's there. He did it. I know it. Did anyone check the ball joints?'

'I don't know what they checked. All's I know is, they didn't find anything.'

'Where's the wreck?'

'Scrapped, I bet.'

'Scrapped?'

'Processed out of the system, anyway. That's what they normally do.'

'Who?'

'Tow yard. It's theirs now. Normally they ask the deceased's family if they want it, and when it's totaled like this, the family always says no, so they sell it off for scrap. Why?'

'You've got to get your Accident Recon people over there to look at it again before it's scrapped.'

'Out of my hands. Out of police custody too.'

'Which tow yard?'

A pause. Kenyon laughed. 'Uh-uh. Forget it.'

I tried another approach. 'If you search Kurt Semko's apartment, I'll bet you find some tubes of something called LME. Liquid Metal Embrittlement agent. Issued to the U.S. Army Special Forces.'

'LME, huh? Well, here's the problem, see. There's not going to be any search. No evidence of a crime means no investigation means no search warrant. That's the way it goes in the real world.'

'He's got the stuff there. I've seen it. That's your evidence.'

'Let me explain something to you, Mr. Steadman, because you obviously don't know how the system works. If you want to get a search warrant, you have to get a judge to sign off. The judge isn't going to sign off unless there's what you call probable cause.'

'I've *seen* the stuff in his apartment.'

A pause. 'I don't know what you saw, but my instinct about you is that you're an honest fellow. Are you willing to be my informant?'

'Confidential, sure. But not named. No way in hell. Kurt knows people all over. He'd find out. Kurt bugged the room you and I talked in at Entronics, you know. He heard every word we said.'

'Jesus.'

'The guy is dangerous. So you see why I can't go on the record as your informant.'

'Doesn't work that way, Mr. Steadman. Judge uses something called the Aguilar–Spinelli test.'

'The who?'

He sighed. 'Basically, it means that you can't issue a search warrant based on plain old hearsay. If the warrant application's based on information you get from an informant, you've either got to list the name publicly or establish a long history of reliability. As a confidential informant. Which obviously you don't have. Now, if you're willing to put your name on the search warrant –'

'Forget it. Not going to happen.'

'Then there's no search warrant.'

'Don't you want to solve this case?'

'Look here, Mr. Steadman. My hands are tied. As far as the state police goes, there *is* no case anymore. I'm sorry.'

'So Kurt's just going to get away with this?'

'I'm sorry, Mr. Steadman.'

I called directory assistance, got the number for J & A Towing – the company that had towed away Trevor's car – and gave them a call.

'You have my brother's Porsche,' I said to the woman who answered the phone.

'Okay?'

'Name is Trevor Allard.'

'Hold on.'

When she got back on, she said, 'Hey, looks like we already talked to your brother's – widow. She said she didn't want the wreck. She gave us the go-ahead to sell it for scrap.'

'Shit,' I said. 'That was my brother's car.'

'The wife was listed as the next of kin. It's probably been picked up already. Wish I could help you.'

'Can you find out if it's been picked up yet? I'm sorry to bother you – it's just that – well, it was my brother's car. And if I can salvage anything from it – well, there's, like, a sentimental value. He really cared about that car.'

'Hold on.'

I waited.

A man picked up. 'This is Ed.'

'Ed, my name is –'

But he kept talking. 'We followed all the proper procedures, sir. We notified the next of kin, and she authorized us to scrap it. The wreck's scheduled to be picked up this afternoon by Kuzma Auto Salvage –'

'You still have it?'

'Like I said, it's scheduled to be picked up.'

'Listen. This is really important to me. What do you get from the salvage company for it?'

'I really couldn't tell you. That's worked out between them and us at the time.'

'Ballpark.'

'Could be a hundred, two hundred bucks.'

'I'll give you three.'

'You really want this wreck, huh?'

'If I can salvage something from it – anything – for my brother's sake –'

'I don't think three hundred bucks is going to motivate anyone, know what I'm saying. We got a relationship with this salvage company, and we already sold a bunch of vehicles by weight.'

'Ed, is this your towing company?'

'Sure is.'

'Three hundred to your company, and another three hundred to you personally for expediting this sale.'

He chortled. 'That important to you, huh?'

'Do we have a deal? Or do I have to buy it off of Kuzma Auto Salvage, for what I'll bet will be a fraction of that?'

'It's a Porsche, you know.'

'A Porsche or a Kia, it's a heap of steel and aluminum now.'

'Cash?'

'Tow it to my yard in Cambridge, and you'll get six hundred bucks in cash. Unless that Porsche's made of titanium, you're getting a pretty damned good deal.'

He chortled again. 'I'll have one of the guys tow it out to you tomorrow.'

'Today,' I said. 'By two o'clock this afternoon. Before I come to my senses.'

56

My comfortable corner chair at Starbucks was still available.

I sent an e-mail to Yoshi Tanaka's personal e-mail address – it was on the back of his business card, which I kept in my wallet – from *Kurt_Semko@yahoo.com*.

'Kurt' wanted to pass on to Yoshi some troubling information he'd discovered about Dick Hardy in the course of a routine security sweep – Hardy's Hushmail account, the Samurai Trust in the Channel Islands, the trading of Entronics options on the Australian Stock Exchange. 'Kurt' wasn't comfortable reporting this within normal channels in the company, since no one, not even he, the new Director of Corporate Security, would dare take on the powerful CEO of Entronics USA. But he thought Yoshi should know about it. 'Kurt' insisted that none of this ever be discussed over the phone or in person. He told Yoshi not to write to him at his Entronics e-mail address.

I hoped Yoshi could read English better than he spoke it.

If Kurt was telling me the truth – and I had no reason to doubt that he really did have the goods on Dick Hardy, since that was what he was good at – then what Hardy was doing was not only illegal, it was basically disgusting.

I was sure the top leadership of Entronics in Tokyo had no idea what he was up to. The Japanese were far too cautious, far too scrupulous, to play that kind of sleazy, low-level game. The games they played were on a far higher level. They'd never tolerate this. They'd get to the bottom of it, confront Hardy, and bounce him out on his ass in a Tokyo minute.

Trevor Allard's wrecked Porsche was a terrible sight. The front end was so badly crumpled it was almost unrecognizable. The hood stuck way up, the driver's door was just about off its hinges, both front tires were flat. The undercarriage had been ripped apart. Looking at it, you could see that no one could have possibly survived the crash.

Graham and I stood there, looking at it solemnly.

'My landlord's going to have a cow,' Graham said. 'Did I say you could have it towed here?'

'Yeah. This morning.'

'I must have been asleep. I thought – I don't know what I thought.'

'As soon as you find the damaged part, I'll have it towed away.'

'And if I don't find anything?'

I shrugged. 'It'll just have to stay here until you do.'

He wasn't sure whether I was kidding. 'Guess I'd better get to work.'

He got out his toolbox and began dismantling the wreck. After a while, he said, 'This is not fun. No wonder they didn't find anything.'

He removed the front left wheel and poked around

in the dark innards of the wheel well. 'This one's fine,' he said. 'No ball joint damage here.'

Then he went around to the other wheel and did the same. A few minutes later, he announced, 'This one's fine too.'

'What else could it be?'

'This is a tough one. I hate to say it, but maybe I'm not being fair to the cops. Maybe they really did look.'

I made work phone calls in his backyard while he continued to search through the wreck for another hour and a half.

Finally, he got up. His work gloves were covered in grease. 'Nothing,' he said. 'There's nothing. Now I got to get over to Cheepsters.' That was the record store where he worked.

'A little longer,' I pleaded. 'Half an hour.'

'Hand me my cell phone and I'll see if I can trade off an hour now for an hour of bondage later.'

I helped him pull the front hood open – it was so damaged that the electric engine-cover release wouldn't have opened it even if he'd applied an external battery to the fuse box. But there seemed to be nothing there either.

'Damn, this is frustrating,' he said. He opened the driver's side door and wriggled into the collapsed front seat. He sat there for a moment. 'Speedometer's stuck at sixty-five,' he said. 'They weren't speeding.'

He pumped the brakes with his foot. 'They work fine.'

He turned the steering wheel. 'Oh, baby,' he said.

'What?'

'Turns a little too easy. Are the wheels turning?'

I stepped back and looked. 'No.'

'This could be the problem. You're driving on the turnpike at 65 and the road bends, so you steer, but your wheels keep going straight. You'd crash right into the guardrail.'

'What causes that?'

'Could be a couple of things.' He bent down and messed with the wires under the dashboard. With a long wrench, he removed two airbag screws behind the steering wheel. He took a screwdriver to the back side of the steering wheel and removed the airbag unit from the center of the steering wheel, then the airbag connector.

'Air bags didn't even deploy,' he said. Now, with a wrench, he removed the steering wheel nut and bolt. He yanked at the steering wheel, but it didn't move. Then he grabbed a rubber mallet from his toolbox and hammered at the steering wheel from behind a few times, then lifted the wheel straight out.

A minute later, I heard him say, 'Oh, now, this is weird.'

'What?'

'Check this out.' He pulled out a thin rod about a foot long that had a U-joint at one end. The other end was jagged.

'What's that?'

'Steering shaft.'

'Smaller than I thought.'

'That's because it's only half the steering shaft. This' – he pulled out a matching piece – 'is the other half.'

'Broke?'

'These things are made to withstand a hell of a lot of torque. I've never seen anything like it. The steel didn't snap. It looks like it ripped. Like a piece of licorice or something.'

'You should have been a cop,' I said.

On the drive back to work, I called Kenyon.

'State Police, Trooper Sanchez.' Hispanic accent.

I asked for Kenyon.

'I can give you his voice mail, or I can take a message,' Sanchez said in his heavy Hispanic accent. 'Unless there's something I can help you with.'

I didn't trust him, only because I didn't know him, hadn't met him. Didn't know who he knew.

I asked for Kenyon's voice mail, and I asked Kenyon to call 'Josh Gibson' back on my cell.

Then I called Kate's cell from mine. She said they'd just arrived at Susie's house, and that the trip over had gone well. She was taking it easy now.

'We got a call on the voice mail at home from the doctor's office,' she said. 'The amnio results are in, and everything's totally fine.'

'Are we having a boy or a girl?'

'We told them not to tell us, remember?'

'Oh, right.'

'What's going on over there – with Kurt?'

I told her I was going to call her back in a few minutes, from another phone, and I explained why.

The Plasma Lab was empty, I knew. I put my fingerprint against the biometric reader. It beeped and let me in.

Somehow, somewhere, an alarm had probably just gone off, and Kurt knew where I was.

I picked up the phone in the corner office, which

416

used to be Phil Rifkin's, and called Kate on her cell.

'Hey,' I said. 'I didn't want to call you from my office. I'm not sure it's safe.'

'How so?'

'Sweetie, just listen. I've been thinking a lot. And this business about Kurt – I mean, if he's doing stuff like tapping my phone, that's one thing. But this – this thing with Trevor's car – that he'd never do.'

'You don't think?' She was an excellent actress, and she was playing her part perfectly.

'I don't. I really don't.'

'Why?'

'It's crazy. It's conspiracy thinking. The state police have examined the car wreck, and there's nothing there.'

'I think you owe him an apology. You'll see him at the softball game tonight, right? You should tell him you're sorry.'

'Yeah,' I said reluctantly. 'I can't do that, though. I'll get grief from him forever.'

The apology thing I wasn't prepared for. I guess she was improvising. Kurt, I figured, would never have believed me if I told him to his face that I'd decided he was innocent. But it would surprise me if Kurt *weren't* listening in on this phone call. And he'd only believe I was on the level if he was eavesdropping on me.

Whatever it took.

Sergeant Kenyon had left me a message on my cell. I took the elevator down to the lobby, drove a few blocks, and called him back. This time he answered the phone himself.

'I asked around about LME,' Kenyon said without

417

waiting to ask why I was calling. 'You may have something there. Liquid Metal Embrittlement is scary stuff. I don't know where you'd buy the chemical – a welding supply house, maybe?'

'Or take it from an army supply depot. I have a question for you. Let's say I somehow managed to get a piece from Trevor Allard's car that proved something had been done to it, some kind of sabotage. Would that be evidence you could use in court?'

'The car's scrapped, I told you that.'

'Let's just say.'

'What'd you do?'

'I'm asking you if the evidence would be admissible.' I'd watched my share of *Law and Order* on TV. 'You know, chain of custody or whatever it's called.'

'It's complicated. I'll have to get back to you on that. See what the DA's Office tells me.'

'Soon as you can,' I said.

He called back ten minutes later. 'Okay,' Kenyon said. 'One of the prosecutors here tells me that, in this state, chain of custody goes to the weight of the evidence, not its admissibility.'

'You're going to have to speak English.'

Kenyon laughed. 'And I was hoping *you* could explain it to *me*.'

'Sorry.'

'What that means is, it's not a deal killer. Legally, you don't have to show every link in the chain. A good defense attorney will put up all sorts of arguments, but a judge has to allow it. So . . . I've answered your question. You answer a couple of mine. Do you have the piece or not?'

418

'I have it.'

'Okay. And you say it proves sabotage. How do you know that? No offense, but you're a corporate executive. Not a metallurgist.'

'I can't tell you for a hundred percent sure that it proves the car was sabotaged. But I can tell you that it looks like a Tootsie Roll that's been twisted and then torn off. It's not a normal metal break.'

'What kind of piece is it?'

I hesitated. 'The steering shaft.'

'Well, let's assume for the sake of argument that you're right. In isolation, all that would tell me is that the car was tampered with. But I've still got a problem. A major problem.'

'Which is?'

'Connecting it to Kurt Semko. So you've got to establish that he had the means to do this – this LME. That he has or had access to it.'

'He *has* the stuff in his apartment,' I said. 'I've seen it. All you have to do is search his apartment.'

'We come back to this,' Kenyon said. 'I told you before, unless you're willing to be a named informant, we're not going to have probable cause to search. If only there was some other way. He never gave you a spare key to his apartment or anything?'

'No, of course not.'

'I don't suppose he'd invite you over.'

'Not in a million years.'

'Then how the hell can you prove he has it?'

'How can I *prove* it?'

'That may be the only solution. Just as you got the steering shaft on your own.'

'Maybe there's another way,' I said.

There was, of course. Graham Runkel was working on it.

'Like what?'

'I'll have to get back to you on that,' I said.

57

Kurt greeted me with a wave, from a distance, and a friendly smile. I smiled back, just as friendly, said, 'Hey.'

He was on the mound already, warming up. The ballpark lights were on. The opposing team, a motley crew from the Bear Stearns retail group, was already inspecting our bats. The word had gotten around. They obviously didn't realize that, with the exception of Kurt, the remaining members of the Entronics team weren't good enough for a doctored bat to make any difference. But they'd soon find out. Festino was consulting with the other guys.

My cell phone rang. I knew who it was, so I walked off a good distance before I answered it, on the third ring.

'I'm in,' Runkel said.

'In the house?'

'You heard me.'

He had broken into Kurt's rented house in the town of Holliston. I could picture it in my mind, from my one visit – everything about it neat and well tended, very hospital-corners.

'Not a problem?' I asked.

'The doors were double-locked, but the overhead garage door was open. The door to the house from the garage is always the weak link. Easy to pick.'

'No alarm?'

'Rented house like this? I didn't expect it. But count on there being a good smoke alarm system. Landlord would make sure of it.'

'You know where to look?'

'You told me.' His voice was sort of jiggling as he walked through the house. 'The spare bedroom off the family room, right?'

'Right.'

'You care what I use to set off the smoke alarm? Like a doobie?'

Kurt was waving to me again, and so was Festino. 'Come on, Tigger,' Festino shouted. 'The business day is over. We're starting.'

I held up an index finger.

Once Graham found Kurt's cache of stolen weapons and explosives, he was going to open the door to the room where the cache was kept and leave it open.

So that when the fire department came, summoned by the smoke alarm, and broke in, did their usual damage, they'd see the illegal armaments, and they would call in the police. In this age of terrorism, they'd have a crime scene on their hands.

And then we'd have Kurt nailed. No arrest warrant needed, and all perfectly legal.

'Find it?' I said.

'No,' said Runkel.

'What do you mean, no?'

'There's nothing here.'

'Okay,' I said, 'if you're looking at the fireplace in

the family room, it's the door on your right. This hollow-core door. The only one on that wall.'

'I'm there. I see which door you're talking about. But there's no stash here.'

'It's there,' I said, desperation rising. Kurt was walking toward me. I lowered my voice. 'I've *seen* it.'

'I'm in the room,' Runkel said. 'There's a single bed, nothing on it. The room smells a little like gunpowder, maybe. Like there *used* to be something here. But there's *nothing here*.'

'Then he moved it. Look in the basement. Look everywhere else. It has to be there.'

'Let's go, Jason,' Kurt said, maybe ten feet away. 'You're keeping everyone waiting.'

'Don't give up,' I said, and hung up.

Shit.

'You're a busy guy,' Kurt said. 'Who was that?'

'It's a contract,' I said. 'Guy misplaced it.'

'That's annoying. So you're playing first base. Can you handle that?'

'Sure,' I said. 'Kurt. About all that – all that stuff I threw at you. About the car and everything.'

He shook his head. 'Not now.'

'No, I just want to apologize. I was out of line.'

'Don't worry about it,' he said. 'That's the past. Come on, let's get to the field.'

He put his arm around me, like a fellow soldier, the way he used to.

But I could tell there was something about him that had changed. He was hard and unyielding and distant.

He didn't believe me.

*

Kurt had moved his cache of stolen Special Forces armaments and war trophies.

That made sense. The heat was on, and he didn't want to risk a search.

So where had he moved it?

The answer came to me while I stood at first base, and it was so obvious I couldn't believe I hadn't thought of it before. Willkie Auto Body. The shop owned by Kurt's friend and SF buddy, Jeremiah Willkie, where Kurt had taken my car the night I met him. Where he stored all his tools and stuff in the warehouse out back.

That's where I had to go.

I tried to focus on the game. The Bear Stearns retail brokers weren't very good. Without Kurt, neither were we, of course. Kurt struck the first two guys out, and then their third man up, who had been studying Kurt's pitches, managed to hit a grounder to the right side of the infield. Letasky tried for it, but it glanced off his glove. Kurt ran off the mound and retrieved it, then threw it to me.

I caught it, but it slipped out of my glove, and the runner made it to first.

'Come *on*, man,' Kurt shouted, annoyed. Before he returned to the mound, I trotted over to him, pantomimed an apology, and pretended to hand him the ball. He glanced at me strangely, but walked slowly toward the mound, taking his time.

I returned to first base, the ball hidden in my glove. The runner, a pudgy, bespectacled kid, beamed me a smug smile. He saw that Kurt wasn't looking, wasn't even back on the rubber yet. Saw his opportunity to steal second, greedy man that he was.

And as soon as he moved off the bag, I tagged him. He was out.

'Hey!' their coach shouted, running out into the field. 'That's a balk!'

Festino and Letasky and the others were watching with amazement. Festino burst out in raucous laughter, shouted, 'Tigger!'

The umpire waddled onto the field. 'He's out. The old hidden-ball trick.'

'That's a balk!' the Bear Stearns coach said.

'Nothing to do with a balk,' the umpire said. 'You don't even know what a balk is.'

'No one knows what a balk is,' Festino said.

'That's the hidden-ball trick,' the umpire declared, 'and it's perfectly legal. Pitcher was not on the mound. Now, play ball.'

'This is sandlot stuff!' protested the Bear Stearns pitcher. Like this was some professional ball club.

Letasky laughed, said, 'Steadman, where'd you get that?'

'I saw some guy from the Marlins do it against the Expos a couple of years ago,' I said.

As we left the field, Kurt came up to me. 'Classic deception,' he said. 'Never thought you had it in you.'

But I just nodded, shrugged modestly.

Go ahead, I thought. *Underestimate me.*

I excused myself, took out my cell, walked a distance away, and called Graham. The phone rang and rang, six times, then went to his voice mail.

Strange, I thought. The cell phone reception in and around Kurt's house was perfectly good.

So why wasn't Graham answering the phone? I had to know if he'd located the cache of weapons.

I hit redial. It rang six times again before going to his voice mail.

Where was he?

Kurt came up to me. 'Come on, Grasshopper. We're up.'

'One second,' I said. I hit redial again.

No answer.

Where the hell was Runkel?

'Jason,' Kurt said. 'Come on. Time to play. Let's show them what you're made of.'

58

The minute the game was over – we managed to eke out a victory – I took Festino aside and asked him to invite Kurt out for drinks with the rest of the Band of Brothers. Make sure of it, I said. I didn't give him an explanation, and he didn't demand one.

Then, in the car on the way to Cambridge, I tried Runkel's cell, then his home number. Still no answer, which freaked me out a little. It wasn't like him to just fall out of contact. He was a hard-core stoner, but he was basically responsible, and he'd been pretty methodical about breaking into Kurt's house.

So why wasn't he answering the phone? I didn't want to let myself think the worst – that something had happened to him. Besides, I knew Kurt couldn't have done anything to him, since I'd been with Kurt the whole time.

He was fine. He had to be.

I'd been to Willkie Auto Body twice – once the night I met Kurt, and then again to pick up my car – so I vaguely remembered the directions. But I had no idea what I was going to do once I got there. I was pretty sure Kurt's storage locker was in the back building, which was a warehouse for auto parts and paint and whatever else they needed. The front building, which looked like an old gas station that had been retro-fitted, was where the customer waiting area was, and the small office, and the work bays, where they did the frame straightening and spray painting and all that.

Willkie's Auto Body was a desolate, marginal-looking place. It was surrounded by a tall chain-link fence, but its front gate was open. I knew the place was open late, but I didn't know if that meant that there was someone there twenty-four hours, or just until midnight, or what.

The plastic red block letters of its sign were dark, the edge-lighting turned off as if to discourage anyone from driving up. Most of the redbrick front building was dark, too, except for the reception area.

As I turned into the lot, I shut off my headlights, slowed way down, and stayed all the way to the right side of the parking lot, where I hoped I wouldn't be seen from inside. A few feet beyond the front building the asphalt pavement ended, giving way to hard-packed dirt.

The rear building was about a half story taller than the front one. It had corrugated steel walls, painted some light color, and it looked like an ice-skating rink. There were no lights on back here. The only illumination came from the almost-full moon. I killed the engine and coasted to a stop next to a Dumpster between the two buildings.

I waited in the car and just listened for a few minutes. No noise back here either. No one was working. So probably the only employee working was whoever was on the night shift.

I took my gym bag from the front seat and got out of the car quietly. Pushed the door shut.

Then I just stood there and listened a little more. No footsteps. No one approaching. No sounds except, every ten seconds or so, a car driving past. If the guy on the night shift, sitting in the front building, had heard me drive up, he probably assumed it was just road traffic and ignored it.

As my eyes adjusted to the dim light, I could see a Mercedes S-class parked out back on the blacktop, in a marked space. It gleamed like polished obsidian. Probably a just-completed job. Next to it was a sixties-vintage Pontiac Firebird with custom flame-painting all over its body. I could never understand why anyone would want to do that to a perfectly good sports car.

Now I walked slowly to the rear building. There were no windows, just some flat steel doors, each one marked with a sign – PARTS and PAINT MIXING. A cluster of gas tanks, which I assumed were empty, or else they'd be inside. A loading dock around to the side, marked RECEIVING. I walked up close to it. A concrete pier about four feet off the ground, a rusted iron stepladder. On a wooden pallet to one side was a haphazard pile of discarded, long cardboard cartons.

Graham Runkel, an expert in breaking and entering until he got caught, had told me that loading docks were always a point of vulnerability. During business hours especially, when no one knew who was coming or going, in most places. But even at night, he'd said. Loading docks are built for easy access, quick deliveries. The loading-dock door was an overhead, folding-type door, probably steel. Around it was a black seal that looked like rubber. I doubted there were any serious security measures in this building, since all the valuable stuff – the cars – was in the work bays in the front building. It wasn't like people were going to break in and steal an unpainted quarter panel or something.

But the question still remained: How was I going to get inside?

I went back to the front and tried one of the steel doors, just so I wouldn't feel like an idiot when I found out later it was unlocked. It was locked. I tried each of the others, and they were all locked too. Okay, no surprise.

The overhead door was padlocked. I climbed the rusty stepladder to the concrete pier and unzipped my gym bag.

Inside were some basic tools I'd picked up at Home Depot on the way over, including a MagLite flashlight and a fourteen-inch pair of tungsten-carbide bolt cutters, which Graham had assured me would cut through just about any padlock like butter. I bent over to take a closer look at the padlock, and suddenly I was blinded by a bright light.

I looked up.

A high-powered flashlight was pointing at me from about twenty feet away. I felt a jolt of fear, a shot of adrenaline.

I was dead meat.

Shielding my eyes with a hand, I got to my feet. Something had kicked in, some hindbrain survival instinct. 'Hey, where the hell were you?' I shouted.

'Who are you?' A man's voice, a Middle Eastern accent. The voice sounded familiar.

'Didn't you guys hear me?' I went on. 'Didn't you get the message?'

'What's your name?' the Middle Easterner demanded.

'Oh, for Christ's sake,' I said. 'Are you Abdul or something?'

'Yes. Who are you?'

I sauntered down the stepladder, the gym bag on my shoulder. 'Kurt didn't tell you I was coming by? He didn't tell you Kenny was stopping by tonight to get stuff from his storage locker?'

I thought quickly, tried to remember Willkie's first name. It came to me immediately – how could I forget 'Jeremiah'?

'Jesus Christ,' I said, 'I thought Kurt and Jeremiah had this all worked out.'

'Had what worked out?' The flashlight was no longer in my eyes, but down on the ground. He came closer.

'Shit, let me use your phone. And your john, if you don't mind. I got way too many beers in me tonight.'

'Bathroom's out front,' Abdul said. 'Did Kurt talk to Jeremiah?'

'Yeah, yeah,' I said. 'Show me to the john first, or my bladder's going to burst.'

He led the way over to the front building, took out a big ring of keys, and unlocked the back door. 'Straight down the hall, on your right.'

I used the urinal, then took out a pen and Kurt's business card from my wallet. On the back of Kurt's card I wrote, in Kurt's precise handwriting, all capital letters, 'WILLKIE AUTO BODY' and the address. Then, 'Abdul will meet you out back.' And: 'If they give you a hard time, call me. Thanks!'

431

I put the card in my pocket, flushed the urinal, and came out.

'Aaah,' I said. 'Thanks. Okay, now I can think straight. I forgot I have my cell on me – I don't need your phone. Hold on.' I pulled out my cell phone, switched it back on, then called my office number.

'I'm here,' I said to my outgoing message. 'Okay, so when are you going to get out? . . . But you left a message here, right? All right. All right. Later.' And I disconnected the call, then turned off the phone.

I reached into my pocket, took out Kurt's business card, and handed it to Abdul. 'Is this you?' I asked. 'On the back?'

He flipped it over. Read the handwriting. 'You should have just gone to the front office,' he said.

Along the back wall of the warehouse was a row of storage units, ten feet wide and high and twenty feet deep. Some of them were open and vacant, and a few of them were locked with old steel chain snaked through iron hasps and then through big old chrome padlocks. Abdul took out his key ring again and unlocked one of the padlocks.

'If you need anything, come get me,' he said, and he left me alone.

I pulled the iron door open and saw everything there, in neat stacks, in cartons and crates.

Much more, even, than I'd seen that day in his apartment. More than just his antique rifles and replica handguns. An entire pilfered armory.

Colorful spools labeled PRIMACORD DETONATING CORD, in festive orange and yellow, the color of kids' soft drink mix. A box of M60 Fuse Igniters. A box

432

marked CAP, BLASTING ELECTRIC M6.

A pile of blocks about ten inches long by two inches wide and an inch and a half thick, wrapped in olive drab Mylar film. Each one had printing on the top that said, CHARGE DEMOLITION M112 (1.25 LBS COMP C4).

I knew what that was. C-4 plastic explosive.

Kurt's auto tools were there, too, in two tool chests, but I ignored them.

I found a tray containing several small tubes labeled LIQUID METAL EMBRITTLEMENT AGENT (LME) – MERCURY/INDIUM AMALGAM.

I took one of the tubes. My evidence.

Then I stopped and looked over the whole stash and realized there were some other things I could take.

59

When I was more than halfway to Boston, I pulled over to the shoulder of the highway and called Sergeant Kenyon on his cell.

'I have all the evidence you need to arrest him,' I said after filling him in briefly. 'Enough to tie him to the murders of Allard and Gleason.'

'Maybe,' he said.

'Maybe? You're the one who told me if I got the tube of LME that would do it.'

'I did. And maybe it will. And maybe not.'

'For Christ's sake,' I said. 'You're the cop. Not me. Why don't you send some guys over to Willkie Auto Body right now? There's a storage locker out back where Kurt's got enough explosives and munitions to take down the John Hancock Building.'

'Your hearsay isn't enough.'

'Oh, really?' I shot back. 'Think of it this way, Kenyon. If you *don't* do anything about this little tip from me, you're going to be in a world of shit. It'll be a career-ending mistake. Maybe you'd prefer me to just call the FBI, tell them the Massachusetts State Police weren't interested in following up on my report of stolen army munitions? After 9/11, I have a feeling they're not going to get too hung up on procedure.'

Kenyon paused. I heard a rush of static on the line. 'I can send some guys over there,' he said.

'That would be a wise move.'

'Is it provably Semko's storage locker?'

'Talk to Abdul,' I said. 'Squeeze his nuts. Ask for his green card. Maybe ask him about his cell of Arab terrorists. You might be surprised at how cooperative he gets.'

My cell phone beeped. Call-waiting. I glanced at the readout, saw it wasn't Graham; it said KURT.

'Let me call you back,' I said.

I clicked over to Kurt's call, said, 'Yeah?'

Raucous bar noise in the background. Loud voices and laughter.

'Hey there, bro. I just got a call from Abdul. You know Abdul.'

My stomach seized up. I didn't reply.

'And I thought you were starting to get with the program.'

'Kurt,' I began.

'And the funniest thing happened tonight during the game. Some guy broke into my apartment.'

'Oh yeah?'

'Friend of yours.'

'Not that I know.'

'Hmm. Graham something. Runkel?' Casual, almost airy. 'Had your phone number programmed into his cell. Gotta be a friend.'

I felt a chill. He knew Graham's name, knew about the connection. Knew what was on his cell phone.

'Last number he called on his cell was yours. That who you were talking to at the game?'

'News to me,' I said.

'Nosy bastard. Made the mistake of looking in my footlocker. Hundred and ten volts wired to the lock on that baby, my little security measure. Knocked him right out.'

Tears sprang to my eyes.

I bit my lip. 'Where is he?'

'You shouldn't have done that. You just crossed the line one too many times.'

'Where is he, Kurt?'

'He's resting comfortably, Jason, ole buddy. Tied up and locked inside a big old trunk I had lying around, until I make further arrangements. Well, maybe not so comfortably. Not a lot of air in there. Fact, he's probably gone through most of the air by now – you know how panic makes you breathe harder, right?'

'In your house?'

'No. Somewhere else. Call it an undisclosed location.'

'I've got something you want,' I said abruptly.

'Oh yeah?'

'A piece of evidence. A damaged steering shaft from a Porsche Carrera.'

He laughed. 'And now you want to play *Let's Make a Deal,* that it? Do you want what's inside my box, or what's behind the curtain?'

'Let Graham go, and I'll give you the part.'

'You'll give me the shaft, Jason?' Kurt said, laughing again.

'An even trade,' I said. 'My friend for a guarantee you won't be going to prison for life. Sounds like a pretty good deal to me.'

He hesitated for a second, considering. I knew his mind was spinning like a compact disk. He was naturally suspicious, far more than I'd ever be. Everything, anything might be a ruse, a trick. And I needed to sell him on the fact that I really wanted to make a deal. That it wasn't a snare.

I needed to sell him on the fact that I was trying to sell him. This was a mirror reflecting a mirror.

'Sure,' he finally said. 'I got no problem with that.'

I thrust back. 'Sure, *you've* got no problem with that. I hand it over, you hand over Graham, and then you head over to Hilliard Street and kill my wife and then me.'

'Now, why in the world would I do that, Jason? After you've given me such a nice gift?'

If Kurt knew Kate had left the house, he'd have mentioned it. I wondered whether he had any idea she was gone.

'See, here's the thing, Kurt. I don't take anything for granted anymore. This piece I've got – this steering shaft – that's kind of like my power. My weapon. Like I'm one of those primitive Amazonian warriors, and this is my club, you know? Without my club, I feel powerless. I don't like that feeling.'

He paused again. Now he was really baffled. I was going back and forth, whipping between suspicion and what seemed like gullibility. He didn't know which was the real me.

'You saying my word's not good enough for you?'

I laughed. 'It was, once. Not anymore. This steering shaft, it's a key piece of physical evidence. Without it, the police have no probable cause for arrest. No evidence, no arrest warrant. You're good to go. But what about me?'

'Well, think about it,' he said. 'Without your club,

437

you're powerless. Means you're no longer a threat.'

I smiled. That was just what I wanted him to say, precisely the conclusion I wanted him to reach. But I wanted it to be his idea. Like Freddy Naseem; like Gordy. Let the other guy take credit, and he owns it.

'But I know things,' I said. 'Facts about you. In my head. How do you know I'm not going to go to the cops again?'

'How do you know I'm not going to head over to Hilliard Street? Pay the wifey and little baby a visit? So we've got ourselves a little situation here. It's called mutual assured destruction. Military doctrine throughout the entire Cold War.'

I smiled again. Exactly.

'You have a point,' I said. 'All right. So?'

'So we meet.'

'Where? It has to be someplace neutral. Someplace safe. Not public. Not your house. Not my house.'

I knew what he'd say. The old sharp-angle close. *The Mark Simkins College of Advanced Closing.* Maneuver the customer into making a demand you can meet.

'Work,' he said. 'The Entronics building.'

Where he felt comfortable. Where he controlled the situation.

'One hour,' I said. 'With Graham.'

'Two. And you're not exactly in a position to negotiate. You give me the scrap of metal, and I'll tell you where he is. So that's the deal. You don't like the terms, find another vendor.'

'All right.'

'Think it over. Take your time. I've got all the time in the world. Oh – that's right. Your friend doesn't. He has three or four hours' worth of air. If he calms

438

down and breathes normal. Which is hard to do when you're tied up and locked in a box in an undisclosed location, huh?'

60

I called Kenyon back.

'I've just made a deal with Kurt Semko,' I said, and I explained.

'Are you out of your goddamned mind?' he said.

'You have a better idea?'

'Hell, yeah. I'll send a unit over to this auto body shop. Once they find the explosives, we'll easily have enough to arrest Semko.'

'Between getting the unit together and equipped, out there and back, then preparing the arrest warrant, how long are we talking?'

'Six hours, I'd say, if we get a judge out of bed.'

'No,' I said. 'Unsat. My friend won't make it. So I'm meeting Kurt whether you like it or not, and I want you to wire me up. Put a concealed recording device on me. I'll get him to talk.'

'Stop right there,' Kenyon said. 'Number one, our Special Services staff don't work at midnight. There's no one around to do a professional hookup until tomorrow.'

'You telling me you don't have a tape recorder and a concealable mike?'

'Well, sure. But we're talking quick-and-dirty.'

'That'll do.'

'Number two, if you think you're going to get Semko to hand you one of those confessions out of the movies – the old 'Now that I'm about to kill you, let me tell you all about my evil plans so I can cackle wickedly' – well, you got to start watching better movies.'

'Of course not. He won't "confess" a thing. But all we need is an exchange. A back-and-forth. Enough to indicate he did it. And if anyone can provoke him to talk, I can.'

More static. A long silence. 'I don't know about this. I'd be putting you in serious danger. It's extremely irregular.'

'Serious danger? You want to talk serious danger? A friend of mine is slowly suffocating in a trunk somewhere. I'm going to meet with Kurt. If I have to use my own crappy tape recorder and tape a microphone to my chest, I'll do it.'

'No,' Kenyon interrupted. 'I'll see what I can scrape together.'

'Good.'

'But are you certain you can get him to talk?'

'I'm a salesman,' I said. 'This is what I do.'

61

I stopped at a Starbucks and did some quick Internet research just as they were closing. Then I met Kenyon about a half-hour later at an all-night Dunkin' Donuts near the Entronics building. It was shortly after eleven. There were a couple of drunk young guys in Red Sox caps and low-hanging shorts with their boxer shorts showing. A tense-looking couple having a quiet fight at a table. A bum who'd surrounded his table with shopping bags full of junk. Nothing like a Dunks late at night.

Kenyon was wearing a navy sweatshirt and chinos and looked tired. We both got large coffees, and then he took me out back to a new-looking white van. He opened the rear doors and we climbed inside. He put on the dome light.

'This is the best I can do on short notice,' he said, handing me a coil of wire.

'Kurt knows how to search for concealed microphones and transmitters,' I said.

'Sure he does,' Kenyon said. 'So don't get too close.'

'I'll do my best.'

'Then we should be squared away.' He looked at my T-shirt. 'You got something long-sleeved?'

'Not with me.'

He removed his sweatshirt. 'Wear this. Just get it back to me sometime, okay?'

If I'm alive, I'll be more than happy to. I nodded.

'Take off your shirt.'

I did. He taped the transmitter to the small of my back with a wide adhesive tape he wound around my chest. It was so sticky it was sure to rip out my chest hair when I removed it.

'Is he going to spot your backup team? Don't forget, he's a pro.'

'So are they.'

I took in a lungful of air and let it out slowly. 'Is this going to work?'

'The transmitter's going to work fine. Everything else – well, that depends on you. Whether you can pull it off. And that's what scares the shit out of me.'

'I can do it,' I said. 'Is there, like, a panic button built into this?'

'We'll be monitoring the transmission. If you need us, just say something. Some phrase we agree on. And we'll come running.'

'A phrase. How about, "I'm not getting a good feeling about this"?'

'Works for me,' he said. 'Okay, then. We're good to go.'

It took me another forty-five minutes to get ready for my meeting with Kurt. I parked in back of a 7-Eleven that was closed and worked out of the trunk of my car.

The Entronics building was mostly dark, with a scattering of lights in the windows. Cleaning people, maybe. A few office workers who kept very late hours the way Phil Rifkin once did.

I saw that the lights were on in my corner office on the twentieth floor. I'd turned them off when I left for the day. The cleaning staff usually came through around nine or ten, so it wasn't them. Not at one in the morning.

It had to be Kurt. Waiting for me.

62

Fifteen minutes before one in the morning.

I arrived at my office a quarter hour before the time we'd agreed to meet. I set down my gym bag and my briefcase as I entered. The lights were already on. So was my computer.

Kurt had been using it, I assumed, but for what?

I went behind the desk to look at the monitor, and I heard Kurt's voice. 'You have something for me.'

I looked up. Nodded.

'Let's make this fast.'

I stood still, looked in his eyes. 'What's my guarantee Graham's going to be where you say he is?'

'There's no guarantees in life,' Kurt said. 'I guess you'll just have to take me at my word.'

'What good is this thing to you anyway?' I asked. 'It's just a piece of scrap metal.'

'It's worth nothing to me.'

'So why are you willing to deal?'

Last-minute hesitation. Happened all the time in my business. How many prospects had suddenly developed a case of jitters just before signing on the dotted line? Usually when I saw it coming I'd head them off by throwing in some unexpected bonus, some pleasant

445

surprise. It almost always worked. But you had to anticipate it.

'Why? Because I'd rather keep it out of the cops' hands. Not that I couldn't handle it if I had to. Not that my buddies on the force might not happen to "lose" a piece of evidence against me. But I'm a thorough guy.'

'Who says the cops are even going to know what this is?'

He shrugged. 'They might not. You're right.'

'They might not even know it's from a Porsche.'

'That kind of shit they can figure out. All it takes is one smart forensic guy to find traces of mercury or whatever's on there. Or the pattern of breakage – I really don't know. I don't care. But why take the chance? When you and I can come to terms. And both of us live happily ever after.'

I nodded.

Got it.

That was enough. That was as much as I was going to get, and it was enough to incriminate him.

'I'm taking a huge chance,' I said.

'Life's a risk. Hand it over.'

I was silent for a long time.

True sales champions, Mark Simkins said, *can sit there quietly all day if they have to. It's not easy. You want to say something. But don't! Keep your mouth shut.*

When enough time had passed, I picked up the gym bag, unzipped it. Pulled out the piece, which I'd wrapped in plastic and duct-taped up.

Handed it over to him.

'Good,' he said. He picked at the duct tape, unraveled the layers of plastic from the steering shaft. He

446

threw the plastic onto the floor, held up the twisted thick steel rod with a U-shaped joint at one end. Weighed it in his hand, admiring it. It was heavy.

'All right,' I said. 'Where's Graham?'

'You know where the old General Motors assembly plant is?'

'On Western Ave., a mile from here or so?'

'Right. That vacant lot there.' He handed me a small key. To the trunk, I guessed. 'Funny how your life can depend on a little piece of metal,' he said. He walked slowly to the big glass window.

'Like a round of ammunition. It can save your life.' Now he was looking out the window. He swiveled around. 'Or it can kill you.'

With that, he swung the steering shaft at the window.

The glass exploded with a loud pop, a million shards showering all over the carpet. 'Cheap-ass tempered glass,' he said. 'Contractors should have at least sprung for laminated, building this nice.'

'I'm not getting a good feeling about this,' I said to the hidden microphone.

Get the hell up here now, I wanted to shout.

'Jesus!' I shouted. 'What the *hell* are you doing?'

Cold wind whipped into the office, a smattering of raindrops.

'Okay,' he said. 'You've been under a lot of stress. Sudden rise to the top. All sorts of pressures on you, trying to save the division – you didn't know the whole thing was a trick. High-level games. You found out the truth, and it was too much.'

I didn't like the way he was talking, but I knew what he was up to.

'Now a hundred fifty people are going to hit the

unemployment lines because of you. Yeah, lot of stress on you. You're going to lose your job too, and your wife's pregnant. So you do the only thing that makes sense. In your desperate condition. You're going to jump. It's a good day to die, don't you think?'

The wind was sluicing through the office, blowing papers around, knocking picture frames off my desk, off the credenza. I could feel the spray of cold rain.

'Speak for yourself,' I said.

I reached into the gym bag, pulled out Kurt's Colt pistol. An army-issue semiautomatic .45.

Kurt saw it, smiled. Went on talking as if I were pointing a finger at him. 'You've left a suicide note,' he said calmly. 'On your computer. Happens more and more often these days.'

The gun felt heavy in my right hand, awkward. The cold blue-black steel, the rough grip. My heart was knocking so hard my hand was twitching.

'The cops can hear every word we're saying,' I said. 'I'm wired, my friend. Your suicide ruse isn't going to work. Sorry.'

Kurt seemed to be ignoring me. 'One-handed grip?' he said, surprised. 'That's not easy.'

I brought my other hand up so I was holding the gun with both hands. I shifted my hands around, moved my fingers, tried to find a two-handed grip that felt natural.

'You've apologized to your wife and your unborn daughter. That's what the amnio results said, by the way. A girl. Congratulations.'

For a second he almost stopped me. I froze for an instant. But then I went on.

'Like Phil Rifkin's bogus "suicide,"' I said. 'He didn't

hang himself. You garroted him, then made it look like a hanging.'

Kurt blinked. His smile diminished, but only a little.

'Because he caught you coming into the Plasma Lab. To do something to the plasma screen Trevor was demo'ing at Fidelity. You didn't expect him to be in on a Sunday. You didn't know the strange hours he kept.'

'Please tell me you didn't just figure that out,' Kurt said.

'I think I've known it for a while. I just didn't want to admit it to myself.'

My left hand braced my right at the wrist. I had no idea if this was the right form. Probably it wasn't. What the hell did I know? Point and shoot. Pull the trigger. If I'm off by a few feet, it's trial and error, aim again, squeeze the trigger. Eventually I'm going to hit him. A lucky shot, an unlucky shot, I should get him in the chest, maybe even the head. My hands were trembling.

'Did you load it, Jason? Do you even know how?'

Kurt grinned. There was something almost paternal in his expression now, proud and amused, watching the antics of an endearing toddler.

'Man, if you load the rounds in the magazine wrong, or even jam the magazine in there the wrong way, you're screwed. Gun could explode in your hands. Backfire. Kill you instead of me.'

I knew he was lying. That much I knew. But where was Kenyon? Couldn't he hear me? How long would it take them to get up here?

'Good choice of firearm, Jason,' he said. He took a few steps toward me. 'Model 1911 A1 Series 70. Outstanding weapon. I like it better than the Glock, even.'

He came closer.

'Freeze, Kurt.'

'Great safety features. Way better than the Beretta M9 the army hands out, which is a piece of shit. Superb stopping power.'

He came even closer. Maybe ten feet away. Very close. Not a problem now.

'Stop right there or I'll blow you away!' I shouted.

I curled my forefinger around the trigger. It felt surprisingly insubstantial.

'You should have taken me up on my offer to give you shooting lessons, Jason. Like I said, you never know when you'll need it.'

'I mean it,' I said. 'You take another goddamned step and I'll pull the trigger.'

Where the hell were they?

'Boy, the way you're holding that weapon, the slide's going to fly back at you and take off your thumb, man. You've got to be careful.'

I hesitated, but only for an instant.

'You're not going to kill me, Jason. You've never killed a man before, and you're not going to start now. A guy like you's never going to take a human life.' He spoke quietly, steadily. Almost lulling. 'That's a nightmare you don't want to live with. Close range like this, you get sprayed with blood and brain tissue, fragments of bone. It'll haunt you for the rest of your life.'

'Watch me,' I said, and I squeezed the trigger.

He didn't move. That was the strange thing. He stood there, arms at his side.

And nothing happened.

The gun didn't fire.

I squeezed again, pulled the trigger all the way back, and nothing clicked.

Suddenly his right hand shot out, pushed the gun to the side as he grabbed it, wrenched it out of my hands in one smooth motion.

'Friggin' amateur,' he said. He turned the gun around, pointed it at me. 'You loaded it, but you didn't squeeze the grip safety.'

I spun around, ran.

A burst of speed. As fast as I could. Like racing up the steps of Harvard Stadium, like doing wind sprints along the Charles, but with every twitching fiber of my being engaged in a desperate attempt to save my life.

From behind I heard him say, 'Colt's not easy to use, for an amateur. You gotta push against the back strap while you're squeezing the trigger.'

Out of the office, through the maze of cubicles.

He shouted: *'Should have let me teach you.'*

The elevators just ahead. I leapt toward the wall panel, pressed all the buttons, lit them up orange.

'Nowhere to run,' came Kurt's voice, sounding closer. Why wasn't he firing at me?

The bing of an elevator arriving. Thank God. Elevator doors slid open and I jumped inside, heard Kurt's footsteps, punched the LOBBY button, punched and punched at it until the doors, so agonizingly slow, finally closed.

A hesitation. The elevator wasn't moving.

No, please.

Then, a little jolt and it began to descend.

So damned slowly. Floor buttons began to light up one after another, slowly. Nineteen . . . seventeen. The flat-panel screen was dark, and the lights in the elevator cabin seemed dim. I stared at the numbers, willing them to move faster.

Where the hell was Kenyon?

The elevator shuddered to a stop. The orange 9 button frozen.

I punched L again, but nothing moved.

Then everything went dark. I could see nothing. Pitch-black.

Somehow he'd shut the elevator off. Turned off the power. I reached out in the darkness, flailing at the buttons, found them with my fingers. Ran my fingers over them, punched each one. Nothing.

The emergency switch was at the bottom of the control panel. I couldn't see it, but I remembered its position. Was it a button or a switch? I felt along the panel, completely blind, sliding my hands down the two rows of buttons until I felt the bottom edge of the steel panel. What felt like a toggle switch. I grabbed it, flipped it up.

Nothing. No alarm, no sound, nothing.

Other buttons down there. Was it a button, then? I jabbed at the bottom row of buttons, but nothing. Silence.

A wave of panic hit me. I was stuck in total darkness in an elevator cabin. I felt the cold smooth steel doors, the palms of both my hands sliding along the metal until I found the crack where the two doors met.

A tiny gap, not enough to get my fingertips into. Sweat prickled at my forehead, the back of my neck.

In frustration, I pounded at the door. Kicked at it. The steel was cold and hard and unmoving.

Found my cell phone, opened it so the screen illuminated. Punched 911.

That little chirp tone that told me the call had failed. No reception in here.

My heart racing. The sweat was beginning to trickle down my cheeks, into my ears, down my neck. Tiny dots of light danced in front of my eyes, but I knew this wasn't real light. It was some random firing of neurons in my brain. I backed up, swung my arms around, felt for the walls of the elevator.

Closing in on me.

I flung my hands upward, felt for the ceiling, had to jump to reach it. What was up there? Little screws or something? Could you loosen them? Were there panels up there, a trapdoor, an emergency escape hatch?

I felt the brushed stainless-steel handrail that wrapped around three sides of the cabin, stuck out a few inches. Maybe four inches.

I jumped again, swept the ceiling. Felt something round, a hole. Remembered that the ceiling in here had little recessed downlights in it. No protruding screws. A smooth, flat, brushed-steel ceiling with halogen lights in a regular pattern. Which were now dark.

But there had to be an emergency escape. Right? Wasn't that required by code?

And if there was some emergency hatch, and I managed to get it open – then what? What was I supposed to do? Climb up into the elevator shaft like James Bond or something?

The sweat was pouring now. I had to get out of here. I tried to swing my foot up onto the handrail, to boost myself up, but it was too high.

I was trapped.

The ceiling lights suddenly came on.

Then the panel lit up blue, then white, then . . .

453

Kurt's face appeared.

A close-up of his face, slightly out of focus. A big smile. His face took up the entire panel.

'The word of the day is "retribution,"' Kurt said. 'Good word, huh?'

I stared at his face on the monitor. How the hell was he doing this?

'Boy, you are drenched,' he said. 'Hot in there, huh?'

I looked up, saw the silvery black dome in one corner of the ceiling. The big black eyeball of the CCTV camera lens.

'Yep, that's right,' Kurt said. 'That's me. And you look like a drowned rat. No need to hit the emergency call button. I disabled it, and besides, there's no one in the control room. I sent Eduardo home. Said I'm taking over, running some diagnostic tests.'

'What are you going to do, Kurt? Leave me in here overnight?'

'No, I thought I'd entertain you with a little live video feed. Watch.'

The image of his face stuttered, blinked, and the screen went dark. Then another image came up, fuzzy and indistinct, but it took me only a few seconds to recognize my bedroom. The image slowly zoomed in on the bed. Kate lying there. Her head on the pillow.

Strange blue light flickering over her face.

'There's the wifey,' Kurt said. 'Couple of nights ago. Guess she fell asleep watching TV while you were out somewhere. *Desperate Housewives,* maybe? She's a desperate housewife herself.'

My heart was going ka-thunk, ka-thunk, ka-thunk.

'Lots of opportunities to install that camera. Hell, she was always inviting me in. Like maybe she was

454

attracted to me. A real man. Not a pathetic fake like you. A wannabe. You were always the armchair athlete, and the armchair warrior.'

Another scene appeared. Kate and me in bed. She watching TV, me reading a magazine.

'Oh, wait,' he said. 'Here's an oldie. From before she went to the hospital.'

Kate and me in bed. Making love.

The image had a greenish, night-vision cast.

'No comment on your sexual technique, bro,' Kurt said. 'Let's just say I've been seeing a lot of you two.'

'I guess you don't want the other half then,' I said.

'The other half?' The image of Kate switched to Kurt's face. Big, looming close-up. A curious look.

'The steering shaft in the Porsche Carrera is eighteen inches long,' I said. 'The piece I gave you was, what – maybe ten inches? You figure it out.'

'Ah,' he said, chuckling. 'Very nice. Maybe you did learn something after all.'

'I learned from the master,' I said. 'Taught me to play hardball. You want it, you bring me back up to the twentieth floor. To my office. I get it from the hiding place, hand it to you. And then you let me go. I retrieve Graham. And it's over.'

Kurt's big face stared at me. Blinked a few times.

'Do we have a deal?' I said.

He smiled. His face pulled back, and I could see my office. He'd been sitting at my computer. Maybe a camera hooked up to it. Maybe the concealed one. I didn't know. I didn't care.

All I cared about was that this looked like it might work.

The elevator made another jolt, and it started to move.

I turned away from the ceiling-mounted eye. Watched the buttons on the control panels light up orange: 12 . . . 13 . . .

Hit redial on the cell phone. This time the call went through. It rang once, twice.

'Police emergency.' A man's voice, clipped.

'I'm in an elevator in the Entronics building in Framingham,' I said. 'My name is Jason Steadman. My life is in danger. There's a guy on the twentieth floor who's trying to kill me.'

'Hold on, please.'

'Just send someone!' I shouted.

The orange 20 button lit up. A ding. The elevator doors opened.

On the phone, another voice came on. 'Trooper Sanchez.'

I didn't understand. 'Sanchez? Where's Kenyon?'

'Who's this?' Sanchez said.

I could see a figure in the shadows in the twentieth-floor lobby. Kurt, it had to be.

'Jason Steadman,' I whispered. 'I'm – I know Kenyon. I'm in the Entronics building – you've got to radio Kenyon, send someone over here *now*. Hurry, for Christ's sake!'

'Steadman?' Sanchez said. 'That scum-sucking piece of shit?' His Hispanic accent was even thicker now.

Two figures emerged from the shadows. Kurt was holding a cell phone to his ear. 'Would you like Sergeant Kenyon's voice mail,' Kurt said in his Sanchez voice, leering.

Another man, holding a pistol.

Ray Kenyon.

Kenyon waved it at me. 'Let's go,' he said. 'Go, go, go. Hand me the other half.'

456

I stared in shock. I'd pressed 911. Nine, one, one. I was *sure* of it. I hadn't hit redial, hadn't called Kenyon.

'Jerry,' came Kurt's voice. 'Hand me the weapon. I'll take over.'

Jerry. Jeremiah. Jeremiah Willkie. His Special Forces brother. The one who wouldn't testify against him. Who owned the auto body shop.

Who was 'Ray Kenyon.'

Jeremiah Willkie handed Kurt the weapon. It looked like the Colt I'd stolen from Kurt's storage locker, but I couldn't be sure.

'The guys are never going to believe this one,' said Willkie/Kenyon.

'No, they won't,' said Kurt, and he pointed the barrel at Jeremiah Willkie and fired. 'Because they're not going to hear about it.'

Willkie collapsed to the floor. His left temple was bloodied. His eyes remained open.

I stared at Kurt.

'Jeremiah has a drinking problem,' Kurt said. 'Get a couple vodkas in him, and he talks too much. But he made an awfully convincing cop, didn't he? He always wanted to be a cop. His uncle was a cop.'

'I called 911.'

'It's called cell phone phreaking. Cloned your phone so I could listen to all your calls. And pick up on outgoing calls too. Your old cell, your new one, made no difference. So let's finish our business here.'

He pointed the gun at me. 'Sounds like you hid the part in your office. You tricky, tricky guy. Let's go.'

I walked to my office, and he followed. I entered the office, stood in the center of the room, my thoughts racing. The wind howled. Papers covered the carpet, and piles of whitish glass fragments.

'Well, I know it's not in your desk,' Kurt said. 'Or in your bookcase. Or any of the usual hiding places.'

My eyes flicked toward the briefcase, then quickly away. It was still there.

'Ceiling panel,' I said.

He'd seen my eyes.

'No, I don't think so,' Kurt said. 'Hand the piece over, and you're free to go.'

'I'm not going out that window,' I said.

'Hand me the rest of the shaft.'

My eyes darted again, almost involuntarily, toward the briefcase next to my desk.

'I'll need your help,' I said. 'I need a ladder or something so I can reach the ceiling panel.'

'A ladder?' he said. 'Boy, I sure don't think you need a ladder.' He stepped toward my desk, grabbed the English leather briefcase. 'Didn't I teach you about the "tell"? Those little giveaway signs in a person's face? You're good at reading them, but not so good at hiding them.'

I tried to grab the briefcase back from him, but of course he was much stronger, and he wrested it from my grip. Both his hands were on the briefcase, and as he fiddled with the latches, I took advantage of his momentary distraction, backed away from him.

'Nowhere to run, Jason,' Kurt said, loud but matter-of-fact. I backed away slowly as he flipped open one of the brass latches, then the other, and then my back was against the doorframe. Twenty feet away, maybe.

A tiny scraping sound.

I saw the realization dawn on Kurt's face, an expression of fury combined with something I'd never seen in his face before.

Fear.

But only for a fraction of a second before the blast swallowed him, blew him apart, limbs flying, horrific carnage like something you might see in a war movie. The immense explosion threw me backwards, slammed me against something hard, and as I tumbled I felt hard things spray against my face, fragments of wood and plaster, maybe, and I didn't know what else.

I struggled to my feet, ears ringing, my face stinging.

A block of Kurt's own C-4 plastic explosive connected to the confetti-bomb apparatus he'd put in my briefcase that day. I'd left it in my briefcase and gone back to using my old one.

And he was right that a little C-4 was enough. I knew there was no chance of him surviving.

Reached the elevator banks, then stopped. Wasn't going to try that again.

The stairs. Twenty flights was nothing. I'd learned that. I was in great condition now.

Well, not exactly. My back ached, and a couple of my ribs were sore, probably bruised if not broken. I was hurting, but I was also flooded with adrenaline.

Opened the door to the stairs and started down the twenty flights. Walking, not running. I was limping, and I grimaced from the pain, but I knew I'd make it just fine.

Not a problem. Easy.

Epilogue

Kurt was right, of course.

It was a girl. Nine pounds, twelve ounces. A beautiful, healthy little girl. Well, not so little. Big, in fact. She looked sort of like Jack Nicholson, with the straggly black hair and the bad comb-over. And I'd always hoped that, if we got a girl, she'd look like Kate Hepburn. Like her mom. Oh, well. Close enough.

The baby – Josephine, we named her: Josie – was so big that Kate had to deliver by C-section. So the delivery was scheduled a couple of days in advance, which was, unfortunately, plenty of notice for my brother-in-law to fly in from L.A. to join his wife and Kate and me in sharing the happy occasion.

I was so happy I barely minded having Craig there.

I had a lot on my mind anyway.

The police business took a few days to straighten out. Graham Runkel and I spent long hours at state police headquarters going over and over what had happened that night. Graham told them about how Kurt had locked him into a trunk, where he might have suffocated had I not released him, barely in time.

They wanted to know how I'd learned to make a bomb. I told them Kurt had done most of the work for me, and the rest I'd gotten online. It's amazing what you can find on the Internet.

Now that Kurt was dead, it was fairly easy to get his Special Forces teammates to come forward and talk about what kind of person he'd been. The picture that emerged was consistent, and it wasn't pretty. Just about every one of the cops and detectives who interviewed me said I was 'lucky' I hadn't been killed.

Lucky. Yeah, right.

Not long after Yoshi had passed on to Tokyo the information about how it was that the CEO of Entronics USA, Dick Hardy, had been able to afford his yacht and his house in Dallas, Hardy was jettisoned.

The board of directors voted unanimously to instruct their General Counsel to inform the SEC's Enforcement Division, and that started the ball in motion. The SEC soon brought in the FBI, and then the IRS Criminal Division, and pretty soon Dick Hardy was facing what Gordy used to call a 'gangbang' of civil and criminal and tax fraud charges. He put his yacht up for sale on the *Robb Report* just two days before the IRS seized it.

I was flown to New York to meet with our worldwide CEO, Hideo Nakamura, and about a dozen other honchos, both Japanese and American, to interview for Dick Hardy's job. It was me versus a bunch of other internal candidates, all of them older and more experienced and much more qualified. Instead of just sitting there on the hot seat being grilled by Nakamura-san, I decided to go out on a limb and make a PowerPoint presentation to my interviewers. Hardy had told me how they all loved PowerPoint.

My presentation made a business case for shutting

down Entronics headquarters in Santa Clara, selling off its valuable and overpriced Silicon Valley real estate, and moving headquarters to lovely Framingham, Massachusetts, where Entronics already had a building. All it needed was some repair work on the twentieth floor, where a blast had turned my corner office into a charred cave.

The kicker was my slide showing how Royal Meister's Dallas offices could be sold at an immense profit. The Dallas Cowboys, see, wanted to build a new stadium, and they were willing to pay handsomely for the land.

This impressed them, I think.

I didn't mention that I had my personal reasons. Like the fact that Kate refused to leave Cambridge. She finally had her dream house, and she'd already furnished the nursery, and she simply wasn't moving. So either I moved to Santa Clara without my lovely wife and baby, or I turned down the job. But I wasn't going to tell them that. That would not be good for my image as a killer.

The interviews seemed to go well, if facial expressions are any indication. I didn't understand a word they were saying. Yoshi Tanaka sat by my side the entire time, throughout every single interview, as if he were my attorney.

In the last interview there seemed to be a really heated exchange. Yoshi spoke to Nakamura-san and another board member in rapid Japanese while I sat there smiling like a doofus. They seemed to be arguing back and forth until Yoshi said something, and they all nodded.

Finally, Yoshi turned to me and said, 'Oh, please

forgive me, I'm being terribly rude.'

I looked at him in astonishment. He was speaking in a plummy British accent. He sounded like Laurence Olivier or maybe Hugh Grant.

'It's just that they keep referring to you as *nonki,* which I suppose I'd translate as "'easygoing," and a *gokurakutonbo,* which is more difficult to translate. Perhaps you might say it means a "happy-go-lucky fellow." But I'm afraid neither is a compliment in Japanese. I had to explain to them that your people regard you as ruthless. They speak of you with a certain trepidation. I told them that's what I like about you. You have that killer instinct.'

Later on, as Yoshi and I waited for the hiring committee to finish their deliberations, I blurted out, 'Your English is amazing. I had no idea.'

'*My* English? My dear boy, you're too kind. I did my master's thesis at Trinity College, Cambridge, on the late novels of Henry James. Now there's a *true* master of the language.'

The realization hit me then and there. Of course. How else could he get people to talk so freely in his presence?

'So when I told you all about my big idea for the PictureScreen, and you just stared blankly –'

'In stunned admiration, Jason-san. That was when I realized you were a bloody visionary. I immediately told Nakamura-san, and he insisted on meeting you in Santa Clara. But alas, it was not to be.'

In the end, I was tapped for Dick Hardy's job, and after a few nerve-racking weeks, when Kate and I agreed not to talk about it, they also approved my suggestion to move U.S. headquarters to Framingham.

And move Royal Meister's top performers to Framingham, too – those who wanted to leave Dallas, anyway. Now Joan Tureck was working for me, and she and her partner were quite happy to be back in Boston. So where was I?

Oh, yes. At the hospital, Craig seemed to treat me with newfound respect. He kept talking about the Entronics Invitational at Pebble Beach, what a blast he had last year when Dick Hardy had invited him to join all the celebs, how cool it was playing a few holes with Tiger Woods and Vijay Singh. I guess I was a little distracted, with our newborn baby, but it took me a while to figure out that Craig was angling for an invitation again this year. Now that I was the CEO of Entronics. Poor Craig was sucking up to me.

But I was as friendly as could be. 'We're trying to keep the head count down this year,' I said, 'but I'm sure we can work something out. Just contact my assistant, Franny Barber. I'm sure we can arrange it.'

I have to say that I enjoyed that.

We all sat in Kate's room watching Baby Josie clamp on to Kate's boobs and suck away like a champ. Finally, she fell asleep, and the nurse came and put her in the bassinet.

I gave Kate a smooch, and said, 'I'm married to the greatest woman, and I have the greatest baby, and I just feel like the luckiest man in the world.' I was almost overcome by emotion.

'I thought you said a man makes his own luck,' she said, arching her brows.

'I don't think I believe that anymore,' I said slowly. 'Sometimes the luck makes the man.'

Ethan sat in a corner of the room reading a book about great military blunders in history. This was his latest obsession. Apparently Kurt Semko's remark about the Battle of Stalingrad had got Ethan thinking.

'Uncle Jason,' he said, looking up from his book. 'Are you aware that the First World War was started because a driver made a wrong turn?'

'Ethan,' said his mother warningly.

'Ethan,' said Craig. 'The adults are talking.'

'A wrong turn?' I said to Ethan.

'That's right. The chauffeur to the Archduke of Austria-Hungary accidentally turned into a street he shouldn't have, where some guy was waiting with a gun, and he shot the Archduke and his wife, and that led to a whole world war.'

'No, I didn't know that,' I said. 'But it makes me feel better about my driving.'

Kate and Susie were discussing nannies. Kate said she'd found several promising Irish nanny candidates on the *Irish Echo* newspaper's website. Susie told her that the only nannies to hire were Filipinas. They went back and forth on this for a while, and of course Craig had to join in the dispute. I didn't care one way or another, of course. I kept thinking about Festino's warning about how the Barney song would get stuck in my head, and I'd be forced to watch *The Wiggles*.

But when they started arguing about which was better, a live-in or a live-out nanny, I jumped in. 'I really don't want a stranger living under the same roof,' I said.

'She wouldn't be a stranger once we got to know her,' Kate pointed out.

'Even worse,' I said.

'You really want to be able to leave the baby with the nanny when you two go out,' Craig said. 'That's what was so great about Corazon. We were able to leave Ethan with her all the time. We barely saw him.'

'That's wonderful,' I said. Kate and I exchanged a look.

He didn't pick up on my sarcasm. 'Whenever he started crying in the middle of the night,' Craig said, 'Corazon would come running and change his diaper or feed him or whatever.'

'I expressed my breast milk and put it in the Sub-Zero,' Susie said, nodding. 'All Corazon had to do was heat the little bottles up in the microwave. But you have to stir them well. There's really only one kind of breast pump to buy.'

'I know,' Kate said. 'I've been on every baby website.'

'Can we not talk about breast pumps?' I said. 'I want to go back to the live-in/live-out thing.'

'Why?' Kate said. 'It's decided.'

'The hell it is. Don't even bother.'

Kate saw the resolve in my face. 'Oh, I've only just begun,' she said with that knowing smile that she knew always turned me to mush.

'Uh-oh,' I said. 'Now it's war.'

Acknowledgments

The fictional Entronics Corporation was built out of the bits and pieces of the giant electronics companies I visited and researched, but none was as helpful and as hospitable and interesting as NEC. Its Visual Display division is one of the largest providers of plasma screens in the world, and a great and innovative company besides. Ron Gillies, formerly the senior vice president and general manager (and now at Iomega), was enormously helpful and patient in answering my most outrageous, most dimwitted questions and in allowing me to talk to a whole range of people there, both in sales and in the more technical end of things. He, and his terrific, charismatic successor, Pierre Richer, were a pleasure to get to know. Thanks as well to Keith Yanke, product manager, Plasma Displays; Patrick Malone, district sales manager; Ken Nishimura, general manager; Bill Whiteside, inside sales; Tim Dreyer, public relations manager; and especially Jenna Held. I did not meet a Gordy there, nor a Dick Hardy, nor a Festino, nor a Trevor, nor a Rifkin. Elsewhere, yes. Not at NEC. And if I got any of my facts grotesquely wrong – well, that's why they call it fiction, right?

Other excellent sources in the world of high-tech sales who gave me a feeling for the culture, the stakes, and the challenges included: Bob Scordino, area manager, the EMC Corporation; Bill Scannell, senior vice president, the

Americas, EMC Corporation; and Larry Roberts of PlanView. All were witty, personable, and generous with their time.

Professor Vladimir Bulovic of MIT shared with me some details of his remarkable breakthroughs in OLED flat-screen technology. I've taken some liberties with it, of course.

The best bad guys often require the best sources, and for Kurt Semko, I was fortunate to have my own Special Forces A-Team, including Sergeant Major (Ret.) Bill Combs of the William F. Buckley Memorial Chapter of the Special Forces Association, who introduced me around; Master Sergeant (Ret.) Rick Parziale, former team sergeant of ODA 2033; and most of all Kevin 'Hognose' O'Brien, Sergeant First Class, who served with the 20th Special Forces Group in Afghanistan. It's obvious to them, but I should declare it publicly: Kurt Semko by no means represents the dedicated and brave and genial Special Forces officers I've come to know. On the circumstances of Kurt's court-martial, two of my military-justice sources on *High Crimes* helped immensely: David Sheldon and Charles Gittens. Jim Dallas of Dallas Security passed along his tips on how to track down concealed military records. Linda Robinson's excellent book, *Masters of Chaos,* provided much valuable insight into the Special Forces.

In matters of corporate security, I'm particularly indebted to Roland Cloutier, director of Information Security at EMC; and Gary Palefsky, director of Global Security at EMC. Jon Chorey of Fidelity was also quite helpful. Jeff Dingle of Lockmasters Security Institute provided great details on building security.

On the financial shenanigans at Entronics, I received a great deal of guidance from the redoubtable Eric Klein of Katten Muchin Rosenman in L.A., an expert in mergers and acquisitions. Once again, my old friend Giles McNamee, of McNamee Lawrence & Co. in Boston, helped devise some of my more intricate schemes with his customary creativity.

Darrell K. Rigby of Bain & Company in Boston helped me understand integration-management teams. And my good friend Bill Teuber, CFO of the EMC Corporation, helped in all kinds of ways.

Matthew Baldacci, vice president and marketing director of St. Martin's Press, really belongs in two places in these acknowledgments. Not only has he been a steadfast supporter in a key role at my publisher, but he was also, on this book, an important adviser on baseball and softball. Thanks as well to Matt Dellinger of *The New Yorker,* who, among other things, manages the staff softball team. And special thanks to my friend Kurt Cerulli, softball coach and baseball junkie, for suggesting numerous softball stratagems and making sure I got them right. Daniel A. Russell, Ph.D., of Kettering University's Science and Mathematics Department, advised me on the tricks (and physics) of bat-doctoring. Dan Tolentino of Easton Sports explained the construction of composite softball bats.

Gregory Vigilante of the U.S. Army Armament Research, Development and Engineering Command, helped me to understand Liquid Metal Embrittlement. Toby Gloekler, of Collision Reconstruction Engineers, Inc., helped me finally devise, by a feat of forensic reverse-engineering, an almost-undetectable auto accident. Thanks, too, to the accident investigator Robert W. Burns; Sgt. Stephen J. Walsh of the Massachusetts State Police Collision Analysis and Reconstruction Section (the CARS unit); Trooper Mike Banks of the Massachusetts State Police; and Sgt. Mike Hill of the Framingham, Massachusetts, Police Department. Retired detective Kenneth Kooistra, formerly of the Grand Rapids Police, again helped me on certain homicide details.

On pregnancy and placenta previa, my thanks to Dr. Alan DeCherney, professor of Obstetrics and Gynecology at the David Geffen School of Medicine, UCLA; and to Mary Pat Lowe, an E.R. nurse at the Massachusetts General Hospital.

My gratitude, as ever, to some of my long-term sources and all-around utility players, particularly Harry 'Skip' Brandon, of Smith Brandon, in D.C., and my indispensable weapons expert, Jack McGeorge of the Public Safety Group in Woodbridge, Virginia. My former researcher, Kevin Biehl, stepped up to the plate again (as it were) with some crucial last-minute research assistance.

I'd like to thank, once again, everyone at my publisher, St. Martin's Press. They continue to believe in me and to push so hard to get my books out there, with an enthusiasm that's almost unheard of, and which I never take for granted. At the risk of leaving important people out, let me mention in particular: President and Publisher Sally Richardson; John Sargent, CEO of Holtzbrinck USA; Matthew Shear, vice president and publisher of SMP's paperback divisions; Marketing Director Matt Baldacci; Ronni Stolzenberg of Marketing; Publicity Director (and olive-loaf aficionado) John Murphy; Gregg Sullivan and Elizabeth Coxe in Publicity; Brian Heller in paperback sales; George Witte; Christina Harcar; Nancy Trypuc; Alison Lazarus; Jeff Capshew; Andy LeCount; Ken Holland; Tom Siino; Rob Renzler; Jennifer Enderlin; Bob Williams; Sofrina Hinton; Anne Marie Tallberg; Mike Rohrig (now of Scholastic); and Gregory Gestner; and at Audio Renaissance, Mary Beth Roche, Joe McNeely, and Laura Wilson.

Keith Kahla, my editor, deserves his own set of acknowledgments. Thank you, friend, for everything you've done. You're truly the best.

My agent, Molly Friedrich of the Aaron Priest Agency, was great as ever, as supporter and protector and incisive reader. Thanks, too, to Paul Cirone at the agency.

My wife, Michele Souda, was a valuable reader and editor of the manuscript. Not only did our daughter, Emma, have to put up with an almost-absentee father during the last months of the writing of *Killer Instinct*, but her baseball obsession inspired a key part of this book.

And finally, my brother, Henry Finder, editorial director of *The New Yorker*: you had my back, as they say (but you never would). From the genesis of the story to the final edits, you were invaluable. I can't thank you enough.